Win Win Win

Win Win Win

If You Want to Go Far, Go Together

Daniel Bernardus
Manon Blanke
Lans Bovenberg

Amsterdam University Press

Cover design: Gijs Mathijs Ontwerpers
Lay-out: Crius Group, Hulshout

ISBN   978 94 6372 326 8
e-ISBN   978 90 4855 449 2
NUR   133

Before we start...

There is a high chance you have received this book as a gift. A colleague, a friend, or even a teacher may have given it to you. I hope you take it as a sign of appreciation. But more than appreciation, receiving this book is a sign of trust, trust that you are able to undertake important things and carry them forward even when things turn rough. The undertaking may be a personal collaborative project, or it may mean participating in a wider societal ideal. Ask the one who gave you to be sure.

One question that may be on your mind, as you receive this gift is: should I actually read the book? Let us explain where the book came from and what it tries to do. Then you can decide for yourself.

This book was written in the context of a research project called "What Good Markets are Good for". This project set out to corroborate the hypothesis that societies with free-market economies flourish because—and in so far as—the key market actors (states, businesses and individuals) respect morality and act virtuously. This book has evolved as part of the educational branch of that project. As you may expect from this context, this book explores economics and morality. Making those abstract terms more concrete, it is a book about collaboration and love.

As an educational approach to deeper questions, lecturing is not something we believe in very much. This book was therefore written as a mirror. In the main characters, you'll see reflections on some common attitudes towards what it means to be human, towards economic collaboration, and towards love in a broad sense. Now, looking into a mirror is not always a pleasant experience. Still, it does tend to help improve things. For example, some of the characters in this book may, to put it mildly, irritate you. If they do, we would suggest that you ask yourself why that is the case. Exploring our 'allergies' to certain things is a great way for us to get to know ourselves, to give us courage to take the necessary next step—essential in any durable success.

The book is set in the context of a Dutch liberal arts and sciences college. That fits the educational context of the work. But it is not accidental that the students go to a business contest, where they need to solve a (truly) real-life business case. Also, the book is as much about the relationships of the students with their families as it is about them individually and as a team interacting together. These two points show that the book has relevance for professionals as well. Looking at the main characters, some of their reactions probably have more to do with the university situation in which they find themselves. But the underlying attitudes they exemplify are much more universal. We tried not to lay these on too thickly, though, leaving it up to you to figure them out. All in all, while this book is well-suited for university students, its intended audience is much broader.

It is our hope that this book will help you on your way towards personal growth. For that, we think it is most beneficial to read the book together and discuss what you see in the mirror. Of course, we would advise doing that with people you feel comfortable sharing with. We think the experience will help you deepen your (collegial and professional) friendships.

If you would like to explore the underlying themes in a more direct way, we have also produced materials to help you do that in the "Good Markets" project and beyond. The "Good Markets" project will result in a final book, gathering together all the research done, that may be interesting for you to look at.[1] More specific to the genesis of *Win Win Win* are two booklets by Lans Bovenberg, published on the occasion of two inaugural lectures given to mark his accepting professorships at two different universities.[2] While these booklets were published in Dutch we hope soon to publish a translation into English of the most relevant parts

---

1   At the time of writing the preliminary title of this work is "Markets, Virtues and Human Flourishing: An Interdisciplinary Approach" by Johan Graafland and Govert Buijs.
2   A.L. Bovenberg, (2016) *Economieonderwijs in Balans. Kiezen en samenwerken.* Tilburg University; A.L. Bovenberg (2018) *Where is the love.* Erasmus University.

of these speeches for *Win Win Win* under the title "Economics and Love". Finally, for more insight into the philosophical ideas resonating with the main characters in this book, we refer to the recently published "Freedom in Quarantine" by Leonardo Polo and Daniel Bernardus. In a shortened version, these ideas are in the free mini -course on "The Meanings of Success" that we can send you via www.danielbernardus.com. This is not to say that we wish in any way to limit the interpretative freedom of every reader. But perhaps you'll find our perspective, the result of having spent several years working on and thinking about this book, worthwhile to take along in your journey.

With that said, we encourage you to take the plunge and spend some time with us by reading *Win Win Win*. We hope you will find the reading experience and the discussions you have afterwards worthwhile and helpful for your personal growth.

Daniel Bernardus
Manon Blanke
Lans Bovenberg

PS
For those interested in using this book for educational purposes, please visit www.danielbernardus.com for information on the free use of the pdf version of the book in the context of an educational collaboration.

Chapter 1

"NO!" I screamed as I checked the time. Not today! When will I remember that turning off the alarm "because I'll get up just now" is just not a good idea? While I wrestled with the tight legs of my jeans, I saw a whatsapp notification popping up on the screen of my new smartphone. Claudio. "Hey, can you tell the teacher I'm late?" A quick look at my clock told me our class started three minutes ago, so that was not going to happen. After tumbling down the last two steps of the staircase, I made my way across the street to the university. It was a misty morning, and the six-storied building loomed up in front of me menacingly. Eight minutes late, I awkwardly knocked on the window near the classroom door. The automatically locking doors we had at uni made it impossible to sneak in late without anyone noticing. Dr. Loffels did not bother to open the door for me. Thankfully, a student sitting next to the door let me in. "Thank you," I mouthed. Still, this was very different from what I had hoped the start to this important day would be like. This important day. My independence day.

Claudio came in after me. The same student opened. I greeted him silently with a wave of my hand and a smile, as he shuffled to the last available table. He smiled back. I did not particularly like Dr. Loffels' Social Systems course. It was all so obvious. I know how capitalism works, thank you very much. As my thoughts inevitably drifted away, I looked at the other students. It never stopped amazing me how students from all over the world decided to come here, to Amsterdam, for a whole three years of college. What is here for them that is not in the big cities they come from? For instance, why trade New York, the city of commerce, for this? New York... This summer I would finally see it with my own eyes. It had always been my dream to dress up affluently and walk down Wall Street pretending to belong there—just as my mum had wanted me to. But today was the day for me to send all those old dreams to the dustbin for good. Today was the day for a change of course, a radical change... if only my tutor[3] would allow me.

Dr. Loffels was droning on about contemporary social regulation, and I pulled out my phone to check the time of my appointment. I knew full well it was going to be fifteen minutes after class, but I wanted to be double sure. I was not going to be late for this one. Would she allow me? Would I be allowed to study medicine on top of my current studies? Especially if my course plan wasn't perfect yet?

"Could you please do that in your own time, Miriam?"

I noticed how everyone was looking at me and felt my face heat up. I tried to put my smartphone back into my pocket, but as sure as certain, I missed, and it fell on the floor. A snigger went through the class. God.

*

After class, I met my friend Elena in the hallway and together we walked towards the canteen. I checked my wristwatch every few seconds. Fortunately, no one seemed to notice.

"It's not fair!" Elena furiously took out her bankcard. "Every time I finally decide to eat healthy, they sell delicious sandwiches. Not fair at all."

I had been close to Elena for some time now. She and I were living in the same string of rooms at the dorms, and often had dinner together. This wasn't the first time I had seen her struggle to turn down appealing food. "Egg or chicken?" I asked.

"Chicken."

I quickly bought an egg sandwich and we sat down at a table next to Claudio and his friends. They were sitting on top of the table, playing some kind of weird game involving cards and quite a lot of unnecessary noise. It was strange how little I saw him these days, while a few weeks ago we met up almost every day.

---

3   Tutor is the word used for academic advisors in the Dutch University College system.

At that time we were preparing for the TopStar business contest, one of these prestigious contests in which students are asked to resolve real-life cases in teams, which we had decided to enter. But from the time we heard that our team had not been selected for the final round, the contact between us had not been as intense.

Claudio looked up, greeting me with that quirky smile of his which brings a lively spark to his Southern-European features.

"Thanks for telling the teacher I'd be late, Mir!"

"Don't rub it in..."

"What?"

"I was also late."

"Great minds think alike!" Claudio smiled. He turned back to throw a red card on the table while yelling "YELLOW. Oh yeah". Strange.

Everyone seemed a little tired today; my friends aimlessly scrolled through their Facebook pages. But my mind was hyperactive and kept on wandering to the study plan I had gone over again and again, all night. It contained all the subjects I would need to combine economics and medicine. It just had to fit... but I couldn't quite make it work. Quick check at the time: Only ten minutes to go before the start of the meeting. The plan was nearly there though, it just needed some final touches. If only Claudio's friends would stop making all that noise. I was trying to focus.

After a few minutes, I noticed an abrupt change in the chatter. Emma, a girl who had been playing among Claudio's friends, and giggling and laughing loudly at their game, had suddenly stopped laughing. I had seen her take bites from a sandwich before, in between her spells of laughter. Now her friends were focused on her intently and asking, "Emma, are you ok?" I looked sideways and saw she was sitting on a chair next to the table on which Claudio and his friends were sitting. She was grasping her throat and gagging.

Claudio stood up and hesitantly walked over to her. He patted her on the back softly, seemingly to show compassion rather than to really help. He clearly didn't know what to do.

I suddenly realized that I *did* know. My first steps on the way to the medical profession were immediately paying off: I had just taken a first aid course, and now I immediately perceived what was happening. I stood up quickly and asked her, "Emma, are you choking?"

She tried to speak, but only managed a whisper, and nodded. Right, I thought, what to do now? I was already certified for first aid assistance, and this was clearly the time to step up and take responsibility. Emma was still grasping her throat, and gagging. No time to waste.

I signaled Claudio to step aside, positioned myself behind her chair, kneeling down. "Easy on now. Let's try to force this thing out of your throat." I wrapped my arms around her torso, made a fist and placed it on her belly underneath her ribcage. I placed my other hand on top of that. "Now hang over forward a little Emma." She remained admirably calm and bowed forward. "Now, one, two..." I thrust my fist into her belly, aiming upwards as fast as I could. I could hear the air rushing out of her mouth, and Emma started coughing, gurgling, and spit out a piece of food. And she inhaled! I felt the tension flowing away, as I gently patted Emma's back. "Well done!"

"Wow, Miriam." Claudio now patted my back. "I didn't know the banker's daughter had any other skills next to her bank account."

"Well, now you know I can save people's lives." I told him. As I looked at him, he didn't look so sure of himself as his ironical comment would suggest. There was even a slight blush in his face. So I decided to just sit back and let the adrenaline wear off.

*

After coming to my senses, I looked at my watch, and the adrenaline was straight back up. I was already late for my meeting! And my plan wasn't finished. Why me? I took my laptop and bag, and rushed up the central stairs of the building. I didn't even say goodbye to Emma or any of the people there.

I knocked on the door of the room where Ms. Daniels held her tutor meetings.

"Hi, come in." My tutor's light grey eyes rested on mine. She was one of those people that are sincerely interested in knowing how you are doing. She looked a little worried. "You look very rushed."

"I'm so sorry for being late. Something... something happened on the way here."

"Oh, okay. Do you want to meet at another time? We only have about twenty minutes now."

NO! I wanted to shout, but only just contained myself. "Now is better for me, thanks." The thought of having to wait longer for Ms. Daniels' approval made me very unhappy. There had been enough uncertainty lately. I just wanted the fog to clear as soon as possible.

"As you wish. How are you?" Her calm demeanor only made me feel more anxious.

"I'm good. Everything's fine." I didn't think that came across very convincingly, but it was a try. We talked a little about life at University College International, but I cut the banter short, subtly shifting my laptop on the desk between us. Soon enough, Ms. Daniels asked me about my curriculum. I entered the password and opened the webpage containing the study plan I'd been working on. I turned the laptop toward her, and gestured for her to take a look. The 'UCI planner', which usually neatly shows all courses a student takes in every semester, looked distorted and bigger than usual.

Ms. Daniels frowned. "That looks ... slightly overloaded. What's this?"

Finally. This was the moment I'd been waiting for. I took a deep breath. "Yes, so you see, I would like to do a double major." I had kind of expected her to shout at this point, because I was telling her that I wanted to do two full bachelor degrees at the same time. But she just looked at me. So I started rattling. "You see, I know that here it says there are two January courses at the same time, which is impossible, but I've heard that people can do language courses outside of UCI. So I figured I'd do two Spanish courses over the summer, and then in the next summer write my capstone thesis for the one major, so that in the end there's only three semesters in which I need to do five courses during the sixteen-week period instead of the normal four. I even have a normal course load for three semesters. That's feasible, right? Will you allow me to do this?" Ms. Daniels just sat there and looked at me for several moments. I must have landed her in a tutor's nightmare.

After a while she spoke. "Well, Miriam, I've never had a tutee propose a double major to me. I would have to check what the precise regulations are. In fact, I think people were working on constructing them. But would you permit us to take a step back? Could you explain to me why you would like to do a double major? You wanted to do the economics track, right? So why all the medical courses?"

That was the dreaded question. I had seen it coming. "Right, well, this is really important to me."

"That's fine, but why? Do you want to be an economical doctor?" She smiled kindly, which took away some of the ironic punch, but not all.

"I... I just need you to know how important this is to me." I didn't quite see how I could bring the message across to her without explaining further, but it was worth a try.

"Miriam. Don't worry, I do believe that. I'm just trying to understand. But if you don't want to talk about it further, you don't have to."

I sighed a bit too loudly.

Ms. Daniels offered to check for me whether my plan would fit the rules. At the same time, she recommended me not to do it, because she said it would be very intense. Instead, she suggested I take a minor. At UCI that consists of six related subjects, meant to give students a good idea of their second field of interest. And it would still be something to show to future universities or employers.

"It has to be two majors." I emphasized. How could I ever explain the whole situation to her? She would never understand.

"Alright then, let me look into the possibilities."

"You can't give me a 'yes' or 'no'?"

"I'm sorry, but again, this is quite unusual, Miriam. I really need to look into this carefully." Ms. Daniels asked me to send me the plan I made, and I agreed to do so.

So clearly now, today was not going to be my day. I got up to leave the room.

"Oh, and Miriam..." Ms Daniels reminded me that to do an extra subject next semester, my Grade Point Average would have to be high enough.

The reminder wasn't necessary. Think, Miriam...What could I say? I figured honesty was best. "Yes, I know. I think I can get the grades. It will be a bit of a challenge for calculus though." I had insisted on taking calculus in my first semester instead of a statistics course, but now I was regretting that a little. But it would work, I thought, straightening my shoulders. I would make it work.

Still, as I walked out of the room, I felt I had failed. Still in the fog. Ms. Daniels was clearly doing her best though, I couldn't really blame her.

*

As I walked down the central staircase of the UCI academic building, Claudio looked up from his desk table facing the stairs in the open study space on the second floor, and spotted me. He stood up, whisking off the headphones he wore to block out sounds, and came towards me. "Hey!"

I still had my mind on other things, so I just gave him a feeble smile.

"Just wanted to say 'thanks' for helping Emma and 'sorry' for teasing you." He put on his most amiable face.

"Don't worry." I managed a slightly bigger smile.

"You do look a bit... problematized."

"Yes, well, I'm off to the dorms now." It was only a 500 meter walk from the academic building to the dormitories where it was compulsory for UCI students to live. But I needed the fresh air and slight change of scenery.

"Hold on just a sec, I'll walk with you."

Claudio went off to grab his books and laptop, while I lingered around the staircase. I would have actually preferred to walk alone, but because it was such a short distance I didn't object to Claudio walking with me. As he joined me down the staircase and out of the building, Claudio asked how I was. But he did so a little too radiantly for me. I explained that I just came out of a tutor meeting.

"Oh, I see. It's a worry about a future that will never be. Those are the worst!" He said that as if it were the funniest thing ever. I gave him an exasperated look as I passed through the revolving doors out of the building. As we came out, he continued, "Sorry Mir. So..." he forged cheerfully on, "it's been a while since we've spoken... What have you been up to?"

That was true. The business case competition we were going to attend had given us opportunities before, but now—even though we were in class together sometimes—it seemed as if we were living parallel lives. But I was fine with that, really. "Nothing much," I told him.

"Any nice encounters with those friends of your Mum's?"

I sighed and was silent as we crossed a small bridge on campus on the way to the main road. For Claudio, I mused, everything seemed to be about networking. And from his point of view, my mum was neatly paving the way for me, networking me into the banking world. I think he really was jealous. I wondered what he would say if I told him that this was precisely the reason why I was not going to be a banker. He probably wouldn't believe it. So I shrugged, deciding not to tell him. I glanced sideways at him, a bit uneasily. Even though I met these people only very occasionally, tomorrow was actually going to be one of these days. My mum had asked me to help her out with a banker's meeting she was organizing. And I had already agreed to. No way out now. But at least I could get one over on Claudio. So after a while I started again, "You know, I'll meet them again tomorrow." I was pleased with my matter-of-fact tone.

His eyes opened so wide they nearly popped out of their sockets. "Wow! Can I come?"

"I could ask mum, but I doubt it will work out. Everything is organized already."

"But she knows me."

"She knows a lot of people."

"Yeah." Claudio looked at his fee, and then hopefully up at me. "Will you try though?"

"If you insist."

"Oh Miriam." He sounded disappointed. "Why do you make me beg? Friends help each other out, right?"

I paused, an option occurring to me that I hadn't thought of before. What if Claudio and I exchanged places? He would be thrilled out of his wits, and I would have some extra time to study, and maybe even to hang out with Linde and Elena. I had some hope they'd understand me better. But mum certainly wouldn't approve. She was so anxious for this to go well and had drilled me so thoroughly that a last-minute change of plan would never be an option for her. And of course, her whole idea was to introduce me to these people. Just like her whole idea was to finance my bachelor in economics. Alright, a bachelor at a liberal arts college—she had allowed that—but in economics, after all, so that I could follow in her tracks. If I would just change away from economics, she'd probably freak out completely and stop paying. So if I wanted to study medicine, it would have to be a double bachelor. No other option. But I would make it work. I would. Really.

In any case, I decided not to give Claudio any further false hopes. "Look Claudio, I know you really want this. But I also know my mum. This won't happen."

"Oh."

"But I promise I'll try to arrange something another time." I bit my tongue after saying that, because I knew he was going to keep me to it, and it was much more easily said than done.

"Really? Wow, that's amazing." The radiance came back to his face. "You're great."

"I just said I'll try. No guarantees." But, looking at his expression, I could see that the damage was already done.

"I know you'll make it work; you can do it." We were arriving at the dorms already.

"We'll see," I said as I entered the door to the apartment block I lived in and waved goodbye to him as kindly as I could.

*

For the rest of that day I tried my best to study, together with Elena. After the conversation with Ms. Daniels I felt motivated to get cracking—exceptionally motivated for a Friday afternoon, I thought wryly. But as much as I wanted to, I couldn't focus. I felt too disappointed and unhappy about the fact that I still didn't know whether the plan for my future was going to work out. My thoughts kept on whirling around that source of anguish. My mind knew very clearly that the rational thing to do now was to study Calculus. I had a big exam coming up next week, and several other deadlines on top of that. But somehow my feelings didn't agree. It was exasperating. In the end, I just had to try to process things. Turning to my friend, I asked, "Elena, tell me. Why do we study?"

"Yeah, tell me about it," she mumbled, not looking up from her book.

"No, seriously, I'm asking."

"Oh in that case, why don't I answer you?" Elena turned theatrically towards me, leaning forward with her chin on her hand, in a rather striking imitation of Rodin's 'Penseur'. "I was reading 'Man's Search for Meaning' by Frankl. He says not to ask 'what we want from life', but 'what life wants from us'." She continued in her mock-weighty tone, "And life clearly wants us to study. That's why we study." She stared intently into my eyes.

I laughed at her convincing performance. "Impressive, thanks for sharing your wisdom."

"You're welcome." She bowed gracefully in her chair, and turned back to her study books.

Certainly her joke contained some truth; study was an in-escapable part of what life was asking of me at this point. But the big question was: how much of it exactly? I couldn't let my mum down now, in order to go study something else. She was counting on me. My thoughts led me morosely along. So, no time for Linde and Elena this weekend either. Sigh. Unless I would just decide on easing off on the calculus and meeting the deadlines with minimum effort. But then, how would I meet my tutor in the upcoming meeting? The whole idea of adding medicine as a second bachelor would then be off the table. Just because I wouldn't be allowed to take an extra subject next semester. And I really had to go for the double bachelor, right? Right?

I frowned, feeling a bit recalcitrant about what Elena had said: why couldn't life just be a bit clearer about what it wants? Why not just send some wireless radio transmission into my ear blaring: 'Miriam, you should really study medicine'. I grinned at the thought, but was sobered by another following quickly upon it—what if that is just what happened this morning, when I saved the choking person? Could Life be telling me: 'this is what you're good at! Go for it!' Who knows?

In any case, I reflected that if life wanted me to study econom-ics, then tomorrow might clearly be the day to tell me. A meeting with all the top bankers in the Netherlands: What better occa-sion? Perhaps, I resolved, I should just go there with that attitude. And if life did send the radio transmission, and it would have to be economics... well, that would save me loads of trouble. But of course, if the opposite 'communication' occurred... it would lead to more trouble. I didn't see any other options. Go tomorrow and listen. That's my plan. Listen to the voice of life. And then decide what needs to be done. Barmy.

Chapter 2

I was nervous, which helped me get up fast the next morning. I even got in two hours of studying before having breakfast, getting all dressing up, and leaving. I met my mum at the entrance hall of the conference center. I gave her a kiss on the cheek. The intense smell of her perfume penetrated my nose and I felt a sneeze coming up. Was that a first message: my body rejecting the smell of banking? Oh, come off it, I told myself. I had to give the banking world a real chance today and overcome the instinctive aversion that had been building up in me. I could do it: an open attitude, and then a balanced decision. Yes.

"Let me look at you, darling!" I didn't look half as fabulous in my blouse and black skirt as she did in her business dress and modest jewelry. Well, I suppose differences have to be.

My mum smiled and handed me an official badge with my name and *Organization Assistant* beneath it. Together we went over all the things that needed to be done. "Are you confident?" She asked. I nodded. "Don't let me down, now." As if I needed that reminder.

Of course, I didn't tell her I had sneaked along my *Economic Systems* book, which also needed reading after all, just in case I'd find a little time in a break.

As we stepped through the heavy door into the hall where the event would take place, an elderly man came up to me and shook my hand with both his hands. "Miriam! It's a privilege to meet you again. Jeanette won't shut up about you! Thanks for coming today. I hope you'll enjoy yourself." He winked at us and walked on. That was Bernard Gerritsen, the head of the bank's financial department, who was organizing this day with my mother.

I looked around at the tastefully decorated hall. There were some minimalist modern paintings on the wall, a table with coffee and tea in the corner, and long tables in the center set with stacks of empty plates waiting to be filled with appetizers.

The wine glasses were sparkling clean, but the luxury wasn't as over-the-top as I had expected.

"Would you please start by putting the name cards on the tables, love? Place them to the right of the wine glasses, please." My mum gave me an overview of the room and asked me to have a look at the new table arrangement. "You wouldn't believe how annoyed some people became when they heard they wouldn't be sitting near to a certain person. I have had to change it around six times!"

With the room overview in hand I started my task. I entertained myself by imagining who had been complaining. Had Mrs. Van Doorsom been so desperate to sit right next to the beloved Mr. Dijkeman? And were Mr. and Mrs. Broekhuijze in a fight, and was that the reason there were five seats between them?

I decided to weigh in on the assignment a bit more, and put the name tags in mirror image. That way there was at least some kind of challenge and I had to pay attention. Else there would be a real chance I'd be too distracted and mess things up. And in mirror image, everyone would still be sitting next to the same person, so nothing to worry about.

The ticking of my mum 's heels alerted me that she was coming up to me.

"Darling? Please do mind the overview. Look here, you need to do it the other way around. This here is the entrance. You have mirrored the table, see."

Goodness. "Yes, but…" I tried to explain that it wasn't a big deal, but my mum wasn't listening.

"Miriam, just put things right, I need to fix something else." And off she was.

"Oh. Right, I see, sorry. I'll start over. So sorry." I said, but she didn't even hear. Alright, she was stressed. But then again, when wasn't she?

Hastily, I retrieved all the name cards from the tables and put them in the original order. There were so many people! And my mind started to drift… Perhaps someone would even be able to give me inspiration for my Social Systems essay. Whom would I have to talk to? With such input, that would become an easy A. But no, focus on my job now.

*

At three o'clock I was guided to the door to welcome the guests. I recognized some old friends of my mother's, but others I had to ask for their name. Not everyone took that kindly. Some people looked genuinely offended, as if everyone was supposed to know who they were. A few elderly men and women that I vaguely remembered from some past encounter seemed very interested in knowing who I was and were delighted to hear I was Jeanette's daughter.

"Jeanette's daughter! I remember when she was pregnant. Don't you, darling? Remember when Jeanette was pregnant? And look at her now. What a lovely lady."

I smiled awkwardly.

My mum was rushing around from one person to another, smiling brightly, greeting everyone by name. A little way down the aisle a young man my age was handing out champagne to all the guests.

While I was showing last people in line to their table, a young couple entered. Their faces were red, as if they had been rushing to get here.

"Hi! So sorry. Train trouble. Are we not too late? We should be on the list. Mr. and Mrs. Broekhuijze."

So those were Mr. and Mrs. Broekhuijze! Interesting...

I handed them their information sheet for the day and walked with them to the dining hall. On the way, Mrs. Broekhuijze took me slightly aside and asked, "So sorry, but do you know whether they've made sure that I'm not sitting next to my husband?"

For a moment I gave her a surprised look, but I corrected myself and answered, "Oh yes, certainly."

"I do know it sounds a bit strange, but... oooh!" Mr. Broekhuijze had come up behind his wife and slapped her firmly on her buttocks.

"Hans! Don't do that. Can't you behave for just once?" And turning to me, "you see, he's always like that at these fancy meetings. He doesn't mean it badly, and it's not like I really mind, but I get so embarrassed. I won't sit next to him. Just better to avoid it."

Meanwhile her husband looked at me with an amused grin. He was clearly having a good time teasing his wife.

My mother and Mr. Gerritsen were on the tiny stage tapping a microphone, which didn't seem to produce any sound. A few angry looks from my mum directed toward the technician who was turning some nobs on a panel did the job. She was pretty good at angry looks, I had to give her that. I would know.

Once everyone was seated she took the microphone and welcomed everybody to the meeting. Mr. Gerritsen also said some introductory words, after which the director of the Dutch National Bank, and a professor in economics each gave lectures.

I enjoyed looking at the guests as they were listening to the lectures. Everyone seemed so at ease, and so confident. They controlled all of the money of the Netherlands and they knew it. And I could easily become one of them. I already knew a third of the audience personally. Was that really such a bad prospect?

The director of the Dutch National Bank gave a talk with the ominous title "Be Prepared". His main message was that it was a matter of time before another crisis would strike. The situation in Italy had everyone worried, and it might be the prelude to a new crisis. The message did not seem new to the bankers, and even though this sounded really scary to me, they did not look overly impressed.

The professor from Harvard Business School was more positive. He discussed new trends and opportunities in the area of cryptocurrency. Everyone nodded along now, and some people were even making notes on their smartphones or iPads. I remembered that my mum was currently working on a project involving cryptocurrency as well. She told me she would be able to gain decent returns for her shareholders that way.

*

After the presentations were over, a door to the kitchen opened and several young waiters stood ready with large bottles of wine. They moved through to the guests efficiently, providing everyone with enough alcohol needed to inspire spontaneous reflections about the presentations they had just heard. My mum saw me standing around indecisively and took me to a young woman with a slightly familiar face. "Why don't you talk to her for a bit?"

I shrugged.

"Hey! Miriam, remember me?" She held out her hand. I shook the hand. She introduced herself as Gerda, and explained that she worked for my mum for quite some time now. "It's great that she has organized this day, isn't it?"

I nodded and took place on the empty chair next to hers. We talked for a bit about the presentations. Since I preferred to hide my response to the first one, I said that cryptocurrency seemed interesting enough. Gerda agreed and added that there were lots of new opportunities and that it was interesting to follow the analyses of the value development. "Nobody knows how it will develop, really."

"So are you investing in it as well then?" I hoped that I could find out a bit more about the day-to-day at my mum's practice. That would help me make up my mind.

"Yes, I am. Great profits. I follow the value every minute though, I'm out as soon as it drops!"

"Is it really that unreliable?"

"Yes, you never know what will happen." Gerda went on to explain that, as the first speaker had said, that's also true for the economy as a whole. We may easily land in a recession again and then we need to be prepared. "That's actually what your mum and I spend most of our time on: making emergency plans."

"So the both of you are taking this threat seriously?"

"Of course we are. Well, we're being told to." Gerda elaborated on the need to be prepared, so that the whole financial system wouldn't collapse. That would be a major disaster, with so many people losing their jobs. We need good bankers to avoid that, she argued. "So are you following after your mum, career-wise?"

I smiled candidly, and quickly changed the subject. But her remarks did get to me. Being a responsible banker would perhaps not be very exciting, but it would help keep society stable, and people in their jobs. That was something for me to consider. She wasn't making my decision any easier. But then again, was this something my mum had instructed her to ask me? She might have. Totally. And that shed a very different light on our conversation.

*

After saying goodbye to Gerda, I was rather enjoying myself walking around, smiling at people, taking another glass of that delicious wine. This was actually quite a lot of fun. I couldn't help myself thinking: could I really not get used to this? I was surprised to see how many people started conversations with me, even those I had only first met at the entrance, with the standard conversation opener: "Hello there, aren't you Jeanette's daughter?" Did all these people really know each other? I suppose the top of the banking world is rather small.

During the main course, I was sitting next to an old man who told me funny stories about the greatest business deals he had made during his lifetime. "Do you know what the most strategic product in Holland is? Butter!"

I looked at him blankly, not attaching too much belief to anything he said, much less something so nonsensical.

"What do they teach you kids at school nowadays? Haven't you heard that Michiel de Ruijter himself, our great Dutch admiral, beat the pirates of Duijnkerke with butter?"

I threw him a questioning look.

"Oh my. They were severely outnumbered." He began to tell the story of how De Ruijter gave the order to rub in the deck with butter. When the pirates entered the ship, they all slipped and fell. De Ruijter's men, on their socks, could overcome them. "That's the reason I decided to go into butter. That's why I commercialized Becel. Butter made from plants. Amazing!" He took another sip from his drink. Even though I of course was familiar with Becel from the Dutch supermarkets, this sounded rather far-fetched. I wondered fleetingly whether his drink might not be a tad too strong for him.

The food was absolutely delicious. Steak with truffle sauce, pomegranate compote, salmon patty, something with zucchini… And sgroppino, lemon sorbet with prosecco wine, for dessert. Spoon poised, I silently entertained the idea of regularly being able to enjoy such delicious dinners…

"Miriam, over here!" Recalled from my reverie, I heard the command in my mother's voice. She had every right to be my boss, of course, at least today. But I was starting to have quite enough of it. She called me to the exit to say goodbye to the people that were leaving. And I grudgingly complied.

It was almost ten. Everyone had finished their dessert and their after-dessert drinks and was starting to head home. I stood at the exit wishing everyone a good night and a safe ride home, which, considering the tipsiness of some, didn't seem misplaced. I recognized one of the gentlemen who had taken offence when I didn't know his name at the entrance.

"Good night, Mr. Van der Wal," I said.

"Wallemans," he grumbled. He murmured something into my mother's ear as he passed her. Normally, I might have been flustered by that, but at the moment I just couldn't care less. My attention was quickly distracted by the long stream of people passing by.

While I was biking home, the messages flooded in on my phone. I hadn't had any time today to read them. How many messages would I get as a banker? Probably a great many more… I comforted myself that I would be doing something important for society, have nice parties, and make a decent living. Was that so bad? I would probably have my mum around too, though. And I would be doing exactly all she wanted from me. Sigh. In the end, it was still the same dilemma. I was still torn, perhaps even more so now than before. Looks like my plan to 'let Life talk to me' didn't work as well as I had hoped.

Chapter 3

I went home to my parents' place. Even though I slept in my old familiar bed, I had trouble falling asleep that night. Granted, it may have been the coffee I drank after I came home, because I really did want to watch some TV without falling asleep. I'm afraid that backfired on me. But really, television was a temporary escape from uncertainty. No decision yet about my future. A big part of me didn't want to even think of that, but inside the issue kept on nagging.

Could I discuss this with mum? Of course not! I thought about what would happen in case my mum discovered my doubts about being part of her professional circles in future. She would surely explode. My mum was 25 when she was hired as interim manager for the Western district of her bank. That's only six years from now! Better not to talk with her. Well, even better to small-talk for a bit. How long had it been, I asked myself, since we had had some good mother-daughter chatter? I'd go for that. But then, who could help me out with my future?

I texted my dad.

"Hi Miriam! Was it fun?" he wrote back.

"It was!"

"Were the people nice?"

"Mostly."

"The food?"

"Amazing!"

"Was your mother not too stressed?"

I decided to end the message frenzy and call him up. I told him that she had, of course, been stressed. I had already heard her talking to people about repeating the event next year though, so that was a good sign.

"Repeat it again?" he asked. "Oh no. I really hoped that this would be the last time."

"Why?"

"She's overloading herself, and it's not good for anyone."

"Why don't you tell her?"

"She wouldn't listen."

"How do you know?"

"I just do."

I decided to leave it there. After all, my Dad was not well. He had been staying in hospital for a while now. Cancer. He probably didn't feel up to challenging my mum at the moment. Well, not that he had ever felt like it before he got ill. Not as far as I remembered, anyway. So I just said, "Okay. And how are you?"

"Having a blast." He clearly didn't feel like talking about himself much. Nor did he ever, since he was ill.

I doubted whether to ask my Dad for advice on my future plans, but decided this would be the best moment for him. He wasn't well. And he would talk to mum, of course. And then probably go with her opinion.

"Will you take care of Tim tonight?"

"I will dad." I wasn't particularly looking forward to that, but well.

"Great. Will you come see me again?" I usually visited my Dad on Wednesdays, but the last weeks had been overloaded. We had called, of course.

"This Wednesday, I'll make a point of it."

"Wonderful, darling. I'm looking forward. Very much."

After that we said goodbye and hung up.

*

I was finally about to fall asleep when a smoky smell from the kitchen made me sit up wide awake.

"TIM!"

I found my little brother sleeping on the couch, phone in his hand, while a blue smoke crept out of the oven. When I opened the oven door I almost fainted from the smoke that came out. Coughing, I grabbed the nearest towel I could find and waved it away. The smoke alarm went off. Of course. It took me a full ten minutes to clear the air and keep the smoke alarm silent. In the back of the oven I found two – what were those anyway? I supposed they were once cheese sandwiches. I slapped Tim awake.

"Are you mad? You could have burnt down the house!"

"Oh that... so sorry, I fell asleep." After looking up at me, his stare went straight down to his phone, which he unlocked with his finger and checked for new messages.

"Tim!"

"What?"

"Drop the phone and help me clean the mess up!"

"Oh, should I?" *Should he?*

"I won't even answer that."

Tim groaned and got up to help me clean the kitchen. I half considered making him eat the burnt sandwiches as a punishment, but then remembered that my Dad had asked me to *care* for him. And my budding medical sentiments said that eating burnt sandwiches is not exactly good for your health.

"Did you talk to Dad today?"

"Nope."

"So who *do* you talk to on your phone?"

"Friends. Even yours. See? Look at this." He showed me a message Claudio forwarded to him. It was in Italian and showed an Italian man driving out of a bank with a truck full of money and the slogan: "If you owe the bank $100, that's your problem. If you owe the bank $100 million, that's the bank's problem." He chuckled again as he looked at it. But I wasn't much in the mood for amusement.

I had introduced Tim to Claudio a few months earlier, when Tim had come to UCI for orientation on his future studies. At the time Claudio and I were preparing for the contest together, so introducing them was the natural thing to do. It had turned out rather well. They completely 'clicked' and exchanged phone numbers. Claudio regularly forwarded banker jokes he received from his Italian banker uncle to Tim. Tim really liked the jokes. He spoke a bit of Italian because of our regular summer holidays there, so that wasn't a problem for him. I wondered about Claudio's dedication to Tim though. Was he trying to secure a second entrance to my mum's banking network, in case I wouldn't help him out? Who knows?

We finished cleaning and I went back to bed, and told Tim to do the same. It was another hour before I could actually sleep though.

*

The next morning I again got up early to work on calculus. Early-morning math works for me. It was hard to fight the temptation to turn the alarm clock off this time, but a quick look at my to-do list did the trick.

Still, studying now was less successful than it usually was. Perhaps I was just too tired. So, after Elena's spamming, which went on for thirty minutes consecutively, I finally agreed to join her and Linde for brunch. Who knew, they might be able to talk some sense into me?

When I packed my stuff to go back to Amsterdam, my mother came down from her bedroom. She had been home late the night before, even after the oven incident, because she had been off to yet another meeting. She still smelled of coffee and weak perfume. Even her hair looked tired. She had already attempted to arrange it, but it refused to stay in the neat bun she usually wore. Even so, would she ask about my studies? I thought that in her current state, she would probably like some small talk with her daughter, without any business things to worry about on the Sunday morning. Or perhaps it was just wishful thinking.

I kissed her on the cheek and wished her good morning, trying to sound cheerful and open to conversation.

"Hello darling... Where did you leave yesterday's guest list?"

Oh no. That was the shortest shortcut to business ever. "Well..." I looked around and went through the pile of papers that lay on the table. I searched my bag. "No, I don't have it."

"Oh dear... No, I just wondered because Harry Jacobsen wrote his number on the back. Could you look again?"

So here I was, I groused inwardly, running to do her bidding again. Not even a Sunday morning relaxed conversation. I decided on the spot: it was time to be off already. I did have to say something about yesterday though, and so changed the subject somewhat forcefully, "Tim nearly burnt down the house yesterday."

"Oh, again?"

I hadn't seen that one coming. "Yes, he let two sandwiches burn to coal in the oven while he was dreaming of whatsapp on the couch."

"My goodness. Tim!" But Tim was still soundly asleep, or at least pretended to be so. "When will this boy grow up? I'll talk to him later. Also, I'll go to see Dad in a moment. Will you come?"

"I... I have to go to Amsterdam now. I'll see him on Wednesday."

"You're off to Amsterdam already?"

"Yes... I have plenty of studying to do. And Tim is distracting me. Even when he sleeps."

She sniffed. "Tell me about it. But we'll have to put up with him like this for a little more. He'll come around though."

"I suppose. Do hope so." I gave her a quick kiss and packed my bags.

"Miriam, one thing before you go."

What now? Seemingly I wasn't fast enough.

"Here." She opened her handbag and took out a cylinder filled with Jodekoeken, my favorite cookies. "I bought these for you. I thought you could use some sugar while writing those essays." She put on a big smile. "Thanks for all your help. Give me a hug."

That was really nice of her. If they were in her handbag, she must have gone to the shop especially to get them for me. We hugged, and I thanked her for the cookies.

But still, I needed to be off. High time to get my own life in order. Independently. On second thoughts, perhaps with some help from Elena and Linde.

*

The train was unexpectedly populated; not usual for a Sunday morning. A child was crying, and people were complaining.

Tourists were hauling large cases. The candy vendor had trouble keeping his balance while making his way through the train. Some people looked up at him, and right when he was about to do his salesman speech, they returned to their phones or conversation partners. Most people ignored him completely. He looked overly happy when he was able to sell a coffee to me.

The coffee made me think about the brunch I was going to have in a moment with my friends Elena and Linde. Did I really have time for that? That of course depended on my decision what to do with my future. But then, they would have to help me make just that decision. A Catch-22. What would they say anyway? Would they say I've lost it? I could certainly use some support. How silly, I even felt myself getting somewhat anxious about what they would say. But then again, who else did I have to turn to now?

Upon arriving at Amsterdam Central, I took the free ferry across the IJ, the river north of the station, and walked to the 'Amsterdam Eye', the film museum where I had agreed to meet my friends. It was conveniently located and I liked the vibe of the building, somewhat similar to the UCI academic building. And it felt good to be thinking about the script of my life in a place where the best movies were being treasured.

The Eye bar-restaurant is like a theater, looking out over the water where ships are passing by. Elena, Linde and I sat down at one of the top rows, and enjoyed the view. I told them all about yesterday, the fancy food and the wine. Their eyes started twinkling. Elena and Linde started imagining the three of us sitting there all dressed up and posh in maybe ten, fifteen years.

When we were all sufficiently in the mood, I decided to just throw it out there. "I'm not so sure anymore about being a banker though." I thought this would be a shocker, but the shock didn't follow.

Linde stared in the distance as she sipped her coffee and stared at the water with an amused smile. "The first thing I'd do with my money if I get a decent salary is get myself a cook. Can you imagine having good, healthy food every day? Without the effort, I mean,"

"I think I'd prefer a cleaner, though. I hate cleaning." Elena spilled some coffee on the table and didn't wipe it away, inadvertently illustrating her point quite vividly.

"But a cook! I mean, wouldn't it be marvelous to just have great food at your disposal, anywhere, any time?"

"I think I want to do something really big with my life." I tried to interject.

"You could get super fat; a cook would help both of you get there." Elena laughed.

"Okay," Linde said, "then I'll also hire a personal trainer. The world is not that complicated when you're rich."

"You hate sports." Elena said in unbelief.

"Okay, but I don't have a cleaner yet. Do you know how many calories you burn when doing household chores?"

"Yes, but then again, you're doing arts. How rich do you think you're going to become, anyway?"

Linde laughed and stumped Elena on her arm. Elena yelled. A few other guests turned to look at us.

"I'm learning about persons, and how they relate to each other. That's much more important than anything else. In any case, I'll be richer than Miriam. And if not, Miriam will pay for us anyway. Right Miriam?"

Of course they were still thinking I was going to follow my mum's tracks. But how could I bring across to them my desire to change? I smiled candidly, and ventured, "I don't think I'll be very rich. I'll be successful though. As a doctor."

"Right, then you can cure Linde's obesity." Elena giggled.

"Are you guys going to stay here for a while?" I burned my tongue while drinking my coffee. "I might head back in a bit. Still need to finish my assignment for tomorrow and study some calculus."

"Yes, study calculus all day, and you'll be a great doctor Miriam. I like the plan." Linde pitched in ironically. Right at that moment a waiter came by asking if we would like some more coffee. Linde and Elena eagerly nodded. I declined.

"We could do the assignment together if you want, after dinner tonight?" Elena went on to explain that her Dad was coming to

Amsterdam in the afternoon. They were going to some museum. She checked her phone. "Nobody knows what time he's coming, though."

Linde and Elena moved on to the topic of all the museums they had visited in Amsterdam. And when they realized that didn't provide much stuff to talk about, they talked about plays and concerts. I considered another attempt at letting them in on my new future plans, because I still really felt the need for their input and support. But they were clearly not in the mood for serious conversation. They were nice to be with, but wouldn't be any help for now.

I halfheartedly gathered by stuff before walking over to the counter to pay for my part, but Linde kept luring me into the banter. Linde and Elena didn't look the least bit interested in leaving the place within the coming hour. When they were finally silent for a few seconds I took my chance to get up.

Elena handed me my scarf, which had fallen on the ground. "You really got to go?"

"Absolutely... too much on my plate at the moment. So sorry. Perhaps I'll see you tonight then?"

"Yes! I can cook tonight, if you want to join" Linde offered.

"Well... Perhaps. I had actually planned to quickly cook something myself" I vividly remembered the last time Linde cooked, when she forgot to drain the water for the mashed potatoes. It surely made for an interesting meal. And in any case, it didn't look like they were going to really listen to me at all today.

*

As I was leaving the restaurant, I saw the entrance to the film museum, and was tempted to go have a look. It wouldn't cost me anything to go in; that's the nice thing about this Dutch museum card system: you pay once and most museums give you free entrance. My sensible-self was urging me to go study. Yet another part argued I was not going to be able to focus anyway until I made a decision about my future. And, silly me, that last part won.

There was an exposition about a Japanese filmmaker. They showed some fragments of his films. They all looked pretty slow, he was exploring human relationships. Being serviceable to others, that kind of thing. He often used food as symbols for how people relate to each other. I wasn't particularly interested, but it just made me pause to consider living my life in such a way that people would look at it and remember.

I sat down on a sofa in the exposition, and for some time, I actually managed to focus on my thoughts. But it just didn't seem to add up... I did have the arguments, I did have the idea: become a doctor. Why couldn't I just synthesize and get everything lined up? After all, this was just what my mother did all the time: synthesizing information and then reporting. And not only research, but also rumors she heard on the stock market and from friends in the banking world. She pulled everything together, analyzed it, came to a synthesis and then figured out the perfect strategy. If I couldn't do that for myself, could I even do that for a bank? Would that be easier if you have and actual interest in the topic, or is research the kind of skill one just has or doesn't have? Do I just not have it?

Working in a hospital would be far easier. No uncertainties there, just science. A genetic mutation equals that disease. A certain structure on a brain scan equals those symptoms. A broken bone means that treatment. Easy. Ordered. Neat. I could help cure people. I could even cure my father. But of course, my mum would never pay for an education in medicine. So I *need* to do a double major, get two bachelor degrees at once. It should be doable!

I had had enough of the uncertainty. There was really no one to talk to now, but I had to make a decision. And I went with my gut feeling. It would have to be medicine. So I told myself: go home, dig in and meet those deadlines!

Chapter 4

As I walked out of the museum, my phone rang. An unknown number. The first few digits of the phone number told me the call came from '011', the Rotterdam area. I wasn't too keen on picking up calls from unknown numbers. It was most probably some commercial company trying to sell a new telephone contract. And I had to get a lot of studying done. But when the same number called again a few minutes later as I was unlocking my bike, I became curious and picked it up. It was a certain Ms. Mertens. The name sounded familiar, but I couldn't remember who she was exactly.

"I'm calling about the TopStar Business Contest. I was wondering whether you've received our emails?"

"Eh, what emails exactly?" I was trying to think back to what I had received from them. The last had probably been the message that we hadn't been accepted for the contest.

"Last week's emails."

"Oh, no, let me check." I quickly opened the email app on my phone. There were a few unread emails, but nothing from TopStar. I quickly searched for 'TopStar' but nothing recent turned up. "No, nothing from last week."

"Oh, that's unfortunate."

Below the search results, there was a link to search trash and spam messages. I clicked the link, and suddenly three messages appeared, with 'You're Invited to Join the TopStar Competition' in the title. Wow. "Oh, there's messages in my spam."

"Your spam."

Oh my goodness, how could this have happened? I had been the one responsible for communicating with the contest. And I usually check my spam too, just to be sure, but with all the coursework pressure, I had been neglecting that for a while.

"Well, don't worry. I understand." She explained that they had been trying to reach me, and that they had just reached out to my teammates, because I wasn't responding. "The question really is whether your team from... University College International, if I'm not mistaken?... would like to take the spot that opened up. One of the teams canceled."

"But it starts this week already?"

"Yes, on Tuesday. If you accept, we expect you and your team on Tuesday morning at ten in Rotterdam."

I didn't know what to say.

"Hello? Are you still there?" The woman's voice sounded rushed.

"Yes... Sorry, it's just... Tuesday is really soon! Would you allow me to discuss it with my teammate?"

"All right. But please let me know as soon as possible. Could you call me back at five at the latest?"

I looked at the clock. It was almost two now.

"Eh... Right, okay. Thank you. Sure, I'll call back soon!"

Ms. Mertens broke the connection.

*

I stood motionless next to my bike. Wow, the business competition I had been so excited about. Really prestigious, and with great prize money too. So much that it would even considerably reduce the student loan I'd have to take if my parents wouldn't finance my masters in medicine. I didn't have much time to think, though, because the phone rang again. Claudio. They had called him also, and he asked me whether I wanted to go. I initially doubted a little because of the short notice and my current situation. Claudio didn't seem to have any doubts.

"The prize money is still €50,000! We can both do a master's from that! And more... That's enough to motivate me. Short term or long term."

I asked him whether they had told him anything special, but it seemed that it was the same story. They just needed a quick decision so they could still call others if we wouldn't come. I wondered whether we had been the first reserves they had called.

"Well, I don't know. Maybe others rejected before us?" Claudio laughed. "Anyway, let's both think about it for a bit, and call again in about an hour?"

Suddenly it dawned on me what a great opportunity this really was. All the reasons for signing up came back to me with greater force. I would be able to make a mark, independently! To re-think economics and show the world by applying it to a real-life case in a top business contest. And to gain financial independence in the process. It really was a once in a life-time opportunity! And I said as much to Claudio. "We could call back, but you know, I'm already convinced. Let's do it!"

"I think so too! But, shouldn't we think it over? I mean, perhaps we should check our calendars, right?"

"I don't care about my calendar. I mean, I have deadlines. And calculus. But I'm going. And I need you to come Claudio!" I had to take this chance with all my might.

Still, Claudio told me to calm down and not be so impulsive.

"Whatever. I already know what I want." I told him I was at the Film Museum, and going over to the dorms now. It turned out that he was arriving at Central station. Since we were so close, and the station was on my route anyway, we agreed to meet at the ferries next to the station. After breaking the connection, I decided that this was the once-in-a-lifetime opportunity I had been looking for. But how was I ever going to arrange this, given my current schedule? Could I actually do this without compromising my plan to study medicine? But this was so exciting!

*

After crossing back over to central station, I had to wait a few minutes for Claudio to show up. But soon enough he appeared riding his creaking second-hand bike, which was really too small for him. The comical appearance suited him, though. He greeted me with a jovial wave of his hand. "Miriam!"

I joined him on the bike path, and we cycled in the direction of the UCI dorms. When we had only just started, Claudio saw the music building to our left. "Why don't we go there?" he suggested. I agreed.

I knew Claudio sometimes came to listen to Jazz here, but on this Sunday afternoon it was very silent. It was a new, modern building with large open spaces. "Think of all the music that has been and will be played here. Endless possibilities. This place inspires me."

"So this is where we'll think of our next song then?"

"Exactly!" He smiled encouragingly. "Let's make this work."

The building was quiet, but there were a few people hanging around, mostly students. We sat down at the cafeteria. We were overlooking the same IJ as earlier in the restaurant with Linde and Elena, but now seen from the other side, and from a standpoint closer to the water's surface. "So, I really want to go." I told him.

"So do I, but can we really? Have you checked your schedule?"

We started discussing all the classes we would miss, the assignments due, and any other things we could think of. It didn't take me long to admit, "Look, really, I'm in a bit of a fix."

"Why?"

I hesitated whether to tell him the whole story. He knew about my family situation, of course, but I doubted whether he would understand my attitude towards continuing in economics. I decided to try tentatively. "So, what would you say if I told you I don't want to be a banker anymore?"

"Well, so what? You're a madwomen, 'cause you have the network— but I knew that already." He winked at me.

"You knew what?"

"That you're mad!" He chuckled. "And I don't care, as long as you introduce me to your mum."

"Claudio!" I feigned indignation, although I was kind of happy at his laid-back response. As I sat back and looked around, one of the students who were hanging around started holding up her phone, and seemed to be filming. That was a little uncomfortable, but I decided to let it slide, as she was probably too far away to overhear our conversation.

"What does she think though?" He asked.

"She doesn't know. And she doesn't have to. I'll do this independently."

"What, stop?"

"Double-major." I explained my plan to him to continue my studies and do the pre-medicine track at the same time.

He whistled between his teeth as he heard me explain it. "Wow. Ambitious."

I explained that it meant I needed to do well this term, so that I would be allowed to take extra subjects next semester—or else the plan would fail. As I finished explaining this, I could hear some faint violin notes coming from the distance, which distracted me a little, I turned my head but didn't see anything.

"So, really, you can't use the downtime now." Claudio got me back into the conversation.

"Yes. No. I mean. I want to go to the contest."

"But you can't."

"Well maybe I can. I really want to go. Can't we make it work?"

As we were talking, the music grew louder. It was a single violin playing a tune I recognized: "The Conquest of Paradise" by Vangelis. I turned around again, and now saw a young man with his violin walking towards the café though the open space in the building. There weren't many people in the building, but he did have everyone's attention. The other student was still filming. What was going on?

Of course, Claudio wouldn't be Claudio if he'd let this opportunity pass to joke around. He stood up, pretending to be angry, "Hey, we're talking here. And if you want to do this, where's the choir? Vangelis with one violin is pathetic."

As he spoke, the students hanging around the building started to hum along on the music. Claudio started to laugh demonstratively. "Flash mob in the music building? Like really?" Luckily the students didn't take it too badly and smiled at him.

Claudio chose to ignore them and went back to the conversation. He laid out my plans for me, and figured that it really meant I was trying to hyper-overload myself? And he asked with some reason whether that would even be healthy.

But I countered that the contest would only last a few days and that they might give me extensions. "The contest is prestigious, isn't it? It's good for UCI too."

"But I still don't get it. Why risk your double bachelor?"

At that moment the soft humming of the Vangelis music burst into full volume. I now started to understand why this was called the "music building". The speakers filled the space with booming music. I put my hands over my ears. But I still wanted to continue the conversation.

"Don't you want to go?" I screamed to Claudio. But to no avail. He gestured that we should just wait a bit. But waiting, for Claudio, would never, of course, be passive. Rather, he stood up, and started to theatrically imitate an opera singer who accompanied his singing with grandiose gestures. He soon had even the flashmobbers laughing, and when the music died down, we all gave him an applause and he received it with a deep bow.

The girl with the camera came walking towards us, "sorry, we were just rehearsing a flashmob."

"I could see that!" Claudio exclaimed. "I think I want to join the real thing."

"I doubt they want you to." I pitched in, laughing.

The girl explained that they were only using the video for the rehearsal. But when Claudio wanted to start to ask them all about their plans, I cut him short and explained that we were just in the middle of an important conversation.

"Oh come on." Claudio protested humorously. But, looking at my expression, he conceded and the girl went away.

Coming back to our conversation, I asked, "So don't you want to go?"

"Of course! But for me it's a different story than for you." He explained how he would just love to meet all these new people. "Have talks with students who do flashmobs, that kind of thing." It made him elated to think of all the contacts we'd make. "I'm sure we'll have great fun together, we'll also work together with the other teams and make new friends."

"What?" Was that really all he was after?

"Yeah, I mean, the network you can gain there is super valuable. And it's fun to help people. And good. It's my mission in life. It's what I think. And of course, if we win the prize it's a great bonus."

"So you just want some LinkedIn connections."

"No, I want to make friends."

"Real deep ones."

"Oh bugger off. But I really don't understand *you*. Why do the contest if you risk your double bachelor?"

I tried to put my thoughts in order as I explained it to Claudio. I talked about all the preparation we had done, which I thought was really good. We were really onto something big; with Loffels we were basically re-thinking economics. And now we would get to make our own synthesis: our own, without my mum interfering, and show it to the world at a prestigious contest. "How cool is that?"

"Hm." Claudio didn't look convinced of my argument.

"Not to mention that the prize money would help me get into any masters I would choose." I explained how the money would give me independence. But that would imply that we do need to win. And joining the contest wouldn't mean that I'd give up the double bachelor. It should still be doable, I thought.

Still, Claudio wasn't convinced.

"Well let's see. Shall we just sketch a quick to-do list?" I asked Claudio to take out his laptop and to start making a list of all the things we'd both need to do over the coming days. He hesitantly agreed. Except for the absences from classes that would be recorded during the four days, Claudio had two assignments to hand in, and he had to work one day at his student job. I also had several assignments to hand in, but above all an important calculus test. And then there were my social commitments. There was my meeting with Dad this Wednesday; it was high time I saw him. And Thursday Linde would celebrate her birthday. She was quite excited about the party. "Wow, looks like we have some serious arranging to do." I concluded.

"Maybe seriously too much arranging? Can we really make this work?" Claudio scratched his head.

After talking it over a bit more, we decided to first talk to Loffels in the morning. We thought he'd help us out. Meanwhile we'd tell the contest people to hang on; they would have to understand that making arrangements at such short notice was not easy, but that we were doing our best to go. As for myself, I decided to get started on the social side of things right away, because time was short. Very short. And we just had to make this work.

Chapter 5

I decided that the first obstacle to get out of the way was the visit to my dad. I was too excited about the contest to even dream of studying now, so I thought I might as well go and see him immediately. Perhaps he'd have some good advice too. And it was always good to be with him, even in hospital. I called him to make sure, and he was very happy to receive me. Mum and Tim were there. So perhaps I could settle the whole family thing in one go.

I checked the travel app, and figured out it would be handiest to take the bus where I usually took it when I went to my father. That was close to the dorms, so I could cycle back with Claudio. He liked hearing that Tim enjoyed his whatsapp messages, and wanted to show me some more good jokes, but I told him I had no time to waste. He shrugged and I continued to the bus, which I made just in time.

I knew the route and the way to the hospital quite well, even though I hadn't been for a while. Dad wasn't there all the time, he went home for periods too. He had texted me the precise room, which I found easily. As I came in, I saw Tim sitting next to dad's bed, but mum wasn't there. Dad smiled broadly as he saw me enter. He greeted me with a hoarse voice.

"Hi dad" I kissed my Dad and slapped Tim softly on the back of his head.

He reacted with an indignant "Miriam!"

"Don't whine little one." And to my dad, "I'm quite alright, really. Rather occupied, as usual. How are you doing?"

"I'm exquisitely well!" He talked about how he had just played cards with Tim. "I'm quite sure he was cheating though. I probably shouldn't be telling you this, should I?" He winked at Tim. "Still, I don't think that your opponent being ill is an excuse to cheat, really. Or is it? Last week his best friend also joined our card game. I certainly did not want to point out his behavior then. That sixteen-year-old looks like he can lift a hundred kilos without even blinking!"

"There never are any excuses for cheating, dad," I laughed. "And cheer up, in the event that you do get into a fight, at least you'll have more than enough doctors around."

"Do you think insurance would cover that, though?"

"I'm not sure. So... What have you been up to these days? How are you feeling?"

"It could have been worse." He started talking about a great new TV show he found to watch. "*Breaking Bad,* have you heard of it? Sounds like something I could do. I know how to cook." He mentioned how his neighbor would complain when he turned the sound up too loudly, because it was a bit of a nuisance to him that he really couldn't read the subtitles. "I don't know when they started using the smaller font."

I asked him again how he felt.

"I'm feeling wonderful. Just a little tired, that's all. But what a surprise you came. Weren't you going to come on Wednesday?"

"I was, but something's happening."

"Oh, exciting. I'm sure Tim would love to hear about that, right Tim?"

Tim sat staring at the hospital floor, while fiddling with his phone that he was holding in his hand. He was clearly in the process of slowly going back to his social media, hoping that if he took it easy, no one would notice.

"Right, Tim?"

Tim nodded with a frown and a dejected look, he didn't look to happy about being involved in the conversation.

"Anyway" I continued, "it's really exciting because we've suddenly been offered the opportunity to participate in TopStar. You know, the business contest we were going to join earlier?"

"And that you were not admitted to?" my Dad asked.

"Right. But a team dropped out and now we can join."

"When is it?"

"Well, that's the fix. They emailed us but it got stuck in my spam folder. Now they reached us by phone, but it's already coming Tuesday. So the day after tomorrow."

Tim whistled between his teeth. "Ha, you're coming now so you won't have to come Wednesday?"

I gave him an annoyed look. "I want to see dad, and indeed, I'm not sure I'll be able to this Wednesday."

"I'm happy to see you any time darling. Thanks for coming."

Tim shook his head and now demonstratively took up his phone and started to engage with his messages and notifications. Dad looked at him, but didn't say anything. I wanted to say something, but given that Dad didn't, that felt uncomfortable. Awkward silence.

After a while I asked about Mum. Dad said she had gone to cook dinner and sent her love.

"But are you joining the contest? It's rather last-minute, right?" Dad asked.

"It is. But it's also a great opportunity."

"Will university allow it?"

"UCI invited me for it in the first place. But tomorrow we're talking to the professor who invited us. Hopefully he'll help me to arrange things."

"Hm. I don't think your mum will like it, though."

"Why not?"

"She never thought this particular contest was a good idea, she knows ones better suited to you, where she knows people and you'll be better received."

I couldn't believe my Dad was echoing my mum in this.

"I mean," he continued, "of course you should do what you think best."

"So why don't you tell her that?" I said before I could hold myself back, and on a quite accusing tone too. Not a way to talk to my sick dad.

My Dad smiled faintly. "Perhaps I should."

"Leave Dad alone." Tim said as he looked up from his phone.

"But look darling, why don't you listen to your mother? I know you like this contest, but... she knows her way around. And we'll have less trouble. You know how she gets."

"Don't worry dad. There won't be trouble." I tried to reassure him as best I could, but I had a hard time even believing myself as I said it.

Tim grinned. He clearly saw the trouble coming, and enjoyed the prospect.

I tried to change the subject. I asked Dad about his medication, whether there had been any changes. The medicine he had taken so far made him quite ill.

"I do believe so... it seems that they're now taking me off the snickers. Apparently, they're not that good for me".

"Oh, Dad." He managed to make me smile.

"I'm sorry. I actually have a meeting with Doctor Hofmans in a bit. They'll tell me about the new plans, make new photos, that sort of thing."

"Can I call you later to hear how it went?"

"Of course!"

We talked a little further about things that had happened, but Tim soon had to leave for home, where Mum was cooking him dinner. I also decided to head back to Amsterdam.

*

In the bus back home my mind started spinning again. Was my Dad going to be alright? It was time he became better. At least I had seen him, and that was one less thing to do for this week, but I added a new issue to resolve. How would I talk my mum into supporting my going to this contest? That was not easy, especially given that this whole undertaking was meant to prove my independence from her. She would certainly sense that. So why should I care to involve her at all in the decision process? Really, I felt like just telling her about it after the fact. But that would probably only lead to more trouble, and I felt sorry to make Dad go through that.

After wheeling around the options in my head for a while, I came to the conclusion that my best option would be to inform her before the contest, but only when everything was already arranged. If UCI was fine with it all, then that would give her fewer options to object to anything. Yes, that was best. I should just go and arrange everything tomorrow, and tomorrow evening call mum to tell her I'm going, "if she doesn't mind particularly". What could she possibly say to that?

But that meant that everything needed to be arranged ASAP and extremely well. As I stepped out of the bus I decided to call Claudio. I now felt like we really needed to prepare more for our conversation with Loffels the next morning. I called; he picked up quickly and enthusiastically yelled at me through the phone. "Miriam! I've been thinking long and hard, gave the idea some time to settle in, even imagined spending a night thinking about it while looking at the stars and all, and my final judgment is that we're totally going to make this work!"

I smiled at his enthusiasm. "Good to hear you're fired up. But don't you think we should prepare the meeting with Loffels tomorrow a bit better? Have we even set it up?"

"Yeah, I mailed him. He replied, even though it's Sunday afternoon! This guy is a machine. We can talk to him tomorrow morning first thing."

"Wow."

"I know."

Claudio suggested we go out for a pizza to discuss further. I hadn't even considered the food issue so far, but this sounded like the best option at the moment. So we met up five minutes later in front of the dorms and cycled to a pizza place close by. We went for the American pizza option; Claudio said he liked the lack of pretense. He knew very well what pizza was like in Italy from visits to his family, and he thought no restaurants in the Netherlands he knew came close, even when run by Italians. I thought he was being over-sensitive. But at least the American 'pizza's' didn't give him trouble, because he accepted they were just something else with the same name tag accidentally stuck on them. And they were quick, of course. I actually liked the more 'Italian' ones better, but decided not to fuss about it. I had enough other things to worry about.

After we ordered and sat down, I explained my thoughts to him. It had meanwhile sunk into me that if we would go, we'd already have to leave in two days' time! And there would be so much to arrange before then.

"Right, so you're overloading yourself. That's what I told you. But calm down." Claudio thought that if we'd inform our tutors it really wouldn't be a problem to get extensions. "I have the same deadline as you on Thursday, remember? Dr. Tuzikov is extremely chill, I'm sure we can hand it in next week."

"And what about preparation? When do you plan to do that? If we don't prepare we don't stand any chance!"

"I don't think preparation will take that long." Claudio reassured me that we have all the texts we need, all the theories... "Hell, we even made presentations about books and drew up our 'master plan', remember? We're MPs!" He proposed to just go over the material and be ready in time. We would start tonight, and meet tomorrow night to go through everything together. I agreed that would be the best plan.

Then I started about the social stuff. "Linde won't be happy if I cancel on her birthday party, and have you thought about what you'll do about work?"

"Don't worry about that. I'll say I'm ill."

"Say that you're ill? But what if they find out and fire you?"

"They won't fire me! Miriam, tell me. Why suddenly all the problems? You were so determined before!"

"Sorry. It's just that..." I explained how my Dad and my brother weren't very supportive. And how sure I was that my mum would not like it at all. In short, I needed to have everything prepared perfectly to keep out of trouble.

"Ah I see. Your mum." Claudio offered to call the organizers, if it would ease some of my stress, and say that we would like to join, but with the disclaimer that in case we weren't able to work everything out, we might still cancel. "Or," he grinned, "I don't say that out loud but just think it. What can they do about it, right?"

"Thanks. But I'd feel better if we prepare the conversation with Loffels perfectly. Shall we do that now?"

"If you insist. I think it will be fine."

In the end, I convinced him and we made an extensive overview of everything that needed to be arranged: assignments, exams, teachers to discuss those with, what to say to our tutors. Everything. While it wasn't very different from what we had made before, still it felt good to have double-checked it all, and to have all the action points written down as explicitly as possible. Now we would have to wait and see whether Loffels could really come through for us, as Claudio had envisioned.

Chapter 6

We walked together the next day to the Academic Building to talk with Dr. Loffels before the first class of the day. "Oh yeah," Claudio said, "I forgot to show you Loffels' message. So cool. He's extremely excited." He took out his phone and showed me the email, saying

> *Hi Claudio,*
>
> *That's amaaaaazing news!!! Never thought that would happen!!! YOU GUYS DID IT. YOU GOT IN! I don't know how, and I DON'T CARE! I'm so proud of you both.*
>
> *Let's meet tomorrow first thing before class at 8:30. Can you make that?*
>
> *LET's GET THIS SHOW ON THE ROAD.*
>
> *Oh, and sorry for all the exclamation, this is just really unexpected and really great news for us. Love it!*
>
> *Greetings,*
>
> *Loffels*

Claudio laughed loudly as he went over the email again. "It's so funny how he apologizes for losing it. He is certainly on our side."

Smiling, I certainly had to agree with that! We arrived five minutes early and waited outside his office. It was a shared space, but no-one had come in yet at this time in the morning. It was completely dark. Loffels soon showed up though, with a broad smile on his face.

"Wow, you guys really know how to make a Monday morning look up! *So* looking forward to our conversation."

He opened the door to his office with his keycard, and we walked in after him as he put up his coat. His desk was easily identifiable by a family picture. Two young boys lay happily in the arms of Dr. Loffels and his wife, and a large dog dominated the foreground. It was somewhat hard for me to picture the strict, passionate-about-work Dr. Loffels as a family man. I often wondered if teachers' teaching style would be representative of how they raised their children. If that were the case, I felt sorry for Mrs. Dunna's children. Loffels didn't take too long to organize his things, and said with another big smile "Shall we find somewhere to sit? I bet there's some meeting rooms free." He even closed it off with a completely over-the-top wink of his eye. I had never seen him so excited.

As we walked with Loffels to the meeting room right next to his office, I felt the compunction to immediately pour out all of my worries straight away. Still I kept quiet. Loffels offered us some coffee, which we accepted. He went to the machine and soon came back with a large mug of coffee for each of us. He sat down at the far side of his desk and looked from me to Claudio and from Claudio back to me.

"Wow." he said again. "You are going to join! Okay, there is a lot of stuff we need to arrange then. Did you both revise the theories we discussed earlier? And the master plan? I hope you did. I spent some time on it yesterday, to get everything fresh in my mind."

"Sir..." I interrupted. "I'm sorry, but there are still some significant obstacles. See, I have all these exams and deadlines coming up, and..."

Dr. Loffels waved his hand. "Don't you worry about that now, Miriam. If you can make a little schedule for me when you have what, I'll go talk to your teachers myself."

"Are you sure?"

"Of course I am! Now about our strategy-"

"Sir, if you don't mind, I'd first like to be sure about my deadlines, and especially my exam. And also that the rescheduled deadlines don't clash with new ones. I can't really afford to have everything pushed back only one week, because the week after I have other deadlines. Could we ask the teachers straight away?" I gave him the overview of assignments and teachers we had made the day before.

I noticed Claudio was trying to suppress a smile.

"What?" I demanded, scowling at him.

"Nothing." His hand covered his mouth.

"What is it?"

"Nothing, really. It's just... God, you're stressed. If Dr. Loffels says he will arrange this with our teachers, he will! And it's" he looked at his phone, "8:40 in the morning. You can see there's no-one here, right?"

Dr. Loffels opened his laptop. We couldn't see what he was doing, but I hoped he was looking at teachers' schedules to see if those who we would need to speak to were already in the building. How could Claudio be so matter-of-fact about all of this?

"Did you already arrange time off from your job, then?" I asked him.

"Nah, I'll go by there today. If you haven't fainted in the meantime because of the weight of all this pressure, that is."

"Are you not worried about anything, ever?!"

"Not about this. Miriam, its *school*. We are leaving school for a *career opportunity*. We are not in jail, they can figure something out."

I turned my head away from him and focused on the apartment building across the street that was visible through the high window. My mind kept on racing over the to-do list we had made and how it would all fit. Meanwhile, I thoughtlessly took a big gulp of coffee, burning my tongue. Again. I sat up as if stung and suppressed a yelp. In an awkward attempt to justify my sudden movements I took two bags of sugar and emptied them both in my cup. Claudio watched me and shook his head in amusement.

Finally Dr. Loffels looked up from his laptop.

"Okay, if you really want to get this done first Miriam, let's do it. Then we can meet later in the afternoon to discuss our strategy. So these are the teachers you need to speak to?"

"Yes, well, the deadline from your course is tonight. If we need time to prepare, maybe it is possible to first of all..."

"Of course. What else?"

I really wanted to know what the new deadline would be, so, after some insisting, we agreed on one. We discussed other deadlines. Some of the teachers of these courses were from the same department as Dr. Loffels, and he promised he'd talk to them during the coffee break and email us directly.

"But your test this Wednesday... Mrs. Dunna, I see. She should be around already. I think it would be better if you go see her yourself. She's not too keen on answering emails asking for a re-sit, I've heard from my tutees. She should be in her office. Perhaps you could stop by before class."

I looked at the clock and saw that our next class would start in fifteen minutes already. Well, if I could get this taken care of before then, my mind would at last have some rest. I thanked Dr. Loffels for the coffee and we agreed to meet again during the lunch break. Claudio stayed behind. Obviously, he didn't worry much about further arrangements. He would get it all done. *Claudio.*

*

Mrs. Dunna was a tiny Italian woman. Her class policy was crystal clear: talk when she is talking, and you're requested to leave the room. Eat when she's talking, and either you buy cakes for everyone next time, or you're again requested to leave the room. Students are welcome to go to the toilet when she is talking, but in that case they shouldn't bother coming back either. I knocked on the door to her office, which was ajar. The office was huge, shared with about 16 people, but Mrs. Dunna was the only one there. She was bending forward, taking out pens from her bag and humming a song to herself. She looked up, through her glasses that were almost falling off her nose. I introduced myself as a student in her calculus class, and said I would like to talk about the exam.

"Remind me of your name, please?"

"Miriam. Miriam Schipper."

"Right."

Hesitatingly, I started "Another student and I are planning to participate in a business contest later this week. It will start on Tuesday and it will last until Friday. It is a really prestigious contest, extremely popular, so it's a very significant honor that we will be allowed to participate. The only trouble is that, well, in case I would participate, I wouldn't be in Amsterdam on Wednesday..."

"Sounds like a lot of fun."

"So would it perhaps be possible to take the exam at another time? Sometime next week perhaps, or even coming Friday? Well, rather not Friday really, next week would be much better, but would that be possible?"

"No."

I stood still.

"Excuse me. No?"

"No"

"And may I ask why not?" My voice had lost its kind edge.

"I'm sorry, Marly."

"Miriam."

"It's too short notice. I won't have time to make a new exam, and I hope you understand I don't want to give the same exam to you later. That wouldn't be fair to the other students."

I tried to ask for some kind of possibility to retake the exam. What if people would fall ill on Wednesday, for example?

Mrs Dunna explained that if people are truly too sick to make the exam, of course there are ways for them to retake it later. "I'm sorry, but you're just going to join a fun contest. I can't let everyone who goes on a fun trip just retake an exam."

"Excuse me, but that is not my fault!" I tried to explain that we didn't plan the contest dates, and they only told us yesterday that we could join, and that it is not just a fun trip either. "It is a very educational experience, and very important for my future career. I will have the opportunity to meet a lot of important people, and it will be great for my curriculum. So this is not just some fun outing."

"If you would have come to me earlier, we might have been able to work something out, but you can't just show up two days before the exam asking me to do it at another time."

Again, I emphasized that we only found out yesterday.

"Like I said Marije,"

"Miriam."

"If I would have known earlier, we could have worked something out. I'm sorry, I understand this is something else than beach holiday, but where do I draw the line?"

"If I understand you correctly, it would have been better to call you on Wednesday morning and say I was too ill to take the exam."

"Then you would have been lying. Now you're not. Congratulations. If you disagree with my decision, you can write a letter to the board of examiners and ask them for a re-sit. But I'll doubt you'll have much luck with them."

I had to force myself to thank her for her time before I stormed off, making my way through all the students entering the classroom. They gave me confused looks. Perhaps it's not so common to see someone with a red face and way too much energy storming out of a classroom at 9 in the morning. I was just in time for my lesson, and texted Claudio the news.

"Ms. Schipper, put your phone away please!" Sounded the loud voice of my big books teacher. Great. Wonderful.

But even without a phone, of course I couldn't focus on the class at all. What if I couldn't cancel the exam? Then I would have to choose: either the double bachelor and the chance to enter med-school, or the contest and the possibility to finance med-school. Great choice. And no choice really, because mum would never allow me to go if she knew I was missing a calculus exam because of the contest. What a wonderful day. Ugh.

Chapter 7

I joined Claudio and Dr. Loffels late during the lunch break. Perhaps it was because there were new types of sandwiches in the canteen downstairs and it took me way too long to make my choice. Or perhaps it was because I wasn't too keen to tell them about my conversation with Mrs. Dunna. Claudio and Dr. Loffels were discussing some Greek myth that Claudio had read about. I couldn't quite follow his throwing around names of gods, goddesses, mountains and nymphs. They didn't even notice as I quietly slipped into Dr. Loffels office and edged into a chair. I just stared at the painting again, until Dr. Loffels greeted me and asked me how my conversation went.

I wasn't in the mood for any circumlocution. "Not well. I will not be allowed to retake the exam. And I have to take it. So unfortunately, I cannot join the contest."

They both studied me. Claudio broke the silence.

"Oh, come on! You're going to let one tiny exam hold you back from entering this contest? Who is the teacher, Mrs. Dunna, right? Ah, the Italian lady." As if automatically, he switched into his heavily accented Mafia mode. "I tell you what. We wait for her after school, in the parking lot. We'll put on masks and bring instruments. We are going to make her an offer she can't..."

"Claudio, may I remind you this is my coworker you're talking about?" Mr. Loffels grinned, but corrected himself.

"I'm sorry, sir. I was... just joking."

Dr. Loffels frowned and folded his arms. He thought for a while, and then took out a piece of paper.

"Miriam, listen. You're going to see Mr. Drieberg this afternoon. Do you know him? He's the head of studies for social science, a very kind guy. I'll write a note to explain the situation to him. He will help you, okay? You're in my class at 4; do you have any more classes?"

"I don't."

"Okay. Then after the lunch break you should go see him, alright? If you tell him that I support your choice, it will definitely be fine."

"Thank you." I took his note, which was barely readable. But at least it had Dr. Loffels' signature, so if what he said was true, this should be enough. That filled me with new energy. Dr. Loffels pulled out his reader with all the texts we had discussed previously during our preparation sessions. I grew more and more excited as we went through them to discuss the key issues and our "master plan". I even realized it hadn't sunk away as much as I thought it had, and I remembered most arguments, and the model inspired by game-theory we had been constructing. It was a lot of fun to go over the key ideas again, and before I even realized the lunch break came to an end.

Claudio left for class, and I went straight to Mr. Drieberg's office. The meeting with Drieberg went very well, he was as kind and helpful as Loffels had predicted. He said he would talk to Mrs. Dunna to explain to her the importance of this contest for UCI and see whether that would help. He did emphasize that teachers have the authority to decide in these cases, and that he was only helping to clarify the situation. He said that there were other mechanisms to overrule the teacher, but they would take a considerable amount of time. Still, given Loffels' optimism, his attempt to clarify was enough to give me new hope.

*

As I was leaving Mr. Drieberg's office, my phone rung. It was mum. I doubted for a moment whether to answer. She wasn't quite the person I wanted to talk to at this moment. But given her busy schedule, I couldn't make her call back another time. Also, I had some time before the next class. So I picked up and greeted her as kindly as I could.

"I'm sorry to disturb you" she started, "but I was wondering whether Dad has already told you about what happened yesterday."

"I was with him in the afternoon, but... no. What happened?"

"Did he say anything about his meeting with the doctors yesterday?"

"Yes, he did tell me. I haven't heard how it went though."

"And have you asked?"

"Oh…" Guilt crept upon me. I heard a deep sigh at the other end of the line.

"Miriam, things are not looking up. They've made new scans and they don't look good."

I had to sit down. My heartbeat suddenly accelerated. "What do they show?" I asked, but didn't actually want to hear the answer to that question. In a way, of course, I did. But then again I sort of hoped to hide from it.

My mum explained that the last treatment was supposed to attack and remove all the harmful tissue in his leg. The doctors now saw that it hadn't. Although they didn't see any signs of growth, the treatment didn't have the desired effect on the cancerous tissue. The new pills didn't seem to be helping boost the iron levels in his blood, either. They were still way too low.

"What does that mean?" I asked.

She went on to say that they had no idea why the pills didn't work, and that they would have to run more tests. Now, they were probably going to run the same treatment as last time, but with a higher dose. There were still several other options they might try as well, though. He would probably have to go in for surgery next week. But nothing was certain yet, there was no final plan. She was going to go there tomorrow to help discuss the best route to take, and in the meantime they were going to run more scans. Mum talked more softly than usual, and her voice had also slowed down. It was as if I were a patient and she was explaining the treatment I would undergo to me.

"Oh my…" I didn't know what to say. I was so lost in thought for a while, that I almost forgot I was still on the phone with her.

"In any case Miriam, I'd really appreciate it if you would visit him on Wednesday. He certainly will, too. Of course, he will say that you don't have to come—you know how he is. I am absolutely positive he would really appreciate it if you do."

"Yes mum, I understand."

"I need to go now. I'm sorry to have to break the news to you. I love you."

"Love you too mum."

Why was this happening? The doctors had of course warned that the therapy Dad was getting didn't work for everyone. But why not for him? Of all people, he was the one who most deserved it. And I clearly had to support him. He needed me.

*

I felt very mixed up, there were so many things coming at me at once. I aimlessly walked around the academic building and found Elena and Linde sitting in a project room. Their study books were spread around across the whole room, but music was playing loudly and the ground was covered with sheets of paper. What was going on? I decided I did not want to know. Instead, I lay down on the table like a patient at a psychiatrist and sighed loudly.

"You look stressed," was Elena's authoritative judgment.

"I am stressed."

"Tell me all about it. How are you feeling? If you would be a color, what color would you be, and why?"

I turned over on the table to face her, and I very nearly crushed the brownie she bought for lunch under my body. She could only just save it. Again, I told the whole story about the contest, including the latest updates about my angry mother, my ill father, the hateful Mrs. Dunna and the helpful Mr. Drieberg.

"First of all," said Linde. "Don't worry about that exam. That is really going to be okay. Mrs. Dunna just likes to be all strict and bureaucratic, but she can actually be quite nice. It will work out if Mr. Drieberg goes to talk to her."

"We'll see." I returned to my previous position, lying on my back again.

"Second of all, you are kind of wrinkling my notebook, but that's okay. I'm really sorry about your dad."

"Thanks. I'm sorry about him too." I told her I was confident he would recover, but that it was all just a big bummer. I really wished for him to come home again and that he wouldn't have to go through this whole agony.

Linde nodded empathically. She started to reflect out loud about what my mother had said. She understood that my mum didn't want me to join the contest, but she questioned whether my Dad really wanted me to give up the contest for that visit. "I have only met him at your birthday, but he seems like the nicest man in the world. He wants whatever makes you happy, and if that means joining the contest and a visit on Friday, he wouldn't complain at all."

"Why don't you tell my mum? She'll be convinced." I tried my best to say that as flatly as I could. But of course Linde was used to my irony by now.

"She just wants you to stay. But you said it yourself; your Dad is with you in principle! I'm sure he meant it, and if you go and your mom gets mad at you, he'll stick up for you."

"Maybe, but... Shouldn't I give something back to him? I feel like I should be there for him now."

"My father always says that kids don't understand unconditional love until they get kids themselves. Your Dad is great; he will be fine with it." Elena said. She squeezed me in my arm. "You really do want to go, don't you?"

"I do" I smiled.

"Then go for it, girl! And if you win, your mom won't have anything to complain about. And me neither, because then you can buy us dinner."

"Yes, you would like that, wouldn't you?"

"Okay, maybe lunch then."

"Lunch? No problem, that's a deal!"

I got up from the table, pretending to be 'cured', but still doubtful on the inside. What a day. I really needed to start making the social arrangements, if this was going to work at all. So I stayed in the project room with Linde and Elena, until Linde left for a meeting with her tutor. She would have a difficult talk as well, I thought. Her school results were not as she would have liked, and she was nearly failing one, and maybe even two courses. And failing a course on a "prestigious, superior" college like this one is of course frowned upon. You can even be asked to leave the College altogether if you fail more than one course. We wished her luck and then tried to study for a bit, but the conversation quickly turned to Linde's birthday.

It was an important topic, because, as Elena remarked, when it comes to her birthday, Linde is like a five-year-old, so excited. We decided to brainstorm about the best presents to buy for her. Linde wasn't very subtle about dropping hints, so we knew the present she would most enjoy was to do something fun with the three of us, such as going to an adventure park or going canoeing. But these options were perhaps not too exciting in the Netherlands.

"Helicopter flight?"

"She's been there."

"Skid control course?"

"I don't think she has driver's license, now does she? I'm sure that would make for some very interesting skidding."

"Parasailing?"

"YES."

There's always a trade-off between price and conditions. The cheap vouchers on auction sites make conditions extremely tight. The first parasailing vouchers we found were only valid until next Tuesday. That was not going to work. While scrolling through some more auction sites, we accidentally ordered a cake with a picture of our faces, a set of party poppers and a board game.

Before I knew it, it was time to head off to Dr. Loffels' lecture. Now here was a man who knew to keep his projects separated. In class he greeted me as if I were just another Social Systems student and not someone he had spent hours and hours discussing readings with. Or as someone who, in his very own office this morning, almost had a mental breakdown because of a contest project he was involved in. I'm afraid to say the lecture was boring, as on some other occasions. I didn't dare to check my phone anymore though. Being called out once a day was enough for me. It was therefore only in the break that I saw Mr. Drieberg's email.

Chapter 8

I stared at my phone in disbelief as I read Dr. Drieberg's message.

"Dear Mirjam,

I am sorry to inform you that there will not be an opportunity to redo the Calculus exam that is planned this Wednesday. I discussed the issue with Mrs. Dunna and I agree with her that it is not possible to make a second exam on such a short notice. Exceptions will be made only for those students who can prove they are too ill on the day of the exam, and not for students who voluntarily choose to miss it.

I hope you understand this final decision,

Kind regards,
Jan Drieberg"

I had to walk to the lady's room because otherwise my classmates would have noticed how my eyes were filling with tears. I just couldn't handle it any more. And it was just unbelievable! How hard is it to make another freaking version? Were there really no old exams lying around that I could take? I mean, even if it were the same version, how many students would be able to remember the exact numbers in all the questions well enough to tell me about it? This was so absurd. Anger started welling up in me, but I decided to keep it in check. No use getting into any more trouble now. I had enough as it was.

Dr. Loffels probably felt that I received some bad news, because he didn't bother trying to include me in the class discussions after the break. I am usually quite active in those, but today I didn't feel like participating at all. I tried to direct my anger into a mind-race over all possible alternatives. *Final decision...* There's no such thing as a final decision. Mrs. Dunna herself had mentioned the Board of Examiners. I briefly thought about trying to send them a letter but concluded that success would not be very likely, taking into account the experience of my friends. First of all, the Board usually takes several weeks to reply to any request, and by then the result it would either be irrelevant or too late. Second, they were extremely bureaucratic. If they couldn't base an argument on some sort of written document, they would not at all likely proceed with it. Bureaucracy. Great.

*

At the end of the class, Dr. Loffels gestured for me to wait a moment, and asked me what was happening. I told him about the final decision, and he looked genuinely upset. I decided not to tell him about my private issues. There wasn't much use anyway. Loffels told me that he was sorry about the exam and that he wouldn't want to ask me to completely miss it.

"I know... don't worry about it. You have done the best you could. You haven't heard back from the other teachers, have you?"

"Yes, in fact I have." Loffels told me they were all completely fine with the extension. Dr. Verweegh did want me to hand it in next week, because it is important to do the assignment before the next exam in his course, but Dr. Luft was open to discussing the deadline with me. "And I know that we said Monday, but if that really doesn't suit you, I wouldn't mind if you hand it in later."

"Oh, thank you." Finally some good news. "What do you think I should do about the exam?"

"That is completely up to you." He talked about how Claudio was enthusiastic about the contest, but he thought he'd understand if I would decide not to join after all. He finished by asking, "Have you looked at alternatives?"

"Yes, I heard about a contest at Neyenrode business school. Looks less attractive though."

"Very well. Why don't you talk to Claudio for a bit and decide what you want to do. I'll be in for another hour or so. If you decide you want to go through with it, we'll talk further about your argumentation."

*

I dreaded having to walk up to Claudio with this latest news. He was indeed already completely carried away by the idea of joining the contest, and I heard him talking to his friends about it from the other side of the canteen. He was standing in front of them, arms spread.

"Honestly, I believe we would be able to win this thing. We have an amazing strategy. Can't say too much about it! But it's original, it's refreshing, it's new. And, not to forget, we're going to meet all the people we need to boost our careers. It's... Hey Miriam!"

"Hi there."

He put his warm arm around my shoulder. "I'm telling you, guys. We are going to network ourselves into the business world of the future. Aren't we, Mir?"

"Certainly... Could I have a word?"

"Always."

We sat down in the corner of the cafeteria. "Look Claudio, I don't know how say this. It's bad news. I won't be allowed to retake my exam... and my Dad is getting worse,"

"Your dad.. and you won't? Oh... Why?"

"Not sure. Well, about the exam I am. Because they're too lazy to make a new version."

"Oh... That sucks. But your Dad is more important."

"I know... I'm really sorry about the contest."

"No worries. You can't just leave your Dad alone. I get that."

"Linde thought he wouldn't mind if I went. But even if he didn't, I can't go to the contest and take the exam, can I?"

We sat down to think about that for a little, but some quick calculations showed that I would lose four hours in public transport, so I would basically lose Wednesday. It wouldn't be worth joining and then not joining half of the time. We'd definitely lose.

"Sure. Okay. Well. Too bad. We tried. Want to look for other options then?"

"I don't know. Would be nice, but I'm not convinced."

"Look at this." Claudio pulled up his mobile phone and showed me the latest cartoon his uncle Luca sent him over whatsapp. It showed a fat Italian sitting on a sofa that had split in two under his weight, eating Pizza, with the name of an Italian bank next to it. "Uncle Luca's making fun of himself. That's the bank he works for."

It was nice of him to try and cheer me up again, but it didn't really work.

We did end up going to Dr. Loffels' office to discuss the theories, because we were too distracted to do anything else. We had some fun for an hour. The pressure of having to leave for the contest tomorrow was no longer there, so that we just had discussions about all the interesting material we had covered. Dr. Loffels even bought us some sandwiches that were left in the teachers' office. When he confided that he wasn't entirely sure whether they were his for the taking, or whether they were Mrs. Dunna's who had just forgotten to take them along, that made us even more eager to eat all of them.

*

I left the fun meeting with Claudio and Loffels with very mixed feelings. We just had such a great time going over all the interesting stuff that would be useful in the contest, but I felt there was no way I could go and miss a Calculus exam. And then there was dad, of course. In in an impulse, I took out my phone and called mum. I greeted her tersely.

"Hi Darling, what's the matter."

"Could I also come to see Dad today?"

"Today? What a nice surprise! Of course. Tim and I will be going to see him in a bit. You're very welcome to join."

Well, that was settled. I felt tired of worrying about all the decisions, and Dad was probably the person who would understand me most, even though he was really the one needing the understanding at the moment. I took my bike and rode to the bus stop. Because bus 320 goes every 10 minutes during peak hours, I didn't have to wait long. And half an hour later I was at the hospital.

"Miriam!" My Dad looked really happy to see me. "You've come again so soon!"

"I have a visit lag to make up for."

My Dad grinned. "You've made up for it already. But give me a kiss."

I gave him a hug and a kiss, and not long after Mum and Tim walked in and greeted him likewise. I actually managed to kiss Tim as well this time, as well as hugging and kissing Mum of course.

I didn't know whether to raise the issue of the medical developments, but Mum did the job for me. "René, will you tell Miriam about the medical results? I already informed her briefly over the phone."

"If you insist." My Dad sighed and told me more or less the same story Mum had told me before. The current medication wasn't working, and the latest news was that they were indeed going to try a higher dose before moving on to something else. "Do you know of any cute rat names?"

"Beg your pardon?" I asked.

"Well, since they seem to be treating me like a lab rat, I might as well take on a second name." He smiled ironically.

"René!" My mother didn't appreciate the joke, but I couldn't help chuckling.

"I'm so happy Miriam came today, don't you think darling?" my Dad said to my mum.

"Wonderful, very happy." She said smiling at me. "You should do that more often."

That last remark stung me. Couldn't she just appreciate that I was here now?

"Oh, come on; don't be like that darling, you know she's been busy with schoolwork, and now this contest." Again, my Dad stood up for me. At least he understood.

"Contest?" My mum was surprised.

My goodness, this certainly wasn't the best way for her to find out. I felt blood rising to my head quickly.

Dad looked at me and said, "Oh, you didn't tell her yet?"

I felt stymied, and couldn't answer him, my cheeks flaming.

My mum also turned towards me, "What didn't you tell me yet?"

I hesitated, but forced myself to say, half nonchalantly, "Oh, this contest we were admitted to, but..." my mum didn't allow me to continue.

"The contest I didn't want you to go to?" She said on an accusing tone.

Oh how I hated it when she talked to me like that. I started to answer, "Yes, but..."

"And you were considering joining again?" she looked at me intensely. This was quickly turning into a full cross-examination. She was making me feel like a criminal.

"Well..." I looked away. I should have known better to come to the hospital with my mum there.

"And have you talked to the Neijenrode people?"

This was the final straw. I had intended to tell them that I was giving up on the contest, but this distrustful interrogation was too much for me. I stood up and looked her straight in the face. "No. I have not talked to the Neijenrode people. And you know what? I am not going to. I am going to my contest. I have just come to say goodbye to dad." I walked over to him, hugged and kissed him again, whispering "sorry, dad." And marched out of the room, while Tim and Mum looked at me in astonishment. Good for them.

*

As I walked out of the hospital, I took my phone and called Claudio.

"Mir! What's up?"

"Claudio. We're going." I told him as matter-of-factly as I could.

"Yes! I knew it! I definitely did not call that lady off. I knew you would change your mind! Yes! I knew it! Oh, I want to hug you right now. I'm hugging the phone instead, if that's okay."

"No, I mean we're going to this contest in May…"

"… What?"

"Got you there! We are leaving tomorrow, Claudio!" I yelled at him. "Pack your bags!"

"Damn you! Yes! I definitely already packed my bags. Oh, I'm so excited! Yes!"

We agreed we would meet at 7:15 tomorrow morning, taking into account one of us would only show up fifteen minutes late. We had received a confirmation email saying that someone from the organization would be available to pick up us by car, with a phone number. I called and arranged the pick-up at 7:30 at the Mind Park station, around the corner from the UCI dormitories.

When the bus arrived to take me back to Amsterdam from the hospital, the logistics of our trip to the contest the next day were already arranged. During the ride home, everything that had just happened kept on spinning through my head. I still felt angry at mum, a bit sorry for not saying goodbye to Tim, and most sorry for having to let Dad go through all this now that he was not well. But there was nothing to be done now. The contest it was.

Was there any way I could still pass calculus? I did some quick calculations. Because this exam counted as 20% of the final grade, and my previous tests hadn't been my best, I would have to score pretty high on the next tests to pass the course. It wasn't desperate, but I would have to give it my all and probably cut down on my social life. Not that that was anything much to cut down on: catching up on the extended deadlines had already eliminated the prospect of most of it for the coming months. That made me feel guilty towards Elena and Linde. But, again, nothing to be done now.

*

I was exhausted after that long day. Fortunately, I didn't have to cook. The sandwiches I ate with Loffels and Claudio had been filling enough. I prepared some fruit and put it in yogurt. Conventions about what kind of food is for breakfast and what is for dinner are meant to be broken. My phone reminded me that I was supposed to go to a concert with Linde, but when I texted her about it, I was glad to find out she had forgotten. I didn't particularly feel like standing and shouting all night, especially not before the contest. But it was a nice opportunity to invite her over for tea instead. She came. A month ago, she had discovered a wonderful new flavor at the local Turkish store, and we had been addicted to it ever since. We still hadn't figured out what kind of tea it was exactly, since the descriptions were in Arabic and we couldn't be bothered to ask anyone about it. I just hoped it wasn't octopus arms, or frog droppings, or something of the kind. It was a mystery how Linde found this tea and she carefully kept the secret. Her latest explanation was that a prince presented it to her in a dream.

We were sipping our tea and mindlessly watching some comedy show on television. Or was it a drama show? The fact we weren't sure showed how unengaged we were with the show.

"I know why you are so quiet," she said.

"Really? Tell me."

"You're bummed out that you can't go to my birthday"

"I am."

"But you're still joining the contest."

"Yes."

"And when you get back?"

"I'll need to work like crazy."

"Have you actually thought about this?"

"I've worried about it."

"But you're still going?"

"There's no other option."

"Why?"

"Long story." I didn't feel like explaining, so I hugged Linde and felt bad about the prospect of having less time to spend with her and Elena.

I couldn't get myself to go to bed just yet. So we watched The Lion King, curled up on my couch underneath an old, smelly blanket. It was raining outside, which added to the coziness. So then we watched The Lion King II. And then The Lion King III, which I didn't even know existed. It was quite as bad as you would expect from a second sequel to a perfect movie. We ate grapes and Linde spoiled some of the surprises she had in mind for her birthday party. It made me wonder how many of these were true and how much of this was wishful thinking, though. I believed there would be a cheese fountain, but how she would arrange the display of a t-shirt recently signed by Coldplay? Really?

It was 2 in the morning when I realized I still needed to pack my bag. What would I need to bring? The lady hadn't said anything specific, but surely lots of paper, pens, pencils and erasers would come in handy. I might as well pack double the amount of writing supplies because Claudio would probably forget his. Then a tooth brush and pajamas. The number one and two on the ranking list of 'Things People Forget When They Go on a Holiday'. A list compiled by me, based on experience. My laptop. Charger. Phone charger. More paper. Calculator. It didn't all fit in my backpack, so I had to reload everything into my small suitcase. I double checked everything before I finally crawled into bed.

It was 2:30 when I finally went to bed, and suddenly realized with a start that in only a bit more than four hours, the first day of the contest would start.

Chapter 9

I did not feel rested when my alarm clock went off. It sounded louder than ever, disrupting the wonderful dream I was having. The moment I woke up, I had already forgotten what exactly the dream was about, but I remembered that it was nice. It had something to do with the sea, and with people. It is a pity how you can never keep those dreams in your memory long enough to enjoy them a bit longer. Usually I snooze the alarm at least five times, but now I woke up with that tired yet excited feeling you get when you go on a holiday. I opened the curtains to let some sunlight in, but it was still dark outside. The rain was tapping against my window and it only strengthened the excitement to go away on a trip.

I thought it would be a good idea to roll out of bed, but the execution didn't go as planned. I landed hard on the floor. I squawked in protest; *what a great way to start this day,* I thought. But in the end it woke me up quickly, and the bruise wasn't too bad.

My phone battery had dropped below 12% and I quickly plugged it into the charger, hoping that half an hour's time would be enough to have enough charge for phone calls, in case something went wrong along the way. Speaking of phone calls... I sent a text message to the group chat of my friends. They would probably not read it for at least four hours, hours of sleep I would have to catch up on another time. I texted Claudio to see if he was already awake. Last seen: 4.39. When would be the last time for me to call him, if he didn't wake up in time? I guessed I could drop by his room? Focus Miriam, I told myself. I had already laid out the clothes I wanted to wear today. Casual chic. Not too formal, but still businesslike. When I put the clothes on, though, I felt that I looked like I was trying way too hard. Should I go for the blue blouse instead of the white one? Blue would be better, yes. Now the shoes... Oh no. What shoes?! I now realized I had left my business-boots, as I liked to call them, at my parents' place. Oh bugger, oh ... I found a pair of heels, but they were way too party-ish, weren't they? I only had ten minutes left before meeting Claudio. Desperate times call for desperate measures. I called Linde, three times before a sleepy voice finally picked up.

"I'm coming by now to get your shoes!" I yelled, as I struggled to put on my coat with one hand as my other hand was holding the phone.

"Hm? Whatever..." Was the sole response I got. I assumed she fell back asleep already.

On socks, with my coat half open, I then ran down the stairs and furiously knocked on Linde's door. No answer. I tried the door, and it was open. It was dark inside and it took some time for my eyes to adjust. I walked over to the bed and tapped Linde on her shoulder. She barely responded.

"Linde! Where are your black shoes that I like? I need them. It's important."

"They're somewhere over there..." It was difficult to hear exactly what she said, but I understood enough. It didn't take long before I found them, put them on, thanked her, even though I am not sure if she fully realized I was there, and then made my way downstairs.

*

7.15 Exactly. Since the rain was still pouring down onto the sidewalk, I first peeked outside before I ventured out to where I had agreed to meet Claudio. Happily, no thunder and lightning any more. But there was no Claudio in sight. I walked outside to make sure, but he wasn't there. How typical. I checked my phone and saw that he hadn't been online this morning. Come on... I called him, but no response. He didn't even pick up the fifth time I pressed the green button underneath his name. My stress levels began to rise. Could I leave my suitcase out here while I dashed up to his room? I ran towards the elevator, and then decided I didn't want to risk it. I walked back, took my suitcase, and anxiously waited for the elevator to come down. The excited, happy feeling I had woken up with just half an hour ago had seriously deteriorated. Maybe this was a bad decision. Maybe I should just go back to bed, wake up in a few hours, and this stress would all just be a hazy dream. I could just go to my classes, make my deadlines, do my exams, say 'sorry' to mum, meet my family and friends and all would be fine.

The elevator doors opened. I was so in my own world that I half bumped into the person that walked outside.

"Sorry," I mumbled.

"Where do you think you are going?" A familiar voice. I looked up. Thank goodness. "Claudio!"

He laughed and greeted me with a hug.

"You already look stressed, and we haven't even started yet! Have you forgotten anything? I can wait outside with your suitcase, if you like?"

"No, thanks, it's fine." We were still in the hallway and both looked outside for a moment before looking back at each other.

"You could have picked some better weather, tjeemigminemig" Claudio said, expressing his disapproval in Amsterdam slang. I smiled. We both closed our jackets as high as we possibly could before stepping outside.

As we walked down the street towards the Mind Park station huddled up against the rain, we were silent for a while, before Claudio gave me a start. "You know, I'm having my last-minute doubts."

"You what?," I sputtered.

"About whether we should go."

"What? Why?"

"Tim messaged me yesterday. He asked me whether I'm going with you. Seemingly your mum is 'not amused' about us going."

My mouth fell open in astonishment. "Tim messaged you?"

"Yeah." And he quickly added, "I told him I was going."

"And now what?"

"Well, I just…" he paused for a few seconds. "I just don't want my relationship with your mother to start like this."

"Oh, is that what this is about. Well, don't worry." I stopped in the middle of the sidewalk and got out my phone. Bending over forward to shield it from the rain, I searched for Tim and wrote him a message. It said: "The fact that I'm going is not Claudio's fault, it's mum's fault." I briefly showed it to Claudio and pressed 'send'. "That should do it." I told Claudio. "Now let's go."

Claudio didn't look too convinced that this was the solution he'd been hoping for, but sure enough he came along with me.

When we arrived at the parking spot next to the station, we decided to walk up the stairs to the station waiting area, where we would be dry and had a good view of the surroundings. We were a few minutes early. Claudio asked who was picking us up, and I reminded him that it's this girl who was working at the Erasmus. I forgot her name, but thought it was something like Patty or Patricia. Because she lived in the Bijlmer, South-East Amsterdam which is quite close to UCI and was going to Rotterdam by car, she had offered to come by here to pick us up.

"Oh, that's really nice."

"I know."

I was now entirely awake—Tim's message to Claudio having accomplished the job started by my bruised backside. It made me more determined than ever to show the world that I could handle this; me, not my mum's network, not even her approval. This competition would be mine. I was going to win. I would show them. "Look" I started to say to Claudio, "shouldn't we go over our 'master plan' once more, now that we're actually joining? I mean, we haven't had that much preparation."

"If you insist."

"Well, of course I insist. But you should also."

"It's 7:30 in the morning Miriam. My little grey cells still need their coffee. And it's not really a big deal anyway."

"What?"

"I mean, we're going to network our way into business! As long as we do a decent job we're fine."

"No we're not! We're going to show the world that we have something new to say. Something different. Something inspiring."

"Something they'll hopefully like. But if they don't, then we'll just go with the flow, right?"

I couldn't believe he was saying that. I mean, he had talked about this networking thing before, but I thought we'd always agreed on the approach. "No, we'll not!"

"But you want to win, right?," he pursued.

"I do, of course!"

"Then you need to do something that the jury will like. They decide, you know."

"We just make them like what we do. And if we're not original we don't stand a chance. We're the *liberal arts* team. We have to be out-of-the-box. It's what we do."

"Yeah, well. But it has to connect somehow." He paused and then, "You know what?"

"What?"

"Why don't we ask this Patricia girl what she thinks about our approach? She works there, right?"

"She does," I admitted.

"Great, so we can get some inside info. If that works, then we go for it. If she thinks it's way out of line..."

"She won't!"

"We'll see." He seemed so assured.

"If you're not in on this I'm calling Loffels."

"I'm scared" he said ironically.

My phone rang; an unknown number. It was the girl, who introduced herself as Patience, saying she was running ten minutes late. I quickly checked the time and saw we would still be quite comfortably on time. We had wanted to make double-sure not to be late, so we had a considerable margin. Claudio suggested I ask for the type of car; she only said it was a red car.

We decided to quickly grab some coffee at the local supermarket at the other side of the station. It wasn't officially opened yet, but several employees were already busy replenishing the store. Some of them were fellow-UCI students and they were kind enough to let us make use of the coffee machine. The coffee was hot and it was just what I needed on this rainy morning. By the drumming noise on the roof of the waiting area it sounded like the rain shower was only intensifying.

After getting our coffee, we rushed back to the parking lot; happily most of the road was underneath the train tracks and therefore dry. As we approached, we saw a tiny red car pulling up in the middle of the entry to the parking lot, blocking the road for absolutely everyone who would want to pass by. Luckily it wasn't too busy. A tall slender girl with flowing dark hair and an even darker skin color got out of the car and stood next to it. She looked nice enough, but would we really have to drive in that car? Yes we would. Independence from the banking world would have its downsides. But off we went.

Chapter 10

With the typical nervousness of meeting someone new who is there to help you, we made our way down the tunnel underneath the tracks to the parking lot. In the pouring rain, we shook hands.

"Hi, I'm Patience," her voice sounded sweet and her hand shake was weak. Her curly dark hair was already dripping of wetness, and her brown eyes inspected us curiously.

Personally, I didn't feel like a lot of conversation except for saying my name. I just wanted to step inside the warm car. Claudio apparently did not. After he introduced himself he thanked her a million times for picking us up.

To be frank, the car looked like a wreck. There were scratches and dents all over and the model looked like it was built in the eighties at the latest—or even the seventies. The color was a type of red they don't use any more in the car industry. I tried to contain myself. I really should not complain, after all; this girl just drove all the way here to pick up two people she had never met before and definitely knew nothing about, except that they were joining a contest. Well, a contest she was helping to organize to be more precise.

Claudio and Patience were still chatting. I saw how Patience awkwardly made attempts to get back into the car, but Claudio kept asking her questions. "Would you consider discussing this inside the car, perhaps?" I asked Claudio with all the charm I could muster.

Patience looked at me gratefully. We put our suitcases in the backseat of the car, which left a tiny spot for me to sit in. Claudio took the front seat next to Patience and we drove away. I felt a feeling of excitement taking hold of me. We were on our way! Ready to get this adventure started! I tried to start the conversation, but clearly Claudio needed first to chat with Patience a bit more. Understandable. She was studying Film and Literature in Leiden. She was in her second year already, and lived with her parents still, since it was only a half an hour by train to Leiden from the Arena, where she lived. I didn't participate very actively in the conversation, which naturally happens when you are the only person sitting in the back seat.

I thought my time might come, but Claudio kept tossing questions at her. What kind of work was she doing, and didn't she want to join the contest herself instead?

Patience explained that she had been looking for a side-job to finance her studies, and that one of her teachers had put her in touch with the Erasmus University. This teacher was part of the preparatory team; he was there to critique the text of the case. Since the beginning of this year she had been involved in logistical operations, like arranging the hotel for the participants to stay, arranging the catering, and keeping in touch with all different parties that were involved in preparing the case study the participants would receive and the practical planning of each day. Officially, her tasks had now ended, especially because in the search for sponsors, others had taken over the day-to-day logistics. But Patience had wanted to come today to see the result of her work, and perhaps lend a bit of a helping hand behind the screens. Her studies weren't very busy at the moment, so she thought she might as well come. And she could start by driving us there, which already make her feel useful.

"You already know what case the participants will need to solve, then?" Claudio asked.

"No, I don't, actually. I wasn't involved in the content of the contest." she explained. She said that she worked with totally different people than she was used to meeting. If it was up to some people, they would let participants work for twelve hours a day on the case. She found that quite amusing. "Luckily I was able to talk some sense into them that they needed to keep track of the time."

"Did you work with important business people, then?" Excitement was audible in Claudio's voice.

"Yes, I guess I did. I didn't know them beforehand. Business is not my favorite topic, I have to admit."

"Would you have joined the contest yourself, if you could?" I asked, in an attempt to involve myself in the conversation again.

"Before starting this job I would have said no. But now? Yes... Yes, I think so. Maybe I could offer some new 'cinematographic' angles on the case." She smiled.

In an attempt to steer the conversation towards discussing our approach further, I mentioned that neither Claudio nor I studied business. I hoped she got the hint that therefore we needed some discussion time now. But my comment was apparently too vague.

"Oh no, not all participants study business. But many of them do, of course."

I was just gearing up to provide further hints to move things along, when Claudio asked, "How many teams are joining?" He had turned in his seat, laying back and facing her like a dog facing his owner.

"I believe there are six teams, including you. They're from all over. Is it just the two of you, though? Or are other people coming later? I must have seen your application, but I'm afraid I can't remember."

"Absolutely, it's the two of us... Why?" Claudio asked. This was actually interesting, so I leaned forward. The belt was hurting me, and I twisted a bit in my seat.

"Oh... Well, I guess that's fine. A bit on the small side though. The other teams have four members, and one of them has five, I believe."

I looked at Claudio and hoped he would look back at me, but he didn't. Dr. Loffels hadn't made any mention of a required group size. But being with fewer in a team would give us a competitive disadvantage, I thought. So he might have informed us about it!

*

We had just turned up the motorway. The car windows didn't fully close at the top, and the wind that blew past made loud and strange noises. It was difficult to continue involving myself and following the conversation. I stared out of the window. How was I going to talk to Claudio like this? I really felt that I needed to! Rush hour was well underway, and there were many cars on the motorway. We were in the slow lane, so I saw meadows flashing by, with a cow here and there. It must be awful for them to be outside in this weather. Do cows have water-resistant fur? I hoped for them that they did. Patience and Claudio were talking loudly in order to understand each other. My eyes followed some raindrops that were chasing each other on the outside of the car window. What to do?

"Are you okay, Miriam?" Patience tilted her head backwards, but even then needed to nearly scream at me to make herself understood. "Would you like something to drink? I brought you some water. I also have peppermints, if you like."

"Yes please! Could I have some peppermints?" Does peppermint actually contain any calories? I hadn't had any breakfast yet. Claudio followed Patience's instructions and found a roll of peppermint in the glove compartment. He held it out to me, but I shook my head. I had given up on trying to be part of their conversation. There was too much interference to hear well. At the next stop I would have Claudio switch places with me, though. I barely had any space for my legs or my feet. But it was about time we started to discuss the content. The contest was nearly getting started.

I tried to intervene. "Claudio! We really do need to discuss our master plan a bit further! Can we do so?"

"Our master plan! Yes, of course, but we first need to explain some of that to Patience!"

Oh my. That's indeed what we had agreed on, but I thought Claudio would have understood that Patience wasn't going to help us much, given her background. But seemingly, that didn't dawn on him yet. And now we were just going to lose time talking to her.

"Did you hear Miriam, Patience? We have a master plan! Let me tell you about how that came about. Would you like that?" Patience smiled and nodded. "Alright. It all started with an inspiring lecture at UCI by Dr. Loffels, who has coached us in the preparation for this contest."

I was starting to bite my nails in irritation, but there was little else to do than to sit back and hear him out.

Chapter 11

Claudio's story. University College International.
Nine months earlier.

It all started with a 'Who's in Town' lecture, one of these extracurricular lectures that are organized at UCI. Loffels had read a book by Bruni called "Reciprocity, Altruism and the Civil Society. In praise of heterogeneity" by Luigino Bruni. The professor wanted to transmit its contents to any interested students, because he thought we might get inspired by it. I don't think Miriam was there, but I went because I thought seeing an economist talking about altruism would be a nice freak show to attend. And I have to say, to my shame, I fully had the intention to make as much fun of him as I could.

The start of the lecture was as idealistic as I had expected. Loffels explained that this book criticizes the view that characterizes mainstream economics and game theory. That view holds that there is only one type of reciprocity in economics: that based on repeated interactions on the basis of individual self-interest. Instead, Bruni's book says that reciprocity is complex and multidimensional, that people sometimes also show unconditional behavior with regard to others. And in making this clear, Bruni is trying to change the world for the better.

When I heard this talk about changing the world, I was like: "Oh really?" I had just quit my job at a supermarket, where everything looked very formal and correct on the outside, but behind the screens my colleagues and I were not being treated well. The managers were always trying to squeeze us out: to get the most work out of us for the least possible pay. That wasn't much fun, but it's the economy, right? Was one book going to change that? I felt rather skeptical.

But Loffels continued to explain that there is now a range of evidence that better working performances are achieved in those environments where more value is given to the quality of relations. That was interesting to me, because if there's evidence, people may listen. He said that workplaces where bullying and 'mobbing' take place also lead to bad working performance. Makes sense.

Still, Loffels explained that this is not at all what we would expect based on standard economic theory. There we would expect that relational gains correspond to economic losses. "So isn't it time to update the theory?" Loffels asked. He mentioned that this is especially important because all studies on happiness show that relationships importantly contribute to our happiness.

There he had a point. I certainly knew that bad relationships at the supermarket were not making me or anyone else happy. And so again, there were studies. But economics is economics, right? Self-interest reigns! Loffels didn't seem to agree.

*

Loffels went on to explain that there have been several attempts to make sense of relationships in economics. Philosopher Martin Hollis and economist Robert Sugden have tried to show in different ways how relationships are 'rational', coming up with something Bruni calls 'we-rationality'. That means that people think about 'us' rather than only about 'me'.

That made me think about how we talk about 'us' in our family. Or even the 'Cosa Nostra', 'our thing', as the Mafia dons that I like to imitate at times call their organization. So it seems that this 'we-rationality' definitely happens in society.

Loffels mentioned that another approach to describing relationships in economics is to see them as 'relational goods', with different authors defining differently what that exactly means.

That sounds somewhat logical, because economics looks at the world from the perspective of an agent choosing goods. Still, it also seems somewhat counterintuitive to call a relationship a 'good'.

In any case, Loffels explained that Bruni is proposing another route in this book. It contains a description of reciprocity in which different forms of reciprocity exist and interact with each other. Some of these forms of reciprocity are unconditional; but those that are not unconditional are not necessarily selfish. "Friends help each other, right?" he mentioned.

This was my chance, so I asked, "What do you mean friends? In economics? Will Apple give me an iPhone because I'm their friend?" I got some giggles from the room. Nice start.

"Apple won't, but your friend the baker may give you a birthday cake."

"Yeah, 'cause he's my friend. Not because I buy his bread."

"And what if you became friends in the bakery?"

"Then that's good for us."

Loffels said we'd come back to this later. So I kept my silence, but I had drawn first blood.

Loffels explained how Bruni goes on to contrast British with Italian, or more specifically Neapolitan thinkers. He especially contrasts Adam Smith, the person we usually consider as the founding father of economics and who lived from 1723 to 1790, with Antonio Genovesi from Naples, who lived from 1713 to 1769. For both thinkers, the market is an important social force, a civilizing force. For Smith, where there is freedom and markets establish their typical institutions, there trust, truthfulness and all civic virtues will blossom. It also happens the other way round: civilization takes markets along with it. The Neapolitans agree: they see economic activity as accompanying civil life and understand trade as a highly civilizing factor. They see civil life as a place where civic virtues can be fully expressed.

But Smith and Genovesi don't agree about everything. Where they grow apart is the type of relationality that they see as being proper to the market. Smith says that the market, even though it is a place of virtue, is not really the place for friendship. He says *"In civilized society he [man] stands at all times in need of the cooperation and assistance of great multitudes, while his whole life is scarce sufficient to gain the friendship of a few persons."* Seen like this, friendship is not a part of ordinary market relations, there is rather a weak type of market relationality.

This was going my way, so I spoke up again, "Right, so I can be friends with the baker, but not with the butcher, the electrician and the Samsung sellers too! Even though they can think I'm cool of course..." There was no response from the crowd this time. Not funny enough Claudio...

"Ah yes, so you seem to be quite Smithian in your approach." But Loffels explained that to understand him well, you need to see that he was contrasting a market-based society with feudalism, which Europe was just climbing out of. And of course, the population was growing and cities were getting larger. Friendship is then just too rare to build a large society on, in his view, and there is sacrifice and risk involved in a friendship.

"Sacrifice and risk?" That sounded pretty dramatic to me.

"Well, reflect a little." But in the end, Loffels decided not to go into this issue; he said that's really a different book. Loffels thought that for now it was enough to understand that in his historical situation, it was very important for Smith to affirm that *"Society may subsist among different men, as among different merchants, from a sense of its utility, without any mutual love or affection."* The market introduces egalitarian relations based on mutual utility, against the illiberal hierarchic relations of feudalism.

I now remembered another book I had read called "the Wound and the Blessing", where personal relationships were described as being a blessing, but also inflecting wounds. And because I could hardly start ridiculing Smith, I stopped interfering for now. There would be other opportunities.

Loffels continued saying that this was Smith's view, but that Genovesi disagrees, because for him, the person is constitutively relational, and there is nothing worse for a person than being alone. Genovesi says that the human person has a certain special type of sociality, namely reciprocity, which sets human beings apart from animals. Therefore he thinks market relations are relations of mutual assistance, and so they're neither impersonal, nor anonymous. This way of seeing the market also leads to his emphasis on trust, not only in individual persons, but also in something he calls 'public confidence'. Because the market is part of civil society, the concept of public confidence is an directly economical concept. And whereas friendship for Smith is a chosen private relationship among specific individuals tied by affective bonds and trust is impersonal, Genovesi rejects this distinction. For him, ethical confidence and friendship share in the same rationality that is a precondition for the harmonic development of civil society. The separation between private and public is therefore much less strong in Genovesi than it is in Smith. The private and public domains share the same logic for him, namely the logic of reciprocity.

Loffels made clear that Bruni's book follows this same line: the market is an instance of civil society, which can be distinguished but not separated from the more genuine reciprocity of friendship and gift. These various forms of reciprocity don't rule each other out, but reinforce each other.

I saw another chance to interrupt, but unfortunately another student beat me to it.

"So Genovesi doesn't separate work and private life, like people usually do here?"

"Not as strongly, no. Perhaps he would also say that taking your conflicts at work home is not a great idea. But he would say you can become friends with your colleagues or clients."

"I've never studied friendship in an economics class."

"True. Bruni explains why, but we'll leave that for now. The point is the 'intrinsic value of sociality', meaning that a market interaction can be seen as friendship, which is not opposed to civic friendship. That idea is mostly missing from economics today. Bruni goes a different path with this book."

I was rather taken aback that Loffels said this, because he was already placing himself in the position of a critic of mainstream economics. I would first have to understand his criticism before I could effectively ridicule it, wouldn't I? So I decided to listen first.

Loffels went on to explain that the rest of Bruni's book is about mathematically simulating the interaction of four game-theory strategies. The first strategy is non-collaboration. The second is the cautious collaboration strategy. The third is a 'brave' or philia (friendship) strategy. Finally, there is a strategy of gratuitousness. The rest of the book is dedicated to studying, conceptually and mathematically, how these strategies interact with each other, and what that means for society. Among other things, he finds that heterogeneous strategies are important for the friendship culture. He finds that cautious reciprocators only contribute to the spread of reciprocity if there are also some unconditional cooperators present, who activate them. So cautious collaborators only really benefit civil life if they live symbiotically with unconditional actors. But, Bruni also says, to really understand the message of the analysis, you need to dive into the mathematics. In the lecture, we only did that superficially.

The rest of the lecture I found interesting, but I didn't manage to intervene much more. When I wanted to leave the hall, slightly disappointed by my lack of success, Loffels called me over. He invited me to a private conversation the next day. That was a surprise! I was curious, so I went.

*

When I showed up for the meeting the next day, Loffels took me to one of the small meeting rooms on the top floor of the UCI academic building. They're pretty small, and have this really big window so everyone can see you, but it does give some peace and quiet to talk. I wondered what was going to happen in this conversation; he didn't seem too mad at me for my interventions during the lecture.

After welcoming me and even offering me a cup of coffee, which I gratefully accepted, he started saying, "You seemed very engaged during the lecture yesterday."

Very engaged! I didn't see that one coming. But I suppose it was true. In response I put on a big smile and said, "Yeah, you had an original angle."

"Did you like it?"

"I don't know what to make of it yet. But really, it was Bruni's angle, wasn't it? Do you agree with him?"

"More or less."

"So how do you see economics then?" I was getting kind of curious.

"Ah. Good question." Loffels sat back in his chair, hands behind his head, and started to talk. "I agree with Bruni that economics is about reciprocity in relationships. People think economics is about money. It's not! Money is only a mechanism to help people collaborate with each other. That's why I like money. It brings collaboration."

I had to let this change of perspective sink in for a moment. But it was so counter-intuitive that I had to ask, "How do you mean? Economic actors are supposed to be self-interested, right? Like *Homo economicus*?"

Loffels took the opportunity to explain that even though an economist might start thinking from the *Homo economicus* model, they were always trying to make different *Homo economicus* collaborate with each other. He said that the whole idea behind economic science is that win-win agreements are possible. This means that two people can collaborate out of self-interest, and each of them can still win.

"So it's okay if everyone's greedy?"

"Self-interest is not necessarily greed. It can be very legitimate. I think 'Greed is good' is a mistaken interpretation."

I was getting a bit confused.

Loffels could see that, and tried to explain further. Classically, he said, economists have tried to make *Homo economicus* collaborate in two ways. The first of these he liked to call hierarchy: the government can force people to collaborate. The second is usually called competition; he liked to call it 'free exchangeability'. If people can choose with whom to collaborate, that will stimulate people to collaborate well.

"Okay," I said, pursuing this, "and left-wing and right-wing people prefer different mechanisms."

"Correct, but there is another mechanism."

"Really?" That had me interested.

"I like to call it 'voluntary commitment'." Loffels clarified that this voluntary commitment could take place on a small scale, for example through friendly relationships. It could also take place on a larger scale, when people freely commit to a certain 'identity'.

"Oh, that's why big brands try to make themselves into a 'lifestyle'?"

"Correct!" And Loffels concluded that to answer my question about how he saw economics, he would say three things. First, economics is about getting people to collaborate with each other; if people collaborate in win-win ways, things are 'in balance'. Second, sometimes things go wrong. People are neither so rational nor so immoral as *Homo economicus*; rather, they have a limited rationality and a limited morality, which means things can go off-balance. Among other things, that may lead to win-lose, lose-win or even lose-lose agreements. And third, economists identify mechanisms to correct imbalance through mechanisms of hierarchy, free exchangeability or competition, and voluntary commitment, like through friendly relationships or feeling part of a certain identity.

"Wow, thanks. Is this why you invited me here?"

"Ah, no, I wasn't actually trying to lecture you more." He laughed, saying, "that kind of just happened."

"Why then?"

"Well... actually, I am looking for engaged students to enter into a prestigious business case competition."

Chapter 12

I had heard Claudio's story before, so I stared out of the window and attempted to catch some phrases. The noise in the car made that even more difficult. We had meanwhile embraced the idea that in real markets, people can relate to each other voluntarily. It became one of the backbones of our 'master plan'. If you pay some attention, you see it everywhere.

"Don't you think this is cool Patience?" I started, leaning forward to insert myself in the conversation from the depths of the backseat, once Claudio finished. "We're actually re-thinking economics with Loffels. And now it's up to us to implement that in a contest!"

"Cool." Patience nodded.

"Yeah, we do need to still talk further about the translation to business though. Could we get started on that?"

"What, the two of you?" she asked. "Sure, no problem."

We drove past a sign that told us there was a parking lot with restaurant a few kilometers ahead. That got Claudio completely distracted from any further talk.

He loudly yelled, "Stop for food!"

That reminded me that I could use something myself; not too many calories, of course. I should have brought something to eat, but had forgotten in the stress of the early morning. Seemingly, the same had happened to Claudio.

Patience almost swerved the car onto the wrong lane and apologized for our bodies thrown against the side of the car. "Shall I stop there?"

"Yes, please!" I exclaimed. "Oh... Could someone please pay for me? My ... purse ... is ... in ... my suitcase! I'll ... pay ... back!" I hoped the spaced message would get across to the front seats. It did, fortunately.

"Of course, no problem!" Patience was softly singing to herself as she took the next exit. I was sure I could make out some food-related words in her song. It was lovely to stretch my legs after being crammed into that little car. Claudio almost instantly ran inside the restaurant. I tried a "Wait for me!" but it was already too late. I stayed behind with Patience, who was struggling to get her purse out of her coat.

"We cannot spend more than ten, fifteen minutes here. We don't want to be late." I told Patience.

"I know. We will be fine." Somehow, she seemed a bit too calm about it for me. That worried me a little, but I decided to leave it there.

The boot of the car that was parked next to us was open. Two little girls, around five and seven years old, were sitting inside and waving at us. Their blonde curly hair shook wildly as they did. "Hey! We have candy! Would you like some candy?"

I resolved to talk to Claudio when he would be finished at the restaurant, and walked over to the girls with Patience. I saw them proudly sitting on a bright pink blanket, with a half-empty bag of candy in front of them. One of the girls held a jar that contained a few coins. I now noticed a young man was standing on the other side of the car. He was dressed in a neat looking blouse with sporty shoes. When he saw us coming closer to the car he stopped to smile before he turned back to his phone conversation. The girls proudly began to organize their candy in front of them on the blanket. "Look, we have chocolate, and this blue one... But I don't like that blue one. Emily does, but I don't. I like the red ones better. Do you want a red one? They cost 50 cents. We are trying to save up for a dog. Dad says that a dog is expensive, but if we can earn a lot of money ourselves, we can have a dog." The youngest girl was focused on laying out all the candy precisely on a straight row as she spoke to us.

"That looks delicious! Let me see if I have some money for you. What kind of dogs do you like?" Patience was still fidgeting with her wallet. I didn't think I even had coins on me anymore. Who uses coins these days?

The girls' father walked over to us. "Hi, I see my daughters have made two new victims with their salesmanship," he laughed. He turned to his girls. "You can't just ask anyone for money, honeys.

I told you we will go to the jumble sale next week. Maybe there you can sell some of the games you don't use anymore. But don't go selling your own candy, now. There's no need."

"It's fine, really! I'd love to buy some candy." Patience finally opened her wallet. "Oh... I'm afraid I don't have any coins on me. I'm so sorry."

"Don't worry. Maybe these nice ladies can have a little piece of chocolate anyway, girls?"

The girls nodded excitingly, and they pushed a chocolate bar into our hands with their chocolatey little fingers.

"That is so sweet! Thank you so much!" I held my hand up for the girls to high five it and enjoyed seeing them gather all their strength to high-five me.

Over their heads, their father whispered to us: "We are going to pick up a dog today!"

My face broke into a large smile. We thanked the kids and their Dad again and finally headed to the restaurant.

*

It was an old place. The walls smelled of smoke, and the floor contained the same design pattern my grandmother used to have. I saw how the cashier was furiously typing in all the product prices instead of scanning them. It looked something like a roadside restaurant that you sometimes see in vintage American films.

Claudio was walking around there as if he had to make the choice of his lifetime. He was intently looking at the price tags.

"Are you well?" I asked.

"Yes, yes... Just.... So many choices!"

This was clearly no time to talk, so I let him be in his own world as I headed straight for the sandwich section and was delighted to see they had exactly one carpaccio sandwich left. That one would be mine! I waited till Patience had measured out the exact ratios of fruit she wanted in her yoghurt bowl, and then we headed to the cashier. Claudio followed us with a large slice of pizza. As we walked away, I heard that familiar noise when

Claudio tried to pay for his bread by card: no balance. Patience asked me if it was okay if she would go outside already. I nodded and said I would wait for Claudio. She couldn't stand the awful smell in this place, which was understandable.

He silently swore to himself. The cashier looked as if this was the so many-th person to whom this happened today, and it was barely half past 8. Claudio pulled out his phone and tried to log in to his bank app, which didn't go so successfully with the place's Wi-Fi. He had to type in the password three times before he got it correct, and the connection was weak. The woman behind him in line pushed Claudio aside and put her sandwich on the cash desk.

"Excuse me?" Claudio looked up from his phone with a puzzled look on his face.

"Go away if you can't pay," the woman replied. I wasn't sure if she literally stuck her nose up in the air or if I was only imaging she did. The cashier laughed and handled her transaction.

In the meantime, Claudio had finally managed to log in and saw that his balance was exactly two cents short of the pizza's price. He yelled that to me and the cashier just laughed again. I saw him typing furiously on his phone, trying to transfer money to himself from his savings. But that didn't seem to work. The Wi-Fi disconnected again, and he was pushing buttons with more severity as more and more customers were helped.

"Excuse me, I know this is an odd question, but maybe you could lower the price for him?" I asked the cashier as it was quiet for a minute. "It's only two cents, after all. Won't matter in the cash total, since the price is rounded up for most people if they pay by cash."

The cashier looked at me as if I had lost my mind. "Eh, no?"

I was taken aback. "Oh... right.

As Claudio was still struggling and there were no customers in line, I saw how the cashier turned to her colleague, said something, pointed to me and they both laughed. My goodness. Is there any way to file a complaint here?

"I'll ask Patience to pay for you," I told Claudio and I hurried away to where Patience was sitting on a bench outside. I couldn't suppress a giggle as I described to her in what kind of stressed state Claudio was trying to get himself a pizza slice.

"Can't they just lower the price for him? It's only two cents," Patience remarked, as she pulled out her bank card.

"Exactly, that's what I said! As if anyone will care about two cents. Let the boy have his pizza."

"Here. My PIN is 2321." She handed me the card.

"Oh... right, thanks. Don't you want to pay yourself?"

"Nah, I'm good here."

I rushed back inside and made my way past the growing line of customers. At the cash desk there was a box with little bags of crisps. "I think we deserved one," I said, as I paid for Claudio's pizza slice and also included two extra bags of crisps. As we walked outside to Patience, I was too distracted by what happened to insist on our much-needed discussion to him. I nearly hit myself in the head a moment later for forgetting that.

*

We enjoyed our food on the bench sitting next to Patience. Claudio seemed happier than ever with his fresh slice of pizza. He didn't even care it had gotten quite cold in the meantime. The rain had stopped, and, unexpectedly, the rising sun even shone through the clouds. You never know what happens to the weather in the Netherlands. We didn't give ourselves much time to enjoy the sunshine though; we wanted to be well in time for the contest. A game of rock, paper, scissors decided that it was my turn to be in the passenger seat. Thank God for those extra ten centimeters for my legs. As we walked to the car, I tried to attract Claudio's attention, but he had already restarted his conversation with Patience. I suddenly had an idea."Patience, when I was sitting in the back just now, I couldn't hear very well because of the noise. The windows didn't shut well. Is there any way to fix that?"

"Oh yes, sorry. They just need a little love." And she walked to one of the windows, opened the door, and turned the knob while pushing against the glass from the outside. And indeed, it closed completely. Two other windows followed. I hoped the ventilation would work well enough to at least give us some air. But now there was a real chance that Claudio and I could talk business in the car.

We weren't even back on the high way when Patience said: "Uh oh."

"What?!" Claudio and I turned to her.

"It's no big deal... We'll just have to stop again at the next exit."

"What? Why?"

"The tank is almost empty."

"Couldn't you tell just now?!"

"No, I told you, this car is quite old. The signal doesn't work well until the tank is extremely close to being empty."

That sounded really safe to me.

"Fine... Okay. The next one is in twenty kilometers," Claudio said. I looked around and laughed at the sight of that tall guy trying to stretch his legs horizontally across the car seats.

"Yeah, now you laugh... You do know that a new pit-stop means a new game of rock, paper, scissors, right?"

"You would like that, wouldn't you?"

The car fell silent, and even though it would have been the moment to start talking to Claudio about the strategy, my eyes kept on going to the gas signal. My worries kept me distracted.

The gas station we entered at the next exit looked even more ancient than the one we had just left. In what kind of place are we?! Far away from Amsterdam, clearly.

There was no restaurant, only a tiny shop with a few candy bars, which I'm rather sure were not sold anymore in most shops. An old man was reading the newspaper and didn't look up when we made quite a lot of noise trying to detach the fuel pump from its holder. While Claudio was filling up the tank, I followed a cat with my eyes, as he snuck into the store and jumped up onto the cash desk. The man put his newspaper down and stroked the little animal's head. It purred.

"Claudio, I think the counter is not working," Patience said. She pointed to a screen on the fuel pump, that should count the liters of fuel as they are being poured in, but it only increased a little. It was behind on the liter count, in either case. "Shall I go tell the guy while you fill up?"

"How do we know it is not working, though?"

"It is not keeping track of the liters properly"

"Yeah, I know... But how do we know it is not increasing?"

Patience looked at him with pinched eyes.

"What? Don't judge me. I'm just a student, ignorant about the world of fuels," Claudio turned back to the pump.

"Well, I'm telling in either case. I don't want to know how many people have taken advantage of this before you." Patience walked over to the little shop. The old shopkeeper was so focused on scratching the head of the cat that he didn't notice her walking in. She knocked on the window. I watched her from a distance, and then back at Claudio. He had turned a bit red and pretended to have all his attention focused on the pump.

"Excuse me... Sir?" sounded Patience's pitched voice.

The man looked up and a smile revealed his almost toothless mouth. "Hello, lovely lady! How may I help you?"

"Well, my friend over there is filling the car, but... We think the counter is not running properly. It doesn't record all the liters of fuel we put in."

The man looked surprised. "How honest of you. Let me have a look."

I could hear his bones cracking from where I was standing as the old man got up out of his chair and walked with Patience to the car. The cat trotted along and slalomed between the man's clogs. Claudio had already filled the tank and he waited as the old man came closer and inspected the thing. He was chewing on his own cheeks as he did so.

"There does seem to be something wrong indeed... I will have a look at it today. Thank you for making me attentive of it. Seems like you three got lucky now!"

"No, no, sir, we'd like to pay for the whole tank," Patience said quickly as she already got her bank card ready.

"You are too kind, lady. It is fine, really. See it as a discount for noting the problem. That way we all win a little, don't we?" He gestured Patience to come back to the shop to pay for the gas. I believe that little discount saved us more than half the original prize. Patience couldn't help but buying some extra candy as a way of thanking the man.

Well provisioned, we then crawled into the car again. I was happy to note that Claudio forgot about the whole rock, paper, scissors game and voluntarily took back his place on the back seats.

"So ladies, can you hear me from back here?" Claudio asked when the car started driving.

"We can." Patience replied.

"Claudio, I told you some time ago, we still need to discuss our plan further."

"We do. Do you mind Patience?"

"No, not at all. But is Bruni's 'Reciprocity' book the only book you used for your preparations?"

"No of course not," Claudio responded. "We also looked at Bruni's other book, for instance, 'The Wound and the Blessing' and then several other ones."

"Oh I know that one!" Patience exclaimed.

"Do you? Tell me about it."

My goodness. That was clearly spontaneous Claudio again. When would we ever get around to our final preparations? I was starting to feel I should never have decided to join this contest last-minute. This way we'd never win.

Chapter 13

As Patience started to explain what she had learnt from "The Wound and the Blessing", I received a text from Tim. *"Mum's really happy you're going. NOT! X-("* I decided not to reply. But I also decided, again, to make the most of this contest. I had to start talking to Claudio soon. No time to waste.

Claudio didn't seem to share my sense of urgency. He said to Patience on in an upbeat tone "Wow, you read the book? I didn't know it was famous."

"It was a thing in my community for a while. So I read it and really liked it."

"Really? What did you like?"

"It's a bit personal. It's special for me, because I think it explains much of the difference between Ghanaian and Dutch culture."

I sighed deeply. I would certainly like to hear more about her cultural roots, but not now. This could last ages.

But Claudio was at it again. "Really? Interesting. Tell me!"

"Okay, very simply put, Ghanaians think more about 'us', the community, and Dutch people think more about 'me'. I mean, not exclusively of course, but I think that in general the community is more important to Ghanaians than to Dutch people." Patience tried to glance backwards at Claudio "Is it strange what I'm saying?"

"Sorry Patience, but would you keep your eyes on the road please?" Driving in a shabby car was more than enough of a scare for me. More safety stress was not necessary.

"Sorry." Patience stared straight ahead.

"It's not strange, please continue." Claudio had bent forward to hear her better.

"Yes. I remember one thing he said. Bruni said that in Europe before modern times, God would mediate relationships between people. So: I – God – Others. But then modern thinkers replaced God by either 'the market' or 'the state'. I think Adam Smith replaced it by 'market' and Thomas Hobbes replaced it by

'Leviathan', which means the state. So now, my relationship with others is mediated either by contracts or by the state."

Claudio nodded.

Patience went on to explain how Bruni compares these mediations. He says that in mediation by contracts or the state we do not receive gifts, nor do we depend on anyone with a name, unlike the mediation by God; it's impersonal, which also means there is less risk of injury. He also says that a personal meeting always has two sides; on the one hand, there is a wound, because the other person can hurt me, but at the same time the other person can also be a source of blessing to me, which gives joy. "Are you still following me?"

Claudio rubbed his hand over his chin thoughtfully and says, "Yeah, it's the title of the book, isn't it? Persons can be a wound or a blessing to other persons when they meet each other."

"Yes."

"And then the point is that early modern thinkers like Machiavelli and Hobbes, had a really negative vision of man. They really emphasize the wound, and want to avoid it. They don't really see the blessing."

I didn't really see where this was going. Claudio had prepared this book, so I didn't know all the details. We hadn't thought it necessary for both of us to read all books. Therefore, I just had to ask. "Are you saying that they've introduced the market and the state to get rid of the personal contact? And with that they got rid of both the wound and the blessing?"

"Yeah, that's it." Patience answered.

"Could you please clarify what are you trying to say then? Are you making the argument that we should get rid of the market and the state and put God back in their place?" If this was the kind of input we were going to get from Patience, we'd better stop talking right away.

Patience looked down, taking her eyes of the road briefly.

"Oh, no Miriam" Claudio tried to save the day by putting on his Italian accent in an attempt to be funny. "We are talking about *Bruni's* argument."

Patience smiled at him, again taking her eyes off the road. "Yes. And I remember Bruni does actually answer your question Miriam." She went on to recall how he says that getting rid of the market is not a good idea, because the void that it leaves is often filled up with power relationships where the strongest exploit the weakest. But he also says the market doesn't have to be anonymous, and can become a place of personal encounter.

"Oh, so it's a more personal approach to the market?" That actually sounded interesting and quite in line with what we were going to do.

"Yes!" Claudio was starting to really warm up to the discussion. "But perhaps there's something missing." Claudio recalled how in a history of economics book he'd been reading, it said that Smith and his contemporaries didn't just 'replace God by the market' but rather distinguished between the private and the public sphere. The private sphere was the place where personal relationships could flourish, which in turn would create the conditions for moral behavior in the public sphere. So when Smith talks about people who come into the public sphere and seek a certain self-interest, they are already socialized and disciplined by the private sphere. I nodded; that was a relevant change of perspective.

*

"See Miriam," Claudio continued, "how interesting it is to talk to people about these things? And we'll be doing that the rest of this week! Cool!"

"We'll be doing that a bit, but we'll mainly work on our own story, I would say."

"Oh Miriam. Don't be such a loner."

"Are you a loner when working in a team? We have something to share with the world, you know."

"And the world has something to share with us," insisted Claudio.

I was starting to feel uneasy with the sense that Claudio wasn't 'in' on our project at all. He didn't seem very keen on sharing the 're-think' of economics that we had been working on with Loffels with the contest participants. That had me worried. For now, the Bruni book went into the right direction. That's why I asked Claudio to continue explaining about that book.

Claudio gladly complied and explained how Bruni says that nowadays, in western society the market is starting to affect all spheres of life, more and more. And he says that the market should start to include gratuitousness, free gift, and not only contracts, to bring this human dimension back.

I just had to go along for a bit. "He talks about free gift in the marketplace? Oh yes, that's like the 'Reciprocity' book you just talked about. But you were not very happy with that, were you? I mean, gift is not very *Homo economicus.*"

"That was when we just started." Claudio went on to say he'd thought about it since, and that Bruni gives some quite convincing arguments against that paradigm. At the start of the book, he writes about the idea of something being just business, and therefore not personal and also not ethical. He gives the example of a scene used in many movies, where a killer tells his victim: sorry, this is just business, nothing personal. He then concludes that that's not possible, a murder is always personal, and the idea that something is outside of ethics would at least have shocked Adam Smith.

"Really?"

"Yeah, and then the studies." Claudio went on to mention the studies of behavior Bruni writes about, that make clear that in practice, personal relations do make a difference. For example the 'trust game' used in an experimental setting in which a subject can choose to risk losing money by giving it to another subject. That other subject gets three times as much as the first subject gave, and is then able to give back some of the received money. *Homo economicus* would not give anything, but people in experiments usually do. That result is probably greatly influenced by personal relationships.

He explained that later in the book, Bruni writes about the Neapolitan economic tradition, where the market goes together with being related to other people, and what he calls civic virtue —that is, good social habits which take others into account.

"What about Corporate Social responsibility?" Patience asked. "That is also not very self-centered, is it?"

"That's right. Bruni talks about that too. But there's even more." Claudio mentioned that studies about self-reported happiness clearly show that money only makes you happy until a certain point, and that beyond that point, it may even make you less happy. There are more ways to show people are not just self-centered.

At this point, I have to admit I got sucked into the discussion a little. I had to think about mum's colleagues. "Please just let me digest this one moment. You ... sorry, Mr. Bruni, is saying that money makes people less happy?"

"Yes, beyond a point, if you're working all the time, money takes time away from relationships and things you like doing."

Ouch, was that remark aimed at me? "Well, I would say people want to reach something. And if they do, it makes them happy."

"That's not what the data suggest." Claudio countered. He explained that Bruni also proposes not only thinking about material goods, but rather also about relational goods, which he describes in quite a bit of detail, the characteristics these goods have, and so forth. "But perhaps that's not our main focus now."

Patience asked, "Do you remember what he says about love in society? That came back in the other book. That was interesting."

"True. I remember two key ideas." Claudio went on to say that, nowadays, the market is governed by only contracts, but that Bruni would prefer the principle: 'let not the contract do what friendship can do; let not friendship do what love can do.' Instead of seeing love as a 'scarce resource' that needs to be saved up for private life, it should be seen as a virtue, a good habit that grows through practice. In this way the love he calls agape or gift-love can start to influence everything: contracts, friendships and gifts themselves.

Ah. I didn't quite know what to think of this. But clearly Patience did.

"Well said. I like that!" She explained that when she went to Church with her Ghanaian community, there is a time for them to bring their gifts. "For us, that's a joyful time, we sing joyful songs and we dance." And she explained that, in her experience, they were trying to be loving towards each other, because of God. So the 'I – God – other' scheme Bruni talks about, they are still trying to live from that.

"But what does that say about the market?" Claudio asked.

"I do buy shoes." Patience giggled. "But also, I don't know, I take some of these good feelings to the shop. I try to love the shopkeeper, with small things, like I love the people in my community, I think." Patience continues softly. "Or at least, I try."

Claudio smiled at her. "So you're already trying to bring some of that gift-love into the market. I'm sure Bruni would be happy about that."

"This is something we should go tell the people at the contest, right?" I tried, testing Claudio a bit further on his commitment. This seemed like a point he was in favor of.

But Claudio had a surprise in store. "Wait a minute. Patience. You seem to know this book quite well, and you haven't seen the case, have you?"

"No, I haven't."

And there it came, he just blurted it out. "The other teams are bigger. Don't you want to join our team?"

*

Well, that was impulsive Claudio again. Socializing without bounds. But I saw an opportunity to make the most of this. So I started: "Shouldn't you consult with your teammate first, before you make an offer like that?"

"Oh, do you, eh...

"No, I don't object, but I do think that if Patience wants to join we should clarify to her what it really is we want to do."

"Yeah, well, that's clear right?"

"Is it? It's clear to me. I want to apply our re-think of economics to this business case. But you?"

"Me too! Well..."

"Well what?"

"Well, if that's well-received of course."

"And if not?"

"You want to win this contest, right?"

"Yes, that's really important."

"Well, then we should do as the jury wants us to. If that's not re-think, then re-think is out of the window."

That remark hit me straight in the face. I had to retaliate right away. "What? How can you say that? Our re-think is a winner!"

"Maybe it is. Maybe it isn't. We'll see. But if we talk to the jury and they're not buying it, we'll need to change. That's how contests go, you see."

I started to feel angry at him; he wasn't making any sense. "How can you say that? What do you mean "talk to the jury"? We cannot know what the jury thinks before the end of the competition, can we?"

"Don't you remember the set-up? There is a jury feedback moment halfway through. I think we should let that determine our final approach."

He had a point there. But still, I was disappointed in his half-hearted approach to our grand strategy. "So, you don't want to go all-out for the re-think?"

"We should do our best at that, but we should also have a second option at hand in case they don't buy it."

The things he was saying now made some sense. Of course, juries do like to pick what they know and support. But then, if it wasn't going to be for the surprise element, we'd never win against the business schools. And then there was our limited time. "Look," I continued, "the re-think project is pretty ambitious. It's true that the jury may not like it. I hope they do. But if we don't go for it all-out from the start, it certainly won't work out. We have very limited time, so we should just draw up our plan and stick with it. What do you think Patience?"

Patience had been quietly listening to our discussion. "About the plan?" She asked.

"Yes."

"Both views have something going for them. I'll let you decide."

Right, well that could have been expected. "Would you consider joining our team at all?" I continued.

"Yes," she replied, "I think it would be a lot of fun. If the organizers permit it, of course."

"So would you prefer being on a team with one or the other strategy?" I just had to try again.

Patience smiled, "I'm fine with either."

"Good. Now, if you do join, would you want to win?"

"Of course."

"And if I may ask, why would you want to win?"

"Miriam!" Claudio interrupted. "Why the cross-examination?"

"You're inviting someone on the team. We just need to make sure we're all on the same page. So Patience, what motivates you to win this contest?"

"Hm." Patience thought for a while. "For me it's simple. You both really want to win. I really want to help out. So I'd be really happy to see you winning."

"Oh. Thanks." Was that really sincere? It did look like it. "Right" I continued, "but you're undecided about the strategy to follow."

Patience nodded, agreeing.

"Well, Claudio, it seems we will need to battle this out together. Re-think all out, or re-think while re-thinking about it. I don't think the second one will work at all."

Chapter 14

I was considering how to convince Claudio of my strategy, when suddenly Patience pulled up the emergency lane. The car shook before it came to a full stop.

"Come on, not again..." Patience muttered to herself.

"What's going on?" I asked.

"Motor trouble. Once every few months I get an error message saying there's motor danger, and then the car just starts trembling and stops." She sighed. "Oh no." She put her hands in front of her face and bent forward in a gesture of despair.

"Right." Given the state of the car, I wasn't really surprised, but this wasn't quite the trip that we had hoped for.

Claudio asked Patience, "So, what do you usually do in situations like this? You seem to have some experience."

Patience head sank deeper into her hands, the palms of her hands now touching her forehead.

"What's the matter?" I asked.

After a little while she inhaled deeply, looked up at me and said slowly: "I should have..."

"What? What's the matter?"

Patience hesitantly told us how the car had broken down recently, and it had done so before. Her Dad usually fixed it; he was not a car mechanic, but had pretty good hands. He had fixed it this time, but she had known that she should have had it repaired properly this time around, after the repetitive breakdowns. "It's just that... I didn't."

Wow. Great. I tried to comfort Patience as well as I could, while I tried to think what to do. Call a mechanic. "Are you with the ANWB?" That membership would mean she could call for free support.

Patience nodded. Phew.

"OK, let's call them. Do you have a number?"

"Yes, but we should get out of the car first. Sitting here is unsafe and not allowed. I *have* done this before." Patience seemed a bit more composed now.

"But it's raining!" Another raincloud was just passing over our heads.

"It is what they indicate, Miriam," she explained. "Staying is not safe. If a car is not paying attention, they could hit us from the back. You can use my umbrella, if you want."

We gathered up all necessary things, put on the alarm lights, got out of the car and stepped over the crash barrier. We walked over to the grass next to the emergency lane. I was clamping onto the umbrella, and Patience and Claudio got as close to me as they could. I felt miserable. The main question that occupied me now was: were we even going to make it to the contest?

*

I looked at my watch. It was nearly 8:30. Google maps told me that we were near the city of Breukelen, just a few minutes walking from the train station, actually. That was something of a blessing in disguise. I asked Patience to call the ANWB, and while she walked off to make the call, I asked Claudio to check the time it would take from Breukelen to the Erasmus School of Economics.

"What, by train?" he asked.

"Yes, have a look just in case."

He gave an amazed look, but still took out his phone to look up the information. Meanwhile, I checked the time by car from here to the Erasmus. It came out about the same. Without traffic, the car was 15 minutes faster; with heavy traffic the train was faster by the same amount. I even looked up a taxi, but the cost put me off quickly.

"What time should we be there by, again?"

"Ten."

"And Loffels said they were going to be strict on starting times, right?"

"Yeah."

I remembered that, because I had thought putting that explicitly in the description was treating your participants like little children. Seemingly they had had some bad experiences in the past.

"But this is force majeure. I can call them, if you like." Claudio continued, putting on his don Corleone accent, "And-e if they donnotte listen, I will calle la famiglia."

I smiled but ignored the joke. "Well, is it force majeure? We can still take the train, it leaves in 20 minutes, and arrive on time."

"And Patience?"

"Well, she'll have to..."

"She's on the team!"

"Not officially yet."

"How can you say that? She's kind enough to give us the ride."

"That's true. She also didn't have the car fixed properly."

"Miriam!"

I explained to Claudio that I was fine with Patience joining the team, even though this episode made me wonder whether she has the grit and determination we need to succeed in the contest. But the main issue for me was that we couldn't risk losing the contest altogether. "If we want to win, we'll first have to get there! In time!"

Patience came walking back with her mobile in-hand. "They'll be here in ten minutes."

"That's not bad" Claudio said.

I did a quick calculation. "Ten minutes. They'll need to figure out what the matter is, so if we wait to hear the verdict we'll miss the train."

"The train?" Patience asked.

"There's a train station a ten-minute walk from here. There's a train leaving in twenty minutes, which will get us to the contest on time."

"Oh, well, then, go get the train." Patience said matter-of-factly.

"No!" Claudio exclaimed. "You're part of the team! I'm not leaving you alone here."

"I just want to help, I can also come later. Really, it's not a problem."

"It is a problem! Three is a company. If this contest will be the three of us, it will be the three of us from start to finish. I'll not leave you alone here. I'll just call the organizers to say we've had an accident, and if they don't understand that, then I'm not sure I want to be on their contest. But of course they'll understand."

Patience looked at me with an apologizing look. "I didn't want to get you guys into trouble."

I nodded in acknowledgement. "Claudio, you're being irrational. Look, if we take the train it's more efficient and we reduce risk. We make sure the two of us get there in time, and once the car is fixed Patience can join us. We can still do the contest together."

"If you call that being rational, it's not my type of rationality." Claudio turned to me fiercely. "Look Miriam, it's very simple. If you'd like to be on time to explain relational economics to these people, I suggest you take the train. On your own."

I didn't see that one coming. I gradually noticed some blood rise to my cheeks. Claudio had won this one. I couldn't just walk away now. Of course not. So we waited in silence for the mechanic to arrive.

Ten minutes later, the mechanic actually pulled up onto the emergency lane. That was something! We walked over to the driver and Patience explained the situation to him.

"That sounds familiar... Mind if I take a quick look?" The guy asked. Patience led him to the bonnet and the guy bent over forward so much that his hat fell off. He took his time to inspect the car without saying anything, and I was just beginning to wonder whether the side of the highway would be a good place to do so much inspecting. Just when I was going to say something about it, the chap said: "It's a tiny problem. I can fix it on the spot."

I wasn't even listening to the rest of his words. *Thank God!* The excitement of the day immediately came rushing back to me. Claudio looked at me with that half smile of his and I had to smile back. It wasn't so bad waiting anymore. The guy took out his gear and started working on the motor, taking some things apart and then putting them back again. He was telling Patience what the problem turned out to be. I didn't recognize half of the technical words he used, but I think he said last time the job wasn't finished properly.

Only ten minutes later we were good to go again. We could still be in time!

*

Once back in the car, and safely driving on the motorway again, I sighed deeply. "Wow, looks like we're going to make it."

"Together." Claudio added on a satisfied tone.

"Yes." I sat wondering for a little while. Would Patience have enough background knowledge to really appreciate our strategy? "Patience" I asked, "have you heard about game theory?"

"Yes I have. And it was in the book Claudio mentioned earlier. By Bruni, right? But now, I'm just happy I'm on the road again."

"Very happy. You're right. And quite correct too, there was some game theory there. Do you have any clue why?" Her remark that she was in film and literature studies and not very technical got me thinking. So I also asked, "Have you done any maths?"

"Maths? Yes, in high school of course. No maths subjects in university, that's not part of the literature curriculum."

"I see. So you wouldn't know why Bruni is using game theory?"

"Miriam!" Claudio chimed in from the back seat, "are you testing Patience again? Why?"

"I'm not testing, I am helping her. Our strategy is inspired by game theory, so she has to feel comfortable with that. We can't just plunge her into an unknown world and then expect her to excel, can we? That wouldn't do, it's not fair at all. Right, Patience?"

Patience just glanced at me sideways and didn't say a word.

"Oh come off it, Patience is saving our lives today. Let her focus on the road. And it's not like we're using rocket science here, Miriam."

"No, it's not rocket science. And Patience can think and drive, she's been doing it all the time. So Patience, have you ever heard of the Prisoner's Dilemma?"

"Yes."

"Good, now just to make sure we're all on the same page, would you be so kind to explain it to me?"

"This is not an exam!" Claudio sounded quite agitated. What was his problem?

"It's no problem." Patience sounded quite calm. And without any hesitation, she started to explain the prisoner's dilemma perfectly.

I was stunned. "How do you know all this?"

Patience smiled at me showing her white shining teeth. "I always liked maths at high-school. So recently I wrote an essay on "The Beautiful Mind" on the life of John Nash. It has a scene which illustrates game theory, but basically messes it up. I liked the topic, so studied it to explain well what was going wrong. I got 9 out of 10 on the essay. It was fun."

"Amazing! A literature student with a knack for math! You're our perfect team member!" Claudio was beside himself. "Please do join Patience; this is going to be great."

"There's quite a lot more she needs to catch up on though." I said.

"You're right! Let me tell you about the time we discussed 'Give and Take'. That one has also left its marks on our strategy. And of course why game theory is important to us."

And once Claudio gets started, there's no stopping him.

Chapter 15

After I agreed to be on the team, Loffels also invited Miriam to join. He thought the two of us would be suitable candidates to represent UCI in the contest. We divided the work of preparation between us.

Loffels had asked me what motivated me to join the contest. I said that it would be a good opportunity to meet interesting new people, and make new friends. After that he recommended me to read 'Give and Take' by Adam Grant. That would be part of my preparatory work for the contest, and given my motivation, he thought I'd like to read it. He had me curious.

I read the book, and I liked it. There were some ideas there that I thought were very applicable to our approach to the contest. I was going to champion the 'friendly' approach, and Grant would help me do it. Or that's what I hoped.

We met one day in his office to discuss the book. I remember quite well. I had prepared myself, and did my best to build my argument around the content for Miriam and Dr. Loffels. That day it was nice outside, a very cold but sunny day in early march. Quite a few people had gone off to ice-skate, because some lakes had frozen over. Skipping those pleasures of winter and walking with Miriam into Dr. Loffels' office instead, made me feel very dedicated. Everything for the good cause! If you want to be beautiful, you need to suffer, they say in the Netherlands. And we were going to have a beautifully friendly competition.

After having settled in to a small meeting room with some hot chocolate this time, I quickly got started. I first had to get Miriam on her toes. "Alright, so at the beginning of this book, Grant says that some people behave as 'takers'. That means they get more than they give. They can also be 'givers', who give more than they get. But there's a third category, the 'matchers', who try to give and get equally. Grant wants to know how successful these behaviors make people. So what do you think? Who is least successful?" I looked at Miriam.

"Not sure, hopefully the takers?" Miriam was quick off the bat.

"Sorry! I'm afraid it's the givers."

"Oh really? Interesting."

"Now for even more interesting. Who is most successful?"

"I suppose the takers?"

"No, surprise! It's the givers again." I got her there.

"Sorry? Givers are least AND most successful? How can that be?"

"Aye, Señorita, you-e need-e to think-e."

"Claudio." Clearly Loffels didn't appreciate my Don Juan imitations.

"Sorry." I tried to suppress a smirk at my successful attempt to surprise Miriam. But then I went on to explain that the whole book is really an attempt to explain this paradox. In the first chapters, Grant tries to show some advantages that givers have. He talks about advantages in building networks of people that appreciate givers and how givers can reconnect to those people afterward when they need them. He also talks about the advantage givers have in building good collaboration and letting others share in the appreciation. Because givers think about others more, they are good at motivating people and therefore developing talented people around them. And finally, even though givers tend to have less 'dominance' than takers, which is associated with strength, power and authority, they do tend to develop more prestige, which is built on respect and admiration. They usually build this through what Grant calls 'powerless communication', which means that rather than bossing people around, they listen to people and sincerely try to take their perspective.

I had Miriam interested. "Right. That's nice, but it doesn't answer the question."

"Very sharp." Then I explained that the second part of the book is about trying to understand the difference between unsuccessful and successful givers. What his conclusions comes down to is this: Grant distinguishes 'selfless' givers, who give without thinking about themselves at all, from 'otherish' givers, who think a lot about others, but also think about themselves at the same time.

"Sorry Claudio, those were called matchers, right?"

"Nice try, but not quite." I clarified that the matchers are people that want to have a balance between giving and getting all the time, but otherish givers are actually out to give a lot to other people. Still, they do have an eye on their own interest too, so that for example they don't get a burnout, because they make sure they get enough rest for themselves.

My mind unintentionally wandered off to the sunbathers-in-wintercoats that were taking a break outside.

Miriam also looked out of the window to the frosty and bright street. "I see. Are there other examples?"

"Yes, well, the fakers." I told her how a problem many givers face is not to get exploited by takers or what Grant calls fakers, people that are agreeable, but are really takers. Otherish givers must learn how to draw a line, and at the negotiation table a good way to do that is for them to think they are negotiating for someone else, for example for their families. That will motivate them to be tough.

"What about culture?" Loffels asked.

"Yeah, that's towards the end." I told them that Grant talks about ways to establish a giver-culture. If there are group norms that encourage giving, and if that giving is visible, more people will start to give, and givers are less likely to be exploited. In the end, changing behavior in this way will encourage people that actually have giver values to put them into practice, but if people's behavior shifts towards giving, their values may follow too.

"Any examples?"

I mentioned the website called Freecycle, which Grant talks about, where people give away free stuff to others. People who participate start to feel part of the community. Whereas they may start to join the community by only taking things, many get activated into 'giver values' and start giving too. I also mentioned an exercise called a 'reciprocity ring' that Grant ran in one of his classes; each student would make a request to the class, which could be anything meaningful from their personal or professional lives, and the others would use their knowledge, resources, and connections to help fulfill the request. Both examples really help people shift towards giving.

"Nice!" Dr. Loffels seemed happy with my summary.

"Well, the book really shows giving is a behavior that makes people successful, if only they care enough for their own interest, so their giving is not exploited."

"Right, but does he say what success means for him?" Miriam asked.

"Nice one." I reported that at the end of the book he does say that the concept of success itself changes from a giver's perspective. The success of others also becomes our success, because givers care more about the team effort. The key quote: "Givers advance the world; takers advance themselves and hold the world back." He is saying that the otherish giving he proposes leads to greater success, but also richer meaning to one's life, and a more lasting impact.

I saw that this conclusion made Miriam look thoughtful again. "Perhaps I do need to read the book for myself. It's a new perspective."

"But it makes sense?"

"It does. I still need to get my head around it, though."

*

Dr. Loffels smiled. "Nice job Claudio. But now for the big question."

"What?"

"How does Grant fit into our master plan?"

This is the question I had been waiting for. "I think it's really straightforward."

"Oh?"

"We need to connect to people there, make friends, and help them out."

"May I remind you that these new friends of yours will be our competitors?" Miriam clearly didn't like the idea.

"So what?"

"I was thinking more in terms of the concepts. How can they help us analyze the case?" Loffels asked.

I wasn't very happy that he didn't seem to back my practical approach. But I wasn't going to give up this easily either. "Well, once we make friends, they can inspire us, you know."

In the end, Loffels insisted on talking about the theoretical side. "Let's think a bit more about friendship." He didn't really say my practical approach was wrong, he just brushed it aside. For now, I decided to swallow that and see where this was going.

Thinking about friendship is in itself something I like to do a lot. I read quite a bit of philosophy about the topic. My favorite is Aristotle, because for him friendship is one of the most important things in life. Of course, his friendship ideal is so high, that it's hardly possible to find a real friend in this life who reaches that standard. Aristotle talks about friendships of utility and of pleasure, which you can find quite easily. These friendships occur between people that seek mutual benefit or that want to have fun together. But then there is the 'real friendship', friendships based on searching the good together. In this relationship, friends try to help each other be the best version of themselves. The friends help each other reach what he calls 'Eudaimonia', the happy or good life, sometimes called 'human flourishing'. They help each other be the fully realized versions of themselves, realized in a 'virtuous' or best possible way. Those friends are hard to find. I wondered whether Loffels would start talking about this approach.

To my surprise, Loffels started talking about game theory. He said that we could use simple games to illustrate the importance of friendship for economics. "Let's start with the prisoner's dilemma."

The prisoner's dilemma? Really? For friendship? I thought that was about people caring a lot about their own utility. But okay, Loffels surprised me before on this issue, so I would give him the benefit of the doubt.

*

Loffels had prepared some slides, which he showed to us on his laptop screen. Because the room was so small, the three of us could see that well enough. The first slide just showed a classical prisoner's dilemma, which goes as follows. Two prisoners are held captive by the police and are interrogated separately. The police doesn't know which of the two is guilty. Each prisoner can either say that the other prisoner is guilty (rat out on the other and not collaborate) or keep his silence (collaborate). The years in prison that would result from each decision are shown in the table; in each cell they are first shown for the first prisoner, and then for the second prisoner.

Prisoner's dilemma

	Collaborate (be silent)	Don't Collaborate (rat out)
Collaborate (be silent)	-1, -1	-10, 0
Don't Collaborate (rat out)	0, -10	-9, -9

Payoff: number of years in prison.

He then went on to remind us how people generally analyze a game like this. Because players are not allowed to talk to each other, they can each individually decide what the best option for them is. Say the first prisoner considers the option that the other prisoner is silent. That would look like this.

	Collaborate (be silent)	
Collaborate (be silent)	-1, -1	
Don't Collaborate (rat out)	(0), -10	

The green circle indicates that in case the second player is silent, the best option for the first player is not to collaborate, because then he goes free. In case the second player doesn't collaborate, or rats out on him, the situation is like this.

		Don't Collaborate (rat out)
Collaborate (be silent)		-10, 0
Don't Collaborate (rat out)		(-9,)-9

So again, the best option for player one is not to collaborate. In this case, not collaborating gives him one year less in prison. The tragedy of the game came out in the following screen Loffels showed us. Because the game is symmetric, the other player is in the same situation. That leads to the following 'equilibrium' solution.

	Collaborate (be silent)	Don't Collaborate (rat out)
Collaborate (be silent)	-1, -1	-10, 0
Don't Collaborate (rat out)	0, -10	(-9, -9)

So the 'rational' thing to do for both players is not to collaborate, even though both would be much better off if they did collaborate.

"And what does this have to do with friendship?" I asked.

"Wait a minute, we'll get there." Loffels went on to explain that economists use this game as an allegory for what happens in society. People don't always collaborate out of themselves, even though we would all be better off if we did. So things are 'out of balance' if we leave them alone.

When Loffels talked about being 'out of balance', that triggered memories about our earlier conversation. I had thought about that in the meantime, because I thought it was interesting. So I asked, "Does this have to do with these mechanisms we talked about earlier, like competition and stuff?"

"Nice one!" Loffels enthusiastically raised both his thumbs. It was clearly one of his favorite topics. He reminded me that his preferred way of speaking was to talk about hierarchy, free exchangeability (his way of saying 'competition'), and voluntary commitment. Those are three ways which economists study to help people come to mutually beneficial collaboration. And, he said, you can illustrate their effects through game theory.

For example, say in the story of the prisoner's dilemma, the police would give a 'fine' of an additional two years of prison every time a player doesn't collaborate. In that case, the whole game would change. Then it would suddenly always be beneficial for players to collaborate, and the 'equilibrium' would shift to collaboration. Of course, giving an extra fine doesn't make any sense in the original story of the dilemma, but it does illustrate one way in which 'hierarchy' can help people reach collaboration. Loffels mentioned that a game in which collaboration is the only equilibrium is no longer called prisoner's dilemma, but rather the 'invisible hand' game. So introducing hierarchy can really change 'the name of the game'. The same holds for free exchangeability, but illustrating that needs slightly more complex, multi-player games.

"So let's look at friendship and love." Loffels continued.

"Love?" Miriam asked.

"Well, in classical terms, friendship is a form of love."

Miriam looked surprised.

"Philia, right?" I asked. Reading Aristotle was bringing me some advantages here.

"Yeah, that's what the Greeks called it. They also talked about eros, storge, and agape. Those were all forms of love they distinguished."

"But distinguished without separating!" I had talked about philosophy with a Spanish uncle of mine, a philosopher, who always insisted that in philosophy, one had to be careful not to confuse distinguishing with separating. He would show me a coin, and then say: how many coins are these? When I said: "one" he would ask whether we could distinguish any different sides to the coin. I then said "heads and tails". And he would ask whether the two sides meant that there were two coins. And I would say "of course not!" And then he would be happy and satisfied. We had the same conversation several times, and I always played along, because I thought it was fun to see him so happy afterwards.

Loffels clearly wasn't so familiar with this point, because he just said "Yeah, whatever." He went on to say that he would describe the situation of the prisoner's dilemma as 'eros' love. Eros, after all, was the love of desire, not only sexual, which is the connotation 'erotic' now has, but more broadly it can be seen as need-love. It's the love that needs to receive from others. And the prisoner's dilemma has a lot to do with optimizing what you receive.

I could see that.

Loffels also mentioned that 'agape' could be seen as 'gift-love'. In game theory terms, the closest thing to it would be the invisible hand game, in which people always collaborate with one another. He said that interestingly enough, the equilibrium of collaboration would then not be because of hierarchy, through fines or other punishments, or through competition, but rather through voluntary commitment. People who love one another in an agapeic way, freely help each other out.

That also sounded reasonable enough. But now I was getting curious. "So what about philia then?"

*

"For friendship we need a different game." And he showed us some more slides on his computer. "This is the stag hunt game."

Stag hunt

	Collaborate (be silent)	Don't Collaborate (hare)
Collaborate (stag)	2, 2	0, 1
Don't Collaborate (hare)	1, 0	1, 1

Payoff: what every person has shot.

Loffels told us the story. Two hunters go out hunting stags (a stag is an adult male deer). Shooting a stag is difficult. They need to be patient, and they only really have a chance at killing it if both shoot at the same time. If they do, they both get a lot of meat (indicated by '2'). If, however, one of the hunters loses his patience, he can shoot a hare, which will give him some meat (indicated by '1'). However, if one hunter shoots a hare, all other wildlife will be scared away, so that the other hunter can't shoot anything anymore and leaves empty-handed. If both hunters lose their patience though, they can both shoot a hare at the same time.

"Nice story, but friendship?" I couldn't quite make out the connection.

"Well, look at the dynamics. This is what happens when player two collaborates."

	Collaborate (stag)	
Collaborate (stag)	②, 2	
Don't Collaborate (hare)	1, 0	

"See? For player one it's best to collaborate. And when player two doesn't collaborate..."

		Don't Collaborate (hare)
Collaborate (stag)		0, 1
Don't Collaborate (hare)		①, 1

"... it's best for player one not to collaborate, so..."

	Collaborate (stag)	Don't Collaborate (hare)
Collaborate (stag)	(2, 2)	0, 1
Don't Collaborate (hare)	1, 0	(1, 1)

"... because the game is symmetrical, there are now two equilibria." Dr. Loffels flicked through the screens as he described the game.

"So you can either collaborate or not collaborate, and both are stable?" Miriam asked.

"Exactly."

"So where's the friendship?" I persisted.

"There's several things." Loffels then explained that it's possible to transform a 'prisoner's dilemma' type game to a stag-hunt type game by increasing the payoff if both collaborate. Friendship gives extra joy to collaboration. So if we take a broader interpretation of the payoffs—and go beyond years in prison or the amount of meat to perceive that there might be a payoff that also includes something of psychological joy, for example—then friendship can transform what was a prisoner's dilemma into a stag-hunt game. Friendship increases the joy of collaboration, and so increases the psychological payoff.

"Right, the joy of friendship." That was a very Aristotelian concept, but of course very clear from daily experience too. I had to think of my uncle Luca who kept on sending me all these Italian jokes via whatsapp. And I had tried to convince Miriam to send him some whacky photos of her, but she didn't think it was funny. Oh well...

"And the next thing is the collaboration itself. Friends collaborate, but not always." Loffels clarified that friends expect other friends to do something in return for them. If that happens, friendship and collaboration continues. But there is also fragility: if your friend doesn't reciprocate, you 'lose' in some way. Then there is risk of changing from the collaborative to the non-collaborative equilibrium.

"Interesting." Miriam clearly liked the approach. I had to think about it a bit more.

"So this game is really a game of trust," Loffels continued. And he pulled up this slide on his laptop.

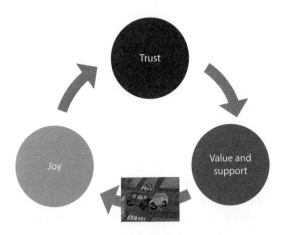

"This is the positive cycle of trust. But as you see, there can be accidents. And then people can fall into the negative reciprocity cycle."

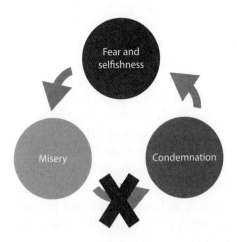

"What's that cross?" I asked.

"That's where the negative cycle can be broken. But only if someone puts up with unanswered collaboration for a while." Loffels said that only if people are willing to put up with others to regain their trust, can the non-collaboration equilibrium move towards the collaboration equilibrium. That's another thing the stag-hunt game illustrates.

"And you think friendship is like that?"

"I do."

I didn't quite understand how this story was going to help me make friends at the contest. And also, I didn't get how this related to all the other things I had studied about friendship. I decided to challenge Loffels a bit. "Sorry, but what kind of friendship are you talking about? Is it a friendship for utility, for pleasure, or for the good?"

"What do you mean?"

"Well, Aristotle distinguishes between these different friendship types. They have a different purpose."

"Oh, well, that doesn't matter."

"How do you mean? These friendship types are very different."

"I don't see the difference. Whatever purpose there is, friends collaborate in the same way."

"Right. So this model is not about what friendship is, but about what friends do? I mean, what they do together in society?"

"I suppose you could say that."

"Cool!" Miriam clearly liked the model. "I'll need to give some thought as to how we can use this to analyze business cases."

"That won't be easy." I wasn't convinced.

"It's an excellent challenge!"

"Go for it!" Loffels encouraged her.

So there we were. My attempts to just go to the contest to make friends had only led us to a theoretical model of friendship. What good was that going to do? And Miriam was all excited to elaborate the theory. Oh, well, let her do the theory. I'd go for the public relations. Pity that we seemingly won't work on that together though...

Chapter 16

Patience had been listening intently to Claudio as she was driving. She was fidgeting a little, and seemed somewhat uncomfortable.

"So, you think it's true?" Patience asked Claudio, as he finished telling his story.

"What?"

"Economics being about relationships and all that? About friendship?"

"You're not?" Claudio reminded her that Bruni, whom she had liked, also made this point.

"Well, it would be great if it's true, and whenever it's true. It's just that... too often it's not."

"So you think it's immoral? Or amoral?" I asked.

"Oh, then we should tell you about 'The Moral Economy'!" Claudio suggested.

"Moral economy?" The peaceful agreeable expression that had characterized Patience's face so far suddenly changed sharply. "I don't believe in that at all!" She exclaimed.

Claudio looked surprised at her sudden outburst, and tried to joke about it, putting on an American slang accent and saying "Heyyy, what your problem lady?"

But Patience didn't appreciate the move. She stared straight ahead as she said angrily, "My problem is that people were deported to the Americas as slaves, in the name of improving the economy. Is that moral?"

Claudio whistled between his teeth, but that enraged Patience even more.

"What are you whistling at? You don't think that's a problem?"

"Yeah... no... I do." Claudio was clearly taken aback by Patience's sudden explosion. A tense silence fell over the car.

I considered for a while what to say. Of course, I couldn't even imagine what it would be like for people to be sold as slaves, transported under horrendous conditions to the other side of the ocean, and there put to work forcibly. In comparison with that, my life was a paradise. In the Netherlands people would talk of "wage slaves", people who do their jobs only because they need an income. Now that was already a much milder form of 'slavery', and I wasn't even in that category, because no wages were binding me yet. But still, I felt I was struggling to loose myself from fetters; different but real. And though I knew feeling sorry for myself wasn't the way forward, I did feel it allowed me to empathize, though only very slightly, with Patience's point. How could I ever bring that across though, without seeming the most spoilt brat ever?

Because the silence continued, I chose to break it as best I could. "I know I can't even start to get my head around it, but I feel very sorry."

"Thanks." Patience quickly glanced sideways at me.

But Claudio seemingly hadn't understood not to push the issue. He resumed, "So economics is all about slave trade? Hasn't that been abolished?"

Patience had regained composure, "It has, but it still exists when money is more important than people."

That made me reflect.

Without any further prompting, Patience went on to talk about Congo. She said that over the last 20 years more than 8 million people were killed there by people that call themselves 'the government'. Europe is a bit critical, but European countries that have economic interests there are not. They send a UN peace force, but that just peacefully stands by while everything happens. "Don't talk to me about morals and economy," she concluded with a quiver on her lip.

Claudio jumped in again. "But you're not really denying that economics is about relationships, are you? You're saying that they should go together, but that people often mess up big time?"

Patience looked skeptical, but said "That's one way of putting it."

"We're not saying anything different."

Because Patience kept silent, Claudio started to explain what we are trying to do: to show people that even though in the real economy there are instances, and even very painful ones, where people act from self-interest, it's still not true to say that people only act from self-interest. "You wouldn't say everyone is selfish, would you?"

Patience looked uncomfortable. "Not everyone, I suppose."

"Right. So if we can show that economics doesn't have to be about selfishness, we can help others also to think about good relationships in economics. Do you think that's a good idea?"

"As long as they're not naïve. What about all these people that don't care about others and exploit people?"

"Of course Patience. Why would you think *Homo economicus* was thought up in the first place? It's convenient for maths, but there's truth to it. People can be very self-centered."

She nodded at me, and showed with some relaxation in her body that she felt understood.

"Right," Claudio said, "they can be, but aren't always. And it's about time Economics took that into account. In the "Moral Economy" book Bowles also shows that governments shouldn't think of their citizens as '*Homo economicus*'. That can be damaging."

"What do you mean, damaging?" Patience said challengingly.

*

Claudio was up to the challenge, and started to explain. "Bowles talks about intrinsic motivation." He gave the example of volunteers in the boards of sports clubs, who help society be more social. But he also explained that this is very fragile. "If suddenly one person on the board would get paid by the government, the others wouldn't want to work for nothing anymore. They would feel that's unfair."

"Hm."

"Bowles calls this 'crowding out' of social preferences." Claudio went on to clarify that sometimes giving subsidies, and making things financial, can have the opposite effect to what is intended. And that's because people are not only '*Homo economicus*'. They also do things out of themselves, and "often recognizing people for what they've done is much better than paying them."

"The government should take advantage of people's goodwill, you say?"

"Take, advantage; take advantage." Claudio muttered. "It's not 'us-against-them' you know. We all make society together. Have you heard of this kindergarten in Israel?" Of course she hadn't. Claudio told the story, which runs something like this. The managers were worried that people were not picking up their children in time. Therefore, they introduced a fine for people picking up their children late. What was the effect? The people only came later, because now they felt they were paying for their children to be there longer, which made them feel entitled to longer childcare hours, and 'crowded out' their intrinsic motivation to be there on time.

Patience shook her head. "So you see: money makes people asocial. Relational economics is too hard."

"That very much depends." He went on to say that Bowles talks about some big projects in the state of Athens, in which it was seen to be honorable for rich people to participate. And they did. "Think of all the private initiatives, people running a small business to help others and make a living. Or think of churches, often built through donations. That's also economy."

Patience looked doubtful, "A church is part of the economy?"

"Of course! There are people doing things together, there's even money involved. But of course, economics about is much more than donating money in church." He elaborated how economists tend to assume that in a certain transaction, contracts are 'complete'—that is, they cover all parts of the transaction. But in reality, this is hardly ever the case, contracts are always incomplete. "There morality also kicks in. Will I treat my business partner badly, just 'cuz the contract forgot to specify that I should treat him well? Of course not."

"Sounds nice, but ethical? Maybe you just want to get repeat business, so you treat someone well. That's nothing more than self-interest." Patience was pretty sharp here, I had to admit.

"Maybe it is, maybe it's not. Maybe I'm a friend. Or maybe that's just who I am: I treat others well. That's completely ethical."

"Why was that important again?"

"Governments have to take into account social motives. They should be careful not to 'crowd them out'. Even more, they can 'crowd them in'."

"What's that?"

Claudio explained how Bowles makes the point that a liberal state has institutions like rule of law that make the consequences of trusting someone that doesn't collaborate less bad. So instead of losing everything when someone cheats on me, I can sue that person, and that person can then be forced to collaborate with me.

"Suing people doesn't sound friendly."

"Maybe not," and he went on to say that people want to avoid lawsuits, and that creates an atmosphere in which people collaborate with each other. There is like a 'generalized trust' in society, which makes the society function well. And in this atmosphere of trust it is also easier that people do things for others 'just because'. "That's 'crowding in' of social preferences."

"Ah."

"So are you convinced?"

"Hm. People want to be someone. Someone good, most of the time. So they also act accordingly—most of the time. Some people don't. I wonder whether any theory is going to change that."

Claudio seemed to get a little tired from pushing. He let her question hang in the air. Perhaps it was the wise thing to do.

*

After a few moments of silence, it became clear Patience hadn't quite finished with the theme. She asked Claudio, "Thinking back to Grant's book that you talked about. What is the biggest taker you ever met?"

"How do you mean, the biggest taker?"

"Well, we're supposed to be talking about real people right? Grant talks about 'takers'. Have you ever met a real person like that? A real taker? Like bigtime?"

"Ah, yeah, well, let me think. Ha! I just met someone who wouldn't let me have a pizza slice because I was 2 cents short.

That's not very giving. But let me think of someone else. It's not really a very nice thing to say of someone."

In spite of myself, I had to think back to my fancy dinner with the jetset of the Dutch banking world. But were these people really the takers they were made out to be? I couldn't imagine it was all of them, there were some pretty normal people there. But then the portrait painted by documentaries like 'Inside Job' was quite different. There may have been some genuine takers there. On stock markets perhaps also. And medicine? Suddenly I had the example.

"Okay." I said "Have you heard of this man who bought a patent for an aids medicine, which was being sold for $13.50 per pill, and raised the price to $750 per pill? He wasn't responsible at all for developing the drug; he just bought it and made money off it, over the backs of sick people."

"Wow, that's pretty hefty taking." Claudio bobbed his head.

Patience looked at me sideways in amazement. "Did someone really do that? That's... I don't even have words for that." She focused back on the road, clearly impressed.

"Okay, but we can't leave it there." Claudio said. "If we talk about Grant, we should also have examples of the 'otherish givers' he mentions. You know, people that are successful and do good."

I decided to give him the stage: "I'm sure you have some nice ones."

Claudio was stroking his chin to look intellectual. "Yeah. It depends a bit what you mean by success, but in the jazz scene you have a few."

"How so?"

He explained how there are some really successful Jazz musicians who raise the admiration of other musicians. Of course, other Jazz musicians get curious how they do it. So they ask them for their secrets. And amazingly, they tend to share the secrets, even on YouTube. "I have a friend who is a Jazz guitarist; he watches these YouTube videos to improve his technique. They don't have to do that; they could also just sit on their success."

Patience looked slightly interested.

I asked, "Any more otherish givers? Like really successful and really good?"

Claudio went on to mention some examples Grant himself gives. A successful Basketball coach who really cares about his payers. Or Adam Rifkin, a successful entrepreneur who tries to do five-minute favors to everyone who asks for them."

Patience slowly came out of her defensive attitude as Claudio gave these examples. She even nodded a little as he finished speaking. Then, thoughtfully, she muttered under her breath, "I should really go and tell my family some of these things."

I didn't quite know what to make of that remark. I figured it couldn't hurt to ask, "Is everything well with your family?"

I saw Patience's new-found positivity drain away again, as she stared more intently at the road. "It could be worse."

I was a bit puzzled what to reply to that. In the end I said, "Does it have to do with this book?"

I saw Patience swallowing, and doubting whether to answer. I didn't dare break in. In the end she did start to speak, "You have to know that I have a very good family, they are very good people, especially my parents."

I didn't really know what to say, but in the end I said, "I'm sure."

"Yes. Indeed. Sure. But my mother and my father, you know, they are givers. They give. And they give a lot, and they keep on giving."

"Very impressive."

"Impressive, but in the end they cannot do it and it all breaks down, you see."

"Oh."

I didn't really know what to say or do after this. I looked sideways and saw Patience's lip quivering as if she was going to cry. But she took a deep breath and the quiver went away. "They are having a very difficult time now, but it is because they both want to give too much. That can happen. Perhaps I can tell you another time. I need to drive now."

"OK. Time for something else. The strategy?"

Chapter 17

"Yes!" Claudio smiled at me radiantly. "Let's hear it Miriam, what are you waiting for? Shoot!"

Oh, finally. "Great! So, I found a way to tackle the case. I just want to know whether you're on board with it."

"Let's hear it."

"Alright, here we go." I explained to them that I had been thinking about the game theory approach that Loffels had proposed to us. The games were pretty helpful, because they illustrated something about different types of behaviors people can have in professional relationships. Still, that wouldn't be enough to tackle something as practical as a case. In a typical case, there would be more than two players, for instance, and the relationships could be more towards the 'eros' type with one player, and more 'philia' or even 'agape' with another. "So we need to translate it to practice."

"And how would you do that?"

This was the moment I'd been waiting for. I demonstratively opened my bag, took out a piece of paper, and handed it to Claudio. "This is how."

Claudio opened the paper and saw my quickly but carefully prepared table.

Stakeholder	Relationship factor	Utility (payoff)	Total
'Me'	1	5	5
Nr 1	0	3	0
Nr 2	-0.5	6	-3
Nr 3	0.5	-2	-1
<etc.>			
total			1

"What? What does that mean?" he asked.

"It's really cool. Let me explain." I told Claudio that this was a wonderful way to analyze go/no-go decisions in the case. I had basically extended the game to multiple players, which was probably needed because cases often involve multiple stakeholders. Also, I had introduced the 'relationship factor'. The relationship to 'me' was one, by definition. For another stakeholder, zero means 'I don't care' about that stakeholder, or 'eros' love. If another stakeholder has a relationship value of one, then it's a case of 'we-rationality' or 'agape' as Loffels called it. But it can also be something in between, something even higher, or even a negative relationship, if people really don't like each other.

Patience was half listening as she focused on driving and watching the road.

"And what about philia, friendship love?" Claudio asked.

"Good one." I had thought about that, and because Loffels had said that philia increased the utility of the collaboration through psychological payoffs, I thought it would be enough just to increase the utility a little when friends were involved. So I explained that to Claudio.

"Ah."

"What do you think? Do you like it?"

"Honestly?"

"Eh, yes?"

"I think it's nonsense."

"What? Why?"

"It makes me think of Bentham. I don't like Bentham."

"What are you talking about? I'm trying to analyze cases here! And who is Bentham?"

"Don't you know? Study some philosophy!"

Of course, I'd heard about Bentham once or twice, but I didn't quite see why at the brink of starting our case competition he had to criticize my wonderful method to win it by only invoking the name of Bentham. "I don't have time; I want to win this competition!" I countered.

"Miriam, Bentham made tables like this." Claudio went on.

"Good for him!"

"But people stopped using them afterwards."

"Bad luck for them." I was a little less energetic on this one.

"And they had good reason to."

"Oh. Like what?"

"Where shall I start?" Claudio reminded us of one of his two favorite uncles he was in regular touch with. This wasn't Luca, the banker in Italy, his father's brother, whom he joked with over whatsapp all the time. But it was his philosopher uncle Pepe in Spain, his mother's brother. With him he had deep conversations. After talking to Loffels about love and game theory, he had wanted to talk to him about what had been discussed. They had had a long conversation over Skype, and this uncle had sent him several articles afterwards. One explained the origins and development of utilitarian theory in economics. In it, he said, they gave several reasons why people stopped using these tables. "So if you want to win, don't go there."

I wasn't about to give up that easily though. "I want reasons!"

"Wow. I have to think." After briefly reflecting he started to explain that Bentham wanted to lay the foundation his ethics on overseeing all the consequences of an action. If the sum of the consequences was positive, then the action would be considered good. He used tables such as this one to make a 'bookkeeping' of all the consequences. The thing is, though, it's really impossible to oversee all consequences of an action—and so the table would always be incomplete.

"But that's not what I'm doing!" I interjected.

"Why not?"

"Well, I just try to understand why someone makes a decision. And this helps. It's not an ethics framework."

"But everything we do is ethical; at least that's what Aristotle thought. But ok. Point taken. You're just trying to analyze the pros and cons of someone's decision. But you're not out of trouble though." He went on to ask how I could ever translate consequences into a number, especially if these 'utilities' could also be psychological, as I had been saying. He also said that by putting a number on it, I made it seem very precise—much more precise than it really is, and so he thought that was misleading. Claudio felt that I would be more likely to emphasize consequences that can be measured, while really unmeasurable payoffs are also important—not only for friendship, but for many other things.

Wow, he really had a point there. I didn't know what to say.

"I'm not going to work with this table Miriam. End of discussion."

*

Claudio took out his phone and started tapping and swiping the screen. Not much later he gave it to me. "Have a look here" he said "It's from Luca".

I was looking at a seemingly endless whatsapp conversation full of silly pictures and videos, but what Claudio was pointing at was a text message reading "I hate people who steal my ideas before I think of them."

"That's your problem," he grinned.

"Not funny." He was trying to cheer me up, of course, but I wasn't in the mood. I had indeed been thinking a lot about my approach, and I had imagined how Claudio would be enthused about my ideas. Now that he wasn't, I felt really disappointed. And really, if we weren't going to do this, how was our 'master plan' going to work out in practice? I decided to confront him with that. "So what's your alternative?"

"Alternative?"

"Yes, alternative 'master plan'?"

"Oh, we just make friends. Talk to people. And then we'll find an inspiring solution. We have enough knowledge to fall back on. It will come to us, don't worry."

Don't worry? Was he serious? He just wanted to waltz into this competition, and see what happens? This would lead to a mediocre result at best. Didn't he see that this was about winning? Or at least, that winning was what I was going for? But was he? He didn't seem to be. And then Patience. I couldn't see her be the one on the team to push for excellence. So, in this situation, did I really want to continue? I could still go back and prepare for my exams. Perhaps that would be the better option.

"Miriam?" Patience broke her silence.

"Yes?"

"Can you show me the table? Or explain it to me, while I'm driving?"

I was surprised by her interest, given Claudio's stark rejection. But I explained what the table looked like and contained.

"Oh. So couldn't we improve it a little?"

"How would you mean?"

"Well, take into account Claudio's objections."

"In a table though?" Claudio didn't sound convinced.

"Yes, why not?"

"I already told you why. Using numbers gives an inaccurate impression of accuracy."

"And if we used categories?"

"Like how?"

"Maybe a Likert scale, you know with five categories?"

"From -2 to +2?" I suggested. "From very negative to very positive?"

"That could be a way."

"But you'd still do the math." Claudio objected.

"So?"

"So is it real when you add someone's 'very positive' psychological payoff and subtract someone else's 'very negative' monetary payoff, and end up with zero? What does that mean?"

It suddenly came to me. "Very simple. It means that those two payoffs are equally important to you when making your decision."

"And if they're not?"

"Then you can modify with the relationship factor."

"Ah."

"Very good Miriam!" Patience exclaimed. "We can make this work."

"One minute." Claudio didn't look happy. "The table says nothing about the type of payoff. If we just have the categories it will be very hard to see what we're really comparing. It's just confusing."

"Well, let's de-confuse" Patience suggested.

I was really happy to see her stick up for me. She clearly hadn't taken my wish to take the train personally.

"How?" Claudio asked.

"Well, what kinds of payoff are there?"

"Many kinds." I said.

"Yeah, but still: fundamentally three types." Claudio seemed confident.

"Three types?" I had never heard about that.

"Absolutely." He explained how his uncle Pepe had also sent him a book of the Spanish management thinker Perez-Lopez. This thinker had elaborated a pretty detailed action theory, which thought about different ways in which people could be motivated to do something. And he basically distinguished three ways: extrinsic, intrinsic and transcendental motivation.

"Transcendental?"

"It's the word he uses." Claudio went on to explain that extrinsic motivation refers to anything outside of us that can motivate us. Things like money, recognition, prestige and so forth. By intrinsic motivation he meant motivation about things that affect us internally, like intellectual learning, or becoming better at something. He added that this was a little confusing, because other economists use the word 'intrinsic' in a different way, but that's life.

"And transcendental?" I insisted.

"The third one." He said that he himself preferred to refer to that as 'relational' motivation. It basically means that you would like others to improve, and that motivates you.

"So, like a good teacher who is really motivated to make you learn?"

"Exactly!"

"So can we add this to the table?" Patience asked.

"With a Likert scale?" I proposed.

"I suppose so," Claudio agreed. "So what would it look like then?" He took out his laptop and gave it to me. "Show me."

I thought about it for a moment, and then made this table.

Stakeholder	Relation-ship factor	Extr.	Intr.	Rel.	Utility (payoff)	Total
'Me'	1	+2			2	2
Nr 1	0		+1		1	0
Nr 2	-0.5			+2	2	-1
Nr 3	0.5	-1			-1	-0.5
<etc.>						
total						**0.5**

"Better?" I asked. I showed it to Claudio. "These numbers are a Likert scale from -2 to 2". I also informed Patience of what I changed. I was glad to see she kept her eyes on the road.

"Hm." Claudio still didn't look convinced. "What do you do when there are more motivations at the same time?"

"You use your brain," Patience stated forcefully.

"What does that mean, you just add them?"

"'Just doing' anything isn't using your brain. You have to think what is most important. Or whether things combine."

I was amazed by her assertiveness. "Can you explain?" I asked.

"Of course." She said that sometimes she wants to go to the movies with a friend, and it would be good for her studies too, but she has to save money. "What do I do? I use my brain! I think what is most important for me at that moment."

"Oh, and that depends on the situation."

"Of course. On the film, the friend, the price, but also the circumstances. They don't always weigh equally."

"I get it." Claudio said. "We're not putting in any fixed rules, we just state the different motivations, so we can think about them, and then make a decision based on the situation?"

"Exactly!" Patience was radiant. "So do we have a plan?"

*

Wow. I was impressed and surprised at Patience's attempt to make this work for everyone. Maybe she wasn't such a bad team member after all.

Claudio said, "This is better, but not convincing yet."

I couldn't believe his stubbornness. "What now?"

"This is still just a table in which everything counts equally. But in reality, some things are just more equal than others."

"What?"

Claudio mentioned a famous paper of Amartya Sen from the 70's called "Rational Fools", in which he criticized the dominant approach of only looking at 'preferences' in economics at the time. He called attention to the fact that some people are just 'committed' to things. "So if you would have offered Nelson Mandela Robben Island with all the wealth, prestige and pretty women in the world, if only he stopped fighting for his cause, he wouldn't have accepted."

"What does that mean?"

"Sen calls this 'metapreferences.'" Claudio explained that there are some motivations that are just on a higher order than all the other ones, because someone is committed to something.

"Can't we put that in the table too?" Patience asked. She wasn't about to give up.

"How?"

"I don't know, just put an 'M' when someone has a metapreference for something? And understand that this explains their choice?"

"I suppose so."

"Great! Happy now?"

Claudio kept silent for a while. He was clearly thinking deeply. After a while he spoke. "Look. I really don't want to rain on this parade, but there are just some things that a table will never capture."

Patience sighed. "Why be so difficult?"

"'Cuz it's true!" He reminded us that already during the discussions on friendship with Loffels, he had had to think of the different goals friendship could have for Aristotle: utility, pleasure or living the good life together. The goals we have when we do something are really important, he said. They make what we do good or bad. A murderer and a surgeon can stab the same type of knife in someone's chest in the same way, but the one is trying to kill, and the other is trying to cure. That's not the same, even though the effect may be the same, for example, the person could die in both cases.

"Oh, so the payoff is the same?"

"Yes, but we don't accuse the surgeon of murder, we accuse the murderer."

"Still, can't we capture that somehow with the table? We have different motivations and metapreferences now." Patience was less forceful this time.

"The 'why' is the most important thing in any action, Patience. It's not in the table. I don't want to be tied down by maths."

This time, Patience didn't insist any more. And I didn't know what to say either. Anyway, we were already in Rotterdam by now. The start of the contest was near. Little use backing out now. And perhaps, with Patience supporting me, we could still go somewhere.

Chapter 18

It was 9:55 when we pulled up the driveway at the hotel across from the university. Just in time. At the registration desk, Patience talked to a lady whose voice I recognized from the telephone conversations. And not long after, it was confirmed that she could join our team. Great news!

It turned out that Patience and I would be roommates too, which I liked. After settling into our rooms, we went down to the opening ceremony, where the Dean welcomed us. He said he was especially proud of the diverse representation of countries and types of schools, and he impressed upon us that we were part of the lucky few to be allowed to participate. The project leader Jeannette van Es introduced the program to us, emphasizing the option to submit work Wednesday afternoon to get some preliminary jury feedback by Thursday morning. She also introduced the judges: Mr. Jacobsen, Ms. Bentley and Mr. Rekels. When Harry Jacobsen introduced himself, a shock of recognition went through me. I knew that name! It was the person whose number my mum was searching for! My goodness, was there then no way to escape my mum's network? But Ms. van Es even showed us the trophies we could win, the sight of which upped my excitement considerably.

We had an amazing lunch afterwards, talking with the team from Riga. They didn't seem to present the most fearsome opposition; Claudio had a good time with them of course. After lunch, Ms. Van Es announced that she would now hand out keys to the project rooms. As soon as I heard about the project rooms, I got up from my seat and couldn't help jeering at Claudio and Patience, still lounging over lunch conversation. "What are you both waiting for?"

They followed my example. I rushed to Ms. Van Es to get the room keys, and was there told, to my chagrin, that we would have to wait for the others to walk to the project room site together. Biting my tongue, I mustered all my patience, which was soon rewarded. We were led across the building to the project rooms.

Our room was very business-like; it had white walls, with a whiteboard on one of the walls. At the far end a projector screen was hanging on the ceiling, but it was currently rolled up. The chairs were typical office chairs, quite comfortable really. The oval table in the center had a projector and a small stand with tea bags, sugar and creamer on it, and now three bags with the logo of the Erasmus University printed on them. Inside, we found a folder with the program, a list of participants, and the case. We couldn't wait to get started. This is what the case said.

*

A failed takeover bid

Please note that in this case all names of people, companies and countries have been changed to respect the privacy of the people involved. The case is a dramatized version of real events.

When Roy Olson drives his top-tier SteadyCar into SteadyCars HQ and walks to the entrance, the people he meets on the way greet him with strict politeness. Olson is technical director at SteadyCars, a Norse car producing company, a position that his father held before him. SteadyCars owes its technical standing, to a great extent, to his family. SteadyCars were also the first to introduce the airbag for driver safety.[4] The people are proud that a SteadyCars automobile can be assembled with half the number of pieces than the competitor FlashCars have to use. The management is also happy with these feats, since fewer pieces per car means, for example, a strong reduction in operating costs. The Olson family has been, and remains, important for SteadyCars.

Still, the respect for Olson and his family background does not translate into a warmhearted attitude towards his person. Behind

---

4   This example is fictional; the point is that the company was a technological forerunner.

the formal greetings lies a distant, disgruntled attitude instead. Behind his back, people call Olson the "Tiger Fish", evoking a fish with a big mouth and small ears. And this aspect of Olson junior's character is not appreciated—neither by the employees, nor by the top management. Today, as Olson is heading for a private meeting with Eirik Larsen, SteadyCars' CEO, he knows the communication issue will be on the agenda, as it has been in previous meetings.

The meeting turns out to be shorter and more dramatic than Olson had expected. Larsen informs him that the atmosphere in the company around his person has not improved—rather, it has worsened—and that it does not look like the conflicts that have arisen are solvable within a reasonable amount of time. The management has therefore decided to relieve him of his duties.

Even though this has been in the making for some time, the managements' decision comes as an unpleasant surprise to Olson. He is compelled to leave the company that he and his family have such a large history with —a company that is home to him.

New opportunities

Some time after his dismissal from SteadyCars, Olson gets a call from a headhunter. A vacancy has opened up for the CEO of Flash-Cars, one of SteadyCars' competitors. Olson has to think the offer over. FlashCars has a track record that is much more problematic than SteadyCars. The company is not doing well, and is in need of a turnaround, which is why the current CEO has been fired. The company is also based in Britain, with a culture that Olson is not used to. It is very different, and in some aspects antithetical to the Norse culture. He does not have as big a business network in Britain as he has in Norway.

After thinking things over, Olson decides to apply for the job. He is presented to the FlashCars directors, and they accept his nomination. Olson becomes the new CEO of FlashCars in January 1992 and gets the assignment to restructure the group and to bring more focus into the company's portfolio.

A new situation

In his new function, Olson takes some time to get to know FlashCars, but also starts building his network in Britain. One of the people he gets to know is Mr. Walker, the CEO of TireDeals, a British tire company. The two CEOs find themselves in similar situations. Walker is implementing a large-scale restructuring of his company. While Olson is just starting, Walker's restructuring is going well; despite the associated costs, the net profit has risen by 82% over the last year, and sales also look stronger. Walker's popularity in TireDeals is mixed; while people do not like the harsh measures he proposes, cutting costs and jobs, they do admire the turnaround in the company that this is producing.

There are also structural links between FlashCars and TireDeals— for TireDeals owns a significant non-majority share in both FlashCars and SteadyCars. SteadyCars is a wanted stock, because of the steady revenue it produces. This is especially handy for TireDeals, because the company cannot easily collect large amounts of money from the stock market. This situation is due to protection constructions that prevent further flotation. TireDeals is owned by the Swiss magnate Luca Bianchi. Bianchi is the owner of multiple companies, some of which he made great himself. Bianchi has great ambitions: he wants to own the greatest tire imperium and to outdo his rivals. His ambitions are well known to his subordinates.

Another shareholder in FlashCars is StrongSteel. StrongSteel is a British steel-producing company. Next to being a shareholder, it also provides steel for FlashCars cars, and has a close relationship with this company. In general, big industry in the UK is being led by a reduced group of people on the boards of several of these companies. This is the British 'economic elite' that is in close contact with British political leadership. In practice, this construction means a "safety net" for British companies. In case something goes wrong with one big company, others will jump in to help turn things around.[5]

5   This situation is of interest to the case, but it is not to be taken to be the real situation in Britain.

Olson is steadily getting introduced to his shareholders, but as a newcomer, his place in the British 'economic elite' is far from secured.

Meanwhile at SteadyCars

SteadyCars has been, and remains a well-to-do car producer that makes a steady yearly profit of approximately €1 billion. It is a family business, built up by the Hansen family, in a culture where family ties are important, also in business. The older Hansen generation has worked for the company themselves, and has therefore built up a bond with the company. Jon Hansen, for instance, has sold for SteadyCars in Africa. SteadyCars sold cars as well as military equipment there. Jon Hansen is an influential man in Norway, because the family owns multiple large companies, and he therefore employs a significant percentage of the Norwegian population in his companies. The Norwegian government regularly talks to him when important decisions need to be made. He is well aware of his social responsibility towards his native country. Jon Hansen is no longer actively engaged in running SteadyCars, but he is active as an owner of the company and influences the decisions around the ownership of the company, together with the younger generation. The younger generation Hansens has not been actively involved in the running of SteadyCars. They have followed financial and MBA educations, and are used to working from a position of ownership only.

SteadyCars is a popular company. It has built up a great brand loyalty with its clients, which are drivers that drive SteadyCars cars for many years. The company actively communicates with them and involves them in discussions about technical innovations that they would like to see in future cars. It has also started an academy, especially for SteadyCars technicians and dealers.

SteadyCars also has close ties with worker associations, and has found a way to deal with the fluctuations in the car market. In consultation with these associations, it has decided to school all its workers for alternative jobs. In this way, when the car market is low, workers can take on other tasks in the Norwegian economy. When the market rises, these people will be easily readmitted to Steady-Cars. This arrangement works well in practice and is positively seen by the workers and worker associations; it also allows SteadyCars to retain a very constant revenue stream, even in a fluctuating market.

The Proposed Takeover

Surveying the situation at FlashCars, the corporate environment he finds himself in, and the situation at FlashCars, Olson decides to seek formal collaboration with SteadyCars. In September 1993, one and a half years after Olson has taken the lead at FlashCars, he writes to Eirik Larsen, the CEO of SteadyCars, proposing a €10 billion takeover of SteadyCars by FlashCars. The bid is being backed by StrongSteel and TireDeals, who see it as an indirect way to gain influence over SteadyCars. To the surprise of Olson, after his initial meeting with Larsen with friendly intentions, SteadyCars makes sure that Flash-Cars' bid is perceived as hostile and brought in the media as such.[6] The workers unions oppose the deal, and also SteadyCars' owners, the Hansens, are not willing to collaborate. This situation leads to a series of negotiations with the owners of SteadyCars, led by Olson. After months of negotiating, the resistance is so great that FlashCars decides to retract its offer in January 1994.

Unexpected consequences

While the talks are ongoing, it comes out that also the owners of TireDeals are not happy with the way the bid has been managed. Bianchi asks his CEO Walker to resign over his involvement in this

---

6   During a friendly takeover, the boards of the companies involved meet and discuss the process, which shows the willingness of both parties to collaborate. In the case of a hostile takeover, no conversations take place, and the existing management is "bought out" without their consent. Hostile takeovers generally require a larger financial investment.

proposed deal. Walker had agreed to back the deal without communicating about it with Bianchi. Notwithstanding his successful management of the TireDeals turnaround, Walker needs to go.

Olson does survive the talks, but the situation at FlashCars remains very difficult. Next to the financial situation there are corruption scandals popping up as he goes along. And his strategy to turn around FlashCars by the merger with SteadyCars has definitely failed.

Olson decides to resign from his post two years after the failed takeover bid, in 1996. The reasons given for his resignation are the internal corruption scandals, for which he is formally, though not personally, responsible.

Later developments

After Olson leaves, FlashCars tries again to take over SteadyCars, but SteadyCars declares the bids to be illegal. The conflict escalates and the governments of the respective countries are involved in trying to reestablish peace. In the end all these efforts are in vain, and the takeover does not go through.

Several years down the road, TireDeals takes over FlashCars cars, and gradually also enlarges its share in SteadyCars. In 1998, TireDeals has a majority share in SteadyCars, and in 2001 a complete takeover ensues. The TireDeals side of the talks around this takeover is directly managed by Bianchi. The Norwegian populace and workers unions are unhappy with the takeover, which was made while Jon Hansen was withdrawing from active participation in the ownership management. The decision to sell is mostly taken by his sons.

The collaboration between FlashCars and SteadyCars remains difficult because of cultural differences. Under the pressure of management, though, it does seem that synergy between the companies is possible, in practice.

Meanwhile, Olson finds a new job as CEO of a Swedish motorbike manufacturer. He leads his new company to success by making it a technological forerunner and expanding operations overseas.

Finally, as he arrives to work in the morning, both he and his employees have reason to smile.

Questions to be answered

1. What do you think went wrong in the failed takeover bid?
2. Who do you think is the key responsible person for the failed bid?
3. Formulate (a) lesson(s) you draw from this situation to avoid similar mistakes in future.

*

After reading this case, I could already see the tables flashing over my computer screen. An analysis of all the key actors in terms of all the stakeholders, and what would motivate their decisions. Amazing! But I also knew that I had to hold my horses a little. No use getting into conflict with Claudio straight away. Maybe better to first listen to him? After all, he is a smart guy—and perhaps he might come up with something interesting? And then integrate the tables later? Claudio was thinking and waiting patiently! Finally Patience finished reading.

"Ah." She sighed as she put down the paper. "So what do you guys think?"

I thought for a second, and said, "very complicated."

"What?"

"Complicated!"

"What 'd you mean?"

"I mean... look at this. So many actors. How do we connect them all?"

"I suppose you mean: we really need that table." Claudio saw right through me, of course.

I thought I'd better keep silent after that comment.

"Can't we just get started?" Patience asked.

"Miriam?" Claudio asked.

Attack is often the best defense, so I just asked, "What do you think?"

"I think we can make sense of this. There's plenty to talk about."

"Right, it's really interesting." Patience said.

"Great." I don't think my intonation was very convincing, but what could I do?

We agreed to all try and think about the case for ourselves in the afternoon. We would reconvene in the morning, exchange our insights and prepare the 'midway' presentation. During the afternoon, collaborating with the others would be up to each of us. I decided to retreat to my room to try and make the best of it by myself. Claudio and Patience remained in the project room. I'd stay away from the tables for now, not to upset Claudio.

Chapter 19

Before I knew it, it was time to have dinner. Claudio sent me a whatsapp message to remind me. Nice of him. I took my time packing my laptop, my notebook and my pens. I had advanced a little, but not being able to follow my approach still bothered me. My head suddenly felt as if it was filled with cotton wool.

I was able to catch the group as they left the university building. We were all led to a restaurant just off campus. I looked to my side, where Patience and Claudio were walking and chatting excitingly with all the other participants. I was still too focused on the business case to let my mind rest a little. That clearly wasn't their problem. I was quite surprised, given all the opportunities that presented themselves to him for making new acquaintances, when Claudio came over to talk to me. He asked how I was getting on with the case, and I told him: "fine". We chitchatted a bit more, and he was his friendly, lighthearted self. I don't know whether he just wanted to dissipate the tension that had built up in the car a little. In any case, just when I thought he would go back to socializing with others, he said: "By the way have you spoken to your mum?"

Even though he had evidently tried to ease into it, I was quite taken aback by this change of subject. "Ehm, no," was all I could reply.

"Maybe you should."

What was he thinking? Was he really so worried about his relationship with my mother and her contacts that he now wanted to meddle with what was happening in my family? "Would you please mind your own business?" I retorted decidedly.

He looked dejected, but didn't push the subject further.

When we arrived at the restaurant, it wasn't exactly as I had expected. Sure, it was nice. Comfortable chairs next to a long line of small tables that were already set. But the atmosphere was very 'abstract', with concrete walls and some weird postmodern decoration, which made me feel a little out of place. The kitchen was completely open, and the cooks were already at work. On every table there were two wine glasses, positioned as if they were already toasting. That was a nice touch.

As we entered, Patience and Claudio were talking to two guys from another team, and they sat down at the table next to them. I rushed over to capture the chair at the head of the table next to Patience and Claudio. I threw Patience a quick smile, and received a warm, long one back. I was trying to look for words to start a conversation with Patience, as I didn't feel like going through this dinner without a conversation partner. Right when I was about to ask her whether she had been involved in arranging this lovely place, Claudio asked her something to draw her back in the conversation with the guys.

Thankfully, I took the wine that a young waiter was offering me. Would the others know this was a Wellington Pinotage? My mother had taught me to distinguish between different types of wine at quite a young age. I think by the time I was legally allowed to drink I could already distinguish between different regions in France. It was something I didn't like to talk about, but I was secretly very proud of this skill.

I didn't feel comfortable sitting there, next to the ever-social Patience and Claudio, who were conversing with different people now. I hoped the first course would be served soon. Right then, the sound of someone tapping on a microphone sounded trough the hall. We looked up to see the older woman who had welcomed us to the hotel earlier that day standing before a small, improvised podium. She looked fabulous in her green dress and loaded with golden jewelry.

Her address wasn't anything special, and contributed to my sense of unease. She reminded us of the timetable for the contest, including the pre-submission to the jury on Wednesday evening. Nothing new there. I starting to feel like I might benefit from some conversation.

As she was finishing, I took out my phone to text Linde and Elena. But Claudio, seeing that, started to talk to me. "Is your phone more important than us?" he quipped.

I put away my phone uncomfortably.

A waiter stood up and asked who had indicated a preference for a vegetarian meal. A few hands went up. He then started to take small plates with salad from the kitchen to the table. Everyone was served a fresh salad within minutes. Patience's eyes excitingly followed him. She was clearly very impressed by their dexterity. And by her questions about the food, it didn't look like she had been in many restaurant dinners before. She actually asked Claudio if he ever had such a fancy dinner. Claudio told a funny story about how his uncle tried to organize a fancy dinner once, but he was a terrible cook, so although the whole set-up looked amazing only burned food was served. I had already heard this story, but Patience hadn't. She laughed and told a story about Christmas dinners at her own family. It's difficult to really keep up with a conversation if you are all sitting next to each other, so I just focused on my salad instead. It was amazing. What followed was a well-prepared steak, with potato wedges and salad on the side. I didn't talk a lot. Claudio and Patience were having a great time, I think. I wasn't. After the few remarks we exchanged among ourselves, they went back to talking to the neighboring guys. Seemingly, Claudio still felt they were more interesting than me.

When the crème brûlée had been served for dessert, though, Claudio turned back to me. Saying that I had been awfully silent. I just shrugged. Perhaps he might ask himself why? But I didn't say anything. I didn't want to ruin their good time.

The wine had made him even more open than usual, and he made the mistake of addressing 'the issue' again. "Miriam, you should really make up with your mum, you know." He said in a low, half-joking voice.

That was just the straw that broke this camel's back. All the discomfort of the evening came welling up in me and mingled with the image of my mother telling me not to go to this contest. I stood up and said, "Have a nice evening." I think I even managed to make it sound nice. Luckily most people were taken up with their own engaging conversations, so not too many looked around as I marched out of the restaurant back to the hotel.

*

I was alone in the hotel room for a while, when Patience came in. "Are you okay?"

I nodded. I was feeling a bit calmer, and somewhat ashamed at having marched out of the restaurant like that.

"Do you want to talk about it?"

I shook my head. It was nice of her to ask though, so I did give her a smile, which she appreciated. I told her I was going to continue work on the case for a bit. She nodded and went off to freshen up. I took my papers and tried to focus, but didn't really manage.

When Patience came back into the room, she saw I was being distracted. "Claudio told me about your dad." She said. "I'm sorry to hear about him."

So now he was opening up my private situation to other people. "Did he tell anyone else?"

Now Patience shook her head. "But maybe we can do something nice for him?"

"For starters Claudio can respect his privacy." But I realized she didn't deserve this tone, so I apologized. It was sympathetic of her to think about doing something nice for my dad. I told her so, but also said that I didn't really feel like it. I wanted to focus on the case.

"As if you're focusing," she said ironically.

She had a point, so we talked it over a little and spontaneously agreed on making a video for him. She took out her phone, and started filming as soon as I had said I was ready. It wasn't anything special, I just told my Dad to hang on and that I was thinking of him here in Rotterdam. We also showed him the nice view of the river from the hotel window.

When we finished, Patience asked, "May I have his contact?" She would app the video to him directly, and thought she might send him some things later to cheer him up.

I thought he wouldn't mind, so I gave it to her and introduced her to him with a message. He sent me a smiley back, and when Patience had sent the video, we both received three thumbs up. He asked to know more about Patience, so I made a picture of her, with her phone in her hand as if she was filming, and send it to him. He liked that too.

I texted him that I was going to get back to the contest now, and told the same to Patience. Perhaps I my focus wasn't optimal, but I might as well try.

*

It soon proved to be a vain attempt. Reflecting a little, I remembered how little I had slept the night before, and I considered going to sleep early, so as to be fresh the next day. Patience also went off to take a shower. That decision made me feel a bit calmer, but just as the calm settled over me, my phone went. I watched the screen. It was mum.

I considered whether or not to answer. I wasn't at all in the mood to talk to her. If I would answer at this time, I probably wouldn't sleep tonight. But then again, if I didn't answer, I would probably start worrying about that too. In the end I caught it, just before it would have switched to voicemail.

The conversation started nicely enough. Mum greeted my affectionately, and I tried my best to respond in kind. She had seen the hotel room video I sent to dad, and said it looked nice and that he was happy with it. But soon enough she went off on the dreaded tangent.

"Darling, are you sure you're making the right choice being there?"

I felt the anger welling up in me. Hadn't she learned at all? I didn't respond for a while.

"Miriam?"

"What do you want me to say?" I said, trying to hide my emotions.

"No, it's not about you saying anything. I just want you to think about what you're doing."

"And what do you think I'm doing?" I said, a little more incisively than I had intended.

"Well, I think, eh…" there was an uneasy silence, "What I think probably doesn't matter."

"It does matter." I insisted.

"Oh." Another silence. "Well, then I ask myself… I ask myself whether you're acting very responsibly, you know, given the situation."

"Responsibly?" I couldn't believe she was accusing me of irresponsibility. "Sorry, but I'm being very responsible."

"Going to a contest where you and I know hardly anyone? At this time with so much going on? Not long ago you were complaining of your study load. That makes me wonder."

"Perhaps you should keep on wondering."

"Stop playing games with me, please. Why don't you stop this adventure? People need you here, and you need to think about your future. Bet on safe horses."

That was enough to detonate me. "Think about my future? My future? *Your* future you mean!"

"What?"

"Now you're acting surprised?" I said fiercely. The bathroom door opened, and I could see Patience's head peaking around it. I gave her a stare and she quickly retreated. But on a calmer note I continued, "Look mum, I really don't want to talk about this. I have taken my decision and that's it. Please do live with it." I hung up the phone.

Chapter 20

I had expected to sleep badly after the phone call with my mother, but the lack of sleep of the night before and the comfortable bed weighed in more heavily, and I fell asleep almost instantaneously. I woke up a good nine hours later through Patience's alarm. Thank goodness for that, because I had forgotten to set mine. We got up and dressed, showered and went down for breakfast. There was a wonderful breakfast buffet, and even though I still wasn't feeling totally fit, the good night's sleep had done wonders to my mood. The morning sunshine peeking in through the windows made me feel more confident that today we were going to pull off the analysis of this case. Claudio also looked well-rested. I tried to get over my misgivings of the night before, and actually managed some nice banter over breakfast. Not soon after, we made ready to get started. I turned off my phone, to make sure there wouldn't be any interruptions from home. I'd had enough already.

I had been trying to make some progress in the afternoon by myself. It had probably been the tiredness, but I hadn't put much together as yet. I still wanted to make my tables, but not at the cost of offending Claudio. Without a concrete plan, I feared that the analysis would become too vague or at best not stand out from the other teams. But I figured the sensible thing for me to do now was to listen. Claudio was a smart guy, he would think of some useful things. But then afterwards, I'd have to make my move. "So people, what have we come up with?" I asked, after we had re-installed ourselves in the room.

"Are you sure you wanna know?" Claudio smiled and went on to present his first approach. "Okay, I say we start by looking at love."

Patience and I smiled.

"Yeah! I've actually tried to think in terms of our preparation! Don't you love that? Why don't we think about the love types? I'd say that it's easiest to start with eros."

Patience looked surprised, "You mean, who is being self-interested?"

"Yeah."

"Okay. What do you think?"

"I have my list, but you can start. Miriam?"

I had to think briefly, but then said "Right, so let's see. We can start with our main protagonist."

"Who, Olson?"

I nodded.

"Right, he's just trying to save his ass."

"And his company" Patience added.

I followed through, "Correct, it's going under."

Patience asked "So is that eros?"

"Well, that's his job, isn't it? Saving the company?"

Claudio nodded, "Yeah, he does need help. Need-love."

Patience frowned, "But not just for himself, also for his people."

"So?"

"He's taking care of others."

I had to think about that one, and asked "You'd say agapé?"

"Well, more like storge, of a company kind," Patience said.

Claudio stroked his chin like a wise old man, and stated, "So, basically he's taking care of his own. But he still needs help."

Patience sighed. "So complicated."

Claudio smiled. "It gets better. He has like a negative philia too."

That confused me. "A what?"

Claudio insisted, "Yeah, with Larsen, the other CEO. It's like a negative friendship."

Patience hummed.

After talking it over a little further, we came to the conclusion that the protagonist was always going to be complicated, so we'd better start somewhere else and work our way upwards. But it was clear from the start that these different love types would not lead to clear-cut distinctions. They all had to do with each other.

Still, after some more discussion, it turned out that a few of the characters more clearly showed eros than others. We agreed that Bianchi, the owner of TireDeals, with his ambition to conquer the world had a clear emphasis on eros, as did Walker, his CEO and obliging servant, as well. Another candidate was the headhunter, but we thought that character was less clear because of his small role in the story.

Claudio took the initiative again. "So much for eros. Why don't we just analyze people? Let's go for another big fish."

"Who'd you like?" I asked. I fully supported the idea of analyzing people. It was leading us right to my tables. But surely Claudio must have seen that too?

He continued, "I think Hansen is interesting."

"True, very interesting." Patience nodded.

I didn't like Hansen much, so I said, "What about him then? He's a bit surreal, isn't he?"

"Surreal?" Claudio asked.

"Right. He doesn't cash in on his company."

Patience hummed again, in agreement. "Good guy."

"But why?" Claudio looked intrigued.

For Patience this didn't seem complicated. "It's obvious. He loves the company. He worked there. He loves his country. It's important for him."

But I was still confused, and asked, "So that's storge again?"

"Uhm, almost agapé."

Claudio frowned, "Agapé? What is he giving?"

"I suppose, stability?" I ventured.

Patience was confident, "And he's putting in effort to make sure this doesn't go through."

Claudio scoffed, asking, "In the best interest of..."

"His company, his country, his people. It's big storge. Bordering on agapé."

I couldn't see this. "Right, gift-love by not giving away the company."

"He's guarding it against the wolves."

"Interesting." I couldn't see it that way, but Patience was very adamant.

"It's like a... metapreference. What we discussed in the car yesterday morning?"

I had to think about that one. It came back to me that those were motivations that are on a higher order than all the other ones, because someone is committed to something. So Claudio was saying Hansen was intrinsically committed to the company. That could be. But soon we went on discussing the other persons involved in the case. It was clear that Hansen's sons, not nearly as emotionally involved as their father, sold off the company. We saw a leading role for eros there.

After a while Claudio remarked, "We're only missing one person: Larsen."

"He appears very little," I said.

"Yeah, but he's interesting."

I shrugged.

"I mean, his relation with Olson is interesting."

"Right, that's your negative philia thing."

Claudio banged his hand on the table, and accompanied that with a "Yep."

Patience didn't get it. "So what do you like so much about it?"

"There's just a lot to it. Look how they call this guy. I mean Olson."

Recalling the derogatory tag, I said, "The tiger fish."

"Yeah. What does that mean?" Claudio asked.

That was easy for Patience, "Well, it says right there. An animal with small ears and a large mouth."

"So?"

"So he wasn't a good listener, and told everyone what to do."

"Yeah, my way or the highway" Claudio added.

I didn't quite see where this was going, "And that's interesting because..."

"Didn't you study any Aristotle?"

Aristotle. That's Claudio for you again! I couldn't help but remark, "He's been dead quite a while, hasn't he?"

Claudio dryly acknowledged this saying, "True. That's probably why people still study him so much."

Sigh. I pushed him, "What's your point exactly?"

"If you study his Nicomachean ethics, you'll see that habits are really important. You know, they make us who we are. And this guy had pretty bad habits."

"Why are they so bad? He knows what he's about."

Patience added, "His father was also in the company."

"Alright, so he's probably a good technician. But even good technicians miss things, and if you don't listen to your people..."

"What, they're not going to like you?" I sneered.

"Well, that for starters. But a company is complicated, and if you don't take everything into account, you're going to make wrong decisions too."

Patience nodded. "You're saying he's missing important information by not listening."

Claudio hummed in agreement. "And people will notice. Tension will build. And after a while it's not sustainable."

Patience complemented the story by saying, "And he gets fired."

"Right, but then what happens? He goes to meet Larsen again."

I tried to imitate him, slightly mockingly, "Right, but then from a rather different position."

"True, he's the CEO of MAN. But how did he ever come by the idea that Larsen would really want to collaborate with him?"

Patience sat back and looked up at the ceiling. "Perhaps Olson still liked SteadyCars. After all, he grew up there."

Oh that all sounded very fluffy. I threw in some business sense. "Or it was just a strategy—I dunno, friendly takeovers are cheaper?"

Claudio remarked, "Whatever it is, he doesn't seem to realize that his relationship with Larsen is not going to allow much collaboration."

"And why wouldn't he see that?"

"The tiger fish. Small ears, big mouth. He's probably rather over-confident."

"So he just doesn't see," Patience concluded.

Claudio nodded. "That could well be. His habits haven't made him very sensitive to others."

"Right, Aristotle." I started to see that now.

We agreed that we had discussed the motives of the most important actors. Time for a break. Luckily there was a coffee machine around the corner, which we were allowed to use for free. Quite luxurious, really. I looked out of the window towards the other big buildings on the university campus. Impressive. I was enjoying myself in the discussion, I was happy we were discussing all the actors. In my mind, I was already going over the stakeholders I would have to put in the tables, and what relationship factors to assign them. But would Claudio give in?

*

We didn't give ourselves too much time. After refreshing ourselves and taking our drinks, we quickly headed back to our conference room. Of the other teams, we didn't see a trace. They were obviously busily engaged in their conference rooms as well. As we came back to our oval table, I decided to jump in and voice my doubts straight away. "I have something to say."

"Say it," Claudio invited me.

"Right. Look here. We've done a good job identifying all the motives and love types of the people in the case. But..."

"Yeah?"

"Really, it's still vague. Not very scientific."

"Miriam. Does it have to be?" Did I imagine notes of exasperation in his words?

"I know you like philosophy and Patience studies literature and all, but I study economics."

"And medicine."

"Right, I want to do science."

Patience smiled, but added softly, "Are you sure it's needed in a business case?"

"Why not?" I asked.

Claudio looked straight at me. "You want your tables, right?"

To be honest, I didn't quite know how to respond to Claudio's remark. I still didn't want to upset him, but I was just feeling too uncomfortable with the vagueness thus far.

"Can't we do some tables?"

"But these motivations are really complex. How are you going to capture that in a table?"

"We came up with something already. I can try."

"And if you fail?"

"I won't. It's just going to be… really convincing. There's a wow-factor to a model. It's scientific. It's cool… It's a winner."

Claudio and Patience looked at each other. Claudio, of course, wasn't convinced at all. Patience shrugged and smiled at him.

"So how long will it take you to make the tables?"

Wow, he was actually giving in. "If you want I can just go ahead and elaborate a proposal. With what we said now, I can elaborate something in a couple of hours."

Patience and Claudio looked at each other again. Patience kept on smiling sweetly.

"Well, whatever. We can incorporate them in our overall story. Which will be richer."

Patience agreed, "Yeah, no problem. But what do we do in the meantime?"

I hadn't really thought about that. But Claudio wasn't going to help me with the model—that much was clear. And we just had to have a model. We had to make this scientific. Hmm, I thought, it would be better to give them something good to do. "Why don't you guys look at the institutional side of things? So far we've talked about the people, but we shouldn't forget the institutions either." I suggested.

"Good point, and perhaps we should also start preparing something to hand in for tonight." Claudio remarked.

Patience agreed, "We can do that. Summarize our discussion so far and include something on the institutions."

We agreed to meet after lunch, discuss what we did and submit our work at 6. In the end, Claudio and Patience stayed in the conference room to work on the document to be handed in. I went back to the hotel, to my room. Because I was still feeling fit, I was confident that I would be more productive there than the day before. And I could now finally work on my tables. They would be scientific. They would be cool.

*

I only had to cross the street again to get to the hotel we were staying at. When going up to my room, I saw cleaners in the hallways, and realized that I had left my room in quite a mess for them, and not put a sign on the door either. When I came in, my bed was made and some packaging that I had left around had been cleared away. There were still some clothes strewn around the room though. I decided to first clean everything up. That would help my focus. It wasn't too much work either. But I sure did have more work on the case. So I got cracking.

The first question was: whose decisions should I analyze with my tables? In our discussion of this morning, two figures in the case stood out: Olson and Hansen senior. Both of them were taking a lot of people into account. Olson, seemingly, because he had to. If he wanted to take over SteadyCars with FlashCars, he just needed the help and collaboration of others. But Hansen Sr could have just cashed in, and thought about himself. Instead, he chose to make others part of his game. He took into account the interest of his workers and his country, for instance. That was a really interesting aspect of love, and I could illustrate that with my table.

A second key ingredient was to include the 'relationship factor', that helps someone decide whether they want to collaborate or not. Clearly, this would be an important factor to explain what went wrong with Olson. If he had a big negative on the relationship with Larsen, that would mean a no-go for the deal. The table would be able to illustrate that too. The thoughts I had developed during the morning session served me well now.

I got straight to work on the tables, and really, it went surprisingly well. It was quite a bit of work, though. With half an hour to go before lunch, I was happy with what I had produced. Still, I didn't feel very well. I just ignored my feelings and dived back into the work. In an hour, I managed to write out my main findings, and even digitized it into Excel. Lunchtime had already passed, but still, I couldn't but note that my progress was fine. Would they like it too? And why was I not feeling as well as I should, when I had just successfully hit my target?

Chapter 21

I was late for lunch already, but still decided to walk outside briefly to get some fresh air. The area around the hotel was quiet and spacious, with trees and grass. As I walked out, Claudio came running after me, wearing his backpack; he must have seen me from the restaurant downstairs. He asked me where I was going, and I told him I had just finished my tables and was going out to stretch my legs. He asked whether he could join me and I agreed.

We talked about our progress in the project a little, but Claudio quite suddenly changed the subject. "So, do you have any clue what's the matter with Tim?"

"Tim?" I was surprised at his asking after my brother. "Why?"

"Don't know. He always responds to my shares and has fun with them, but..."

"But what?" It was somewhat surprising to me that Claudio should think beyond superficial appreciation, so I was curious about what would follow, even though I was trying to avoid thinking too much about home at the moment.

"He doesn't be seem to be doing much more than that."

"How do you know?"

Claudio explained that he had started to be worried about how Tim would take the whole family situation as it was developing, and had decided to give him a call. Even though Tim hadn't been very keen on talking, Claudio had made out from his responses that except for going to his classes, Tim wasn't doing anything much these days.

I nodded in recognition.

Claudio went on to say that this situation worried him a little, because if things were difficult at home, there wasn't anything to distract him.

"Good point. Can't be helped."

"What?"

"Sorry Claudio, but that's just the way he is. And can we talk about something else?"

"Why?" Claudio looked exasperatedly back at me.

"It's a sad situation, but I have other things to focus on now."

"It's about your brother!"

I could have started to explain all my vain attempt at activating and educating him during the weekends at home, but I really didn't feel like that either. So I just shrugged.

Claudio's mouth dropped open. "I can't believe your attitude."

I shrugged again, and to force a change of subject, I walked over to the nearest tree and started hugging it. "Look Claudio, it loves me!" I expected him to laugh, but, uncomfortably, he didn't.

"Family is important, Miriam."

I let go of the tree and wiped my clothes, which retained some stains. I should have known. Irritated, I walked over to him and looked him in the face. "It is. But not now." I said as decisively as I could. I walked away from Claudio and took a few good deep breaths of fresh air. "Lunchtime." I started heading back to the hotel.

"Oh Miriam," Claudio unexpectedly sang at a seductive tone, "look what I have here."

Despite myself, I looked around to see, and I turned to stone. He was holding the trophy of the contest in his hand, which had been displayed to us when we had just come in. He was holding his open backpack in his other hand.

"This is what you want, right? Here, you can have it." He held the trophy out to me.

I remained a statue for a little longer, unsure what to do. In the end I muttered, "You're not supposed to have that," as I turned around to face him.

"I know."

"Then put it back."

"I might" he said in a playful voice. "But only if..."

I felt anger welling up inside as I considered what he was trying to do, "If what?" I said fiercely.

"If you explain to me what's happening," he said, deflated and emotionless.

I grumbled on the inside, and then something snapped. I paced up to him. "Alright, I'll tell you everything." I said, looking him straight in the eye. "Everything you don't want to know. Tim's just a lazy teenager. He does nothing but lie on the couch and play with his phone. This drives Mum crazy—that is, if she's at home at all, of course, and not off to one of her appointments. And dad, who should be correcting him, is in hospital, as you know. Are you happy now?"

Claudio looked dejected.

"It's time for me to have lunch now. Please put that thing back." I told him, and marched inside.

*

I decided to have lunch quickly, also because most people were finishing up or had already left. There was still more than enough leftover in the buffet to fill my plate. I went and sat in a corner, trying to go unnoticed. I noted that it was already twenty to two, and at two we had agreed to meet in our meeting room and discuss our progress. So I had to eat fast to be in time.

But I hadn't been eating for very long when Patience walked into the restaurant and looked around for me. When she saw me alone in my corner, she came straight at me. I greeted her and explained my situation.

"I understand. But there's something urgent."

"Oh."

"Don't you have your phone on you?"

I checked, and I did carry it on me, but it was still switched off. I showed her.

"Oh. Well, your Dad is trying to reach you."

I bent down towards the table and put my head in my hands. What was happening now?

Patience came over next to me, and put her hand on my shoulder. "Come on, girl."

"Do I really need to call him?"

Patience nodded. "Better sooner than later."

"Do you know why?"

"Actually, we did talk a little. But it's better that he tell you," She said softly and smiled compassionately.

I took a beat to let that sink in a little, and it sank to my stomach like a block of ice. What would have happened to dad? I silently continued eating, while Patience stood by, waiting. I asked her to sit down, but couldn't say much. It was nice of her not to try and start a conversation, but just to be there. As I finished my lunch quickly, I tried to gather the mental energy for the call.

I stood up, thanked Patience and excused myself, telling her I was going to make the call outside. Walking out, I leaned against the tree I'd hugged earlier as I turned on my phone. I saw a number of missed calls from my dad, and then from my mum and Tim, as well as three voicemails and a text asking to call back. They clearly hadn't spared any effort to reach me. Even Patience and Claudio had called me, but that was around lunchtime. I decided to call Dad directly, and the phone hadn't rung twice before he picked up.

"Miriam!" He greeted me, clearly making an effort to sound bright, but with an unmistakably weak voice. "Where were you hiding?"

I apologized and explained I had turned off my phone to be able to focus. "What's the matter dad?"

"Did Patience tell you?"

"Not much."

"She's nice."

I hummed my assent. Then we said nothing for a while, the ice block now lodged in my throat to keeping me from talking.

My Dad resumed, after a short while, with audible effort, "Look, darling, eh, these new eh, Snickers aren't very tasty." He attempted a chuckle, but it ended in loud coughing. "Here's the nurse."

He passed the phone to one of the nurses who must have been standing near to him. She explained that mum and Tim had just gone off for a bit, but that they had been trying to reach me to tell me about what happened to my father. She suggested I call them to get the story, because my Dad was very feeble. I asked whether she could update me. She hesitated a little, but when I insisted she explained that my father had had a strong negative reaction to the new dosage of medication. He had become even weaker than he had been before. The doctors hadn't decided what to do yet, but the most likely thing was that they would take him off the medication directly. It was proving too much for him.

I sighed, and had to muster courage to ask, "So, is he in danger of..."

"No, not directly, no, fortunately. But he is not at all well. Oh, he's asking... Here's your father."

"Miriam?" His weak voice was back.

"Dad?"

"Don't... don't worry. Do... your thing. I'll be perfect. Just think of me, and of us."

I felt tears welling up in my eyes. I didn't know what to say.

"Will you think of us?"

"I will, dad." I whispered.

I heard a heartfelt and happy, though fragile, humming on the other side of the line. "Love you, darling." And he hung up the phone.

*

I looked at my watch and it was nearly two. But I couldn't just go on like this. I leaned with my two hands forwards against my tree, sinking my head onto my arms. I started to sob slowly. I hadn't been standing like that for very long, when I felt an arm around my shoulders. It was Patience, and I turned to hug her. She hugged me back and comforted me.

After a short while, I inadvertently looked at my watch, and saw it was now well past two. "Claudio is waiting. We should go," I told Patience, releasing her and drying off my tears with a handkerchief I fortunately kept in my pocket.

"Are you sure?" she inquired.

I nodded.

"Your Dad sounded very weak."

"He was."

"So shouldn't you be with him?"

"Maybe. He told me to go on."

"Did he?" She gave me a baffled look.

I managed a faint smile. "He's amazing."

"But still…" Patience looked away from me and stared into the distance thoughtfully.

I reflected a little. Of course, I would love to go and support my Dad at this time. Would he even like that, though? Of course he would. But at the same time, what he had asked me was sincere, I had no doubt. Just think of me, think of us. Perhaps if I sent him some progress updates, pictures and more video's, he would also enjoy seeing me make progress in the competition. He was like that. And, as the nurse had said, his life wasn't directly in danger… I could go and see him right after the contest.

As these things were turning over in my head, my phone went. Claudio. "Hey ranger, you turned on your phone!"

"So I did." I said, trying to sound composed.

"That's a very stupid thing to do for kids coming late to meetings, you know." Claudio sounded his cheerful old self.

"Is it?" I smiled despite myself.

"Yeah, that way they'll always catch you. Especially if you pick up. Where are you guys?"

"We're coming over." I said confidently.

Patience gestured, and I handed her the phone. "Just a minute Claudio. Something's come up. We'll be over soon." She hung up and handed the phone back to me. "Are you really sure?"

"I am."

"Your Dad needs you, you know."

"We'll send him more videos."

"He needs you near him."

"He would have told me so."

She looked at me with a frown. "He's ill, and a good man. He doesn't want to impose."

"Patience!"

"Okay, okay. Your call."

I ran up to get my work, and we walked together to the meeting room. Patience didn't look very happy with my decision, but luckily she didn't insist further.

Chapter 22

When we arrived at the meeting room, Claudio was waiting there for us. He had already gotten us some tea, very kind of him. He asked whether everything was well, and Patience said she'd update him afterwards.

"So how's the production?" Claudio asked.

I managed a terse smile. "Fine. I have some tables for you."

It was kind of him to try and sound enthusiastic about the tables he hadn't favored, as he said, "Wow, amazing! Let's see."

So I gave them the paper that I had worked on, immediately adding, that perhaps it would be easier if I went over the set-up again. They agreed and I walked up to the whiteboard that was attached to one of the side walls of the meeting room. I picked up one of the black markers that were lying on the ledge underneath the board, but didn't start writing yet.

"Right, so what I've done is to make tables that show how people arrive at the decision to collaborate or not. Right? So, that basically depends on the stakeholders you include in your decision, what they think about the situation, and your relationship to them."

Claudio nodded agreement.

"For now, I made two tables, one for Olson and one for Hansen."

This was the time for me to take the cap off the marker and start writing. I wrote

Hansen

Stakeholder	Relationship	Perceived Utility of the deal going through				Notes
		ext	int	rel	U	

"We'll start with Hansen. Here we'll list all the stakeholders involved in his decision. This is the relationship he has to them" I indicated the 'relationship' column, "and this the utility that Hansen thinks that the stakeholder has in the deal." I indicated the 'perceived utility' column. "Of course, he doesn't precisely know what the utility is, but this is what he estimates, given the situation and his knowledge of that person."

Patience looked up at me and said, "May I ask a question?"

I nodded.

"Can you remind me of the different motivation types?"

Claudio started "Those were based on a book I read.[7] This guy distinguishes between extrinsic, intrinsic and what he calls transcendental motivation. Basically that means: motivation from the results you get from doing something, motivation from your personal gain by learning from the process, and finally motivation from what others gain by learning from the process. So the last one I just call 'relational'."

"Right, and why did we add those to the table again?"

I replied, "It just helps you think about different ways people can be motivated."

"And I suppose 'U' means utility? That's what you make of what came before?"

I continued, "Yes, but remember: we agreed not in any linear way. You said we should think about that in every circumstance. And that's also why we need the notes."

Patience sat up and said, "Oh I remember now. It depends on the situation: the different payoffs and the circumstances, right?"

Claudio responded, "True. Even the same person may change their tastes." He explained that if you look at happiness studies, they show that money only makes people happier up to a certain point. If you have enough, then other things, like relationships, take over. Money may even harm happiness if earning it eats up the time you have for others. So if people are smart and care for their happiness, even their taste for money changes.

I was a bit surprised, "That's what the studies show?"

"Yeah."

7   J.A. Pérez Lopez. *Teoría de la Acción Humana en las Organizaciones*. RIALP 1991.

Patience continued, "So, you're reinforcing the point that we should see what a person values most in a given situation."

"Correct. And it's not linear. It's complex, but not very complicated to understand, I think."

That sounded good to me. "Complex but not complicated. I like it."

"Exactly. But institutions are less complex than people, that's what Patience and I have been talking about, right Patience?" and he smiled a warm smile at her.

*

I took the paper from Patience, who had been looking at it last, and went on to complete the table, explaining every step of the way. I wrote the stakeholders I identified from the case, which we had discussed in the morning session: Hansen's own interest, Larsen, the workers' union, the Norwegian government and country, SteadyCars itself. And one by one, we went down the list and discussed how important that stakeholder was to Hansen, and how Hansen would see those people affected by the deal.

Hansen himself, we had discussed earlier, wouldn't mind the income of the deal. The 'relationship factor' for Hansen with himself is '1' by definition. So for him, it would overall be positive. Unless, of course, we would say that he had a strong 'metapreference' for not selling the company. There were some arguments in the case that pointed to that, as we had discussed earlier—like the fact that he had worked there himself, and that the family had built up the company. He may somehow have felt too attached to the company to sell. But for now, we decided not to go that way, and said that he for himself wouldn't mind the money, but that he did care about others.

So then we went through Hansen's relationship with all the other people: the deal would be good for Olson, but his relationship with Hansen is not very good. It may even have been slightly negative, because he had been fired from SteadyCars. So overall,

Olson negatively influences his decision. Hansen had no wish to help Olson.

Hansen had a good relationship with Larsen, his CEO, we presume, but of course he cared about him less than about himself. We gave that a relationship factor of 0.3: a rough estimate. Larsen was facing the prospect of losing his job in the takeover, especially if it would be inimical, so the deal is not good for him. Larsen also sees that this deal is not good for the company. So Larsen is another 'minus' on the overall balance.

Then the company SteadyCars as a whole. Hansen had built this company, and he worked there. He cared about it a lot. We decided to say that he cares about it as much as he cares about himself. Again, that was an educated guess, so we put the 'relationship factor' at 1. SteadyCars is doing fine, with steady profits, so there was no real need for the takeover on their side. But Hansen knew his company, and foresaw the cultural differences between the two companies. He thought that the takeover would bring more problems internally than it would solve. Something similar holds for the workers' union, because they were quite happy with the current situation. Things could only get worse. So overall, his care for the company and the workers made him resist the deal even more.

Finally, Hansen also cares a lot about his country: he is well aware of his social responsibility, the case says. This deal would mean that one of the biggest employers in Norway is no longer in Norwegian hands. That would not be good for the country, probably decreasing tax incomes and also prestige. So that's the final minus on the overall balance sheet.

After talking them through everything, I could give them the paper again. I also showed them the excel version, on my laptop, which looked like this.

Hansen

Stakeholder	Relationship	Perceived Utility of the deal going through				Overall	Notes
	/ Weight	ext	int	rel	U		
Hansen himself	1	++		-	2	2	Let's say he wouldn't mind the money
Olson	-0.2	++			2	-0.4	Cares about saving himself & FlashCars. Has left SteadyCars in conflict, not a good impression
Larsen	0.3	-		-	-1	-0.3	Good relationship. May lose his job in the takeover.
SteadyCars	1		--		-2	-2	He has built up the company and wants the best for it. He foresees a culture clash with FlashCars.
the workers' union	0.5	-			-1	-0.5	There are good relationships; the takeover may put those at risk.
Norwegian govt and country	1	--	--		-2	-2	He feels responsible for Norway. Would mean less tax income? Less prestige?
Grand total						-3.2	Balance is negative, decides not to do it.

Clearly then, Hansen could have taken the money, but he cares enough for other people and his company to block the deal.

Patience and Claudio came to stand behind me to see the table on the computer.

Patience said, "Looks nice. Just so I understand: in the first row we have '++' for extrinsic motivation, and '-' for others, but still we put 2 in the overall score. What was our thinking?"

Claudio responded, "We just decided that Hansen, if it were about him, would be quite happy with the money. What happened to the others wouldn't completely ruin his own party. So we just left it at the two plusses."

"I see, but then the other lines show that he does take into account the others."

"That's it."

I was happy with this progress. "Great! So what's next?"

"Wait a moment." Claudio frowned.

I think my heart lost a beat. What now?

"We're still running into the same problems." Claudio continued.

"Which ones?" I asked.

"So we have utility categories, right? That looks good. But what about this relationship factor? What does it mean that it's 0.3 and not 0.4? Again, it looks very precise, but really it isn't."

I sighed inwardly. So even though he seemed to be collaborative earlier, Claudio really still wasn't on board.

Patience came to my aid again, "But here, the overall picture is clear, right? He is negative about the deal."

"Well that leads to the next problem. We can't really say, because we haven't analyzed the 'deal' scenario yet. We have to compare alternatives."

"Ah." I had to admit he had a point there. Then I had a brainwave, "But can't we just capture the difference between 'deal' and 'no deal' in the utility? So the utility itself is relative? Between scenarios, I mean."

"Eh," Claudio had to think on that. "I think not."

"Why not?"

"Well, we have complex motivations, right? So we need to consider every scenario thoroughly. There might be a shift in motivation types between scenarios, or a different dynamic between the stakeholders. It's better to think about that explicitly."

He scored again. So, well, we had to extend the table. This is what we came up with for the "no deal" scenario.

Hansen, 'no deal' scenario

Stakeholder	Relationship / Weight	Perceived Utility				Overall	Notes
		ext	int	rel	U		
Hansen himself	1			+	1	1	He is OK, happy for others that things are going well.
Hansen family	1				0	0	His family is OK
Olson	-0.2	--			-2	0.4	Is in trouble with FlashCars, and needs a solution.
Larsen	0.3	+		+	1	0.3	Is happy with a well-performing company
SteadyCars	1				0	0	Things are fine, normal.
the workers' union	0.5	+			1	0.5	Happy with current arrangements
Norwegian govt and country	1	+			1	1	Happy with SteadyCars
						3,2	Balance is much higher in this 'No Deal' scenario than in the 'Deal' scenario.

"Right, so now it's clear why Hansen is not going to go for the deal, if he considers all the stakeholders." I stated confidently.

"In very precise numbers" Claudio remarked sarcastically.

"Come off it, man" Patience said emphatically, "we are actually showing something here. This just makes clear that if Hansen cares about others, he'll not go for the deal."

Claudio sighed. "Alright. Let's have a break."

"Yes, give us a break." Patience smiled.

"Oh, she's actually cracking a joke" he said with sarcastic enthusiasm, but accompanied it with another warm smile.

Claudio clearly still wasn't terribly happy about the approach. But we were getting somewhere, and his criticism had actually led to improvement, so things could be worse.

*

After a short break, we continued with the second table I had started preparing: that of Olson, the second protagonist of the case. With those two people, we agreed that we would have the core of the action in the case covered.

Looking at the case, we thought that Olson was mostly interested in getting himself and FlashCars out of trouble through this takeover. They would be merging with a well-to-do company, which would generate income for the joined company. But also, it would give a push to FlashCars to do things the way Olson was used to: the way things were done in SteadyCars. That last point wasn't explicitly in the case, but we decided it sort of made sense. After all, Olson grew up in SteadyCars, his family had been in the company for a long time, and he knew things well around there. He didn't leave of his own initiative, so he must have liked it somewhat.

We considered whether he was really trying to get back at Larsen with this takeover. In the end it seemed a bit strange that, if that were the case, he would go in for friendly talks with him at the start of the takeover. So we decided that was not the leading motivation.

Still, this thing of going in for friendly talks after being fired also showed that Olson didn't quite see reality objectively. He may have thought that this deal would also be good for SteadyCars, or at the least be a matter of indifference—otherwise, he wouldn't have started these talks. His nickname of 'tiger fish,' with small ears and a big mouth, would again help to explain this attitude, we thought.

Finally, we thought Olson didn't personally care much for the people backing him, though he would care a little because he needed them. Perhaps most about TireDeals, because it was the most powerful party. In any case, he thought this deal was good for them, because they would get more ownership of a company that is a 'cash cow'. And that interests them. So that's good for Walker, and also good for Bianchi.

In the end, our table looked like this. Olson saw this as a great deal!

Olson, 'deal' scenario

Stakeholder	Relationship	Perceived Utility of the deal going through				Overall	Notes
	/ Weight	ext	int	rel	U		
Olson himself	1	++	+	++	2	2	Cares about saving himself & FlashCars.
FlashCars	1	++	+		2	2	Would like to help the company, is his job.
SteadyCars	0.1				0	0	Has a family relationship with the company, still good feelings. Doesn't see the problem, is neutral for SteadyCars from his perspective.
TireDeals	0.3	+			1	0.3	Will get ownership of a 'cash cow' through investing
Bianchi	0.1	+			1	0.1	What is good for Tire Deals is good for Bianchi
Walker	0.1	+			1	0.1	What is good for Bianchi is good for Walker
StrongSteel	0.1	+			1	0.1	Will get ownership of a 'cash cow' through investing
Bottom Line						4.6	All systems are go!

The 'no deal' scenario was not so difficult. He would remain in trouble with FlashCars, so it would be very negative for him and his company. TireDeals, Bianchi and StrongSteel, as shareholders, would carry some of the burden of that negativity. For SteadyCars, it would be no problem; it would remain fine as it was. And Walker was doing well at his TireDeals job, so for him the situation would remain positive. Those thoughts resulted in this table.

Olson, 'no deal' scenario

Stakeholder	Relationship / Weight	Perceived Utility				Overall	Notes
		ext	int	rel	U		
Olson himself	1	--			-2	-2	Is in trouble with FlashCars
FlashCars	1	--			-2	-2	FlashCars is in trouble.
SteadyCars	0.1				0	0	SteadyCars is doing fine
TireDeals	0.3	-			-1	-0.3	Problematic shares is not good
Bianchi	0.1	-			-1	-0.1	Problematic shares is not good
Walker	0.1	+			1	0.1	Is doing well with TireDeals
StrongSteel	0.1	-			1	0.1	Problematic shares is not good
						-4,2	Inactivity = death

So all in all, we agreed that Olson was very much in favor of the deal, also when he took account of his relevant stakeholders.

Patience started walking around the room. "Strange how wrong he was about Bianchi and Walker."

Claudio took that up. "He didn't evaluate the situation well. If you don't listen, that's what happens. See how things between people can be complicated?"

"Sorry?" I asked.

"We were talking before, Patience and I, about how goals of institutions are simpler than those of people. Companies just make money."

"Purely extrinsic motivation?"

"Basically. Perhaps they want to have good relationships or increase their internal efficiency, but in the end it boils down to profit."

"Always?"

"There may be exceptions... but they confirm the rule."

"And that's different for people?"

Claudio and Patience both nodded.

"People can really care about others." Patience said confidently.

Chapter 23

Patience's words reminded me that I should be keeping in regular touch with my dad. I asked whether we could take a break and make another video for him. Claudio asked why, but Patience quickly responded that he was having a rough time and could use some cheering up. Claudio remembered I had said that he was in hospital, and was fine with that. We thought for a moment about what to say and where to shoot it, and Claudio proposed making it an over-the-top comical newsflash about the deliberations of team UCI in their secret headquarters, attempting to take the TopStar trophy by force (force of arguments, of course). Patience doubted at first whether that would be appropriate, but in the end we went for it.

Claudio played the reporter. He made a real performance out of it. He started outside the door to the office, and in a hushed voice described the sinister plans being forged behind that door, while filming himself with his phone. He put his phone against the loophole in an attempt to peek inside, but then came to the conclusion that this reporter was going to face the situation head-on in all its depravity. As he entered through the door, filming, Patience and I looked up and started waving at the camera, I told my Dad we were working hard at the contest and were going to dedicate the victory to him. At the end, Claudio turned the camera back to himself and asked, "Incredible, have you ever seen such deceptive criminals?"

Claudio messaged the video to me, and after having watched it and laughed about it, I sent it through to my dad. Soon enough, he replied with thumbs up and a big smiley. Film project succeeded, we got the Oscar.

*

It was time to get cracking on the work again. We had gone through most of our analysis now, but had to still come up with an overall conclusion. "So what about the main question?" I asked.

"Main question?" Claudio mirrored.

"We were supposed to say what went wrong, right?"

"Right."

Then Patience intervened, "But maybe it didn't go wrong."

That confused me. "What?"

"Well in the end Hansen senior just loved his company, his people, and his country so much that he blocked the deal. Very well done!" Patience explained.

"You think it's good the deal didn't go through."

"Yes, I do!"

Claudio stroked his chin, "But it did happen later, in a way."

"Yeah, that's a pity."

"Wow." She actually thought it was a pity the deal went through later? "But why was the deal bad, if everyone was duly compensated?"

"Oh, I don't know. I just sympathize with Hansen who cares about his company."

"You do make it sound like a metapreference" Claudio observed.

"Well, whatever. He cares about his people, that's what I like. It's in the table, right?"

"Yeah, but if the situation changes later? The table will change too."

"I guess you're right." Patience sat down again.

We still agreed to give this approach a shot, and wrote down that it was actually a good thing for the deal not to go through at first, given the relationships of the decision maker. We were really curious how the jury would react. I wasn't quite sure that this was going to fly, but I decided to go with it and see where it brought us. We finished writing everything up, and had something presentable by six o clock, the deadline. It looked quite slick, actually, Patience had made a nice cover design. As we handed our work to the jury, I reflected on our hard work that day. Would it lead us anywhere? To victory? The feedback on the following morning would hopefully give us some indication. I couldn't wait to hear.

*

We had about half an hour before dinner, but looking outside, I doubted where to spend it. Patience and Claudio had gone straight back to the hotel. I thought it would have been a good time to explore the campus a little, were it not for the ominous clouds that came floating over Rotterdam at that time. I checked the rain radar on my phone, and indeed the showers that had started a little while ago would only get heavier the coming thirty minutes. It even showed some risk of thunder and lighting. That was enough to get me out of my exploration mood, and I hesitated in the entrance hall to the academic building. I didn't even feel like walking over to the hotel, although I would have to, eventually, given that the dinner would be served there tonight. So it was something of a relief to me when my phone rang. That is... until I saw who was calling. It was mum again.

All kinds of thoughts shot through my head. What was it now? Would she again try to convince me to stop the contest? Was it just about dad? After all, I hadn't talked to her about his current situation. I decided that given what was happening with dad, and given that I didn't have too many other things to do anyway, I might as well pick up. So I did.

Mum greeted me affectionately, and she didn't sound angry. I greeted her calmly, but was aware that a little tension was noticeable in my voice.

"You heard about dad, did you?" she started.

"I spoke to him."

"Did you?"

"And sent a video."

"Yes, he showed me. Very nice."

"Did he enjoy it?"

"You made him smile. This teammate of yours...eh"

"Claudio?"

"Yes, Claudio... is very funny."

"Mmm." So far so good. But what was she calling for? I thought I might as well ask about dad. But as I was asking, I heard some movements on my mother's side of the phone.

Tim had burst in to the room she was calling from, and was asking whether I was on the line. When he heard that was the case, he exclaimed, "Miriam, tell Claudio he's a genius! He has to become a crime reporter!" And he laughed in a rather over-the-top way. My mother hushed him, and sent him out of the room again.

"So how is Dad taking everything?" I decided to take the initiative to bring the conversation forward.

"As always, I suppose. He tries to joke about it, but this time he hardly has the energy, even for that. He is not well at all."

"Have the doctors already taken him off the medicine?"

"Yes, this afternoon."

"Oh good. The nurse said he would recover then, right?"

"Hopefully, but Miriam, he is really ill."

"I know."

"He needs you here."

Well, there we went again. I could have seen it coming of course. But anyway, I could counter. "He told me to stay and think of him. That's what I'm doing. It's why I sent the video."

"That was very nice of you..."

I didn't reply, and an awkward silence ensued. Thoughts started racing through my mind. Was I doing the right thing? Did my Dad really mean what he said? Might the nurse be wrong, would he die soon? Would I regret taking his advice for the rest of my life? As thoughts flashed through my head, my unrest grew.

In the end, my mum spoke. "Look, Mir, I know how you feel about the contest. It's just that, I feel very strongly we need to be together now. Your Dad doesn't want to impose, and he doesn't. And he wants the best for you and your contest. But really, if it's not for him, then please come for me. I need us together now."

To be honest, I hadn't expected her to take that tone. It caught me by surprise. And my initial inclination was to comfort her. But I held off a little, as my mind started spinning more. There was more awkward silence. My mum needed me together with her? Us together as a family? Did that actually mean she was cancelling her business meetings? I decided to ask, "You won't be away for meetings if I come?"

"Well... not... not all the time..."

What? I couldn't believe my ears. She was making an emotional appeal for us to be together while planning to go to her business meetings?

She continued "... but they will be short. And I'll explain, they're really..."

"Mum!" I exclaimed with force, and saw that people going into and out of the academic building looked at me with curiosity or irritation. So I walked to a quiet corner and continued, "You cannot do that!" I said forcefully, but in a hushed voice.

"I know I can't; it's just that I have to."

That was it for me. I tried to suppress the anger that was welling up in me once again and managed to say quite calmly, "Well, you always do, don't you. I'll tell you what. I have a contest I HAVE TO attend to. I am very sorry if that makes you feel bad. But quite frankly, I think there's only one person to blame. Have a look in the mirror tonight, and you might catch a glimpse of her." I hung up.

As I put my phone in my pocket, I noticed I was trembling. Outside, a lightning bolt cracked, and the thunder rolled over the campus little more than a second afterwards.

*

When I hesitantly started to walk out into the storm, to get to the hotel before dinner, a girl with bright red hair came up to me from behind as she was exiting the building. I recognized her as one of the students I had seen Patience and Claudio talking to. I believed she was from Paris. This hypothesis was confirmed as soon as she started talking with a thick French accent.

"Hi... You're Miriam, right?"

"Yes?"

"Hi, I'm Pauline. I saw you were talking on the phone just now. Having some conflicts in your team?"

Excuse me? Where did this Pauline get the courage from to talk to me about that? More importantly, what gave Patience and Claudio the right to talk to her about me?

"We're collaborating fine," I answered.

"Okay. I mean, I don't want to interfere. I just wanted to remind you that teamwork is part of the final assessment."

Excuse me?! I was baffled. Why did this girl start to meddle in my affairs?

Without responding, I walked out of the door and ran to the hotel, shielding my face from the rain as well I as could. My face was red with anger. As I entered the lounge, Claudio was sitting alone on one of the couches. He was looking at one of the television screens, texting and then calling someone. His head hung low and his legs were crossed. Nothing like his usual open attitude. So what should I do now? Go and talk to him too? I didn't much feel like talking to anyone.

Before walking out of the lobby, one of the television screens near the exit captured my attention. They were showing an extensive discussion program on the current situation in Italy. Tensions between the Italian government and the Europe had been building for a while now, with the government being accused of overspending. Interest rates had been rising steadily for a while, and there was now talk of rating agencies downgrading Italian state obligations. Banks were starting to be tested. Wow, that would probably be tough on Claudio's uncle. Good thing that my mother was in Dutch banking. They would perhaps notice a little, but clearly not as much. Anyway, this was not the best news to be cheered by. But then, who watches the news for good cheer?

I went up to change my clothes, wishing I could change my mood with them. I couldn't remain angry all the time. For one, that was just too tiring. This was one of the evenings in which the pressure of the contest was off, in expectation of the Jury's feedback. I might as well take my mind off the home situation a little, and at least try to have a good time with all the interesting people here. Maybe Claudio did have a point on the way here.

Chapter 24

The next morning my alarm clock woke me up. Patience had gotten up early and was not in the room any more. I had hit the shower when someone knocked the door to wake me. Appreciated. Overall, I hadn't slept too badly; seemingly I still had had some sleep to catch up on. And the night before had been fun. I had actually started to go around and meet people and drank a few beers with them. Perhaps even one or two too many, but happily no hangover today. During the night I had woken up once or twice and started to worry about everything. Fortunately, the tiredness had still been too strong, and those episodes lasted only a short while. I felt I had enough energy to face this day. And to make progress. But what would the jury say?

I was at breakfast early. Looking out of the window, the storm was over, but the weather was less sunny than the morning before. There were clouds overhead. It wasn't very grey, but some of the lightness of the atmosphere at yesterday's breakfast had gone. I opted for a more normal breakfast. Some cereals, bread, butter and cheese; a glass of milk: I've got to admit I'm a stereotypical Dutchie when it comes to breakfasts. Just as the others started to arrive, I decided to go already to our meeting room and re-read the case. Full focus. I wanted to have everything in my mind as fresh as possible when the jury report came in. They would make a tour of the meeting rooms between nine and ten in the morning. It was 8:30 when I started reading.

A bit before nine, Patience and Claudio walked in. They didn't look very cheerful or well-rested. We greeted each other and I asked them how they were feeling.

Patience answered, "Okay, thank you. But have been better."

Claudio wasn't any different.

"Did you sleep well? You look tired." I asked and looked at Claudio.

"Yeah, not too good."

"Am I bothering you?"

Claudio smiled and shrugged. "No, other stuff. But that's for later."

"Right."

Patience started to say, "We just spoke to the jury..." when someone knocked the door to our meeting room. "We'll be the first ones they visit, I wanted to say, but here they are already."

The three jurors walked in. They were all elegantly dressed, as they had been on the night of the introductions. They smiled and said "Good morning" as they walked into the room and took a chair. Ms. Bentley took the lead.

"You are the University College International team?"

We nodded.

"Oh yes of course, you must be Patience. How nice of you to join their team. How are things?"

Patience smiled. "We are very well, thank you." She clearly had the talent to be really charming if she wanted to. And she was now.

"Good to hear. Now, we need to be brief, because the other teams are waiting. We've written a report with feedback on your submission. We'll give that to you in a moment when we finish." She took out a piece of paper from her briefcase, put it on the table, and laid her hand on top of it.

For a moment, I was completely fixated on that sheet. What would it say?

"In short, we think your approach is very original. You've looked carefully at the motivations of the different actors. That's interesting. You've also looked at the institutions a little. And there was a very interesting approach to visualizing the motivations of the two main actors through a novel methodology."

I felt my heart beat faster. They liked my tables! Ms. Bentley paused a little.

"But overall, I'm sorry to say, we were rather disappointed with your submission."

What? I noticed my hands getting sweaty.

"You come to the conclusion that overall, given the motivations of the actors, it's actually a good thing for the deal not to go through." She glanced sideways at Mr. Jacobsen.

Mr. Jacobsen leaned forward and said in a soft but intense tone, "You need to realize we are at a business school here. This is a business case competition. The fact that this deal did not go through was a major setback for the investors, for the companies backing the deal. You can't just say it's no big deal. Because it is."

Ms. Bentley took the word back. "You don't seem to take into account the institutional interests at stake here. This was one of the biggest company takeovers at the time. The stakes were really high. It didn't go through. And we're asking you: what went wrong."

I felt my head turning red.

Mr. Rekels, the third juror, sat back and chewed his pen. And then he said, "Correct. And from an economical perspective you seem to forget what your mentor at UCI always emphasizes. Economics is about collaboration. If people or institutions are different from each other, we have a solution! The great thing about money is that it can compensate people for inconvenience. It can create collaboration where there was none: between people and institutions that are very different from each other."

Mr. Jacobsen sat back, and took over again in a matter-of-factly tone. "Analyzing the intentions and the love of the main players is all very nice, but we want to see real problems. As far as we are concerned, you're quite far behind on the other teams. So you have catching up to do. Give it your best shot guys."

We were dumbstruck. We hadn't seen this coming. Not this bad.

Mr. Rekels smiled at us faintly as the three jurors got up to leave the room. Ms. Bentley slid the paper with the jury findings our way. As they left, we also got up and shook their hands. My handshake wasn't very firm. Claudio's was, and Patience managed to keep calm and still smile charmingly. But now her charm only irritated me. Look at where it had brought us. The door closed after the last juror. It was the three of us again.

My heart was pumping, and my head must have been red as a tomato. "So now, what do we do?"

Claudio spoke up. "First we calm down Miriam."

"Calm down? Didn't you hear what they said? We're behind! We don't have time to lose!"

"Miriam. Take it easy."

"I beg your pardon? I'm not going to take it easy." What was this chap thinking anyway, bossing me like that?

"Alright. Then why don't you not-take-it-easy somewhere else for a moment?"

"Or take a glass of water, I can get you some." Patience already started to stand up out of her chair, but I beat her to it and paced towards the door.

"I'll get the water, thankyouverymuch."

With that I marched out of the door and slammed it shut behind me.

*

I did actually go to get some water. And I did try to calm down. But that clearly didn't solve our problem. How could we have gone with Patience's solution for our final analysis of the case? She was studying film and literature, for crying out loud. At least they liked my tables. Well of course, they were good. But we weren't even close to an adequate analysis of the case. How were we ever going to win this? All this fight with my mum, for nothing? And in the end I would just have to go crying back to her, and tell her I'm sorry and I'll never do it again? That I'll eat out of her hands forever more? No!

We were still going to win this contest. Mark. My. Words.

But how? I unclenched my fists, trying to relax. Should I just do my thing and completely forget about Claudio and Patience? At least I would hand in something decent. What would I say? First of all that the deal went wrong, of course. But that wasn't more than 'return to start'. That's what we'd been given before we even started our approach. Our 'master plan'. Oh, how 'masterful' it looked now. But still, there was plenty to it. I could get a decent approach to the case from our plan, and supplement it with some business insight of my own. That would work. They liked the model. They would like this. They didn't like Patience's work, however sweetly she smiled. Hmmm.

I decided to return to the meeting room. Whatever it was going to be, I couldn't just break away without informing them. They'd have to give me room. So I went back to see what would happen and swung open the door.

"Miriam!" Claudio even managed a smile.

I marched straight ahead to my seat and sat down.

"You look better." he continued.

"Do I?"

Claudio just nodded and Patience smiled faintly. Time to get to business.

"So, what do we do?" I asked.

"Something makes me think you have a plan." Claudio tried to say this in a funny conspiracy mode. And he managed, actually. Claudio. I couldn't help but smile.

"We'd love to know the plan." Patience added. Well, right, that was a good attitude on her side to start with. But would she still want to if she knew what my plan was?

"I have a plan. And you?"

Claudio replied. "Yeah, nothing special. Just try to work with the feedback."

Patience hummed in agreement. "It's pretty detailed, it's good. Look at the document. We can do something with it."

"Really?" I said. "So you're willing to switch around our whole interpretation and think like business people?"

Claudio took this up. "Well, we'd have to see to what extent we agree with them."

"Oh, is that right? It might well be that we know better, of course."

"We can have a different perspective."

"A different perspective?" I tried to speak calmly, but I was still more intense than usual. "Weren't you the one to say we should go with what they say? Especially if they wouldn't like the tables? And now they like the tables and we can have a … different perspective?" I said the last words slowly and with emphasis.

Claudio chuckled. "And weren't you the one to say we should stick to our guns, irrespective of the jury?"

I didn't laugh, but asked, "What do you say Patience?"

At that moment my phone buzzed and sounded. I had forgotten to turn it off. I took it to do so, but then I saw that the messages were from Linde, telling me "You go girl! Show these money grabbers what you're worth!" I smiled and realized that today was her birthday, and I hadn't sent her anything yet. I quickly unlocked my phone and sent her a "congrats!" with as many hearts as I could.

Meanwhile Patience hesitantly answered me, "Eh, we should listen to what they say."

As I got my absent mind back to the conversation, "Sorry. Listen. Right. But then what?"

"See what we do with it."

What did that mean? "And you're saying that that could be the complete opposite of what they say?"

Patience looked to the ground, while Claudio said, "Well, we should conclude something we support. Something that follows from our analysis..." and after a slight hesitation "... from the tables."

I felt they were playing with me, trying to convince me to see things their way through circumlocution, which made the anger rise in me again, but I managed to calm it a little before saying, "Right, a conclusion that follows. That we can support. " I paused. For effect. And then continued, "Now let me tell you something. I have come to this competition to win." Another pause. "Let me repeat. I have come to this competition to win." I looked at them both intently and added, "Do you understand?"

Claudio was turning on his chair; Patience crossed her arms and sat back with a look of disdain.

"Now if you would prefer to do your own feel-good thing, go ahead, but I'd prefer you to do that in your own time."

"Woho, your own time? What, are you paying us to be here now?" Claudio turned to me fiercely.

"Let me put it like this. I think we should listen to what the jury tells us. But not just listen. We should do as they say. Like it or not. They are judging us. They can make us or break us. They can make us a success. They can make us a failure. And. We. Are. Going. To. Succeed." I stared at them again. "Is that clear?"

Claudio kept on staring at me. "I don't know Miriam."

"How much clearer can I be?"

"I don't know whether this is our approach."

Patience added, "Your master plan."

I insisted, "We'll use our master plan. But we'll add on top of that anything they ask."

"And if what they ask goes against our master plan?" Patience asked.

"What are you talking about? They're just talking plain business sense. How can…"

Claudio interrupted, "Very simple Miriam. It's a question of priorities."

"We talked about it while you were out." Patience remarked.

"Right. So our priorities don't agree with those of the jury, and we prefer to keep our priorities rather than win the contest, is that it?"

"They are very important." Patience said.

"Winning is very important!"

Claudio kept on staring at me. "That's clearly your priority."

I didn't know what was happening to me here. Were these people actually telling me that they preferred losing the contest over changing their view of the case? What kind of dogmatism was this? Who did they think they were anyway?

"So. Then. Here it is. If you don't want to win this contest, would you mind, please, stepping aside and letting me do it?"

This startled Claudio. "D'ya want us out?"

"That's not precisely what I said. I want you to either work with me at winning. Or leave. That's what I want."

Claudio stared ahead at the wall. Patience sat shaking her head softly. Then she stood up. "I cannot do this." And she walked out.

Chapter 25

When Patience had left the room Claudio turned towards me. His voice was lower than usual.

"Really?" That was all he said. And he gave me a piercing look I'll never forget. It made me feel very bad about myself. I quickly looked away.

"It's okay, I don't mind. We can finish the project on our own. She doesn't need to help."

"She *wants* to help. She is part of our team Miriam. We need her input. She's been supporting your approach, for crying out loud!"

"She's nice, but her conclusion was useless!"

"But we agreed to go with it! And she has something to say too. Why don't you *listen* to her?"

"She just doesn't have the background or the preparation. We've just seen that! She's leading us astray. We can do things better on our own, just the two of us, as we planned."

"Maybe just do things all by yourself then, if you know so well. You're unbelievable. Just to let you know: I'll talk to Patience, tell her we need her input. You do your stupid project thing. We'll talk again at lunchtime."

I didn't feel anything about Claudio leaving the room, except having a sense that it would be easier this way. No more interference from his philosophical ideas. I finally felt calmer. I did not listen to the voices in my head saying that this wasn't right. We needed to win, didn't we? I never minded doing group projects on my own, if that meant that the results would be better. I looked through all the notes we made together and quickly shoved them away. I took out a fresh new sheet of paper and organized my own notes and ideas on it. I was really getting somewhere, I knew it.

*

When lunchtime was approaching, I decided to go back to the hotel to refresh myself. I already felt calmer and better now that all my thinking was on paper. Thinking over the situation a bit more, I decided it might not be such a bad idea for Patience to be with us after all. The jury did like her, so if she gave the presentation there would be bonus points for that. The only challenge would be to have her agree with my approach to things. But I knew I could be convincing if I wanted to. I just needed a bit more of a political approach. And Claudio was right, she had been supporting me. Probably Claudio had already talked Patience into continuing anyway. Claudio would take care of that.

As I walked into the hotel I saw Patience, who was standing at the reception desk. A blue suitcase was standing beside her. I walked over and tapped her on the shoulder. Teary eyes turned back to me. "Are you... okay?" I asked.

The shake of her head was so small that I barely noticed it. I looked at the suitcase, and then back to her.

"What are you doing?"

"I'm leaving." She spoke so softly that I had to ask her to repeat herself.

"You're *what?*"

"It's not because of the contest. Or because of you."

"Did Claudio talk to you?"

"He did. But it's just... I need to go home to see my parents," she continued. "They need me."

"Oh. I don't think Claudio will like that."

She looked at me with a look I hadn't seen before. Her kind eyes had turned sort of dull. "They are my *parents*. I can't leave them alone, I hope you understand that. Claudio does. It shouldn't be such a big of a deal, right? You had planned to go to the finale alone with Claudio in the first place."

"Sure, but... You're part of our team now. You can't just leave."

"Am I, though? What part of my input have you actually used to fix your analysis? I would have loved to help you out, even if you wouldn't let me, but family first."

All the while, the receptionist was standing behind the desk looking awkwardly from Patience to me and back to Patience. When we were quiet for a second, she took her moment to hastily whisper to Patience that she needed her signature for the early sign-out. Patience seemed happy to be able to focus her attention away from me. She signed a form, gave me a faint smile, and then picked up her suitcase and started leaving the hotel. After taking two steps, she turned around to me, and said, "I may even go and visit your father. Would you mind if I did?"

Go and visit my father? What did that mean? "What?... Why?"

"I think he likes me and he can use some cheering up. You could even come with me if you like."

"But weren't you going to your family?"

"Yes, they need me for a bit. But not all the time. If things go well, I may still come back tonight or tomorrow. Would you like that?"

I didn't expect this gesture from her, so I felt blocked and couldn't speak. But I nodded in agreement.

"And will you come with me to see your dad?"

"I can't."

"Okay. I'll see whether I'll come back. No guarantees." And she walked away.

I didn't know what to say. Did I want Patience to be part of the team? Yes and no. Her role would be to play the kind-hearted art-lover who could give our presentation that final nice touch that showed our human side. I felt worse about her leaving than I had expected, and didn't know if it could be attributed to the fact that she was just a good presenter. Would she come back? Probably not. Mindlessly I wandered into the lobby and took a seat. I saw the red-haired girl from yesterday and deliberately sat down at another table. I had no intention to face her today, tomorrow would be early enough to bash their presentation if I were given the opportunity.

*

After a short while, I got my act together, and freshened myself up for lunch. I decided to look for Claudio as soon as I could, to make sure we could talk things over and work further on the case this afternoon. Time was certainly starting to press. I had made some progress this morning, but I did really need his feedback. He would give that, of course. After all, Patience's problems with her parents were beyond both of us. We just had to accept that and move on. I was sure he'd understand that.

As I walked into the lunchroom, I quickly spotted Claudio talking to some other Parisian friends. He seemed to be imitating their French accents, and actually asking for their help to improve the imitation. "Goodmorning, darling, would you drink a glasse of wine on the Eiffél Towér with me?" I heard him say. He seemed to be having fun. Clearly he had overcome his downcast mood. That was good. I could use a bit of the usual Claudio. But as I walked towards him and he saw me, he did greet me, but the radiance left his face. He was suddenly the serious Claudio of this morning again. Oh well. We still had to talk. "Are you busy, or shall we have lunch?"

"No, one minute." He made a few more remarks to the other students, and came with me. The lunch buffet was still a bit busy, so we decided to order a cup of tea from the bar and sit down at a table in a quiet part of the room. I tried to smile to him, but his gloom had definitely returned. So I tried to start the conversation. "Patience left."

"I know."

"She told me you talked to her?"

"Yeah, I did." He picked up his teabag, untied the rope, slowly dropped it in the hot water, and started pulling it up and down with his full attention.

I decided to follow suit. But then I asked, "So what did you say to her?"

"What d'ya think?"

"I suppose you tried to convince her to join us again?"

"I first apologized, Miriam—and if you haven't done so already, I suggest you do."

"Apologize?"

"What, is that not in your dictionary?"

"It is, but what for?"

"Oh, come on. You haven't been very considerate, now have you?"

"Patience left because of her family. Right, so she didn't think I wanted her on the team. But I did. I just wanted us to follow a winning strategy."

"Winning strategy. And that means: 'your way or the highway'."

"It means: the jury's way."

"The jury's way." Claudio took out the teabag from his cup and put the dripping thing on the small platter next to it. "She won't be coming back, I suppose?"

"Don't know, but it didn't look like it."

Claudio looked around and noticed that the buffet line had shrunk. He proposed that we go and get some food. I agreed.

Walking towards the buffet table, Claudio put on his smile again. I envied his ability to put on or take off his good humor as if it were a piece of clothing—and felt a bit sorry for myself that he wasn't 'dressing up' for me very much these days. But that would pass.

Just as we walked up to the buffet, one of the employees was renewing the platter with boiled eggs. She was in her early twenties, and looked good in her uniform, with a city-wise air about her. Claudio didn't hesitate. "Wow, look at all these eggs. The chicks around here must be really fertile." And he winked at her. Goodness.

But she didn't as much as blink, and retorted "and the hens seriously impotent. If these would've been fertilized, they wouldn't lie here." And she went off without paying him any more attention.

Claudio looked at me and grinned, indicating with a hand wave how touchy he thought she was. What a guy. He filled his plate to the brim, and I decided on a normal lunch, even though I wasn't feeling very hungry. There was some serious work ahead this afternoon, so I figured I might as well fuel up. I'd just need to get Claudio's nose in the right direction again. But surely, that would work out.

*

As we sat down at the table again, Claudio went back to his earlier lackluster ways. "Are you ok?" I asked.

"Fine."

"So what do we do?" I pricked my fork into the nice-looking potato salad.

"Wait for Patience."

"What?"

"Wait till she gets back." Claudio took a chicken wing in his hands and took a bite from it.

"We don't have time for that."

After taking a few more bites, and putting the bone back on his plate, Claudio just said, "I don't care."

His words baffled me. 'I don't care?' —what does that mean? What does he not care about? "You don't care about winning the competition?"

"No." He shook his head and started full speed on the rest of his plate.

"You don't care about how I feel about this competition?"

"Hm." He brought his hand to his face and stroked his chin, swallowed and said. "Not for now."

"Not for now?!" I couldn't believe he was saying that.

"Not until Patience is back."

"And then you'll start caring?"

He nodded and continued working on his rapidly emptying plate.

"Did it ever occur to you that even if she came back, that means that we don't have any time at all to prepare our case?"

Claudio looked up from his plate and said emphatically, "I told you: I don't care."

"No, you told me you would care if she came back, but now you're saying... you're telling me you don't care even then." I had started stuttering as I felt bitter tears welling up, but I struggled against them. No, no, no, I was not going to burst into tears. Not here, not now.

"Oh come off it, Miriam. You don't need me. You can prepare this thing by yourself. At the presentation, Patience and I will just stand there and pretend we've been the perfect team together. That's what you want, right?" He forked the last bits of salad into his mouth and started chewing on them.

I couldn't believe what he was saying; at first I could only open my mouth in astonishment. But that soon passed, and I felt my earlier bitterness turn into anger. And this time, I didn't manage to control it. "You moron. Of course I need you. But you're not getting your way and now you're leaving me alone." I stood up from the table, took my napkin and threw it next to my plate. And I marched off.

*

I went straight up to my room and flopped down on my bed. I didn't know how to feel any more, with a whirlwind of all my emotions raging through me. I just felt everything except good. A text message from Elena. "How is it going?"

That did the trick. Uncontrollably, a tear rolled down my cheeks. My face became redder and redder as I tried my best to stop more tears from rolling down. I hoped that no one would come back into this room. Yet, at the same time, I hoped that Claudio would come back and finally realize how I felt about this whole situation. That he would apologize; say he would work with me, that we would work on an amazing case analysis together, and that everything would be fine.

I decided to text Elena. "Disaster. Patience left. Claudio ditched me."

The reply was almost instantaneous. "Whaaat?????" And then "Well, at least you can still eat pizza and gelato and won't find any horseheads in your bed. Italians."

I had to smile, despite myself. Elena called me just then, and I told her the whole story. That helped me to calm down a little. But when I hung up, I broke down and cried again. It was over. Definitely over. On my own, I was never going to win this thing. I wasn't going to prove myself to anyone. None of my plans would work, not here, not at university. I felt miserable. The only thing that helped was crying. So I cried.

Chapter 26

After crying my heart out, I felt a bit better. But what now? What was I going to do this afternoon? Give it a desperate try after all? No use. But what then? Just give up and start working on some UCI assignments to advance my road to a medicine degree? Plenty to do there. Talk to people here? Visit my dad? I didn't feel well enough to make any decision just yet.

I scrunched down into one of the sofas in the lounge, looking at the television screens. They always put on news channels here. Accidents. Fighting. Politics. Developing crisis in Italy. At least I wasn't the only person in the world to feel bad.

I felt the telephone vibrate in my pocket; I slowly pulled it out and looked at the screen. It was mum. Sigh. I decided to take the call. "Mummy?"

"Miriam, where in Rotterdam are you exactly? At the university?"

"At the hotel closest to the university. Why?"

"Right, I think I know the one you mean. Just across the Kralingse Zoom, right?"

"Eh, yes."

"I'll be there within a few minutes."

"You'll what?" I tried to answer, but she had already hung up.

I could have gone into a panic, but feeling down has its upsides. That didn't happen. But why on earth would she come all the way to Rotterdam to see me? To tell me off? To drag me home? Well if that were the case, I couldn't really care less at the moment. If there was going to be a scene, it would at least be one-sided. No frantic defenses on my side. I did figure it would be a good idea to just stay in the lounge. Perhaps the public setting would inhibit her a little.

After a bit more than ten minutes I saw her car pulling into the parking lot in front of the hotel. Quick as always, she parked, got out of the car, and paced decidedly towards the hotel entrance. It didn't take her long to spot me. "Miriam!"

"Mum!" I got up and walked towards her and gave her a slightly formal hug and kiss. "You came all the way here."

"I did. I thought you would be working on the case."

I wasn't in the mood to discuss that situation with her, so I decided on the evasive option. "We've been working on it a lot these days."

"Wonderful. Miriam, could we find somewhere more private?" Right, so the lounge effect would not work. Judging from her mood though, she wasn't going to be telling me off. I'd just have to wait and see what this was about.

I proposed that we take a walk outside. The clouds I had seen at breakfast were still there, but it was pleasant out. We could walk along the sporting complex at the other side of the road. It wasn't exactly nature, but there were some trees and it was green. When we were underway, she sighed, and remained silent for some time, crossing her arms and looking at the ground. That was not at all like her. What was she going to say?

At last she looked up at me and broke the silence. "I thought about what you said."

"What?"

"That I should look in the mirror."

"Oh." I hadn't really thought she would. "And?"

"And I think you have a point. I came to say I'm sorry."

"You..." I was speechless.

"Yes. I have been very taken up with my work. More than I should. Even now. I am sorry."

I wanted to say something in return, but the words just wouldn't come to me.

"You don't have to say anything, darling. But will you allow me to explain something?

I faintly assented with my head while my mum took another breath.

"It's something important for my future, for your future, and even for the future of Europe."

Wow. Again, I didn't know what to say.

So there was more silence before my mother went on, "Even though you've been away from home much the last months, I think you have noticed that I've had to work very long hours lately, haven't you?"

I nodded.

"There were good reasons for that. I think you remember from our meeting that people were very worried about the situation in Italy. And as you may have seen, the situation is worsening. Actually, it's worsening faster than we thought. The Italian banks are a having a very tough time. They are in need of help, but the ECB is refusing, it's cutting them off."

Why was she starting about Italy? I was confused. "And so?" I asked.

"And so." She sighed. "You know I love Italy. And that I have learned through being with them, that there are many good people there. That can be trusted. Even though they're different from us."

I cast my mind back to all our holidays in the country house off Lake Garda. She had really put a great deal of effort into learning Italian and interacting with the locals. I had often heard her go on about her discoveries of the Italian mindset. They are much more relation-minded people than we are, but usually trustworthy, was her conclusion. The image of the whole of Italy as a Mafioso gang, which we sometimes have in northern Europe, was not justified, she thought. "I remember that," I agreed.

"Well, this is what is happening. I saw how one of Italy's oldest and most respected banks was heading for trouble. Because of the political situation, the ECB was hesitant to help them. So I thought they could use a little help from their friends."

"You what?"

"I thought they needed help, and that we could give it. Actually, this idea wasn't completely selfless. I figured that in the end, the ECB wouldn't allow such an institution to collapse. That would be like another 'Lehman Brothers effect'. So I figured helping them would be a good investment in the long run."

"So what did you do?"

"Here we go. I set up a deal for my bank to take over a substantial part of the Italian bank. And everyone agreed. The deal was signed."

"Great, and then?"

"And then it came out that their problems were much larger than I had anticipated."

"So?"

"There is a real possibility that this bank will collapse."

"Wow."

"And that probably means the end of my employment."

"Really?" I should have felt shocked, but my shock-capacity had already been exhausted. So I just asked, "And now?"

"At the moment, I have done all I can do from here. Really, they need to clean up their mess. But that will require a different attitude from the bankers. I am not sure how fast they'll be able to change their mindset. And if they're not fast, they'll go down."

"Can't you help them with that?"

"Miriam, do you think they will take it very kindly if some Dutch bankers barge into their bank and tell them how to do things from now on?"

"No, but you could be gentle about it, right? Like you've told me in the past: listen to them, apply your 'Indian talking stick'." My mum had told me about how this 'Indian Talking Stick', a technique to facilitate active listening, had gotten her out of trouble in the bank on several occasions, and turned difficult situations into constructive opportunities.

"If I were invited, it would be different. But I can't just present myself and say: let me tell you how to do things. I cannot even go there to listen. What would I be doing there?"

"But if you were invited, you would go?"

"Of course. My career, an also the future of my bank depend on it."

"Oh my."

My mother started staring at the ground in front of her again, her arms now hanging listlessly from her shoulders, which were bent forwards a little. I had never seen her so downcast. And I didn't know what to say.

After a while, she looked up at me. "And you understand that this will affect your future too, don't you? It will be much harder for you to follow in my tracks."

What was I to say now? Tell her that I wasn't planning on doing that anyway? Say that this was the core of the whole issue? Something in me wanted to just throw it out there, but something else in me kept me back. And the latter won. My mum had enough to deal with as it was, with my Dad and her professional situation. So I decided on saying, "Don't worry mum, I'll be fine." But on the inside I was disappointed that even though she apologized, she still didn't have a clue what she was really doing to me. But for that, now was not the time.

"I know you will, darling. But think about what will happen if this bank collapses. Another full-blown crisis. People losing their savings, their pension, and their jobs. Not just in Italy, but in Europe, and perhaps beyond. It's horrible."

"And nothing we can do."

"Not for now, anyway."

*

My mum stayed a while longer, and we talked a bit about Dad and how admirably he was carrying his illness. He had become close with all the nursing staff, calling them by their first names as if they were best friends, and offering them to partake of the cookies that people had brought for him, even though they most often didn't accept. He then would tell them with a wink in his eye that they clearly knew better than he did how to stay healthy...

She told me how impressive it was that he still kept his sense of humor. When they recently had to put him on the drip for a few days, he proudly showed the tubes, saying, "Look, they're making me a cyborg-avant-la-lettre. I feel so hi-tech!" And they had been laughing together for quite a while about many things. The last few days he had clearly lost a lot of his energy, but today he had been a bit better. And he had been very happy for her to go and see me.

She said she felt guilty, because she should be supporting him in his difficulties, and she was trying to not burden him too much, but she suspected he was quite keenly aware of what was going on. I just assented to that. In the end, it was really him that was supporting us both through all the trouble, by listening to us, and being so lighthearted about all his own trouble. She wished that she could be a bit more lighthearted herself, and so did I. Strangely, I felt a bit better now that I was not the only one to have her world collapse.

Mum made a little attempt for me to come along to see dad, but that would be giving in to her too much. I resisted, and she didn't push. Of course, I didn't tell her about the trouble we were having with the team. In the end, we went down into the restaurant and had a cup of tea together. But not too long after, my mum said she had to go, to take care of dad. Her work would be a bit quieter now that things were out of her hands, and she had some more time for him. She asked me to come and see him when I finished the contest, and I said I was already planning to. We gave each other another hug and kiss, and she was off again. Quite the visit.

*

That afternoon was clearly lost to any sort of productivity. It's strange how feeling down sucks away all your energy. And it was all just too much for me. Things would need to settle down in my head and heart before I could even as much as think again. I decided to go out and see the harbors. I had never really taken the time to see what Europe's largest harbor looked like. I went and took a boat tour, getting on board near the futuristic-looking Erasmus Bridge. I imagined it being a man kneeling down, holding up the road ahead of him with rays that emanate from his heart. It made me think of my Dad a little, even though his rays weren't probably as strong as those of the Erasmus Bridge.

The boat tour took us along a small part that was left of the old city of Rotterdam, nearly completely destroyed at the start of the Second World War by German bombs. But there were also the new parts: Rotterdam had now become a hubbub of architectonic activity. All the modern buildings that didn't pay too much attention to the buildings around them sometimes made me feel like I was walking in a theme park. But soon these buildings gave way to great silos and container transfer installations. Big ships were coming in from the North Sea, and others were being unloaded or reloaded with gigantic cranes. I imagined sitting behind the controls of the crane all day, high up in one of the cabins. I would probably be scared to death because of the height. Not my cup of tea.

I allowed my mind to wander off to think what would happen with these containers. They would probably be put on a truck or a train and transported on—to... the Netherlands, Belgium, Germany? There was now even a train line to China, I heard— although it's likely that quite a few of these containers came from there in the first place. In any case, this was a goods gateway to a large part of the world.

It suddenly occurred to me, that if my mother was right and Europe was heading for another crisis, this could have direct consequences for the people sitting there in those cranes. A slower economy, fewer containers to transport, and also fewer people needed for the cranes. Maybe people would lose their jobs—or at least no new people would replace those who left. More insecurity. Not nice. And those were only the crane drivers in the Netherlands!

I do not recall ever feeling so small. I thought my problems were contained to my own small world, but there was so much more going on. It was probably larger still than I could grasp right now. In 2008 I was in the first year of secondary school. I vaguely remember my economics teacher talking about an American bank that had collapsed, but back then my world was way too small to understand what that meant. The money I knew came from my parents. Every week I would get 5 euros, and I thought that was a lot. I had no financial obligations and could use the entire amount to buy magazines and save for cool shirts. I wouldn't, though. My mother had always taught me how to wisely spend my money, and not buy the first cool thing I saw. My small pocket didn't notice anything from the financial crisis. I kept getting my money, and could still buy things or save up what I wanted. My parents kept their jobs. The stores were still filled with products. I had no idea of the people that lost their jobs or couldn't afford to buy a new house.

Was something similar going to happen now? What did that mean? It was suddenly so much closer, now that my own mum's job was at stake. Would we have to sell the house, and move to something smaller? That would probably be the least of my problems. My mother has never been a house mum. She was always working. When I was little, she worked at home. We were not allowed to walk into her bedroom, where she had made her own office. I once overheard my mother and father talking about old times, when mothers stayed at home and fathers worked at factories, and my mother saying that she would go crazy if she wouldn't be allowed to work. But did she ever think about daughters going crazy when mums were trying to push them to the professional success they had in mind for them? The longer I thought about it, the more frustrating I found it that she had apologized—for entirely the wrong reason!

And all of that was happening in the background. Right now, it wasn't even an option to fully worry about it. I wasn't in the mood. Claudio had quit. I still couldn't believe it. He just walked out on me as if all the talks we had had, all the discussions we had had, all the meetings with Loffels and all the time we had put into reading theories and background research were just nothing. Just like that. Wasn't it obvious that the path we had taken was not the right one? He had read the same jury rapport as I had, right? I couldn't believe he was too stubborn to not admit that my idea to obey the jury might actually be the right way forward.

When I came back to my room, I had to conclude that all in all, the excursion to the harbors hadn't improved my mood much. I had gotten some fresh air, but that was about it. I still wanted to win the contest, but with a team that had fallen apart, and the situation of my parents to worry about, I didn't really see how this could go anywhere.

I did decide to go for dinner with the participants. After all, I hadn't spoken to the others much yet. Perhaps there would be some interesting and inspiring people to talk to. Who knows, perhaps they would light the spark again. How ironic is that, to have to go search for inspiration with your opponents? I suppose it was what Claudio wanted all along. Oh well, desperate times call for desperate measures. And what the heck, this wasn't going anywhere, anyway—so I might as well have a laugh with them.

The only thing was: would Claudio do the same? He would probably be there. I didn't much feel like facing him. He hadn't tried to come back to me. Neither had I tried to contact him during the afternoon. Not after how he had treated me. Alright, so I could go to one side of the room, and hope he would stay on the other. But it would be a forced situation. How could I go and have fun with these other students, if I was worrying all the time whether Claudio would come and see me?

But what was the matter with me anyhow? Would I let a fun night with some international students be ruined by some Italian guy who only cared about looking slick and popular with his friends? I couldn't have fallen so low. You know, I was just not going to care. Not about him. Perhaps my mum was right about Italians not all being Mafiosi, but clearly she wasn't talking about an Italian-Spanish mix raised in the Netherlands. Those were the worst kind. Clearly. So off to the dinner, off to some fun making new international friends. Off we go!

Chapter 27

Just as I was about to leave my room to go to dinner, my phone rang. Patience. Patience? Why would she be calling me? Was she seriously going to contact me again? I thought she hated my guts by now. I hesitated too long whether I wanted to pick it up. It already stopped ringing. What could she possibly have to say? More importantly, where was she now? Did she want to come back? For some reason, I really wanted to call her back, but my pride was in the way. Why had she walked out on me like that after the jury report? I did feel a bit sorry for her parents, though. But in the end, it was something about the way Claudio had looked at me this morning when I had not listened to Patience's story about the priorities that she had spoken of with Claudio. He had looked so derisively at me, making me feel as if I were absolute filth. I never wanted him to look at me like that again.

I called Patience back.

She greeted me with a soft voice, thanked me for calling back, and asked me whether I would like to have dinner with her. Would I? I was just looking forward to having fun with the other students. Today's lunch was enough mealtime tension for one day. I didn't really look forward to having a dinner like that. And by now, the time was surely too short to do anything for the competition. Still, she was offering me the opportunity to make up. I thought that might be the elegant thing to do. I agreed to meet her in thirty minutes at a restaurant not far from the university. I was not going to mix and mingle with the international student crowd then. Oh well...

I got out my phone to look up the best way to get to the restaurant. I saw that it was next to a golf club, a 25 minute walk, so I decided to just get going. The more fresh air the better.

While I was walking, I didn't like how tense I felt about meeting her. After all, I had just been trying to do the best for our team. Setting the winning strategy. Yet, somehow, I felt nervous. What would she want to say?

I arrived at the restaurant a bit before she did. The place was cozy enough and not too big, so that it would be hard for me to miss her. I sat down at one of the tables and looked around a little. The style was rather classical for Rotterdam, with dark-brown tables and chairs, and a bar. It was definitely upper-class, but in a sporty way. Nice. And, looking at the menu, not too expensive. Good.

Patience walked in when I had only been sitting for a few minutes. The feeling of intimidation passed away quickly as she smiled to me in her charming way. Clearly, she didn't have any negativity in her attitude. I wondered how that was possible. After she sat down, a waiter came and we ordered drinks. Soft drinks: she had driven here.

"So, how were your parents?" I didn't quite know whether I should raise the issue, but it was hard for me not to, given that it was the main reason she had given me for leaving.

"Better, thanks."

"Oh great. Are you coming back?"

"I'm here."

"Right." I was wondering how to ask her directly whether this was the real reason for our conversation, but I felt blocked.

"How have you been? Any progress?"

"Not really." I looked down at my shoes, wondering whether to tell her about everything that happened today.

"Oh." I could see Patience hesitating to ask more. In the end she said, "How is Claudio?"

I looked up at her, a bit too fiercely, and said, "Waiting for you to come."

"For me?"

"Yes. He said he won't continue until you come back."

"Really? And so what did you do?"

"I took a boat tour."

Patience suppressed a chuckle. "Wow."

"We can forget about the competition Patience, it's not going to work anymore."

"Really?"

"Yes really. So let's just have dinner and go home."

"To see your dad?"

"For instance."

Patience told me that she had actually gone to see my Dad today, as she had told me when she left. He was feeling a bit better, but was still weak. He had really appreciated the visit, but had been worried to see her show up. He was genuinely concerned for the progress of the competition, because he knew it was important for me. So he had encouraged her to go back. And he had also told her that my mum had visited me today. When she saw in my body language that I didn't much want to talk about that visit, she didn't inquire how it went. She did, however, finish by saying that my Dad was expecting me to not let him down, and make the best out of this competition. We couldn't allow the other schools just to waltz over UCI like that, he had said.

*

The waiter came by to bring us our drinks. He asked whether we had already made our choices for the food. Of course we hadn't, but I decided to just make a choice on the spot, and Patience followed suit. We only chose a main course, selecting from the cheapest ones on the menu. I went for the burger, Patience took the chicken satay. The waiter noted our order and asked, "Students"? We nodded. "Thought so." He smiled at us in a friendly way and went off.

Seemingly, this was the time Patience had been waiting for. "May I ask you something?"

I nodded, leaning back in my chair.

"Do you know why Claudio didn't want to go on?"

"I told you why."

"You mean, because I went away?"

I nodded again, looking straight at her.

"But I mean: do you know why?"

What did she really want? Did she want me to tell her that I thought Claudio wanted to push through their interpretation?

Is that why she came to have dinner with me? I couldn't believe this. I turned away from her and looked out of the window at the golf course.

Patience continued. "Did you try to listen to him?"

"Did I have to? I think it was obvious enough."

"I don't think it's so obvious."

What was the matter with her? I kept on staring out of the window, wondering whether to stay for the rest of the meal, or just to excuse myself. This is exactly what I wasn't waiting for tonight.

"Miriam, don't be like that."

I reacted as if stung. Was she now going to tell me how to behave too? I turned towards her again, and said angrily, "I beg your pardon, but who do you think you are, my mother? And if you want to know about her visit, well, her world is falling apart too, like mine. Tonight I was just going to have a party and go home. You've succeeded in ruining the party now, so let me just..." I took my napkin from my lap and wanted to throw it on the table.

"No, Miriam, stop." Her voice was not very strong, but rather filled with pity. That surprised me. I stopped. "I am sorry to hear about your mother. Do you want to talk about it?"

"I don't."

"Right. Okay. And with Claudio, well..." She looked at me sadly. "We don't have any dogmas. I don't want there to be. I'm here to help."

*

Our conversation turned to an uncomfortable silence after that. Luckily, the waiter walked by our table, on the way to helping some other customers. It wasn't too busy in the restaurant, and he clearly felt like chatting a little. He interpreted our silence as his chance to pitch in. He asked whether we were having a good time, and we said we were. He started to explain about the golf course, about the rich and famous that would come here occasionally, even though the club was open to the general public. Had we ever played golf? We hadn't. Did we like Jazz? Yeah, we sort of did. Well, the golf swing got you way further than the jazz swing, he said, so we really had to try golf. Nice try. He left the table with a sympathetic wink.

When the silence was about to become notable again, Patience reopened the conversation. "I really think... I really think you should listen to Claudio."

"And then what?"

"He has something to contribute, you'll see."

"I know he does. He just didn't want to when you were not there."

"Right. But if we're going to stop, we might as well talk things over. Then at least we leave as friends."

I rolled my eyeballs to the ceiling. Was this about failing, but then in a friendly way? Who cares about that, anyway? But all right, if that was important to her. "If you want. I don't feel much like it at the moment. Maybe later."

"No, tonight, please Miriam. We need to make up as soon as possible."

"Why the hurry?"

"It's just that... otherwise things will turn sour. It's not good."

I was feeling pretty sour already, so I wondered how much worse that could get. But alright, point taken, perhaps if we talked things over I would at least understand a tad better what went wrong, and have a bit more peace with things that way. So I said, "Okay."

"Okay, as in you'll do it?"

"Yes."

"Amazing, thanks so much."

*

From there on in, the dinner became more animated. Our food soon arrived, and we talked about our favorite films and actors. Patience knew a lot, and had really interesting stories about the history of Afro-American actors in Hollywood. She had clearly studied that in depth. And she was very amiable.

As good students, we decided to skip the dessert, and ask for the bill. Then we faced the question of how to contact Claudio. Given the situation, we decided it would be wisest for Patience to contact Claudio. So she did. Seemingly, he was having some after-dinner fun with a few Italian students, but he was very happy to hear that Patience was back. And he agreed to meet up ASAP. We decided that the restaurant at the hotel would probably be the best place to have a drink and talk things over. It would be easier from there to get our things and go home afterwards. If the organizers would let us of course—but then, why wouldn't they?

We got into Patience's car and drove to the hotel, which was only a five minute drive. As we came closer to the hotel, I became more pensive. What was going to happen? What would Claudio say? And why was I so nervous about that anyway? We parked next to the hotel, and walked to the entrance. Claudio was waiting for us outside, greeted us heartily, asked Patience about her parents, and said he had wanted a bit of fresh air before meeting us. Was he also nervous about this meeting?

As we walked into the restaurant, we saw that there was still some juice available from the dinner buffet, which had again been at the hotel this evening. So we all took a glass. Patience noticed that there was also some desert a little further on, and invited me to have some. So we took a plate filled with sweets and fruits, while Claudio looked at us in amusement. We sat down at a quiet table in the corner. The restaurant had mostly emptied out; only here and there a few students were hanging around, discussing something at one of the tables. But they were not close enough to be able to overhear us.

While Patience and I were munching on our first strawberries, Claudio got us started, saying "Great we're all here again."

Patience glanced up at me, as if to tell me that it wasn't as bad with him as I had thought. I didn't answer her look, but kept my focus on expertly skewering a piece of pineapple onto my fork.

Claudio continued, "So what do we do now?" He made it sound as if nothing had happened at all.

Luckily Patience pitched in. "Perhaps we should talk things over."

"What?" he sounded surprised.

"Well, things have happened, and Miriam is rather discouraged."

I intervened, "Not precisely. I'm not discouraged, we're just quitting."

"Eh, right, that's what I mean." Patience looked at Claudio. "She thinks it's no use continuing now."

"Of course not. We don't have time. The presentations are tomorrow." I said.

"And she took a boat tour this afternoon..." and after I directed a killer glance at her she added "which is completely understandable."

Claudio was struggling to get his head around the situation: "You took a boat tour. You no longer want to win?"

"Of course I want to win you..." I bit back my retort. Calling him names once today was quite enough. "But on my own, I can't."

"Oh." That was all he said.

Patience broke the uncomfortable silence, saying "Miriam and I have just been having dinner together. Actually we still are." She smiled and looked at our gradually emptying plates. "And so I think there's something I think she wants to ask you." She smiled encouragingly.

Right, nice set-up. Now what should I ask exactly? I should ask why. But why what? Why he didn't collaborate. I thought a little about how to put this and said, "Yes, I actually do have a question. This afternoon you said you didn't want to continue because Patience wasn't there anymore. The question Patience put to me was: why was that a problem for you? I couldn't answer her."

"Yeah." Patience said soothingly. "I think it's good we talk this over. And let's not argue, please. Let's just try to listen and understand. Claudio?"

I didn't much feel like listening, much less like understanding. I snagged the last strawberry from my plate on my fork and brought it to my mouth.

"Yeah, but does Miriam really want to know the answer? Does she want to listen?"

How did he know?

"For me, I think that was the main problem," he continued. "I can't work with someone who doesn't want to listen."

That got me. I looked at him in astonishment and my mouth dropped open. The strawberry that I had just put into my mouth came sliding down my tongue to the entrance of my mouth where it halted against my front lip and bulged out of my mouth. The effect must have been comical, because Patience giggled, and also Claudio couldn't suppress a grin.

He continued, "So strawberry girl, are you prepared to listen? Because if you are, and if you want to hear, I'd still be prepared to give this a go. What the heck, we're here now anyway, and we don't have anything to lose. It may even be fun!"

I quickly gobbled up the strawberry, and then just sat there. I hadn't seen that one coming. And with my father ordering me to go for it, the UCI honors to defend, and an enthusiastic team, what was stopping me, really?

Chapter 28

After letting Claudio's words get to me for a while, Patience encouraged me, "So, what do you say Miriam?"

I clearly had to say something. But then again I didn't, I had to listen, not speak. In the end, to break the silence, I said, "Right. I'll listen". That's all I managed to come up with.

"Great. That's all I needed to hear." Claudio said. "But I won't stop listening either, and the first question is whether you want to continue. I'm up for whatever you say. Patience?"

Patience just nodded.

"So you take the lead, if you want." Claudio continued.

"As long as I listen?"

"As long as you listen." Claudio smiled broadly.

All the impressions of the past day came to my mind. Europe on the verge of crumbling down. The contest in ashes. But it seemed that somehow the frail phoenix was rising again. If I wanted it to. Well, there wasn't too much hope of winning now. But we could still give it a shot. First I had to tell them about everything that had happened, though. Otherwise I could never focus. And it occurred to me that they would be in the same boat. A lot was happening to them too. So yes, we would all have to listen. "Let's go for it. We'll first have hear each other out, about everything that's been going on. That's the only way we'll be able to focus at all. Are you in?"

Claudio and Patience looked at each other and smiled. I started to wonder whether they had planned this together. No use wondering though. I quickly finished my dessert, and so did Patience. We decided to go to the meeting room over at the university, to have a more professional environment. Our access cards also worked at night, so we were able to go there even at this time of day. And I could use the short walk outside to arrange my thoughts.

*

We walked into our meeting room, and I suddenly realized that it was only this morning, here, that Claudio had refused to go on. It seemed ages ago. I dwelt for a moment regretting all time we lost in between. Would we ever be able to make up for that time, even now everyone was joining again? Of course not. And really, we couldn't just get started. So many things to talk about and listen to first. And we needed a way to get very constructive in a short amount of time if we weren't going to look very silly tomorrow. I decided to use my mum's secret weapon. I proposed the Indian talking stick. That would mean that only the person holding the talking stick could make a point, others could only ask for clarification. And the stick would only go to the next person if the person speaking felt understood. Claudio was a bit surprised, and asked whether this wouldn't take too much time. Listening is one thing, but an Indian talking stick is another. I convinced him saying that he was the one to insist on listening, and this was my way to actually do it. He allowed himself to be convinced. I took a stirring rod from the holder at the center of the table. "This will be our talking stick!"

There was so much I wanted to talk about, that I asked them whether they would be OK for me to hold on to the stick for now. They didn't look too happy about it, but when I explained that in order to be able to listen later, I just had to offload my mind first, they did agree. So I started: "Thanks. I need to tell you something about what happened to me today. Are you ready?"

Patience nodded, and Claudio said, "Let's have it."

I told them what had happened to me with the visit of my mother, how I had thought she had come to tell me off, but then discovered that she wanted to apologize for not being there for me, and to explain that she was in professional trouble. And the problems she was experiencing were not just her own, but also Europe's problems. I told them about the deal with the Italian bank, and how it was hard for her to do anything there now, because she could not just barge in there and change things around.

"Sorry, what's this bank called again?" Claudio asked.

I told him the name.

"Really? Wow, I think that's the bank my uncle works at."

"What? What does he do there?"

"Not sure exactly, but he's pretty big there."

"Oh. Interesting."

"Yeah, do you want me to put your mum in touch with him?"

"Why?"

"Well, you said she couldn't just barge in, but maybe if he invited her?"

"But he would have to want that..."

"If it can save the bank?!"

"I don't know, it's a bit of a long shot, I think."

We decided to leave it there, and I ended up also telling them about the support that my father, in his illness, was giving to my mother. I saw that Patience was touched by that. I finished by saying that I was still somewhat frustrated that she didn't apologize on the core issue between us, but I left it at that. I didn't feel like burdening Claudio and Patience with that.

After finishing my story, and, in true 'Indian talking stick style' had made sure they had understood the key things I had said, I handed the stick to Patience. "I think you have plenty to talk about. If you want to share, of course."

*

Patience took up the talking stick and sat quietly for a while. You could see that she was very concentrated, inwardly, in a way that I had seen few people do. Her eyes were looking down, but she wasn't downcast. She just seemed very composed, but not in a far away-way. You could see she was suffering, but there was a strange sense of peace about her. After about a minute like this, she started to chuckle a little. "I'm sorry that I'm taking my time. I just need to careful about what I say. So I need to ask for some help."

Claudio and I looked at her a bit confused, but she made a calming gesture.

"Don't worry, it will be fine. Miriam is dealing with issues in her family. I know, I visited her dad. But that also reminds me of a lot of things that I have been struggling with the last time. You see, I need to speak of my parents. And before I say anything, I have to say that I love them very much. They are wonderful people. Very good people. They are having a difficult time. It's not easy. Not at all. So I need to support them. I don't want to criticize, do you understand?"

Claudio and I looked at each other and nodded. Clearly, her parents were very important to her.

"What's happening is... for several reasons, my father wants to move to a bigger house. That's very important for the family. Especially now a baby is coming. From my sister. But we cannot. And there have been tensions." Patience paused. "I haven't talked about it so far, because I didn't want to burden you guys. If you don't mind, I will not talk about it too much now."

"Of course," Claudio said softly.

"My father went away on Tuesday morning and didn't come back for a while. But in the end he came back on Wednesday evening. There was a big... scene. They told me, and that's why I went back on Thursday morning. My father went to work on Thursday, and I had lunch with my mother. She is very good. He is very good too. She wants to ask for forgiveness for some things she said to him, but she also needs him to ask for forgiveness and change his ways." Patience paused again, and looked a bit sad now. "It's just that I don't know who should tell him that."

"How do you mean?" I asked gently.

"My mother can't tell him. That would be more fighting, we don't want that. My little sisters are too small. We don't want to involve other people from the church or the community. They would want to help of course, and some know what is happening. But it would be better..." her sadness became deeper "It's just that I can't."

Claudio asked, "You want to speak about this with your father? Wow."

"Do you understand the situation?" Patience asked softly.

"I do. Or at least, I think I do." I thought for a while what more to say. "Are you sure there's no one else?"

Patience shook her head. "Well, there are, but then really everyone will know. That's the way things go in our community. We don't want that."

"And what if you leave things be?"

"It will probably still be okay tomorrow, because my Dad will be away at work. But over the weekend, things will explode again. They usually do. There really need to be apologies, and things need to change."

"Can we help?" Claudio asked.

"Thank you. But I don't see how. They don't know you."

"Right." Claudio scratched his head. "Even Mafioso tactics won't work on this one? I have a few friends in Amsterdam Zuidoost…"

"Claudio!" I exclaimed.

Patience chuckled, but a tear rolled down her cheek. "I just hope and pray there will be a solution. But I don't know what it can be." And she decidedly handed the talking stick to Claudio.

*

Claudio thanked Patience and sighed. He started by apologizing for not being at his best over the last few days. He said that Miriam's relationship with Tim was getting to him more than it should. It reminded him of the death of his little brother. He told us that he was called Giuseppe and passed away when he was 13 years old, because of an aggressive form of leukemia.

"I feel sorry for your loss." I said. And Patience empathized too.

I thought for a while whether to ask him anything more, and if so what to ask. Because I couldn't figure out anything specific, I just went for: "Would you like to tell us more about Giuseppe or about his illness?"

Claudio started talking about how the two of them used to play together. They were very close, and liked each other so much that they never really fought, to the amazement of their aunts and uncles. Giuseppe liked watching the stars a lot, and at night he would look through his telescope and explain his discoveries to Claudio. Stars. Constellations. Galaxies. Meteors. You name it. Now, every time he looked up at the sky, he had to think of Giuseppe.

Another episode that had been impressed on him very deeply was the first time his father told him that something was the matter. Claudio had come home from school. That day his parents had been to the hospital with Giuseppe. As Claudio passed the back yard, his father had walked out to him and said "Claudio, it's bad." This sentence had stuck in his memory, especially because later he had experienced how bad things could get. He lost his brother and his best friend.

After this, Claudio could no longer go on talking. We sat in silence for a while.

Then, Patience took the word and said, "I don't know how much this means to you, but I promise I will pray for your brother—and for you and your family."

"Thank you" he mouthed, and overcoming himself he said "I'm sure he's baking pizzas for me in heaven." And winked at us. Claudio.

*

After this long session, it did become clear to me that listening had actually been a good idea. So much going on, and I had only captured less than half of it. No wonder we had not been able to focus much on the competition. That, at least, soothed me a bit. We were all in the same boat. And now we were really in it together. But it was time to get going again. Time for the content. This morning, after Claudio had walked out, and before lunch, I had actually developed some ideas that took into account all the ideas all of us had had so far, and would still be able to convince the jury. So I proposed kicking off with my proposal, promising to listen to their feedback afterwards. Claudio and Patience agreed.

I explained that it seemed to me that the jury would not support any general conclusions about the failure of the deal as a 'good thing', but surely they would not mind if we said that while the deal was a failure to most actors, the outcome was welcome to others. We could apply my model to all actors, and then show what was important to them, in our view. In this way, we could keep Patience's point on its feet, while also making sure we had taken into account the Jury's opinion, as well as use my model, which the jury liked, to the maximum. Furthermore, I proposed that Patience would present the case. They clearly had sympathetic feelings towards her, and we could use her charisma on stage.

"So does this mean," Caudio asked, "that we need to present your model for every actor, and then draw a separate conclusion for every one?"

"I don't think so. We do need to do the analyses, but we can show the most relevant ones, and give several main conclusions, indicating which actor would support which conclusion."

"Sound fancy."

Also Patience sat up a bit. "Yes, I think that could work."

After making my point, I asked them whether they had understood. Indeed, they both did, and could explain my strategy back to me. So I passed the talking stick to them.

Patience just said, "For me it's important that money is not the only thing that matters to these people. Especially to Hansen. And you can see that in the case. That needs to come out in our analysis."

Claudio agreed with her. When he took the talking stick, he referred to the different love-types that we had studied during the preparation. "That's another way of saying the same thing," he thought. He made the point that people love different things, it can be their own material well-being or success, their development, but also the well-being of others. But he recognized that those were already in the table, through the different motivation types we included. He did insist that we shouldn't stop at the table, but continue to really think carefully about what motivates the people in the case, and the institutional actors.

Also, following up from the Jury comments, he underscored that the fact that money can help people can strike deals that everyone profits from—even though they're really different—is actually something quite beautiful. He wondered whether this realization should not somehow be included in the case. Loffels would clearly want us to mention it.

Patience agreed with him, but did add that striking deals is not the only thing in life. Building relationships is another thing, even though that may eventually also have consequences for the deals you strike.

After having talked everything over, listening carefully to each other, we all felt understood—and agreed that the strategy I had proposed would be a good basis to bring across all these points. And we would have to ensure that the story around it was coherent, too. Great. But now, would we still have time to implement these ideas?

Chapter 29

We had a short break with some drinks, which were sorely needed after the conversation we had had. Then we went back to the meeting room to get started. What should we make of our presentation with the little time we had left?

"I'm sorry to bug you all," Claudio started, "and I know we're short on time. But I'm still not comfortable with this relationship parameter."

"Okay" I said tentatively, not knowing exactly where this was going.

"I mean, I've told you it's too accurate to be real. I don't want to impose, but we should agree on this, right?"

"Should we do this now?"

"Well, if not now, then when? And perhaps you can explain it to us better, and convince me. I'm open, but I just don't see it. Explaining is also good for Patience, by the way. If she's gonna present, she might as well understand."

Patience nodded.

"No problem, but I'll have to explain how I thought of the idea in the first place."

"Go for it!" Claudio said encouragingly.

Right, so there we went. I explained to them how this table was the result of my thinking about game theory. I had thought about extending games by including the relationship to the other player in your own payoff, in a two-player game. I had thought this was important, to capture something of philia and agape love in the model: caring about the other person's wellbeing as if it were your own.

"Right," Claudio interjected, "that makes me think of we-rationality. Thinking about us, instead of just me."

"True, but we-rationality is a special case of my model. Let me show you." I had to search a little in my files, and eventually found a document I had made in the preparatory phase. I showed them the following table, which shows a normal prisoner's dilemma game, but with slightly different numbers. I explained that the meaning of the numbers is not so important for now; what is important is that if we analyze this in the standard way, we come to an equilibrium of non-collaboration: both 'defect'.

P1 \ P2	Collaborate	Defect
Collaborate	10, 10	0, 12
Defect	12, 0	**5, 5**

I went on to explain how I had expanded on this first game by introducing relationships. The way I did that is by making the one player 'care' about the pay-off of the other. Say we have the same game, but each player 'cares' for the other player's payoff about half as much as for their own payoff, so r=0.5. The payoffs change, and we get the following.

P1 \ P2	Collaborate	Defect
Collaborate	**15, 15**	6, 12
Defect	12, 6	**7.5, 7.5**

I pointed out that 'caring about the other' changed the dynamic of the game. We were now no longer in a 'prisoner's dilemma', but rather in a 'stag hunt' game with two stable equilibria: the players can either collaborate or not collaborate. Loffels had explained to us that this was a model for friendship: there was a possibility for collaboration, but through betrayal that could switch over to non-collaboration.

Finally, I showed that if the 'caring for each other' went so far as to appreciate the other's payoff as much as one's own, r=1, we would get to the 'we-rationality' Claudio had just mentioned. The payoffs would then become like this.

P1 \ P2	Collaborate	Defect
Collaborate	**20, 20**	12, 12
Defect	12, 12	10, 10

In this game, there was only one stable equilibrium: collaboration.

Now, how exactly caring for each other affected the game dynamics depended, of course, on the initial payoff matrix—and this was just one example of the more general theory I had elaborated. But explaining that would go too far for now. The general message that I took from it was this: the extent to which you care about the payoff of the other person, influences the dynamics of the game.

"I see that," Claudio said. And he told us experiments confirm that people actually do sometimes care about the other person's payoff. "Did I ever tell you about the time I played game theory pranks on my cousins?"

*

Claudio explained that because his mother is from Spain, where people celebrate the Three Kings that come from the east, they were very amused to hear that in the Netherlands we celebrate Sinterklaas,[8] who comes by boat from Madrid to the Netherlands. They once invited the family over to come and celebrate the feast. Claudio dressed up as Sinterklaas and invited his friend Dauwe to be his assistant, called Piet.

He first called two of his cousins to step forward at the same time. These two boys were more or less the same age, both about nine years old, and usually play together when there are family meetings. They were friends, but never completely at peace with

8   A Dutch abbreviation for St Nicholas.

each other. There would always at least be one instance of some fight or conflict in which the parents had to intervene during every meeting of the two. So Claudio was interested to see how they would do together on a game theoretical challenge. He decided to make them play an ultimatum game.

In the ultimatum game, one player receives a certain initial endowment, and then needs to share that endowment with a second player. The rule is that only when the second player accepts the offer, do they both get to keep the endowment. If the second player does not accept, both players walk away from the game with nothing.

He asked Dauwe to show ten 'pepernoten' (special Sinterklaas candy) to Kiko, the slightly older of the two. He told the boys that Sinterklaas had heard that he and Javi often played together, but had not always been sweet to one another. That's why they now had to play a game together, to see how their relationship really is. He explained the rules: Kiko was free to give as many of his pepernoten to Javi as he liked. Then Javi would have to say whether he accepted them or not. If Javi would not accept, then neither would get any pepernoten. If Javi did accept, then both would get the number they had agreed upon. Kiko quickly spoke up.

"So these," pointing at the pepernoten Dauwe was holding out, "are for me if I give some of them to Javi and he thinks it's OK?"

"Yes. There are ten pepernoten there, how many would you like to give Javi?"

He looked sideways at Javi, who was looking shyly at his shoes. "Uh."

"Do you like pepernoten?"

"Yes!"

"And Javi?"

Javi nodded frantically without taking his eyes from his shoes to the amusement of the family standing around.

"Alright Kiko, Javi likes pepernoten too, how many would you like to give him."

Kiko hesitated for a moment, and then said "Well, four." A slight murmur went through the bystanders.

"Right, so Javi, if Kiko gives you four of his ten pepernoten, will you accept them?"

Javi looked up slightly and nodded.

"Great! Then Piet, please give the boys their pepernoten. Well done. Now you can also both have your presents."

Claudio explained that the outcome was not entirely to the liking of the onlookers. Kiko's mother would have preferred that he had given half of his pepernoten to Javi. But in the end, they did strike a bargain, and Claudio had considered telling Kiko's mother that the outcome that evening was not even the worst possible one. Experimentally, people tend to accept if three out of an endowment of ten are given to them, but they tend to reject two or lower. And actually, if both players would act according to *Homo economicus'* self-centered optimization, then player one would just offer one out of ten, and the other would accept. So Kiko had actually displayed decidedly more social development than *Homo economicus*—and was even slightly more generous compared to experiments.

*

"What does that mean for us?" I asked Claudio.

He explained that in the same way that his nephews didn't act like they didn't care at all about the other (as *Homo economicus* would do), neither do experiments generally show that.

"But this is just one game." Patience said. "I mean..."

"Alright, that's not much. But I did more, the same night even." Claudio described that after these two boys, he decided to call two girls. Teresa was seven and Dolores eleven years old. The family knew them as sweet girls, so he decided to play a game with them that usually has a sweet outcome experimentally, much more than one would expect from *Homo economicus*: the trust game. He asked Piet to give Dolores four chocolate euro coins and explained the rules to her. She could either keep the chocolates for herself, or give them to Teresa. Teresa would get three times as many chocolates as Dolores gave her, so a maximum of twelve chocolates. Then Teresa could either keep these chocolates, or return some of them to Dolores. Even though Teresa was quite a bit younger than Dolores, she seemed to understand the rules very well.

Nearly everything happened as he had hoped. Dolores, who confirmed her reputation as a sweet girl, decided to give all her chocolate coins to Teresa, who therefore received twelve coins. And Teresa, somewhat doubtfully, in the end counted half of what she received and gave them to Dolores—and then she even gave one extra. The aunts applauded. The girls also received the presents Sinterklaas had brought for them, and were happy with them.

"Is that also what experiments usually show?"

Claudio elaborated that in some studies, less than one-fifth of participants in an experimental game like this make self-interested choices. And interestingly, some studies show that businessmen would make more trusting decisions than students. What exactly to make of these results remains an open discussion, but it is clear that also in this game, people don't act only as *Homo economicus* would do.

*

"So if you're convinced that people care about each other's payoffs, then you also like my relationship parameter?" I asked Claudio.

"Not quite yet." After his burst of enthusiasm, he went back to looking at the screen. "The stories I told are nice, but they're not the table." He pointed out that all of the games we had been describing were two-player games.

"Good point. The nice thing is: you can extend my model. For that we need to extend it to more players." I explained that if you would have to write that extension out in a game theory table with all the payoffs, the complexity would soon be overwhelming. The table would have to include all possible outcomes of interactions between all possible players. The number of those interactions increases exponentially with the number of players.

"So can you still do game theory?" Patience asked.

I went on to explain that this was possible, but that it was better to just to take it one player at a time, and show that in a table.

"That's cool." Claudio nodded his head.

"What does that mean?" Patience asked.

"We can make one table for every situation we analyze, and show how each person contributes to the overall situation."

"If we know the relationships and the payoffs." Claudio pitched in.

"Right. We'll need to do what we can to estimate those."

"And that's just our problem, isn't it? How do we know so exactly?"

From here, I didn't really know how to answer his objection further, but unexpectedly, he came to my aid.

"Still, I see the point better now."

"Really?"

"Yeah, and in the multi-player case, you could argue that you need a bit of freedom in this relationship parameter."

"Really?" I said again, but more intensely amazed this time. I didn't expect him to give the answer to his own question.

"Really. I see it now. If you would also categorize the relationship parameter, you wouldn't be able to indicate how important you think the different players are relative to each other."

"Yes, good point." I hadn't thought of it like that, but that certainly was true.

He explained that even though we may not know exactly what the relationship is, we need this parameter to express the player's attitude to another player, also relative to all the others. It's like introducing some 'degrees of freedom' into a model where you need them. And the number just expresses how important the different actors are for the one who needs to decide, relative to himself and to each other.

"And will that help us?" Patience looked a bit confused.

"Sure." Claudio looked at her with some surprise. "It's going to make super clear that the people are not one-dimensional—not even in this case." He grinned.

"That's what you wanted, right?" I smiled at Patience.

"I suppose so. If being not one-dimensional means caring about others."

"Yeah, it can mean that. Brilliant." I was happy to notice we were getting more and more on the same page, and my methodology was finding some approval. I showed them the table header, to remind them how it looked.

Stakeholder	Relationship	Perceived Utility				Notes
		ext	int	rel	U	

"Of course, we already introduced the complex motivation. You know, extrinsic for external motivators, intrinsic for internal motivators, and relational for relationship motivators. And U is the overall utility, the final payoff. It takes some thinking, but the complex motivation is real, though." Claudio was adamant, and we agreed with him.

We also observed how it was difficult to estimate this motivation in others. How would you even do so in real life?

"Listening to them!" Patience shouted exultantly.

That made me scratch my head a little. She had a point. "But only if they're trustworthy."

"True," she agreed.

"It sounds like we're all very happy now, and thanks for explaining. It's cool. But we haven't actually done anything." Claudio brought us back to our senses again. He pitched his voice in terminator style, "A relationship is nice, but there's gotta be payoff, buddies."

*

Really, it was high time to make a plan. We had been talking for half an hour, and really needed to make things concrete. What needed to be done? If we wanted to do this well, in the way we had discussed earlier, we had to do a good evaluation for every actor in the case. "It needs to be evidence-based." I told them.

"How do we do that?" Patience looked puzzled.

"We quote the case." After talking it over, we decided that the only rigorous way to make our approach work would be to gather all text elements of the case that referred to each of the actors. Then we would see how complete this was, and where necessary, supplement information. We'd have to be very careful about that, though, and argue why any supplementation would be necessary and justified. Based on those, we would evaluate the motivations of all the actors in the case, and draw up a table for each of them. And from the tables, we would get the overall evaluation every actor makes of the case. Then we could give our overall impression of whether that actor was in it more for himself, more for others, or was going for a lose/lose or win/win option. We would then have a complete analysis of why the deal didn't go through.

We all agreed that this would be a really cool analysis.

And a lot of work.

For now, we divided up the actors. Everyone would do a few: find the texts and make the table. Patience wanted to take on Olson and everything related to FlashCars. I offered to do everyone related to SteadyCars—quite some work, but I was most familiar with the methodology. Claudio then did the rest: everyone related to TireDeals, StrongSteel and also the headhunter. We would have to do the analyses tonight. Then tomorrow morning we would put everything together and do the calculations. I had all that already implemented in excel spreadsheets, so the calculations wouldn't be very hard. Sometimes technology comes in handy. But we would of course have to look at each other's work, and see whether we agreed with the evaluations we made. That might take some time.

In any case, we had a plan—a crazy plan, admittedly, in the timeframe, but a plan. And even if we wouldn't win, we would still blow the roof off this place with the applause we would get. And looking at all this, I thought determinedly that we still could win. It was cool. We could still win.

Chapter 30

As I sat down to get started on the text analysis after our meeting, the tiredness and the many emotions of the day suddenly overwhelmed me. There was so much buzzing through my head that I couldn't focus. So I decided on a strategy that had worked for me before: go to bed now, and get up early in the morning to do the work. Then my head would be clearer. I talked it over with Patience; she preferred to do the work right away, but we agreed that we would both be quiet: she when she went to bed, and I when I got up. Wonderful! I could go now to 'hit the hay', so that I would be fresh in the morning.

I figured that I would need some eight hours of sleep. It was only nine now, so if I were in bed by 9:30, I could get up at 5:30 in the morning and still have a few productive hours before breakfast. I could do that. I walked to the hotel and went up to the room. I decided to take a quick shower, so that I could wash all the things that happened that day off of me. Hopefully that would give me some peace of mind, with the advantage of not having to wake Patience by showering early the next morning.

The shower actually did me well. All the thoughts and feelings racing through my mind calmed down a bit. But they were still there. And when I had set the alarm and pulled the blankets over my head, they still wouldn't go away. It just kept on spinning... Why would mum have to lose her job? ... Would Europe really crumble? ... What about this case study, was our analysis really going to make sense? ... Would we get the applause? ... Would we win? ... How would our final conclusion be, after doing all the text criticism and calculation? Would things really line up to a clear story? ... Would we have time to pull it all together? Well, in answer to the latter question—we'd only have time if I could sleep now and get my head clear! That would have to be my main objective for now. I tried to convince myself, thinking that the whole success of my work tomorrow, and therefore of the contest, depended on it. So "Sleep", I commanded myself. "Sleep!" Oh, why does that never work?

I started thinking about the rush we were in. Luckily, I had written out much of the theory of my approach already for the report last Wednesday, so we just needed to add the results and conclusions, and reshape the introduction a little. That would be tight, but possible. If only I could sleep now.

I decided to get up and walk three laps around the room. Sometimes that helps me to calm down. It did get some thoughts out of my head, but it introduced others. It seems like the source of worry was inexhaustible tonight. What would my father do? Smile, probably, and try to joke about it. Could I laugh at myself for being the Oracle of Delphi with a never extinguishing source of unintelligible thoughts welling up from deep within me? I tried, but it wasn't funny enough. I needed Claudio to make me laugh. But my father was also always thinking about other people, like my mum, my brother and me. Maybe that would help? More thoughts—caring thoughts about others—to combat worry thoughts? I wasn't sure that would work.

I could at least give it a try. What about Claudio, how was he doing? Not in top shape clearly, because Tim was reminding him of his brother. But he was trying to be his funny self. And he was collaborating now. He was going to support me. He was going to support ME. Shift to caring, Mir: What about him though? How important was this contest for him? In all my anxiety to win, I had never really stopped to consider that. And I had never listened to him about that, never asked for it. I remembered him bragging about the contest to his friends, and saying to them that they were going to win it. But was that just to impress them? Did he really want to win? Or was that just because of me? Because winning was something I wanted to do? I couldn't tell. It could well be that he just thought it was a nice experience, something to learn from, but nothing more. Was that so?

And what about Patience? She definitely wasn't in this to win. She was here to help, she told me herself this afternoon. Did I trust her on that? I didn't really see why not. So she was in this to help. But why did she want to? Out of pure goodness? Or was she escaping from the situation at home? As far as I could judge, working on this competition now was not helping her situation at home at all. But perhaps she didn't want to do anything else because she didn't dare to face her father. Understandable. That was definitely a big dare. I wasn't very much at home in African cultures, but Dutch directness turned full blast on her father would probably not be appreciated. Would I do it, in her situation? I could hardly imagine my father getting into such trouble, but I think I would be able to talk to him. Could I help her do that? Oh wait, but if I did that, she would want to do so tomorrow, and then she couldn't present the contest any more. And her charm was essential for us to have any chance at winning. But then...

I lay down on my bed again. It came back to winning. Why exactly did I want to win? Right... to show I could do it. Independently. But... really... who was going to care? What would the consequences of winning really be? For me, for others? I sat up straight in my bed. This was it. I had to make the call. Should I really want to win the contest? I had to get my thoughts straight. Only then would my mind be calm, so that I could sleep.

And then it hit me. I knew just the method.

*

Yes, that was it. I was going to apply my own method to the GO/NO GO decision on trying to win the contest tomorrow. So far it had been so clear for me: go for it, and full stop. But now I saw there were other people to take into account. How would this work out?

First I had to make up my mind about whom to include. Who would be affected by the outcome of this contest except for me? Well around me there were my mum and dad, my brother (but no, he wouldn't really care), my friends Elena and Linde. Then Claudio and the people around him: his friends (whom he was trying to impress), his family. And then Patience, her mum and dad—not to mention her community, since she was also worried about what would happen to the community if things went really wrong between her parents. I decided that that would be enough for now. I could of course include all sorts of important things, like the effect on the environment, and keep everyone at UCI happy, but I supposed that this particular decision would be CO_2 neutral: no use worrying!

I put all these names in a spreadsheet on my computer. Great. Now the next thing. How strong would I say my relationships to all these people were? Tough one. The relationship to myself is one by default. How much more do I care about the wellbeing of my mum and Dad than about my own? Well, I do think about them as 'us', so because I said to Claudio that we-rationality has a relationship factor of one, I might as well fill out the 'one' there. Patience and Claudio? Well, it's really become an 'us' now too, so I'll also give them both a one. My friends? Same, but they're not really involved here, so I'll give them some less importance. Say 0.5. Claudio's friends? I don't really care how much he impresses them. Zero. Claudio's family? Important, but not very close to me: 0.5. Same for Patience's mum and dad. And the community? I'll count it in a little because it's important to Patience, but only 0.1. Great, good going. I now had a spreadsheet on my computer looking like this.

Stakeholder	Relationship
Me	1
Mum	1
Dad	1
Friends (Elena & Linde)	0.5
Claudio	1
Claudio's friends	0
Claudio's family	0.5
Patience	1
Patience's mum	0.5
Patience's dad	0.5
The community	0.1

What was the next step? I needed to make up my mind what situation or what situations I was going to analyze. This was about GO / NO GO. So those were two situations. But for the GO, there were two things that could happen: either we win or we don't win. And that would make a big difference to the payoffs. So I should go ahead and do two GO scenarios: GO and WIN, or GO and LOSE. What about the NO GO? Was there any risk that Patience would go to her father and not succeed in convincing him? That things would only get worse? Difficult to say, but given how respectful and loving she had been when talking about her parents, and her evident charisma for dealing with people, I thought that would be quite unlikely. She would just have to overcome her initial fears, and then it would probably be fine. Or at least, that was my sense. Right, so perhaps I was being stupid, but for Patience going to talk to her father, I thought a positive outcome at home would be a safe bet. That is, if she would do so soon, so things wouldn't get worse over the weekend, as she feared. So only one scenario there. Right. Three scenario's in total. Let's rumble.

*

The next step in the process was thinking of all the payoffs of different kinds, external, internal and other-related, as Claudio had suggested, and putting an overall number to that from -2 to 2. That was quite a bit of work. For myself, it was quite easy. I would be really happy if we won (+2), really disappointed if we tried and lost (-2) and if we wouldn't try, well, I would still be disappointed, but I actually felt I would be happy for Patience at the same time. So that would compensate, zero overall. My mum? I thought she would react the same way I would, except that she didn't know about Patience. So it would be disappointing to her if I said NO GO. Would she even care though, now? I figured she would. And my dad? Well, really happy if I won (+2), and just happy (+1) otherwise. Then my friends, well happy for me if I won, it wouldn't be a big deal for them if I didn't, and they would be happy to hear the story about Patience's quest to deal with her family. Right, that was the first part. No time to write up the notes that the original table specified. That's sloppy, but that's life…So this then became the first part of the table.

Stakeholder	Relationship	GO & WIN				Overall	GO & LOSE				Overall	NO GO				Overall
		Perceived Utility					Perceived Utility					Perceived Utility				
		ext	int	oth	tot		ext	int	oth	tot		ext	int	oth	tot	
Me	1	++			2	2	---			-2	-2	-		+	0	0
Mum	1			++	2	2		--		-2	-2			-	-1	-1
Dad	1			++	2	2			+	1	1			+	1	1
Friends (Elena & Linde)	0.5			+	1	0.5				0	0			+	1	0.5

I smiled at myself, because it suddenly dawned on me that I was inventing the relation-minded geek. That was going to be me. All the way!

Now it was time for Claudio and his friends and family. For him, I thought, winning would make him happy, but he also didn't seem to care that much, so +1. And that +1 would also be because he was happy for me, probably. If we didn't win, he wouldn't mind so much. And if we wouldn't go for it, and helped Patience to fix her family situation, that would probably make him really happy (+2). With regards to his friends, they would probably like it if he won (+1), but not find one of the other options any big deal (0). His parents had other things on their mind now, so they would probably not be very impressed by any of the possible outcomes. And they didn't know Patience enough to really appreciate what the third outcome would mean to her. So this was the part of the table for Claudio and his friends and family. Good going! I told myself to keep it up.

Stakeholder	Relationship	GO & WIN				Overall	GO & LOSE				Overall	NO GO				Overall
		Perceived Utility					Perceived Utility					Perceived Utility				
		ext	int	oth	tot		ext	int	oth	tot		ext	int	oth	tot	
Me	1	++			2	2	--			-2	-2	-		+	0	0
Mum	1			++	2	2			--	-2	-2			-	-1	-1
Dad	1			++	2	2			+	1	1			+	1	1
Friends (Elena & Linde)	0.5			+	1	0.5				0	0			+	1	0.5
Claudio	1	+		+	1	1				0	0			++	2	2
Claudio's friends	0			+	1	0				0	0				0	0
Claudio's family	0.5				0	0				0	0				0	0

Now the last part. The most interesting part. What about Patience and her family? Patience would clearly be happy if she were part of the winning team, a bit like Claudio, so +1, but the situation of her parents would quickly overtake her (-2). Overall, the win would only be a small patch for the bleeding, so I'd give her a -1 for that situation. If we wouldn't win, no patch, so -2. And what if I helped her to talk to her father? Well, +2 just for learning to do that.

What about her family? The situation was not good, and didn't look much like improving over the weekend, as Patience had said. So the outcome of the contest would not affect them much, they also had other things on their minds, just like Claudio's parents. In the case Patience would not step in, their situation would most probably be stuck in -2. And the same for the community, as they would start to hear about the trouble. What if Patience did step in? Would all problems be out of the way? No, probably not, but given Patience's talents, there would be a good first step towards reconciliation. And that would already be really positive. So a +1 for that. In that case the community wouldn't have to know, so they would not be affected. Great, so this completed the table. This is what the last part of the table had become.

Stakeholder	Relationship	GO & WIN Perceived Utility				Overall	GO & LOSE Perceived Utility				Overall	NO GO Perceived Utility				Overall
		ext	int	oth	tot		ext	int	oth	tot		ext	int	oth	tot	
Me	1	++			2	2	--			-2	-2	-		+	0	0
Mum	1			++	2	2			--	-2	-2			-	-1	-1
Dad	1			++	2	2			+	1	1			+	1	1
Friends (Elena & Linde)	0.5			+	1	0.5				0	0			+	1	0.5
Claudio	1	+		+	1	1				0	0		++		2	2
Claudio's friends	0			+	1	0				0	0				0	0
Claudio's family	0.5				0	0				0	0				0	0
Patience	1	+		--	-1	-1			--	-2	-2	++	+		2	2
Patience's mum	0.5	--			-2	-1	--			-2	-1	+			1	0.5
Patience's dad	0.5	--			-2	-1	--			-2	-1	+			1	0.5
The community	0.1	--			-2	-0.2	--			-2	-0.2				0	0

Amazing. Now everything was filled out. I looked at my watch and it was only 10:30. The whole exercise, at full speed, had taken about an hour. But now the most important bit. What was I going to decide?

*

I had thought about several possible analyses for my tables. But I wanted to take a decision now, and get back to bed as soon as possible. So I went for the basics. What were the overall scores for the three scenarios? Let's see. GO&WIN. I typed the 'sum' command into excel, and got... 4.3. Good, positive. Now 'GO&LOSE', another command and I got... -7.2. Wow. If I lost, I would lose big time. Scary. And then finally... my heart started beating as I typed in the command and selected the cells to be summed up. It was... 5.5! There it was, right in front of my eyes. I couldn't believe it.

GO & WIN	4.3
GO & LOSE	-7.2
NO GO	5.5

So if I was serious about the things I had put into my method, the relationships and payoffs I had put into this table, then the rational thing was for me to opt for the NO GO scenario. To not try and win tomorrow, but rather help Patience to go home and deal with her family situation.

I went over all my calculations again. It was all correct. Of course, I had the layout of this excel sheet from before, and the sum commands weren't the most difficult ones.

I had to think back to Claudio's warning. 4.3 was not too far from 5.5, and not all stars had the same interpretation. Then I went over all the things I had put into the tables. Was I serious about these relationships? Should I down-tune some? Were the payoffs realistic? Were there some more important than others? I thought through everything again, but I couldn't with a clear conscience change any of this, or interpret it away. I could of course just forget the entire analysis and go for my own success. I could. And I would impress my mum if I won. I would. She wouldn't understand it if I went NO GO. She wouldn't. But then there were the other people.

This was it. My mind was made up. NO GO. Well, GO the minimum. And help Patience first. She would get priority. I couldn't believe myself.

I got into bed, and now my thoughts all calmed down. I put my alarm clock later, I was giving myself eight hours of sleep. I wasn't sure whether my approach would turn out the way I planned for Patience and her family. But I was going to do the right thing. And I slept tight.

Chapter 31

It was quarter to seven the next morning when my alarm clock went. I was awake immediately, and out of a reflex turned off the clock instantly. I was vividly aware of Patience sleeping in the other bed, without me even seeing her. But when I looked, there she was. The alarm hadn't woken her up, luckily. She'd probably be sleeping until just before the breakfast, which was scheduled at nine today. So I could still work for two hours, if I was quick now, and I wanted to.

I stealthily took my clothes to the bathroom, dressed myself, brushed my teeth and combed my hair, and last but not least made sure I looked decent. It came back to me how mad my decision of last night really was. Look at everything I had put on the line to come to this contest and win: my double major, which would help me become a doctor, the time for my friends in the rest of the semester, the relationship with my mother. I still wanted those things to go well, and it was now clear that I had risked all going wrong for nothing. Well, for nothing? To help Patience with her parents. But it was the rational step to take, I still felt certain that my analysis last night was well done, because I had checked it so well. And I still felt it was the right choice. I would go for it.

Once I was done, I quietly took the materials I needed and left the room. Patience was still sleeping; I had managed not to wake her. Wonderful. I slipped down into the lobby and saw that the dining room was empty. They hadn't set up breakfast yet; the place looked a bit desolate, but there was enough light and quiet to be able to work. I sat down there and took out the case.

I quickly marked all the text relevant for the people and organizations related to SteadyCars. Having the text base cleared up, I then started assigning payoffs, for the DEAL and NO DEAL scenarios, for the stakeholders I was looking at. Really, this wasn't so difficult when you got used to it. And working under pressure was something I had had a lot of practice in at UCI: not a problem.

Because I felt rested and sharp, I quickly got into the flow, and was working away for quite a while when the personnel came to set up breakfast. By then, I had managed not only to do my own actors, but also all the other ones. It wasn't too hard, because I had been working away at this case for a while now. I knew my stuff. Of course I would listen to what Claudio and Patience would have to say about them, but I figured it would be faster to have my opinion ready already, so that we could compare and only discuss any differences of opinion that we might have. Efficiency. We'd need it today, especially given the fact that Patience's issues would have priority. I had just about finished my entire analysis when the first students started arriving for breakfast. Sigh. Time for me to have some too.

But when would Patience come? And how would I go about telling her about my decision? And now that I thought about it, I really could use Claudio's support on this.

*

Luckily, Claudio walked into the breakfast hall before Patience did, not much after nine. Knowing Claudio, his punctuality was surprising. I walked up to him and asked him how he had slept. Not a lot, but well, he answered. He was a bit surprised when I asked to have a word with him outside, but he agreed and came with me.

On the way out through the lobby, I wondered how to start the conversation. I didn't really know where to start, so when we came out, that's what I told him.

"What's this about?" he asked.

"It's Patience."

Claudio sighed. "What now?"

"No, it's not what you think. It's just that... I think we need to help her."

"Oh. To give the presentation?"

"To talk to her dad. Today."

"What?"

"Yes." How was I going to explain this to him? In the end I resolved to tell him the whole story. I started explaining how I got up last night and did the whole analysis on the three scenarios: GO & WIN, GO & LOSE, and NO GO.

Claudio started laughing. "You're a true geek."

I didn't see that coming, but I suppose he was right, and I smiled too. "Thanks, I'll take that as a compliment." Then I went on to explain to him what came out of the analysis: if we went for it and won, the overall outcome would be positive; if we went for it and lost, the overall outcome would be very negative; and if we decided not to give winning priority, and help Patience fix her situation, that would be the biggest win for the most people, considering everything. So the best option would be NO GO.

Claudio stared at me. "What?" He looked astonished. "Are you telling me you no longer want to win?"

"I do want to win; it's just, not at the cost of everything. If we help Patience fix her situation, I figure she'll do that really well. She spoke really well of her parents, so it should be possible. She has to do it today, though, or, as she said, things will happen over the weekend. So if she talks to her dad, her family will be better off. And I thought that would make you happy too. Right?"

Claudio continued to look at me in utter astonishment. Then, slowly, a big smile came over his face. And when the corners of his mouth had nearly reached his ears and had completely bared his teeth, he leaned forward and gave me a big hug. "Miriam."

Wow. I didn't see that one coming, either.

As Claudio released me, he started to look thoughtful. "Good move Miriam. Now it's time for me to do the same."

"What do you mean?"

"Go have breakfast; I'll join you in a minute." And softly, to himself, he added, "I need to start taking responsibility."

*

When I walked back into the hotel, I saw that Patience was just at the end of the breakfast buffet, and she waved at me as I took my tray, plate and cutlery. She sat down at an empty table, and not long afterwards I was ready to join her there. She had been working late on the analysis, like Claudio, but they had both managed to gather a text-base for every one of the stakeholders they had been assigned, and evaluate their motivations based on that. When Claudio joined us a bit later, we found out that neither of them had found it easy, and there were some instances in which there had been some guesswork. We agreed we would look at those together later. There was some other business to clear up first.

As we were finishing our breakfast, Claudio said to Patience, "I think Miriam wants to tell you something."

"Do you want to do that here?" I asked him.

Claudio shrugged. "Why not?" It was true. The restaurant was not too busy, and the other students were sitting quite far off.

Patience smiled. "Tell me."

Again, I didn't really know where to start. Now, I was quite happy to have talked to Claudio first. I noticed I could really use his support. All I could bring out was, "eh", and I threw a begging look at Claudio. Luckily, he got the message.

"So, Miriam has been thinking about our situation. Right Miriam?"

I nodded.

"Well, actually, more than thinking about it, she has been analyzing it. But then, what would you expect from our whiz kid?" Claudio snorted.

Patience looked confused.

That was enough to get me started. With a mock-dark look at Claudio, I took over and explained the whole story again. I told how I had applied our methodology to our own situation, the GO & WIN, GO & LOSE, and NO GO scenarios. But this time I emphasized that I had included her and her family in the analysis.

"Oh." Patience looked surprised.

"Well, you're part of this project, aren't you? And what you do affects your parents. So, it's logical to include them."

Patience nodded faintly but didn't say anything; I could see she was unsure about how to react.

This was the sensitive part. How could I bring across to her that I thought she would do really well talking to her father? That he would probably listen to her? It was possible that she would reject the suggestion out of hand. Then my whole plan would just fly out of the window. I had to try. I started tentatively. "I thought about what you could do for your father."

Patience reacted as if she had been stung. She looked alarmed.

I looked sideways at Claudio, unsure about how to continue. Thankfully he again understood the cue.

"Take it easy," he said to Patience.

"What are you expecting from me?" She looked at us in disbelief.

"Don't worry," Claudio continued, "we're not..."

"You have no idea about the situation in my family. I told you about it because I had to get it off my chest yesterday. But it has to stay here, among us."

"It will." Claudio interjected.

"And it is not your problem. It cannot be. You don't know what it is."

Claudio and I looked at her in silence for a few seconds. "You're right, we don't," he then said.

I looked at him again in surprise.

"But you do." He continued. "And you are part of our team. We have full confidence in you."

"Thank you," Patience said, but still looked uncomfortable.

"That's why we think you are able to deal with the situation in your family."

"What do you mean?"

This was my chance. "You can talk to your father. You can stand up for what you believe in, and we think you will do very well."

She looked at us in disbelief. "You don't know what you're saying."

Claudio again chimed in, "Perhaps we don't, but again: we have full confidence in you."

Patience started shaking her head and repeated, "You don't know what you're saying."

*

The conversation had stalled, with Patience sitting downcast and silent in her chair. I didn't know what to say. Perhaps that wasn't so surprising, with all my practice at pushing away emotions, I've never been very good when people get emotional on me. But Claudio seemingly also didn't know what to say, and he's hardly ever lost for words. I went over all that happened yesterday in my mind again. Would my final conclusion come to nothing because I wouldn't be able to help Patience? When I thought about it, she had helped me loads yesterday. She helped me to get the team on the road, and to realize everything I was forgetting about. And she had taught me to listen... Right. That was it!

I ventured, "Look here Patience; you're right we don't fully understand your situation. But see this?" I took a metal spoon that was meant for eating yoghurt with, but that I hadn't used in the end, and gave it to her. "This is an Indian talking stick. It is especially fabricated so that you can slap anyone on the head with it who dares not to listen to you when you hold it."

Patience managed a weak smile, which quickly faded away into sadness again.

"You and Claudio told me yesterday that I need to listen. So here I go. Explain to me all I need to know. Only if you want, of course. But I think it's the only way we can help you. And we want to help."

Claudio nodded approvingly at me and then encouragingly at Patience.

Patience took the spoon from me, but hesitated. In the end she started. "Thank you. You are very kind. But there is much that I cannot explain very easily. In our culture, a daughter does not go up to her father to tell him what to do." She sunk into a gloomy silence again.

"And can she listen to him?" I tried.

Patience looked up at me in surprise. "Of course."

"So why don't you do that?"

"And then?" She looked puzzled.

"Well, after you've listened to him, do you expect he will ask you what you think? You told me he's a good person."

"He definitely is. I suppose he might."

"Then why don't you try that? It won't hurt, will it?" I smiled at her as warmly as I could.

Patience couldn't suppress a grin. "So now you're the one telling me to listen."

"I suppose so. When could this happen?"

"Yeah." Patience quietly thought for some time. "It would have to be before the weekend, so today. And daddy will be at work. I think it would have to be his lunch break then."

"Have you ever done that before, talk to him then?"

"Of course not. But that's all I can think of."

"Very good." Claudio pitched in. "Why don't you give him a call?"

We got up, cleared away our breakfast, and Patience went outside to make the phone call. When she came back, she told us that he was happy to talk to her during the lunch break. They had agreed to meet in Amsterdam at her dad's workplace at 12:30. To be well in time, she would have to leave at around 10:30. Because she had just gotten back yesterday, there wasn't much cleaning up to do. That meant we still had nearly an hour for her to work with us on the case, and to tell us about what she had done yesterday. I reminded them of the 11 o'clock deadline for the case report, which meant we had until lunch to prepare the presentation. So we decided to make the best of it. We wouldn't win, without Patience presenting, but we might as well do something.

Just as I thought our plan was all set, Claudio added, "Great! But there's one other thing we need to arrange first."

This morning he kept on surprising me. "What?"

Looking at Patience, he asked "could you go and see Miriam's dad after yours?"

"What? Why?" I exclaimed.

Claudio said that he had just texted Tim to ask whether he and his mum would come see the final.

"You what?" I couldn't believe my ears.

"He said they couldn't make it because they didn't want to leave Dad alone." And Claudio now suggested that perhaps if Patience would go and see him, the two of them might be able to come.

"But I don't want that! And mum has to work anyway."

"She doesn't, remember?" Claudio insisted. "And I asked to be sure."

"Why don't you want her to come?" Patience asked.

"Well, it's not like we're going to be doing anything very respectable."

"She's your mum!" Patience said forcefully, somewhat in disbelief.

"My point exactly!" I replied decisively.

Patience shook her head and sat pensively for a while. She then resumed, "If I understand correctly, you think that your mum will only respect you if you win this contest."

"I don't think so; I know so. Especially because she didn't want me to go."

"Right. If you will excuse me, I have another phone call to make." Patience stood up.

"What?"

"I'm calling your dad, Miriam. Your mum is coming, like it or not. You'd better prepare yourself. You're teaching me to stand up for what I believe in. So here you go. I'm doing it." And she marched off.

Chapter 32

I was a bit cross at Patience, but decided to get over it. Because we had very little time, Claudio and I decided not to go to our meeting room, but to stay where we were and get started. Soon enough, Patience came back, and put a hand on my shoulder.

"Thanks for taking into account my feelings." I couldn't help but saying.

"Don't worry, it will be fine. Trust me," she answered.

It wasn't the time for an argument, so I didn't make any further hassle; the object was to be as efficient as possible. Everyone would get their work, and we'd meet at the hotel room that Patience and I were staying at. There was enough room for the three of us to work there. If some would sit on the beds, that is. Within five minutes we met upstairs.

The first phase was simple but intense: comparing notes. We went through all the actors and looked at the relationship coefficient and payoff that we extracted from the case for every actor. For the relationships that were most clearly described in the case, the estimates were pretty similar. Other relationships, which had to be inferred from the context, showed more difference in estimation. We didn't have time to go into in-depth discussion, so we tried to reach some compromise quickly for all of the actors in both scenarios.

As we went, we updated the values in my computer, because in there I had all the subsequent analyses already pre-programmed in my excel spreadsheet. Thank goodness for all the spreadsheet tricks I had learnt—mostly from my mum. When we reached the end of all our discussions, we could dive straight in and look at the results. Claudio insisted on distinguishing between institutional and human actors, when looking at the results. We did, and this is what we saw.

	DEAL	NO DEAL	Difference Overall Score (pro-Deal is positive)	# Stakeholders
TireDeals	1.7	-1.7	3.4	4
StrongSteel	1.7	-1.7	3.4	4
FlashCars	1.8	0.6	1.2	6
Worker Unions	-2.9	0.9	-3.8	3
SteadyCars	-2.4	1.7	-4.1	5
Norway	-4	2	-6	3
Olson	4.6	-4.2	8.8	7
Walker	4.4	-1.1	5.5	6
Hansen sons (without Father)	1	1.2	-0.2	6
Bianchi	-2.5	-0.5	-2	4
Hansen Sr.	-3.2	3.2	-6.4	7
Larsen	-6	4.8	-10.8	6

The first thing that stood out from these scores, was that the differences in the overall score between the DEAL and NO DEAL scenario were much more negative for everything and everyone connected to SteadyCars than they were for FlashCars, TireDeals and StrongSteel. One notable exception to this pattern was Bianchi, who was not happy about this deal being brokered behind his back. Also to be noted was the much less strong negative stance of the Hansen's younger generation towards the deal, if we analyzed them without taking into account their father (we did that to see what would happen in case he fell away). This last analysis, in our view, helped explain why when Hansen Sr. passed away, the takeover could go through more easily. They cared less about the company, and had fewer problems with selling it than their father had done.

When we looked at the difference between institutional and human actors, it was quite clear that the human actors had the most extreme overall scores, either highest or lowest, but that this went together with the highest number of stakeholders they took into account. In our analyses, human persons took other human persons as well as institutions into account, whereas institutions would mostly look towards other institutions only, leading to fewer stakeholders.

Claudio then stood up and made the point that here we should really be looking into the intentions of the different actors to make sense of the situation. We should also mention the negative relationship that had developed between Olson and the people at SteadyCars, which was weighing down on the deal big time. Our numbers were showing that to some extent, but not too clearly. That was the interpretative layer we needed on top.

At this point, I looked at my clock. We had only fifteen minutes before Patience needed to leave—and forty-five before we had to hand in the report. All hands on deck!

*

We just had to decide on the conclusions we were going to draw from our analysis. It was quite clear to us. The first question was, "What went wrong in the failed takeover bid?" What we saw was that, taking everyone and everything into account, the deal wasn't nearly as attractive for SteadyCars, its management and owners, as it was for Olson, FlashCars, and the ones supporting him. This was already clear from the institutional point of view, but even more so from the point of view of the individual persons involved.

The second question we were asked to answer was, "Who do you think is the key responsible person for the failed bid?" For us, the three main candidates were Hansen Sr., Larsen and Olson himself. If we had to choose, we would go for Hansen Sr., because he had the power to say 'no', and it was clear that after he died the deal could go through. But, actually, we thought it was the dynamic between these three people that played the decisive role.

The last question was: "Formulate (a) lesson(s) you draw from this situation to avoid similar mistakes in future". A first lesson we agreed on was that taking into account all stakeholders could give a richer case analysis. A second, more daring lesson, given the jury's position, was that this deal not going through was bad news for some people, but good news for others. Finally, our analysis showed that Olson could have been more aware of his bad relationship with SteadyCars, and saved himself a lot of trouble.

There were only a few minutes left before Patience had to leave. She used her last minutes going over the text of the introduction and the methods, to see whether everything was clear. Meanwhile I got to work on our results section, copy-pasting some of the graphs from excel and writing some text around it, and Claudio wrote down the conclusions we had just discussed in the final section. Luckily, we had had quite some practice with project deadlines at UCI recently, but this was certainly the tightest deadline we had faced yet.

*

When Patience rushed off after a few minutes, emailing her suggestions for the introduction and methods to me, she gave me a big but somewhat nervous smile. You could see the upcoming meeting with her father affected her.

"Don't you worry, you can do it," I encouraged her.

She walked up to me, tucked a loose lock of my hair that was hanging in front of my face back into place, and said, "So can you."

Claudio got up and gave her a hug.

After that, she hurried off with her suitcase trailing behind her.

Claudio and I worked away at the project for the next half hour, looking at the clock continuously and deciding how to round things off reasonably well within the given time. Five minutes before eleven we gathered everything we had done and written into a single document, saved it as a pdf document, and sent it by email to the jury, as instructed, at one minute to eleven. Incredible. We did it. Well, I had to correct myself here: we did something.

"Shall we go and get a drink? I think we deserve one." I asked.

Claudio agreed, and we walked to the hotel bar. We had two hours to finish the presentation, an ocean of time compared to what we had for the report. But if we wanted to do something good, there was still a serious amount of work to be done.

*

When we got to the bar, we ordered some soft drinks; Claudio, glancing up between sips, said, "You know, I've been thinking about something."

"About what?"

"About responsibility. There's more I could do. Your mother and my uncle."

"How d'you mean?"

"Well, let's see. You said your mother could use an informal way into the Italian bank, right?"

"She just said that if she would barge in there, it wouldn't work."

"Right, but remind me again what the downside would be of trying to bring her into contact with my uncle? I mean, earlier you said it was a long shot—but so what?"

"I suppose it couldn't hurt. And if you insist, Claudio..."

Claudio slapped his hand down on the bar loudly. Throwing his hands wide he ejected, "I insist! We have to try this." He theatrically brought his spread out hands together in front of his face, and rhythmically tapped the tips of his fingers against each other, looking over the tips to say to me in a conspiratorial tone, "we need to save the world."

Oh Claudio. I couldn't help chuckling.

"Call your mother," he went on in the same vein, "it must be done now, or it will be too late."

I shook my head smiling, but got out my mobile phone and rang my mum. She answered immediately. When I explained to her about Claudio's uncle, she was very interested to get in touch with him. I didn't mention her coming to see our presentation; nor did she. After I hung up, Claudio messaged her the contact details of his uncle. He said he would prepare him for the call. Indeed, he soon sent him a whatsapp voice message, again in the funny tone he was used to with his uncle, saying that he was on a quest to save the world and was putting him in touch with the one lady that would make it all happen for him. At the end, he did get serious though, and explained the situation. His uncle soon after sent him a 'thumbs up' in return. You could see there was a lot of confidence between them. We told my mother.

Did we just save the world? It didn't much feel like it. But anyway, we had other things to worry about now, like making a killer presentation.

Chapter 33

We decided to go back to our meeting room after we had our drink, to have a better workspace. We basically faced the challenge of synthesizing everything we had written in the report, but there was more to it than that. The presentation had to be compelling. Even if the report had been rushed off a little, we now still had the opportunity to make our case in an engaging and compelling way. But how to do that?

"We need to tell a story." Claudio said.

"Well, obviously."

"No, I mean a real story. One with a beginning, a middle and an end. One with conflict and intrigue, with sadness and laughter. One with the full emotional palette." He decidedly stood up and walked over to the whiteboard, uncapped a marker and emphatically drew an upward curling line on the board.

"What does that mean?" I asked, shaking my head in amusement.

"I don't know, but it looks creative."

"Great. So what should the story be about? The case itself is story enough, isn't it? It's all about Olson."

"Yeah, but they know that story. It needs to be fresh and bubbling."

"We have one and a half hours, you know."

"Oh come on, it's just a story. What kind of stories do you like best?"

"True stories."

"Really?" He brought his hand to his chin, and looked around in detective style. "Then we need to tell a true story."

Claudio was clearly amusing himself with his theatrical imitations, but I didn't think we were getting anywhere very fast. Telling a true story would be very nice, but there were so many true stories, and where would we get the most relevant one from? I think Claudio caught the hesitation from my looks, because he tried to convince me further.

"Come on Miriam, what's the problem?"

"What's the story going to be about?"

"You tell me: what's our main conclusion?"

I took out the report we had written just now and read the conclusions to him. They were: taking into account all stakeholders to give a richer case analysis; the deal not going through being bad news for some people, but good news for others; and thirdly, that if Olson would have been more aware of his bad relationship to SteadyCars, he could have saved himself a lot of trouble.

And then it hit me. "Oh."

"What?"

"My name is Olson."

*

After my eureka-moment, Claudio and I spent a full hour preparing the afternoon's presentation. Again, it was intense, but it was a lot of fun to be able to work with Claudio like this. He immersed himself completely in the work, and was his funny self. Seemingly, the memory of his brother was no longer troubling him.

Just as we were preparing the final slides and the end of the story, my mother called. I picked up and walked out of the meeting room. When she asked, I told her I was fine and preparing for the final presentation this afternoon.

"At what time does the whole thing finish?"

"Between four and five I think. There's optional drinks afterwards."

"And what are your plans for the weekend?"

"A lot of catching-up on UCI stuff. Why?"

"Oh, right." I heard her sigh.

"What's the problem mum?"

"You're too good of a daughter, that's what the problem is."

I didn't see that one coming, so I blanked, I didn't know how to respond.

"Miriam, listen. The Italian banker you put me in touch with is throwing a party this weekend. It seems a bit counterintuitive, but they're throwing these regularly now, to try and fix the situation. Many important clients of the bank will be there. Among them are some of the accounts that are putting the bank in trouble."

"Oh."

"He is inviting me to come over."

"And will you go?"

"I couldn't ask for a more perfect opportunity. I can get to know the situation in person, literally. And that would be a great step forward."

"You'll go there and fix everything?"

"Well, not like that, of course. I'm not going to barge in. That's just what I'm trying to avoid. It'll have to be Italian-style."

"And listen."

"Yes. And listen."

"Right, but you can do that."

I could imagine her grin. "Yes, we'll speak Italian. They'll love that."

"And then you'll try and see what you can do."

"Quite so. After a while, they may like me a bit less."

"Ah."

"But that's part of the job."

"Right. So this sounds wonderful. What's the problem exactly?"

My mum sighed. "I would need to take a plane this evening already. And I'd only be back Sunday afternoon. I don't want to leave your Dad alone."

"And Tim?"

"I think he wouldn't mind spending some more time with his grandparents."

He certainly wouldn't, I thought, because they always completely spoilt him.

She continued, "But he couldn't be at the hospital with his Dad for so long. He wouldn't manage. And you need to catch up on your UCI work. Clearly."

"Oh, right, I understand. Just give me a minute, will you? I'll call back soon."

*

I went to Claudio and explained the situation to him. He couldn't believe that our phone call could actually lead to this opportunity for my mother to go in and arrange everything. That, indeed, really was something.

But then I had to explain my situation to him. I had put a lot of pressure on my academic situation by coming to this competition. I really wanted to go for the double major, and I had vowed to give it my all once I came back. School before everything. Hobbies, friends, parents—the bare minimum until the semester was over. But now this happened. I couldn't be with my Dad all weekend, of course, only during the visiting hours. But still, that would eat a considerable amount of time that I really needed for upping my grades and finishing assignments.

"So, remind me: this double major, why did you want to do that again?"

"That's easy. I can't stop doing economics. My mum would never let me. But I want to be a doctor."

"Okay. And why a doctor?"

"Because I want to help people. I don't want my life to be just about making money."

"Sure. And that's why you can't help your parents now?"

I nodded. "Long-term preference."

"Long-term preference." Claudio scratched the back of his head. "Have you thought this over after everything that happened here?"

"Well, not really."

"So what do you think *now*, is this still the right way to go?"

"Why would it be different?"

"Oh Miriam." He leaned over backwards in his chair and closed his eyes. "What if... Hansen senior had become a doctor."

"What?" I chuckled.

"Yeah, like cured people. Would that have been nice?"

"I don't know. Was he any good at it?"

"Reasonable. Not particularly talented, but not bad either."

"Then I suppose it would have been good for his patients."

"And for all these people who wouldn't have a job, because he never made his company big?"

"Oh."

"Right." Claudio opened his eyes, bent towards me and said, "What if all Hansen seniors would become doctors? Where would that leave our economy?"

"In the hands of the Olsons?"

Claudio opened his eyes widely, raising his brows, and nodded at me. "And who will you be when you are chasing your long-term preference this weekend? Have you thought of the other stakeholders?"

*

I called back my mum and told her that I checked my UCI schedules, and that I would be okay with spending time with Dad that weekend. It took a bit of insistence to convince her, but in the end she was very grateful. She said she would be asking her secretary to book the tickets right away. She was going to talk to Dad afterwards. Again, I didn't ask her about coming to our presentation, and she didn't mention it.

Claudio and I finished up preparing our presentation. I would be the speaker. It wasn't my greatest talent, and Claudio was clearly far more theatrical, but the way the story turned out, there wasn't really another option than for me to speak. We used the last twenty minutes or so before lunch to do two practice rounds. Claudio gave some incisive feedback. He told me to keep in mind all that Dr. Loffels had told us. Speak clearly, loudly and slowly. It's not the same speaking to someone right in front of you or to someone a bit further away. If someone is further away, what seems unnatural to you comes across very naturally. Take it easy. Pauses are fine, but get rid of the 'ehs'. Look over the audience, just above their heads. I felt reassured that after this vetting session I was prepared enough to feel reasonably confident going into the presentation—even though I would probably need much more practice to do all these things well. For that, there was no time. We emailed our slides to the indicated address, and went down for lunch.

The first person we walked into was Pauline, the girl who had notified me that teamwork was part of the final assessment. She greeted Claudio heartily, and he corresponded likewise. I still felt rather sore about her remark earlier. Pauline asked about Patience, and Claudio told her that she had gone off to fix some problems at home. Pauline reacted emphatically, and showed her concern and understanding, as well as her empathy for our team. To me, it all sounded really fake.

"We haven't seen you very much, Miriam." Did she really want to meddle again? Perhaps someone could suggest to her that her manners could be a bit less direct?

"I had things to see to." I managed a faint smile.

"Right, well for some of us this was more difficult than for others. Some people have just cruised through this."

"I see. How was it for you?"

"Oh, I've had fun hanging out with people. Claudio's been great." She smiled at him. "Patience was very nice too. But there's so many nice and interesting people here. It's really amazing."

"Did you manage to work on the case a little?"

"Of course. Our team from Paris is supposed to be one of the favorites. We don't think so though, we're more here to meet people, but we did the best we could."

But I could see that she said one thing and meant another. She really believed they were going to win, just because it was them. Her slick arrogance repelled me.

As we walked into the lunchroom, it was clear that not everyone was taking things as relaxed as Pauline from Paris supposedly was. Some groups were sitting apart in one of corners, still fiercely debating some point or other in their presentation. Others were quietly waiting in line for the buffet. As Claudio walked in, several people greeted him with a smile, and he greeted them, calling everyone by their first names.

"How do you know all their names?" I asked.

"That's just important. I make the effort." He confided to me. "I also have their birthdays in my agenda already."

"Really?"

"Yeah, of course. When else will I get back in touch with them?"

"Ah."

During the lunch, for the first time I could mix and mingle at ease with the other students. They were, overall, really a nice bunch. I felt sorry about not investing in these relationships earlier. Clearly, Claudio had understood better than me the importance of taking such things seriously. And really, I had a good time. Claudio had told me to, as well. "It has to be authentic," he had said, "or it doesn't count." He explained that making friends is one of the nicest things someone can do, and you can make good friends in professional life nowadays, if you want to. But he also said that nothing kills friendship faster than people who are just trying to 'network' and get the best out of relationships for themselves. But friends help each other out.

As the lunch drew to a close, the tension rose perceptibly in the room. Word was buzzing around about whom would be presenting, and people were wishing each other luck. Some wished me luck, too. I decided to wish the same to several others. I was ready. Sort of. Bring it on.

Chapter 34

As we walked into the auditorium, the stage was appropriately dressed up with banners of the "TopStar" conference. It looked slick and fancy, just what you would expect from an occasion like this. Someone gave us a card when we entered, which could be used to vote for your favorite presentation. You had to indicate your team on it, and which of the other teams' presentations you liked best. The outcome would be used to give an audience award.

Because we were the last team to be added to the competition, they had told us we would also be the last to present. They actually presented that to us as a favor, the 'last mover advantage'. To me though, it felt more like a burden. I had to put up with the nerves during the whole session. The session would only last one-and-a-half hours. Every team had ten minutes to present, and there were five minutes for one or two questions from the audience. After all of the six teams had presented, there would be a twenty minute break, during which the jury would convene and determine the winners. That would be my time to let some steam off. Whatever they would tell me afterwards was by now fine with me, or so I told myself.

Ms. Van Es welcomed us all to the final session of the TopStar business case competition. She, the other organizers and the jurors had enjoyed seeing us wrestle with the case analysis, make friends, and learn from the process and from the feedback they had given us. They were eagerly looking forward to hearing our final presentations. With that brief introduction, she gave the floor to the first team.

What I noticed most from watching the different presentations was the generally slick style. Everyone had clearly practiced smooth delivery, in all likelihood much more than I had. You could tell. Of course, there were the accents. The unmistakably American one from the Boston team, but from the Rotterdam team too, to be honest. Then we had the French with their funny English. The Swiss presenter was clearly a German speaker, but his accent sounded quite charming. The accent I was least familiar with was that of the speaker from Riga. I was therefore the only one speaking with British pronunciation. Oh well, some refinement wouldn't be out of place here.

What was very striking was the difference in content between presentations. I was surprised to see the great differences between the different teams' take on the case. Judging from what we had been thinking about, there were some that focused more on the institutional actors, while others had more attention for the people involved. I liked the people-centered approach from Riga best. They carefully talked about the motivations of the different actors, and also talked about the difficult relationship that had grown between Olson and the people at SteadyCars over time. That point was lost on most of the other teams; some just thought Olson was trying to get back at his old boss. The Paris team, to whom I paid special attention because I now knew Pauline a little better, presented a solid story that tried to paint the overall picture of interactions between personal interests and institutional interests; they concluded that better communication could have overcome many of the setbacks that presented themselves in the deal. There was clearly some truth in that.

A presentation that stood out for its slickness and simplicity, as well as for contrast with our story, was that of the Swiss team. They spoke just before our turn. They took a one-sidedly financial view of the case, and argued that the whole situation had just been a strategy of TireDeals to get a cash cow, and of the Hansen family to sell it dearly. A friendly takeover bid would bring in relatively little cash, so that was the reason it was rejected out of hand. For the second 'inimical' takeover they would already have to take significantly larger coffers with them, but it would still be the merger between two companies in the same branch. A merger with a company from a different branch would be seen as more difficult and therefore even require a greater investment from those taking over. So that's what finally happened when TireDeals took over. The Hansens got the jackpot. So, according to the Swiss team, nothing went wrong—the Hansens just played their cards well. Even though the team presented this very smoothly, the argument rang somewhat cynically in my ears.

It wasn't a surprise to see that the Americans also excelled in a thorough analysis and a smooth delivery. Like the Swiss, they focused mainly on the financial aspect, but gave it an interesting twist. According to them, the Hansens weren't just trying to cash in on their company later on, but had negotiated in such a way that everyone had been duly compensated for their situation in the deal. Hansen Sr. had been prudent in fending the deal off while it was not 'ripe', given the situation in his company. But when everything had been well-arranged, the junior Hansens didn't hesitate to go for the deal. That's the beauty of money, they concluded: when everyone is duly compensated, it can help very different people collaborate.

I liked their take more than that of the Swiss, but because they lacked some depth in their character analysis, I filled out 'Riga' on my voting slip.

But now for my turn.

As I walked up onto the stage, I could feel the eyes of the audience on me as Ms. Bentley announced the team from Amsterdam. I'm sure they didn't look at me any differently than any of the other presenters, but because of the things I was going to say, it seemed to me as if they were trying to look straight through me. This wasn't going to be easy. But well, we had practiced, and by now, I would just stick to the plan. It surely wasn't a winning plan, but it was our plan.

The screen flipped and showed the starting page of our presentation. The title read "In our case". Claudio had thought that funny. I thought it was mildly funny, but no one laughed. Of course, you needed to understand our story to get the joke. It still made me smile a little, and with that confidence I looked up at the audience. But then I froze. At the back of the auditorium were Tim and mum.

*

I stood still for a moment, there was an expectant silence, but thoughts were racing through my head. I hadn't seen them when we walked in; they must have entered silently during the other presentations. I now felt as if saying the things I had planned to say was something akin to climbing Mount Everest. But stopping was no option, either. So I just forged ahead.

"I would like to start this presentation by making a confession. When I came to this competition, I only had one objective: I came to win. Our team was added to the competition last-minute, but I was determined to show the world that I could do this. I rearranged deadlines, cancelled on my friends, put my future studies at risk, even, sorry to say, postponed a visit to my father who is in hospital. I was going to win and prove myself."

A deep silence had descended on the room as I said these things. My mum moved restlessly. I had certainly caught their attention.

"When I came here with Claudio, whom many of you know, Patience Owusu came and picked us up by car. She eventually even decided to join our team, because there were only the two of us, and she thought we could use some help."

"Before coming here, we had elaborated a 'master plan'. This consisted of a novel approach to case analysis, which I will now briefly introduce."

I pulled up the slide on which we first introduced the idea that we were going to use a table to analyze the way every stakeholder would evaluate the 'DEAL' and 'NO DEAL' scenario. I explained that our table would include reference to how that stakeholder would think about three different types of motivations for himself and other stakeholders.

On the second slide, I introduced the extrinsic, intrinsic and relational motivations, and explained how we would use an overall view of these motivations and the circumstances to come to an overall view of the utility for that stakeholder. I explained that the overall utility would be categorized in five possible categories, from very negative to very positive.

On the third slide, I explained the relationship factor as a way to weigh the importance of other stakeholders' utility for the decision maker.

I then pulled up the next slide, which showed the start of our case analysis for Olson, the main protagonist of the case.

Olson

| Stakeholder | Relationship | DEAL | | | | Overall |
| | | Perceived Utility | | | | |
		ext	int	rel	U	
Olson himself	1	++	+		2	2

"This simple table already contains a lot of info. Let's see." I went on to show how we 'coded' Olson's evaluation of the situation for himself into the table. It had a very positive external effect for him, by solving his company's problems, and that translated in to a +2 utility overall. I showed that the relationship to himself is one, by definition.

The next slide contained the other stakeholders.

Olson

| Stakeholder | Relationship | DEAL | | | | Overall |
| | | Perceived Utility | | | | |
		ext	int	rel	U	
Olson himself	1	++	+		2	2
FlashCars	1	++	+		2	2
SteadyCars	0.1				0	0
TireDeals	0.3	+			1	0.3
Bianchi	0.1	+			1	0.1
Walker	0.1	+			1	0.1
StrongSteel	0.1	+			1	0.1
Grand total						4.6

"Most people and companies he cares about would be happy with the deal, because their FlashCars stocks would go up—and he doesn't think it will be negative for SteadyCars, either." I noted how his expectation for Bianchi's happiness with the deal did not turn out to be correct. "But we didn't think he saw that coming."

Finally, I showed the complete table, with also the 'NO DEAL' scenario included.

Olson

Stakeholder	Relationship	DEAL						No DEAL				
		Perceived Utility				Overall		Perceived Utility				Overall
		ext	int	rel	U			ext	int	rel	U	
Olson himself	1	++	+		2	2		--			-2	-2
FlashCars	1	++	+		2	2		--			-2	-2
SteadyCars	0.1				0	0					0	0
TireDeals	0.3	+			1	0.3		-			-1	-0
Bianchi	0.1	+			1	0.1		-			-1	-0
Walker	0.1	+			1	0.1		+			1	0
StrongSteel	0.1	+			1	0.1		-			1	0
Grand total						4.6						-4

I pointed out that, according to our reading of the case, Olson mainly saw the positive effect of the merger for FlashCars and therefore for himself. We thought his main focus was on the external payoffs. This merger would get him out of trouble, he thought. Overall, the utility of the DEAL scenario was way more positive than the NO DEAL scenario for him, so he really wanted to go for it.

I then went on to the next slide, that of Hansen Sr.

Hansen Sr.

Stakeholder	Relationship	DEAL					NO DEAL				
		Perceived Utility				Overall	Perceived Utility				Overall
		ext	int	rel	U		ext	int	rel	U	
Hansen himself	1	+		-	1	1			+	1	1
Hansen family	1	+			1	1				0	0
Olson	-0.2	++			2	-0	--			-2	0
Larsen	0.3	-		-	-1	-0	+		+	1	0
SteadyCars	1		- -		-2	-2				0	0
the workers' union	0.5		-		-1	-1	+			1	1
Norwegian govt and country	1	- -	- -		-2	-2	+			1	1
Grand total						-3					3

Here, I pointed out that the situation was more complex. Hansen cared about his own and his family's income, and in that sense the deal would be good for him. But at the same time he saw it would put Larsen's job at risk, which would mean an uncertain future for SteadyCars, the workers' union didn't like it, and it wouldn't be good for Norway. For all these stakeholders, the 'no deal' scenario would be way better. So taking everything into account, Hansen Sr. opposed the deal.

Now it was time to move on to the complete picture. "We did analyses like this for all the relevant actors in the case. And this is what came out." I showed them the table Claudio, Patience and I had produced this morning.

	DEAL	NO DEAL	Difference Overall Score (pro-Deal is positive)	# Stakeholders
TireDeals	1.7	-1.7	3.4	4
StrongSteel	1.7	-1.7	3.4	4
FlashCars	1.8	0.6	1.2	6
Worker Unions	-2.9	0.9	-3.8	3
SteadyCars	-2.4	1.7	-4.1	5
Norway	-4	2	-6	3
Olson	4.6	-4.2	8.8	7
Walker	4.4	-1.1	5.5	6
Hansen sons (without Father)	1	1.2	-0.2	6
Bianchi	-2.5	-0.5	-2	4
Hansen Sr.	-3.2	3.2	-6.4	7
Larsen	-6	4.8	-10.8	6

I then pointed out to the audience how this deal was overall positive for everyone related to FlashCars and its shareholders, with the exception of Bianchi, but not for SteadyCars and its stakeholders. The table also made clear that, in our perception, Hansen Sr. had a much bigger problem with the deal than his sons had. This an important element of our explanation of why the deal did go through later, even though the entire situation must have changed by that time.

I also made the point about the lesser number of stakeholders in the institutional analysis, because when one starts to think in terms of institutions, it's easy not to assign people with the same importance. On the other hand, from the perspective of the people, the institutions are important. So, the people perspective is more inclusive, or such was our perception.

I continued, pointing out that what these tables don't show is the genesis of the negative relationship between Olson and the SteadyCars people. "It's clear that the tables are just a snapshot of what is happening at that particular moment. But to get to that moment, history had its role to play. Olson was called a 'tiger fish', and had clearly developed habits of not listening and pushing through his views. That lack of relational ability cost him dearly at the point of the case."

I sighed tensely. Time to wrap up, but the worst was still to come.

I looked steadily at the audience. "So, you may say, your Masterplan didn't turn out too badly. Your analysis shows that the deal was much more attractive to FlashCars than to SteadyCars. That's why Hansen Sr. was responsible for blocking it, and he did so with good reason. You also see that the *dynamic between the actors* was perhaps even more responsible than any one actor. And there are lessons to be drawn about the importance of including stakeholders in decision analysis, about the deal not going through being good news to some and bad news to others, and a lesson for Olson: he might have, after all, saved himself a lot of trouble by being aware of his bad relationship to others and working at that earlier."

Was I really going to say what we had planned next? Even with mum and Tim in the room? I felt the sweat moistening the palms of my hands. I took a deep breath, and said it.

"But really, the take home message for me is this: 'I have been Olson, and wasn't aware of it'. In my desire to win this competition, I didn't think of my stakeholders, the other people in my team. Our whole effort came very close to falling apart. You may see the humor in it, but it's only then that I applied my method to our team. There were three scenarios: we try and win, we try and lose, and we don't try. I'll spare you the details, but here's what came out."

Scenario	Payoff
GO & WIN	4.3
GO & LOSE	-7.2
NO GO	5.5

"And here's what we decided: NO GO. Or rather, go the minimum. The one presenting here should have been Patience. She is much more charismatic than I am. But she has gone off to fix a problem at home. Our report should have elaborated much more on precisely why we evaluated the stakeholders the way we did. But we didn't go there; instead, we decided to fix other things in our lives first. What I have told you is the outline of a story that could have been really nice: a deal that went through. But it didn't. I have now chosen to be 'Hansen Sr.'. Thank you for your attention."

After finishing my speech, I looked down at the ground as an uneasy silence settled upon the audience. After a few seconds, though, one person started applauding—and as I looked up I saw that he had even stood up! Soon after, a second person joined in, a third, and then the whole audience stood up clapping—including Tim and mum. It was a standing ovation. I was dumbstruck.

When the applause died down, Ms. Van Es came alongside to me to say that there was time for one final question. My breath faltered as I saw my mother stand up. Taking the microphone handed to her by the assistant, she introduced herself, citing the bank she worked at, also mentioning that she was my mother. "I don't have a question, but I do have something to add to the story. After my daughter has bravely stood up there and said she has acted like Olson, I feel I also have to stand up publicly and apologize. Because the real Olson has been me." Her voice faltered at these last words, and she had to overcome her emotion before she continued in an unsteady voice, "I have always had very high expectations of Miriam, also for her professional future. Miriam came here, probably, to resist my dominance and show she can do things her way. And she was right to do that. I should have been more open and listened to her desires. So Olson was me, and I am sorry." With that she gave the microphone to Tim, bowed her head forwards and shielded it with her arms. You could see she was quietly crying. In the silence that ensued, you could feel people were impressed and didn't know what to do. I hesitated a moment, but then jumped off the stage, ran to my mum and gave her a big hug.

There was another standing ovation.

Chapter 35

The session had ended, everyone left the room except Tim, mum and me. Tim was unsure what to do, but he said he would go and see Claudio and also went off. I didn't know what to say to my mother, but she understood that.

"You know how this happened?" she asked.

I shook my head.

"I went to see dad." She explained how after our phone call she had talked to dad, and after discussing the banking situation, he had asked about why she thought I had gone off to the contest. When she hadn't been able to respond with anything very substantive, Dad had shown her a video message that Patience had sent him in the morning. I reasoned that Patience had sent it just after breakfast, when she had stood up to me.

Mum explained that in the message, Patience had advised my Dad to talk about my reasons for going to the contest without my mum's consent. Patience had explained her impression that I didn't feel understood by my mother, and that this was one of the leading reasons for me to join the competition. I needed some independence and was trying to prove it this way. Patience also suggested that my mum perhaps didn't understand the situation, and that talking about it might help everyone further. "We didn't have to talk much further really, I had to let this sink in, but I saw it was true," Mum remarked.

Patience had also suggested that she would come in the afternoon to be with my dad, so that Tim and my mum could come to Rotterdam. They agreed to the plan—and that's what happened.

I gave my mum another hug, but then excused myself. I was quite overwhelmed after everything that happened, so much so that I had to retreat a little to process what had just happened. I wound my way to the ladies room. People smiled at me on the way there, and told me "wow" or "impressive". I still couldn't believe that this was happening.

I decided to take a short walk outside, and suddenly realized that Patience would by now already have finished talking to her father and be with my dad. I decided to give her a call to ask how it went. She picked up straight away.

"Miriam?" Patience said.

"Yes, how did it go?" I asked.

"Oh thank God, it was so good."

"Really?"

"Yes. I did what you said. I listened and Dad explained everything."

"Oh good."

"And then of course, when he finished, I... I didn't really know what to do."

"And what happened?"

"He just saw that I was uncomfortable and asked why."

"And then?"

"And then I just explained mum's side of the story."

"So what did he say?"

"He said he loves her very much."

"What?"

"Yes: that the situation is very difficult, but that he will do anything to get through it with her."

"Wow."

"Yes, I told you he is really good."

"And did you ask him to apologize?"

"Well, I suggested it, and he immediately agreed it was a good idea."

"Wow."

"Not everything is solved you know, we still have money issues. And there are still investments to be decided about. But I think they really want to tackle things together."

"That's wonderful."

"Thanks so much Miriam, I couldn't have done it without you."

"I can say the same to you!"

"Really? What happened?"

I explained the story to her, and finished with, "We're waiting for the awards ceremony now, but the whole thing was just incredibly well received. I don't know what will happen."

"That's really great. Let me know as soon as you know, alright?"

"I will."

And with that, we broke the connection. Again, I couldn't believe all the things that were happening. I suppose this is what Claudio and I had expected to happen with Patience. But the fact that it actually happened was really great. Now I had to go back to face the other students. Was I ready? Not really, but well.

I slowly walked up the stairs to the lounge where the drinks were held. I first met one of the Swiss students, who greeted me formally, with a bit of distance. But soon other students came to congratulate me on the talk, the Americans with their typical exaggeration: "Wow, what an event, incredibly amazing!" But then we had a girl from Riga who shyly said she had really appreciated my contribution. I could honestly say the same about their talk. That was a really nice exchange.

Then there was Pauline. I tried to avoid her, but she came towards me. There was no getting around her. I was wondering how she was planning to sting me now.

"Miriam."

I looked in the other direction.

"Miriam. Listen. I... also... want to say I'm sorry. I didn't..."

I turned to face her and dryly said, "Thank you." Even though it wasn't the sting I was expecting, I didn't like the idea that she had been in the audience while I was giving my speech, and much less when my mum intervened. And why would she care to apologize anyway? Would I ever see her again?

"May I explain?" she pleaded.

I knew that I should let her talk, but my head was still spinning too much. At that moment, I saw Claudio. I said "Sorry, another time" to Pauline, and walked over to him.

Claudio had been standing back while I received the congratulations of the other people. But when they were finished, he came up and gave me another one of his big hugs. "I'm so proud of you," he whispered. I didn't see my mum there, she had probably retreated as well.

*

With all the congratulating going on, I didn't know what to think while going into the final session with the awards. I was rather confused. Surely, we wouldn't win the award with a presentation saying that we had decided not to present, and that admitted handing in a flawed document. That would just be too strange. Oh well, I just decided to let it all just happen. But I sat down in my chair with a bit of a tremble, telling myself that this really wasn't the most important thing. But my goodness, the tension had come back to me in spades! Mum and Tim came and sat next to me, and it was good to have them there.

After calming everyone down, and making sure everyone was seated, Ms. Bentley took the microphone. She thanked all the groups for their submissions and presentations, and said, "Juries tend to say that the decision on awarding prizes is really difficult. But I don't think they would say so if they would have had to judge this contest before their own. I don't think any of us have ever had to make such a difficult call. All of your contributions have been truly outstanding. Please award yourself with applause."

The audience erupted in applause. The students looked at one another nervously.

"At this point I would like to remind you about the seven criteria that we promised to judge the contest by. The four content-criteria are: identification of relevant facts from the case, the plausibility of the interpretation given to the facts, soundness of reasoning, and cogency of the answers to the three key questions posed and the overall conclusions. The three form-criteria concern the way of presenting and structuring the final report and the final presentation. The last form criterion is teamwork. The audience award, as is logical, was not awarded by the jury, but by counting your voting slips after you saw the presentations.

"Before we give the results of our jury evaluation, in which we've meticulously followed the established criteria, we would like to point out that the jury is not blind to the great difference in the interpretations of the case that have been put forward. One could even speak of a 'war of the worldviews', with a very materialist approach on the one end, and a much more personal, relationship-centered approach on the other. Or perhaps more modestly, we could call it a confrontation between different interpretations of economics and business. Even though each juror has their own convictions, we have tried not to let these interfere with our final decision. Again, we have followed the established criteria.

"With that said, it is time to announce the winner of this year's TopStar case competition. This team had a very business-like way of interpreting the case, but had an open mind towards the relational elements that business and economics involves. Their reasoning was straightforward and clear, and their conclusions followed coherently from their analysis. Their report was impeccably structured and their presentation fluently delivered. The team acted as an organic whole. Please congratulate the winners of this year's TopStar competition: the team from Boston!"

From the start of Ms. Bentley's description I knew that the prize was not going to be ours. Well, again, that was to be expected. We had consciously given up on it. It was no surprise. But, surprisingly, it still hurt a little. Even though they weren't my favorites, the Americans' presentation had made sense to me—and at least it wasn't as cynical as the Swiss. So I applauded together with Claudio, who was of course cheering exuberantly from the start, as the Americans walked on stage to receive their price.

It was nice to see the American team standing on stage radiantly, with their semi-formal, semi-nonchalant manners. They received the flowers, the applause and the cardboard cheque. The audience stood up to cheer them. We joined in.

After the applause had died down, and both the audience and the Americans had taken their seats, Ms. Bentley once again addressed the audience. "Before this case competition started, we had a discussion with the organization about whether we wanted to have an audience award. At this point I can say that all of the jurors are particularly pleased that this year's edition does have an audience award. We have counted all of your voting slips. And the result is not surprising. Let's not spend many more words on it. Miriam has stolen our hearts. The audience award is for the team from Amsterdam!"

A roar went up from audience as everyone immediately stood up and applauded. I stayed seated in astonishment. Perhaps I might have expected this to happen, but somehow I hadn't. I took a few seconds before Claudio and Tim helped me get moving from my seat, and Claudio and I walked up to the stage. As we came up, another roar went up from the audience. I looked towards them and shyly made a gesture of acknowledgement. I hadn't expected this much enthusiasm. The jurors gave us flowers, kisses and even another cheque. In my drive to go for the top award, I hadn't even as much as noticed that the audience award also had some money attached to it. Even though it was significantly less than the main prize, we had still won €10,000. I couldn't believe my eyes. When we had received the award, I gestured my mum to also come up to the stage, and gave her another hug, which was also greeted with applause.

When we had gone back to our seats, Ms. Bentley thanked everyone again, and invited all the participants to stay for the final drinks. The photographer asked to take some extra pictures of Claudio and me, with and without the American team. There was also a short video interview, asking us how we felt after winning the audience award. I thought saying 'confused' would not come across very well, but I was at loss for alternatives. Happily, Claudio spoke up and said we were very happy with the support from the audience, and that I had done a great job telling my story, our story, and relating that to the case. The family situation had made everything memorable. When the interviewer in the end asked how I felt, all I managed to say was 'really grateful'. And I suppose that was the most appropriate thing to say—for so many reasons.

*

We went to the final drinks for a bit, but soon I had to remind Claudio that I should go relieve Patience, and that my father was waiting for my company. My mum was also flying out to Italy that evening, so we had to get going. He understood that I had to leave, but said, "So, perhaps we should discuss this later, but what shall we do with the prize money?"

"Oh. Good point. Why?"

"Do you need it?" he asked.

"Eh. Do you?"

Claudio shrugged. "It's nice, of course, but I think Patience can use it better."

Well, that was something. I was impressed that he should be thinking about that at this particular moment. But I was still too confused to say anything. In the end I just said, "Good idea, is it okay if I discuss it with my family?"

"Yeah, no problem." And then he went back to mafia-mode. "Are they to be trusted though?"

I put on my poshest British accent in reply, "Claudio, what are you suggesting? That my family is adopting your famiglia's ways?"

We both laughed, and gave each other a long hug. "See you on Monday" Claudio whispered in my ear.

I nodded silently as we let go. I got in the car with my mum and Tim.

*

We drove to Schiphol, where my mum would have to take the plane not long after. We parked there. I said I would go to see Dad afterwards, and Tim offered to look after the house.

"Look after the house?" I said in astonishment. I wanted to add 'and burn it down' but I kept myself.

"Mir!" he said fiercely, "You know, without me all this wouldn't have happened. I helped Claudio so that mum and I could come see you. I can be responsible."

There was a point I hadn't considered. Mum and I consented to him taking care of the house, and after saying goodbye to him, we each took the public transport in our respective directions.

I was still quite confused. All the emotions and surprises of the day still needed to settle down in me. What had really happened? I was actually really happy to have some time with my Dad to talk to him. Perhaps he could help me make sense of things. It was around dinner time when I got to the hospital. Patience had messaged me that she needed to leave a bit earlier, so I didn't catch her there. Fortunately, my Dad hadn't dined when I got there, and I was able to accompany him during his dinner.

He was really happy to see me, and gave me a big hug. I hadn't been there for long when a nurse brought some dinner. It wasn't too much, but it looked acceptable enough. "Look at this, you treat me better than in a five-star restaurant", he said, with a wink to the nurse.

As he started on his dinner he asked me how the contest went. I couldn't contain myself, so I just spoke my heart.

"Very good, but very confusing."

"Confusing?"

I explained how mum's apology had come as a complete surprise to me. It was a beautiful thing, but also raised a lot of questions.

"About what?"

"Don't know, about me, what I want, the future."

"I see."

As I talked about the future, his illness hit me again with full force. "Dad, how do you... how do you deal with your... situation like that?"

"Sorry? What does that have to do with anything?" His voice was kind, and I could see he was rather surprised.

"I'll explain. It has a lot to do with everything. But can you answer me?" If I would figure out how he managed to deal with what he was going through, then certainly I could learn how to feel better now.

"Well, what do you mean exactly?"

"You're always so optimistic. Light-hearted, you know." I looked at him with questioning eyes.

"Oh that." He smiled to himself. "I suppose my Dad taught me that. He went through a lot, as you know. He always bore it lightly. I admired that, still do. I try to imitate him. I don't do as well as he, I don't think, but it is what it is."

"You're wonderful, dad."

"Well, very wonderful, but if Patience hadn't helped me, I wouldn't have been able to deal with the situation... between you and your mum, you know. Why don't you explain what happened."

I gave my version of the events and then said, "I'm so confused. I've... I've always tried really hard to reach my goals. That's what everything and everyone is telling me. At school, everything is aimed at high grades. And I need to do well at my studies, so I can be like mum. Have a high position in the bank. That's what she wants for me, right? But now... now I've tried to be independent. And independently, I've tried to do the same: reach my goals, be the best. But, because of everything that happened, I actually stopped doing that. I gave up winning. I didn't go for my goal. And I confessed that in public, too. And what happened then? Mum did the same. People stood up and applauded us, dad! It's so confusing." I felt a tear rolling down my cheek.

"Come here, little lady," my dad said, giving my head a hug while I bent over to him—which was the only remotely possible hug while sitting on his bed with what was left of his dinner in front of him.

When I had bent back up, I continued. "And what you and grandpa are doing to your... to the things you go through. And surely they prevent you from reaching your goals. Still, you don't despair, or even get grumpy. Do you know what made grandpa be like that?"

"Yes. I think I do. Your grandfather was a very religious man. I did ask about this once. He said that for him, suffering was a way to come closer to God and to other people. And that's what made it meaningful to him, what made him happy. He said something about carrying the cross with Christ. I didn't quite understand that. I stopped going to church when I was a teenager. Still, I really admired the idea that suffering can bring you closer to people. I can really see that it strengthens relationships—if carried well, of course. It's happening now, too, at this very moment." He smiled at me with a broad smile, which made me give him another semi-hug.

"So you see," he continued, "the real question is what health really is. And what freedom really is, for that matter."

"What do you mean?"

"Well, the doctors are trying to cure me, and that's important. But still, since I've been in hospital, my relationship to your mother has never been better. And in the past... may I say? ... that had me worried sick at times. Of course, I tried to hide it so that you and Tim wouldn't notice."

"Oh."

"But now, even today, you gave your mother this amazing opportunity to fix her career, and she would even have rejected it if you hadn't come to take care of me. That's just amazing. It makes me feel very whole. And very liberated, even though I'm tied to this bed." While he said this, a nurse walked in. She asked whether he was finished eating. He said he was, and she took away the tray table.

"Good questions." I said. "But I have even more."

"Like which ones?"

"You know, Harry Jacobsen was in the jury, mum knows him. But the jury didn't give us a prize, the audience did."

"Silly girl," my dad smiled affectionately, "what did you expect? Bankers are just people. What would you do in his place?"

I had to think back to the quirky Mr. and Mrs. Broekhuijze. They hadn't seemed very extraterrestrial to me. But how do networks work then? Was I going to ask dad about that now? Maybe not. There were other things.

"The jury said some things that I didn't understand. Ms. Bentley spoke of a 'war of the worldviews'. And then later, when she gave me the prize, she said I had 'stolen their hearts'. Why did she say these things?"

"It sounds like you still have a lot to think about."

"Don't you know what this all means dad?"

"I have my suspicions. But now I'm a bit tired. And have you had dinner yet?"

I said I hadn't, and he encouraged me to go home to Tim. He would take a nap, because he was feeling very sleepy lately. I could come see him tomorrow and we would continue talking about life, and also about what to do with Patience and the prize money. I gave him a big hug, the biggest ever, and walked out of the hospital. I thought about how much less confused I felt now compared to when I came in. And it wasn't that all my questions were answered. It was just... my dad.

I felt deeply and exceedingly grateful.

Chapter 36

It was early July, about two-and-a-half years later, when my mum, Tim and I met Claudio and his family at the Leidseplein in Amsterdam. Earlier that day, we had been to the Carré Theater, where our bachelor degrees in the liberal arts and sciences had been conferred upon us. It had been a wonderful ceremony, and we were still enjoying the afterglow. I greeted Claudio with a casual kiss, and I also gave kisses to his parents. My mother opted for the slightly more formal Dutch three-kisses approach, while Tim gave them all a somewhat shy handshake.

We had agreed to find a restaurant around here together, to celebrate the day's event. Claudio had said he was fine with any type of restaurant, as long as it was not Italian, because his irritation with Italian food in the Netherlands hadn't diminished. "They do their best, but if an Italian cooks it in the Netherlands, it doesn't taste like Italy." So far for an open mind in food issues... In the end, we decided on a place which served food from three different kitchens, so that everyone would have plenty to choose from. It was a nice place; it looked homely enough, even though it was quite big, and had several rows of tables. It felt like an agreeable place to celebrate this evening. And there was room enough for all of us.

When we had sat down, Claudio received a text from Patience, saying that she and her family would be arriving in ten minutes. They had already announced being slightly delayed, and had asked us to find a place. He told them where we were seated. Once we had ordered drinks, Patience and her parents walked into the restaurant. They were received with open arms, and Patience came to sit at the head of the table next to Claudio and me, while her parents moved over to the other side.

Patience's parents started asking about our impressions of the ceremony, even though Patience must have told them something already. We were able to get her a ticket, even though these were quite scarce and strictly rationed at two accompanying persons per student. So in the end everyone present at the dinner except Patience's parents had been there. Everyone was happy with the musical and creative performances in the interlude, the nice speeches, and impressed by the diversity of themes that graduating students had addressed in their bachelor theses.

We soon started looking at the menu, and not long afterward the waitress came to take our orders. Claudio tried to confuse the waitress by first addressing her in Italian, then in Spanish. But she didn't budge at all. When asked where she was from, she said from Poland. She was clearly used to an international crowd.

Soon enough, everyone had their drinks, and was suitably engaged in small talk. Claudio and I had spoken to Patience earlier today, but with all the classmates, families and friends to talk to, we hadn't really had much opportunity to catch up. Not that that was really necessary, we did speak to her regularly, but during the last month she had been especially busy at work. There had been a special event at the local television station that she worked at, and she had been heavily involved in the organization. So even though our last month at UCI had not been that intense, there was certainly some catching up to do. Claudio was very amused to hear her speak about a black-gospel choir that had performed; he started singing, "Oh Happy Day" in imitation. I tried to shut him up quickly, looking around embarrassed at the other guests. But of course, Claudio couldn't be bothered.

*

Everyone was in high spirits when the food was served sometime later. It looked really good, and Claudio even nodded approvingly when he examined his mother's and dad's plate. Of course he looked in dismay at what I had ordered. "How can you eat that?" But, really, I had gotten used to that by now. Just his way of teasing.

When everyone was served, my mum, who was sitting next to me, stood up to say a few words, and asked for a moment of silence. She added, "and perhaps we can particularly remember those whom we would have liked to be here with us today." Her voice faltered at the end of this sentence, and as I looked sideways to her, I saw a tear rolling down her cheek. I felt the emotion well up in me too, as I thought of my dad, who had now passed away two years ago. The wound was still very fresh for mum, Tim and me. Especially the days leading up to an event like this, had weighed heavily, as we thought of how much dad would have liked to be here. Soon enough, the 'fire brigade' had also reached my cheeks, and I gave my mum a big hug.

Sitting around the table with all these people, I thought of how true my dad's insight had been that suffering can unite people. Of course, he and mum had not only supported the idea to give the prize money to Patience and her family, which contribution in the end had only been a drop in the ocean to their troubles, but above all he had invited the family to meet with him and his wife to discuss their situation. Their expert advice, in an atmosphere of trust created by Patience's relationship to me, was what had really helped to calm down the anxieties in the household. And with some solid investments, eventually, their situation had improved considerably. Ever since, our families had been closely connected in friendship.

But perhaps the biggest surprise to me had been the help Patience's family had given my father in carrying his illness. When they learnt he had shared in his youth the same faith that they professed, Patience's father had asked whether he would appreciate having some spiritual assistance. Dad had thought that over for some time, and in the end, he said he would. So they arranged for the Indian priest of the west-African community to come over and visit my dad. He visited him several times, and I was always amazed to see how much good these visits did my father. Of course, Patience and her parents came to visit him too, and he really appreciated their attention. They laughed a lot together. Now, they gave my mum and I understanding looks as we hugged each other.

*

When I looked at Claudio, I saw that he was also struggling a bit. He probably would have liked to have had his brother here. In the past years, though, the theme of his brother hadn't come up as much as I had expected. But now I did think it might be appropriate to ask Claudio, "What would Giuseppe have said today?"

Claudio looked down at his plate pensively for a moment, and then said, "He would have been nineteen by now."

"I'm sure you'd still be best friends." Patience said.

"Probably. So many jokes we didn't make, experiences we didn't have together." He looked up at us and said in an attempting-to-be-upbeat tone, "because of that, I don't know what he would've said."

"Your buddy," was the only thing I could think of.

Claudio wouldn't be Claudio if he let an emotional moment like this last one second longer than necessary. So to break the spell, he immediately told Patience, on a more humorous note, "I have to say, you have an enormous appetite." And indeed, the Argentinian steak before her was not one of the smallest.

Patience was quick on her feet and countered decisively, "Mind your own plate."

"Well, it's not just your plate, it shows a little too, you know."

"Claudio!" I exclaimed.

"Well, it's true," he said while raising his shoulders in a theatrical display of protested innocence. And he did actually have a point. Patience had visibly gained weight, compared to her slender self a few years back.

But Patience took the frontal attack sportingly, and stretched out her arm to Claudio, with the flat palm of her hand facing him, "Well, talk to the hand, 'cause the head ain't listenin'," she sang at him while rocking her head to both sides.

Claudio and I broke out in laughter. "You've watched Oprah too much," I giggled.

*

As the conversation went on, we did come back to the theme of health. Patience told us that in her community, overweight and obesity was a problem that people were being made very aware of. There had been studies on the Ghanaian and Surinamese populations in Amsterdam, which had shown that these populations have a life expectancy of twenty years less than the average Dutch person.

"For us, food is a sign of wealth." She explained. "So when there is plenty, we make plenty of food, and we eat."

"I suppose that in Ghana, food shortage is a problem." I suggested.

"It's a problem. But it's also not a problem. So perhaps you're hungry. But we say, 'if you have God, you have everything.' And we're happy. Here, people are not happy. Not everyone, not most people."

That made me think back to the question my Dad had asked me, and that I had thought about often afterwards, 'what is health'? I had finally decided to major in social science, focusing on economics, but I had also taken a rather significant minor in science, with mostly medical subjects. It wasn't enough to get into medical school, but enough to know a bit more about the biomedical basis of health. But all these classes hadn't answered my father's question. So I said, "My dad, just before he died, told me, 'Miriam, promise me you'll always keep on asking the big questions. Never think you've found all the answers, but also never despair of your ability to find more true answers.'" I smiled at my friends, "Don't you think that's beautiful?"

They agreed it was.

"Well," I went on, "'What is health?' is one of these big questions, I think."

"Well said," Claudio agreed.

"And I think that for people here, it's very important to realize that for your community, physical health is not the highest priority in life."

"That's true. Otherwise they won't connect to my people."

"So why don't we think a bit more about what health really means? I mean, all the different meanings it can have, and what implications that has for talking about it with people."

"Are you thinking of spiritual health?" Patience asked.

"That could be, or healthy relationships," I said, thinking back to my father, "but there may be other important kinds of health that we're not thinking of now."

"And then we do what?" Claudio asked.

"We talk about it with people." I said.

"So why don't we start talking right away?" he suggested.

"What do you mean?"

"Well, we bring people together to talk about this theme. We could make it into a conference."

"Yeah, or our own case-study competition!" Patience exclaimed.

"Nice." I said.

"This could be really important for my community," Patience murmured, thoughtfully.

"And what's in it for you, Claudio? As an economist?"

"Let me think. You could say that our economy is sick every so often, when a new crisis threatens. Or at a smaller level: companies can be healthy or sick. What does it really mean for a company to be healthy? I think that would be super interesting to explore. And there's a parallel, right?"

"Sure." I agreed.

"But that's easy. A company is healthy when there's enough money, right? And the economy—same thing," Patience remarked.

"That's like saying that there's nothing more to health than a healthy body though..." Claudio replied thoughtfully.

Patience looked up at him, consideringly. "Ah."

"Loffels once told me that—and you'll like this—you can even see an image of God in the economy."

"What? How?" You could see he drew Patience's full attention with that remark.

"Well, you know, Christians think that God is a Trinity of persons, three persons, one God, correct?"

Patience nodded.

"So there are different persons that form a unity in love. Well, economics, if everything goes well, helps very different people to collaborate. And the very different persons working together add value for everyone. So there are differences coming together in unison, like the Trinity."

"Out of love though?"

"Well, some form of love, you could say. There are different types, remember?"

Patience looked puzzled.

"Anyway, an unhealthy economy is one in which this mechanism doesn't work well enough or breaks down, I'd say. So that's more than there not being enough money—even though enough money may help the economy work well."

All this was a bit mind-boggling to me, but I found it really interesting.

"Okay, let's think about our plan a bit more. Do we have time?" Claudio asked.

"I have some time over the holidays."

Patience and Claudio said they also did, and we decided to meet about the issue the following week.

Reflecting a little, I proposed in a quiet voice, "Shall we dedicate the project to my dad?" Patience and Claudio gladly agreed to that, too.

*

Claudio mentioning economic crises made me think of the connection he had made between my mum and his uncle. We asked Patience whether she had ever heard the story. When she said she hadn't really, I asked my mother, who had been busy talking to Claudio's and Patience's parents, to tell her the story. I knew I was doing her a favor, because it was one of her favorite stories to tell. Whenever an opportunity would appear at a party, she would talk about it. So much so, that people in our family were quite tired of it. But this was a fresh pair of ears.

My mum eagerly took the opportunity, and explained how things had gone much the way she had predicted beforehand. When she arrived, everything had been nicety and pleasant surprise: to have a friend of the family from the Netherlands come over who spoke Italian, appreciated the culture, and was knowledgeable about finance. She had spent the late Friday afternoon and evening getting acquainted with people, and because the party was not too large and the people were quite open, she had integrated into the company quite smoothly by the end of the first day already.

But not too long after, even on Saturday, business issues would pop up in the conversations. Of course, the whole setting had been created to discuss these in a relaxed atmosphere. And when these popped up, it soon turned out that my mother had a rather more strict view on the measures to be taken than what the Italian businesspeople were waiting for. This had led to one notable 'drama scene', with conversation partners theatrically espousing their unbelief at the solutions she proposed. Things had nearly derailed completely when she had been too direct with one of the most important clients. One of the Italian bankers had then saved the day by pulling open a bottle of Champagne and toasting to the birthday of the client's daughter. Mostly, though, my mum had managed to be patient and to listen, and with her Dutch cool head and feminine tact, she managed to gradually bring across the reasonability of her strict vision.

Of course, after her visit, the bank's problems hadn't been resolved. But the Italian bankers were very happy with the 'wedge' she had driven into the difficult accounts. It had been the start of several conversations that would later lead to a more stable situation for the bank. And the stability of this pivotal bank had in turn been essential to soften the outbreak of a new financial crisis in Italy. Something had happened, but it had been controllable. And, she would always add, it wouldn't have happened without a phone call from her daughter and her classmate. The blessings of relationships in the information age...

*

After the story, and more flowing conversation, when everyone had finished their main course, Patience stood up. She asked everyone, even though she was aware this was a bit unusual, to come stand in a circle in a small open space next to the table. We looked around, and when there seemed to be enough room that we wouldn't bother other people, we agreed to her request. She asked all the parents and Tim to make a circle outside with the six of them, while the three of us were standing in the middle.

As the whole set-up was arranged, Patience started giggling. "I'm not very good at speeches." And she looked nervous.

Claudio put a hand on her shoulder. "Relax."

She sighed. "I want to say that today is a very special day. You have both graduated. You have a university bachelor in social scienccs, from a very good liberal arts college. Well done!"

Everyone standing around the circle applauded.

Patience giggled again. "What I just said you already knew." A chuckle went around the circle. "But what I can say, and what you still will not fully know, is how blessed I feel to have friends like you. And how amazing it is that we have brought together our families. And that we have faced good times and bad times together. It is a blessing, and I am very happy.

"For now, all I want to say is: let's keep our friendship alive, and let us help many more people through it. Thank you."

Claudio smiled tender-heartedly at this short speech, and pulled both Patience and me in to a group hug. And the circle of people standing around us smiled and applauded.

*

If you have enjoyed this book, please consider leaving a review of it at your favorite retailer. We hope this story can help many people grow personally, and that it can lead to interesting conversations with colleagues, friends and family. For that, social support is indispensable—and leaving an honest review is a great way to support the project. Thanks so much!

To further deepen the themes addressed in this book from various angles, please visit www.danielbernardus.com . From there, we will be able to send you a free mini-course on "The meanings of success" which explains the views of success that Miriam, Claudio, and Patience exemplify in three short video's.

Other resources at www.danielbernardus.com include "Economics and Love", a book that further explains the economical thought behind "WIN WIN WIN" and "Freedom in Quarantine", a book that explores the philosophical inspiration for the story. We hope these resources will help you get the most out of your reading experience, as well as your discussions with colleagues, friends, and family.

Educators can visit www.danielbernardus.com for educational resources and a free educational license for the pdf-version of WIN WIN WIN in the context of an educational collaboration.

About the authors

Daniel Bernardus
Daniel Bernardus is a religious theoretical biologist fascinated by life, especially human life. He teaches interdisciplinary courses about health at a liberal arts college in Amsterdam. His PhD in biology was about cholesterol and mathematics. He is crazy enough to dream of a second PhD in philosophy. He has a passion for a healthy human heart, biologically, socially and spiritually. He would like to help people get to know their own hearts and find their way to personal health and personal growth. What he most enjoys is reflecting about big life questions with others in a relaxed setting. This is why he edits the free "Relax, Relate, Reflect about Big Questions" E-zine. If you would like Daniel to send you the E-zine, go to www.danielbernardus.com; you will then also receive a free mini-course on "The Meanings of Success".

Manon Blanke
Manon Blanke is a media technology student, with a passion for storytelling, be it through books, movies, or interactive games. She also enjoys theatre, being outdoors, and a good cheese platter. During her bachelor programme, she helped develop initial ideas and setting up the storyline of the book you currently have in front of you. She aspires to a career where she can combine storytelling with new technologies and can create awareness for modern problems.

Lans Bovenberg
Lans Bovenberg is a professor of economics. He studied econometrics at the Erasmus University and obtained his PhD in economics in 1984, at the University of Berkeley, California. After graduation, Bovenberg lived in the USA, working at the International Monetary Fund. In 1990, he returned to the Netherlands. After working a brief period as a policy officer at the Ministry of Economic Affair, he became a professor of economics at the

Tilburg University and Erasmus University. Between 1995 and 1998, Bovenberg was deputy director at the Bureau for Economic Policy Analysis.

In 2004, he won the Spinoza prize for his research on environmental taxes. Bovenberg was the second Dutch social scientist ever to win this most important science prize in the Netherlands. With the price-money, he founded together with Theo Nijman, Netspar, a think tank and knowledge network for pensions, aging, and retirement. In 2009, literature critic/journalist Tjerk de Reus published: "De balans van Bovenberg – economie en geloof in crisistijd", in which for the first time, Bovenberg's theological vision on economics was accessible for a broader audience.

Bovenberg holds the F.J.D Goldschmeding chair on 'Innovation in Economics Teaching' at Tilburg University, since January 2016. He combines this position since January 2019 with a part-time chair as 'Professor of Relational Economics, Values and Leadership' at Erasmus University.

Acknowledgements

This book wouldn't have been possible without the help of many people. We would like to thank the then-students at Amsterdam University College who participated in early discussions including Simone Stergioula, Artemy Kovynev, Sam de Bruijn, Eleonora Gelmetti, Arsalan Ali Aga, and those who helped out in later stages like Wasutin Khodkaew. Adrien de Boer, Pim Versteegh and Peter Rauwerda have inspired us through good conversations. And then there are the indispensable people who have given feedback on early versions of the book including Nathan Potter, Marcel Canoy, Dieuwe Beersma, Clara Visentin, Ritsaart Bergsma, Thomas Heijnen, Richard Prins and Silvan de Boer. An important final round of editing-under-pressure was undertaken by Jeanne Bovenberg, for which we are especially grateful. An effort is underway to convert this book into an audiobook, which has also had impact on the text. We would especially like to thank Rebecca Scarratt, Francisco Hamlin, Alice Hamberger, Laura Psara and Ellie Swanson for their contributions. Randy Ingermanson's 'Advanced Fiction Writing Ezine' been an important inspiration for Daniel to keep on dreaming and growing as a writer.

Bas van Os has had a pivotal role throughout the project, skillfully helping to guide the project in good times and bad. We are deeply grateful for his always-cheerful helping hand.

Finally our fondest gratitude goes to the leaders of the "What Good Markets are Good for" project: Govert Buijs, Johan Graafland and Eefje de Gelder. Not only has their support throughout the process has been invaluable, but their support to push the project to completion at the end has been decisive.

Bibliography

Lans Bovenberg, (2016) *Economieonderwijs in Balans. Kiezen en samenwerken.* Tilburg University.

Lans Bovenberg (2018) *Where is the love.* Erasmus University.

Samuel Bowles (2017) *The moral economy.* Yale University Press.

Luigino Bruni (2009) *Reciprocity, Altruism and the Civil Society.* Taylor & Francis Ltd.

Luigino Bruni (2012) *The Wound and the Blessing.* New City Press.

Adam Grant (2014) *Give and Take.* Penguin Putnam Inc.

José Antonio Pérez Lopez. (1991) *Teoría de la Acción Humana en las Organizaciones.* RIALP.

Further Reading

Lans Bovenberg, Daniel Bernardus (expected 2021) *Economics and Love.*

Leonardo Polo, Daniel Bernardus (2020) *Freedom in Quarantine.* Leonardo Polo Institute of Philosophy Press.